SWORD CROSSED

BY FREYA MARSKE

THE LAST BINDING TRILOGY

A Marvellous Light
A Restless Truth
A Power Unbound

Swordcrossed

FREYA MARSKE

SWORD CROSSED

TOR

First published 2024 by Tom Doherty Associates / Tor Publishing Group

First published in the UK 2024 by Tor
an imprint of Pan Macmillan
The Smithson, 6 Briset Street, London EC1M 5NR
EU representative: Macmillan Publishers Ireland Ltd, 1st Floor,
The Liffey Trust Centre, 117–126 Sheriff Street Upper,
Dublin 1, D01 YC43
Associated companies throughout the world
www.panmacmillan.com

ISBN 978-1-0350-3928-9 HB
ISBN 978-1-0350-3929-6 TPB

1 3 5 7 9 8 6 4 2

A CIP catalogue record for this book is available from the British Library.

Printed and bound by CPI Group (UK) Ltd, Croydon, CR0 4YY

Visit **www.panmacmillan.com** to read more about all our books
and to buy them. You will also find features, author interviews and
news of any author events, and you can sign up for e-newsletters
so that you're always first to hear about our new releases.

This one's for all the eldest children,
and for Macey and Alex and Jenn,
for being there at the beginning.

SWORD CROSSED

CHAPTER
1

Matti laid his fingers on the polished edge of the bar's wooden surface and forced himself to stop counting sheep. And yards of twill. And looms in need of repair, and outstanding debts.

Instead, he counted today's collection of ink smudges, bruise-black on the brown skin of his hands: six. He counted the number of blue dyes that would have been used in the fabric of the bartender's layered skirt: four, possibly five if the palest shade was true dimflower and not just the result of fading.

The tense throb of pain like a fist clenched in his hair eased, grudgingly, to a quiet ache. Bearable. Normal.

It was busy in the drinking house, the post-dinner hour that usually found Matti heading back to his study to finish the paperwork that a member of his family had tugged him away from in order to eat. Matti counted the number of flavoured jenever bottles on the shelf behind the bar—fifteen—in the time it took Audry to finish serving her current customer and sweep her sky-coloured skirts to stand in front of Matti.

"And here's a face we haven't seen in a while! Something tells me you're here for a celebration, Mr. Jay."

Matti hoped the smile he'd pulled onto his face wasn't the wrong size, or the wrong shade of abashed. "News travels fast."

"Mattinesh Jay and Sofia Cooper. A match surprising exactly no one."

Matti kept the smile going. There was a silence in which Audry politely didn't say, *Pity she's in love with someone else,* and so Matti didn't have to say, *Yes, isn't it?*

Audry said, "Wait here a moment. I've got something in the back that I think will do nicely."

Matti cast a glance over the room as Audry disappeared. His cousin Roland made an extravagant sighing motion and pretended to check his watch when Matti's eyes landed on their table. A burst of laughter came from a dark-skinned woman nearby; she was wearing a dress that rode high at the knee to reveal a fall of lace like frothing water, a northern style of garment that Matti's own northerner mother seldom wore these days.

At the closest table the Mason Guildmaster, Lysbette Martens, was deep in conversation with a senior member of the Guild of Engineers. Martens met Matti's gaze with her own and nodded brief acknowledgement. He was sure she was weighing his presence as consciously as he was weighing hers. This was a place to be seen, after all.

"Here you are. Red wine for young lovers."

Matti turned around again. Audry named the price for the bottle as she uncorked it and set it on the bar. Matti paid her, ignoring the lurch like a fishhook in his stomach at the amount on the credit notes he was so casually handing over. Mattinesh Jay, firstborn of his distinguished House, had no reason not to indulge in one of the finest bottles of wine that money could buy.

No reason that anyone here would know about, anyway.

Matti took the bottle in one hand and hooked three glasses with the other. Making his way over to the table, his mind circled back to dwell on the wrong sort of numbers. The money in Matti's purse was painstakingly calculated: enough for the first round of engagement drinks, and enough for him to hire a top-of-the-range duellist who would step forward in the awkwardly likely event of someone challenging for Sofia's hand at the wedding itself.

Matti's skin prickled cold at the very thought of what might happen if Adrean Vane challenged against Matti's marriage to Sofia and *won*. His family's last hope would be gone. Matti would have failed them in this, the most useful thing he could do for them.

He was so caught up in this uneasy imagining as he wove through the room that he collided, hard, with another person's shoulder. Matti was both tall and broad, not easily unbalanced; the unfortunate other member of the collision made a grab for Matti's coat, couldn't get a good grip, and tripped to the ground with a caught-back *"Fu—"*

Matti tried to step backwards. They were crammed into a small space between tables and there were people moving around them. His first panicked instinct had been to keep the wine bottle upright and the glasses safe, so he didn't have a hand free to steady himself on a chair.

He wasn't quite sure what happened next, except that he ended up wobbling and stepping forward instead, and he felt his boot come down on something that was not the floorboards. A small, pathetic, grinding mechanical sound crawled up Matti's nerves, heel to head, and reached his ears even amidst the noise of the busy room.

"Sorry!" he said at once. "I'm sorry. Was that— Oh, Huna's teeth."

The man on the floor jerked his head up, staring at Matti, and Matti stared back.

For a moment all that Matti could see was the wide, straight line of the man's mouth, set beneath an equally straight nose, and the frame that set off the whole: the dark, luminous copper-red hair that seemed to be trying to grow in about ten different directions.

The man's tongue darted out in a nervous mannerism, wetting his lower lip. Something in Matti's own mouth tried to happen in a yearning echo.

"Would you please *lift*," the man said precisely, "your gods-damned *foot*?"

Heat flooded Matti's face. He snatched his foot backwards with enough force that his heel collided with a chair leg.

The redheaded man stood, his fingers closed convulsively tight around a small velvet bag. His brown coat was shabby and made of a coarsely woven fabric, though his shirt was good and his trousers had probably been equally so before they'd been overwashed into a patchy shine.

"Fuck fuck shitting—*fuck*," the man said in tones of despair, with a lilt to his accent that placed him at least one city-state farther east: Cienne, or possibly Sanoy. He shook the contents of the bag into his palm and ventured into new realms of inappropriate language as he did so.

Enough people had witnessed their collision, or had their heads turned by the stream of expletives, that there were a fair few necks craning to see what was in the man's hand. Matti, at whom the shaking fingers of this hand were pointed most directly, couldn't help seeing for himself the ragged, glinting pile of cogs and jewels and glass. Only the intact cover—monogrammed in a swirling, engraved *H*—spoke of this pile's previous existence as a pocket watch. A very expensive pocket watch, by the look of it.

The man's breath hissed out through his teeth. "Guildmaster Havelot is going to use my arm bones as a fucking *lathe*. He only had it made to order, and he only trusted me to pick it up, didn't he? Two hundred gold. Fucking fuck."

"I'm so sorry," Matti said again. He recognised the name: Havelot was the Woodworker Guildmaster in Cienne. "Truly. I can—" He stopped. The abrupt lack of his words created a silence that seemed to suck noise into itself, as conversations died to murmurs and the onlookers sensed something interesting.

The man looked straight at Matti with a stubborn lift of his chin. His brows, the same absurd colour as the rest of his hair, had sprung up into the beginnings of hope; as Matti's silence grew longer, they lowered again. And then lowered farther. He swept a look down and then slowly up Matti's own outfit, and now pride warred with scorn in the way those maddening lips pressed together.

Matti felt sick. His own coat was made of the finest wool, a midnight blue cut perfectly to his figure, and the rest of his clothes were of the same quality. He was holding a bottle of extremely good wine. Anybody looking at him would make immediate assumptions about the amount of ready money that Matti might have, and the ease with which he would be able to reimburse a poor clerk, if he'd just ruined a pricey piece of artificer's skill that the man's employer had trusted him to travel all the way to Glassport to collect.

Of course they would make these assumptions. That was the *point*.

Matti swallowed and felt the burning heaviness of his purse redouble. He'd be left with enough to a hire a duellist, yes, but not one of the highest skill. It wouldn't buy himself and his family the absolute security they needed.

His friends were looking at him. It seemed like every pair of eyes in the drinking house was looking, and in another moment the murmurs of curiosity would turn to murmurs of disapprobation. *I thought Matti Jay had more honour than that,* they would say. *What's two hundred gold to someone like him?*

Besides, the plain fact of the matter was that Matti had broken the watch. And he couldn't pretend that he and this man with his proud mouth and poor coat, patched at one elbow, were on an equal footing. Even if he were left without a bronze, Matti would still have influence, connections, the weight of his family's name. That was still worth something. For now.

So that was that.

"I—I really am sorry." Matti set the wine and glasses down on the corner of the nearest table and pulled his purse from inside his coat. He kept his gaze on the man's face, on a pair of eyes that were either grey or brown—impossible to tell from this angle—and urgently willed them not to look away. To a degree that seemed irrational, he wanted to banish the judgemental expression from the man's face. "Of course I'll cover the cost. Two hundred gold. Who did the work?"

The man glanced down at the metal scraps in his hand, as though the answer might be hidden in the pile. "Speck," he said at last. "Frans Speck, in Amber Lane."

"He's a fair man. Tell him what happened and he'll rush through the repair job," Matti said. He held out the century notes.

The man tipped the wreckage of the watch back into the bag and closed his hand around the money, slow and wary. His fingertips had rough patches that scraped against Matti's own, sending a tingle up Matti's arm.

"I appreciate it," the man said. He looked less cold now, though still nowhere near warm. "You've saved my life. Really."

Matti forced himself to smile. Forced himself to say, "It's nothing," as though it really were nothing.

The man nodded awkwardly at Matti and tucked both money and bag into a pocket. Then he turned and was gone, headed for the door.

Matti somehow made his way to his table and sat down. His heart was pounding so loudly that he could barely hear anything else, and he wanted to shout at his own blood to be quiet and let him *think*. He needed to be alone in his study. He needed to contemplate his options, and make lists, and pore over the accounts for the thousandth time, in case they transmuted themselves into a picture of prosperity instead of the ugly, desperate reality that nobody outside of Matti's immediate family knew about.

"Two hundred gold," he said, before he could stop himself. "*Two hundred.*"

"We saw. Hard luck," his cousin Roland said, making a face.

Perhaps it was stretching the term to call Roland and Wynn his friends, but they were the closest thing Matti had to members of that category, and the only people he'd been able to think of to form his wedding party. At least the three of them never found it too hard to pick up their acquaintanceship again, even if it had been months since their last conversation.

Wynn turned the bottle of wine to inspect the yellow butterfly on the label. "How appropriate that we're drinking wine from your betrothed's own winery."

"Audry's idea of a joke, I think," Matti said. The word *betrothed* had landed in his ears like a piece of music played in an unfamiliar key; his mind was still turning it over, trying to decide how it felt about the melody. His hand was shaking as he poured the first glass, sending the stream of dark wine shivering and slipping. He'd steadied it by the time he poured the second.

"Huna smile," he said, opening the toasts by lifting his own glass. "Thanks for agreeing to stand up with me, you two."

"Drown your sorrows in this one, and by the time we hit the next bottle you'll remember that you're here to celebrate. And that once you're married to Sofia Cooper," Roland went on, lowering his voice sympathetically, "Jay House will be rolling in enough money to replace a hundred watches."

Except that Matti had to get himself successfully married in the first place. And he'd just lost his best guarantee of doing so.

He let the old, gorgeous wine flood down his throat until a good third of his glass had vanished. He felt lightheaded; it had to be panic, because the wine couldn't be working that fast. Panic and a sense of becoming unmoored. And the image of the man's face, pale and sharply beautiful, gazing up from where he was kneeling at Matti's feet.

"A fair effort," Wynn said, when Matti put the glass down. "But I'll show you children of Huna how it's done." He raised his own glass. "Agar fill your plates and cups."

Matti smiled and drank again, accepting the toast. Maybe the wine was working after all. He could still feel his panic, the wound-up watch of his worry, but he shoved it away into a recess of his mind: its own small, dark velvet bag. It would be safe enough there. It would last until tomorrow. Matti's ability to worry was shatterproof.

For now, he was going to drink.

———— >∙≫∙◈∙◈≪∙< ————

The sun was making a personal project of finding Matti's eyes as he walked through the Glassport streets the next morning. Every gap between eaves and chimneys was a new opportunity for glaring rays to assault his eyelids. His head felt like one of the snow-baubles you could buy in the winter markets, flurried and shaken into a confusion of water and oil and small flecks of metal, and fragile. Prone to cracking. The sunlight was one source of cracks; the rumble of carts and carriages, raised voices, the rattle of machinery—the everyday racket of city life, which Matti could easily ignore on a normal day—was another.

Matti was not a drinker, as a rule. His family brought out the occasional decanter of good spirits if a deal was being struck or they had particular reason to please someone. On those occasions Matti had learned to spin out a glass across hours, to honour the work of Maha's children by rolling each sip over his tongue, and to forget that alcohol had any ability to muddle the thoughts.

He'd also managed to forget that the state of existence known as Maha's Revenge awaited anyone who had, for example, spent the previous night sharing two bottles of wine among three people and chasing all of that with glasses of rosemary jenever. Not that Matti could remember the jenever portion of the evening. He'd made an educated guess at that upon waking, based on the smell of his wrinkled shirt.

Matti had escaped his house relatively unmocked for his delicate state. His family knew where he'd been and what he'd been celebrating. The slight change in the set of his father's shoulders, the new and terrible light of relief in the communication-dense glances his parents exchanged . . . those were a form of celebration too. A piece of lowered horizon glimpsed after a long, long uphill trek, whispering at the possibility that soon their feet might find the road sloping downwards.

Matti had awoken to the twins hurling themselves onto the lump of him in his sheets, delighted to find their older brother abed at a time of day when he'd usually have been awake for hours. Joselyne had chased them away and brought peppermint tea, which had helped the uneasy roil of Matti's stomach but hadn't done much for the head-bauble.

As much as Matti would have liked to stay in bed, or even to sit in his study with a plate of greasy spiced potato dumplings at his elbow, there was something he had to do this morning.

Matti ducked his head to avoid another piercing sunbeam and rounded the corner into the street that held his destination. The city's only agency of swords-for-hire had its office tucked incongruously above an apothecary's shop front, with a narrow flight of stairs leading up from street level. Matti passed through a doorway with the symbol of Pata, patron god of soldiers, guards, and duellists, set as a plaque above the doorframe. The room it led into was small, with a single window looking out onto the street, and it was dominated by a pair of wooden cabinets set on the opposite wall. A man with thinning blond hair sat behind a desk in front of the cabinets, and he was climbing to his feet even as Matti walked in.

"Mr. Jay," he said. "What can I do for you, sir?"

The man's face was vaguely familiar, but even Matti's trained memory couldn't attach a name to it. "I'm afraid you've got the advantage of me."

"Tolliver." He extended a hand and Matti shook it. "Hardy Tolliver. I stood swordguard for your sister's naming ceremony, several years back. This was my father's agency. Now it's mine."

"I need to hire a best man."

"Of course. Is there reason to expect a challenge?" Hardy Tolliver's voice was polite, his face impeccably blank. Matti didn't have the energy to try to work out if Tolliver was being deliberately obtuse, or just displaying professional courtesy. If he knew who Matti was, he might well know more than that, and it wasn't as though Adrean Vane made any secret of either his feelings for Sofia or his enthusiasm for the blade. He'd even set those feelings to music. There'd been a time last year when you could barely walk down a street in the city without hearing someone whistling "Wildflowers Under Glass"; it was the kind of tune that nestled merrily in the ear for days on end.

"Yes, there is," Matti said.

"I can think of a few people on our books who would do nicely." Tolliver waved Matti into a chair, and turned to open one of the cabinets. He began to flick through folders.

"I should probably tell you," Matti said, "I can pay four hundred gold, and not a bronze more."

Tolliver turned back to him, surprise splashed across his face. "We aren't, ah, in the habit of bargaining—the Guild allows for rates to be set—"

"I'm not trying to bargain with you."

Tolliver still looked bewildered. Matti steeled himself and gathered his most businesslike voice. It was the voice of a man who'd grown up in a townhouse in the Rose Quarter, who could count back eight generations of his House's current trade, and whose father was currently in his second three-year term as elected Guildmaster.

It was Matti's voice, even if these days Matti himself rattled around in its cadences like a slim foot in a shoe of overstretched leather.

"Jay House is having a rough quarter. I would appreciate it," he said, "if this fact were not to become public knowledge." He could only hope that wielding this little power would be enough to suppress the Glassport instinct for gossip; if not, *a rough quarter* was more forgivable than the truth.

"Four hundred gold?"

"Four hundred."

"That does rule out a lot of our most talented people."

"I thought that might be the case." The memory of century notes leaving his hands bounced queasily inside Matti's rib cage. "I'd appreciate anything you can offer me within that budget."

Tolliver sat. He opened a leather folder and flicked through some loose pages, moving each one neatly from one side to the other. Then he looked up.

"There's someone. He's new to town. No prior duels to his name in Glassport and I only put him on the books two days ago, so I can't give you a full reference, I'm afraid, but I tried him out. He's not bad; he's certainly better than what he's charging. Probably the best value you'll get for that price."

It took Matti a moment to recognise the second layer of generosity there, no matter the truth of the "value" that Tolliver was offering. Someone new to town and unfamiliar with Glassport society might not recognise Matti as anyone significant. They might not bat an eye at the fact that Matti was paying midrange rates for a best man. It was another way to contain the gossip. It wasn't an outright guarantee of Tolliver's own silence, but it was a gesture. A statement of faith that one day Matti would be in a position to return the favour.

Matti nodded, trying to convey both understanding and appreciation. "Could I meet him before deciding?"

"Absolutely." Now Tolliver smiled the relaxed smile of someone close to a sale. "Right now, if you'd like. He's renting the attic from my wife and me, while he waits for a room that's coming free in a boardinghouse at the end of the week. We're just a few doors down. Wouldn't be a moment to fetch him."

Matti could see no reason to object, and Tolliver's feet were fading on the stairs within a minute. In the sudden lull of thought and speech, Matti's head began to remind him again about the jenever. He stood up and paced in the small space, taking deep breaths that smelled of dust and leather and, faintly, acrid herbal scents seeping up from the apothecary. He felt clearer by the time he heard Tolliver's feet on the stairs again, this time accompanied by a second pair.

"Mr. Mattinesh Jay," Tolliver said in tones of announcement as he entered. "And this is Luca Piere."

Matti's first thought was one of irrational despair: that Huna had decided to twist her knife, because far from assuming Matti to be a man of modest means, the man was now going to think him even *more* cheap.

Then reality elbowed him in the brain, and he felt his expression freeze onto his face.

Luca Piere was no longer wearing his brown coat with the patched elbow. He *was* wearing his good shirt and his thin trousers. And along with those, as he stood frozen behind Tolliver's shoulder, he was wearing an expression of guilt so naked and obvious that Matti remembered, abruptly, that the man worked for Havelot. That he was visiting the city to pick up a watch.

Except that he clearly was not.

Matti's heart leapt into his throat and then slammed back down again. He brimmed with a feeling of foolishness rapidly bubbling into fury. It was a con as old as the very idea of marketplaces: "break" something already broken, and demand compensation. And Matti had fallen for it simply because this man had had the gall to try it on a scale of two hundred gold, with a full audience of Glassport's finest looking on.

Matti opened his mouth to say something—what exactly, he wasn't sure—but before he could, that guilty expression widened into panic, and Piere took a smart few steps forward.

"You've told Mr. Jay he'd be taking a chance on me, Hardy," Piere said. "How about you let us into the practice room and I'll give him a bout, so he can see to his own satisfaction what he's paying for?"

Matti stared at him. Piere's head tilted towards the other door in the room, a mute and desperate invitation. His lips were pressed together hard enough that the already pale skin around them was bone-white. Matti, feeling the power in the room shift palpably in his own direction, found it easier to breathe and to think.

Tolliver looked dubious. "Have you done any duelling, Mr. Jay?"

Matti had never lifted a finger in a violent pastime in his life. But right now, experiencing the unusual palm-tingling urge to get his hands around another person's throat and *squeeze,* he quite fancied the idea of picking up a weapon. Even if he hadn't the faintest clue what to do with it. And he could feel his own sheer curiosity rising like a vine from the rich mud of his rage.

"I'll give him a try," he said shortly.

He followed Piere into a long, narrow room that stretched back away from the street, with light coming from a single street-end window and a series of skylights. The floor was heavily scuffed, and bolted along one wall was a rack of swords.

Luca Piere had stopped in the middle of this room. As soon as the door closed behind Matti, he turned, as though the click had triggered some small mechanism within him. In the daylight, his hair was a riot: a true, bright copper. It looked as though he'd sat in front of a mirror with a curling iron and painstakingly coaxed small pieces of it to curl in different directions. Or else he'd crawled out from a pile of pillows and not bothered to run a comb through it, and gravity had been so amused at the sight that it hadn't interfered.

Matti's hands, which were still tingling to be placed against the vulnerability of Piere's pale throat, now began to take on an edge of interest in the hair instead. About how it might feel for them to be buried in it. About how ideal that length was for *pulling.*

Matti closed them both into fists, and ignored them.

"All right," Matti said. "Now start talking."

CHAPTER
2

Luca cursed the instinct that had led him to stand in the centre of the room. It was a natural response, after years of training, to seek a good vantage point. But he'd forgotten that he was unarmed, that he hadn't bothered to strap on his own sword belt before leaving the house to meet a potential client, and now he'd left Mr. Mattinesh Jay closer to the sword rack. If the man on whom Luca had handily sprung the pocket watch con decided to snatch a weapon from the rack and come at him, Luca would be at a disadvantage. And if someone was angry enough, the fact that these were mostly tipped and dulled practice swords wouldn't make a lot of difference in terms of the damage that they could do.

"All right," said Jay. "Now start talking."

He didn't look like he was going to reach for a sword. In fact, the glance he gave the rack of weapons suggested he was uncomfortable just being in the same room as that many blades.

So of course Luca decided to say, "Pick up a sword."

"What?"

Luca went and chose himself one. Jay's dark eyes followed Luca warily as he tested grip and weight. Luca allowed himself one long held glance, trying to gauge just how angry the man was. He tried for neutrality, he really did, but it still came out sounding like a schoolmaster sarcastically spelling out the obvious when he repeated: "A sword."

"I can't actually use one," Jay said, dry.

"Yes, I'd gathered that. But Tolliver's going to expect to hear swords clashing, and I'm not keen on trying to have a fight with *myself."* He added, "You can take off that nice coat, if you're worried about getting a hole in it."

Something unreadable flashed in Jay's eyes. Then he let out an irritated sigh, turned aside, and began shrugging the coat off.

Luca took the opportunity to look his fill while Jay wasn't looking back. When the coat came off and the man tugged his shirt-sleeves awkwardly up, Luca realised that Jay was both taller and more solid than he'd appeared the previous night. The coat was near-black and tailored to fit like a possessive pair of hands, giving an illusion of a slimmer build, and Jay's round-shouldered posture pulled him in on himself. Luca itched to get in close and curl his hands around those broad shoulders, like his own sword master had done for him, tugging them back and straight. He could spider his hand between the man's shoulder blades, dig in his fingertips, and say, *Now imagine a piece of string.*

Luca shook his head and busied himself with turning the sword in his hand. He was getting carried away with nonsense because Jay . . . drew the eye, that was all, with his clear brown skin and his black hair, long enough to hint at the promise of curls if left untrimmed. Jay was too far from Luca now for the equally dark lashes to be visible, but up close in the drinking house they had been stunning.

Jay folded the coat and hung it over one edge of the rack. He reached for a sword, clearly at random; Luca could have told him that it was too short for his height, but it wasn't like any of that mattered. This was just for cover. Jay walked into the centre of the room, lifted the sword like a stack of plates, and faced Luca down the length of both blades with a renewed look of stubborn nerves.

Luca rolled his eyes. "Calm down. I'm not going to hurt you."

"Oh, so you're no more a duellist than you are working for Guildmaster Havelot?"

"No, I *am* a duellist."

"Just supplementing your income with petty theft."

Luca, feeling that needle further under his skin than he'd like, gave a tap with his sword against the one held in Jay's too-stiff arm. "Yes. I tricked you. All right? I needed the money."

"You think I didn't?" Jay tried, clumsily, to tap back. Luca let his wrist absorb the jarring force.

"Look, Tolliver's agency has a buy-in. I wasn't expecting that, I thought he'd just let me start work and take it out in commission. So that took most of the ready money I had, and I needed something to pay for food and board."

"And meanwhile you've wrangled yourself an invitation to stay with your new agent," said Jay. "You do move fast, don't you?"

"Hardy Tolliver's a decent person," said Luca. "Most people are."

"All the better to take advantage?"

"I'm not— Oh, would you stop holding it like you're trying to chop down a *tree*, Pata *wept*—"

Unsurprisingly, this accomplished nothing more than a further darkening of Jay's expression and another stubborn clash of his sword against Luca's.

"I don't give a damn about your buying-in fee, your board, or any other excuse," Jay said. "That was *my money*. What did you— why did you have to pick *me* to try your tricks on?"

Luca gave him an incredulous look, stepping back and letting his sword tip lower. "Are you joking? You bought a bottle of Cooper Ruby, and you were wearing the best clothes in the room. I do know what money looks like."

Jay's sword arm sagged back against his side. Now he didn't look angry so much as despairing. This wasn't making any sense.

"That two hundred gold was for *this*. For a best man. I'd set aside six hundred, in all. And scraping that much together meant weeks of my family tightening belts that were already tight, which was a fucking laugh to explain to my brother and sister, who are all of *five* and don't really understand why hiring some stranger with a sword is more important than having sweets at the end of dinner. I'm not a damn miser. I'm desperate."

Luca's pulse had picked up, and he didn't know what kind of excitement it heralded. Jay had seemed an obvious choice last night: a handsome face, deep pockets. And he'd been so eager to apologise; so desperately wanting to please. *This* voice, deep and rough around the edges with poorly suppressed emotion, was something different.

"I need a best man who will win any challenge. Guaranteed," Jay went on. "So you're going to hand me my money back, or I'm calling the city guard and they'll haul you up in front of a magistrate."

Luca bit his lip against hysterical laughter. The fucking *irony*, to flee the consequences of his actions in Cienne only to be arrested his first week here in Glassport.

"Or maybe I'll call them anyway," said Jay.

"No! Shitting fuck. Look—" Luca did the only thing he could think of to do, which was raise his sword again. Jay raised his own, startled. Luca stopped messing around with pretence; he stepped in close, engaged their blades, and twisted the sword out of Jay's grip in a matter of seconds. It fell to the ground with a thud and a bounce, off to Luca's left.

Jay stepped back. Luca followed.

He set the dulled point of the sword to Jay's throat, watching the undulation of the skin there, where the line of the neck emerged from the loosened collar of the man's shirt. As soon as the metal touched his skin, Jay went still. Now Luca *could* see those eyelashes, and those eyes as well, opening wide. Jay's lips parted in something that was almost certainly fear, but which Luca's nerves interpreted as something else. Arousal gave an interested twist in Luca's stomach.

It had taken a few seconds at most. There was no reason for Luca to feel breathless, beyond the fact that Jay had given another nervous swallow, and Luca couldn't decide whether to look at his eyes or at the place where the dull bronze of his skin met the white of the shirt.

"Give me the rest of the money," said Luca.

Jay's eyes fell to the sword, then rose. "Are you trying to rob me *again*? How exactly do you think that's going to work?"

"*Hire me,*" Luca said. "As your best man."

"Hire you? Are you mad?"

"You've already said you planned to pay six hundred. Pay it to me."

"Yes, that's what I budgeted. For someone very good."

"I am *extremely* good." Luca gave a deliberate dart of his eyes to where Jay's sword lay, a fair distance from their feet. Jay did not seem impressed. Fair enough. Disarming an inept beginner was hardly an accomplishment.

"Tolliver said you're . . . not bad," said Jay.

Luca let the sword drop again. "Tolliver is a middling swordsman who, if I'm any judge, stepped gratefully behind a desk as soon as the opportunity arose to become a businessman instead. I was barely trying when he tried me out." He was exaggerating, but not by much.

Jay's eyes narrowed. "If you're worth six hundred, as you claim, then why are you charging less?"

Luca couldn't exactly say, *Because I'm trying to keep a low profile.* "Because I'm new. I haven't any record to rely on; there's no point in my entering the market at the top, untested. I need to build my reputation. I can always raise my price once demand is established."

That was the kind of business sense that any child could understand. Jay nodded slowly, but the suspicion hadn't vanished from his face yet. Luca needed to press his advantage before Jay could start poking holes in his story. Or talking about magistrates again.

Now that the sun was higher in the sky, it was warm in this room, which pulled sunlight in through the skylights but had no cracked windows to allow for an exchange of air. Luca wiped his brow. His best idea was going to require some exertion.

"Hold this for me," he said abruptly, and tossed his sword up—showing off—to adjust his grip, catching it by the guard as it fell. He offered it to Jay, hilt-first. It was a thin gesture of trust, here between the two of them where there was no trust at all and no reason for it to exist. Jay took the sword probably more out of instinctual politeness than anything else.

Luca pulled his shirt off over his head, exhaling in relief as the air found the moisture on his skin and set about cooling him. He took the sword back from Jay's unresisting hands, swiped back a few hanks of hair that had tried to fall over his forehead, and went back to his position in the centre of the room. He fell into a ready stance.

"What are you doing?" said Jay.

"Showing you what your money's worth," Luca said, and began.

To someone as ignorant as Jay, Luca could only hope that what he was doing was recognisable as proficient. He was tempted to make it showier, to add a few flourishes and tricks, as though he were fighting off a host of imaginary opponents. But he could hear Master Carriere's heavy, uncompromising voice telling him that this was not a game, that there were no shortcuts, and that respect for the weapon and the body were the only keystones. Luca believed that theatrics added spice to most areas of life, but this wasn't one of them.

He did the simple forms as a warm-up, then the advanced ones. He did them in a perfect line. He did them very, very quickly.

The sun in his eyes was an annoyance, so he closed them. Blood hammered in his feet. He could feel the familiar ache that wasn't pain, but acceptable stress, in his wrist and in his shoulder, after five minutes had passed without his ever lowering the blade fully.

A knock sounded on the door to the room.

Luca whirled, the sound like a hammer on the pulled-tight anticipation of his reflexes. He heard in the silence the quick pant of his own breath.

Jay was staring at him, one of his hands trying to clench around the fitted fabric of his trousers. His gaze dragged across Luca's bare chest before rising, and Luca felt the heat of it even on his overheated skin.

"Is everything satisfactory, Mr. Jay?" came Hardy Tolliver's voice.

Luca held very still. He felt balanced on the edge of a knife; he had no idea which way he might fall.

"I can do this for you," Luca said, low. "You're not the only one who's desperate. *Please.*"

It seemed half a century before Jay nodded and raised his voice. "Everything's fine, Mr. Tolliver. We're just talking. I'll be out in a moment, to sign the contract."

Luca exhaled. His heart eased itself away from the battering it had been giving his ribs. "Thank you."

"Not so fast," said Jay. "I have a condition."

"What is it?"

"I'll pay you the six hundred, as a duellist's fee. And in exchange for not telling anyone the truth of what happened last night . . . there's something else I want."

Luca curled and uncurled the fingers of his sword hand, uncertain. Jay looked embarrassed. No matter what it was, Luca would have to have a good reason to refuse. Jay had a far better bargaining position, and they both knew it.

"Yes?"

"Sword lessons. I want you to teach me."

"You think you can be your *own*—"

"No, don't be stupid." Jay waved a hand. "It's only a few months until the wedding. Obviously I can't learn more than the basics in that time. I don't expect you to turn me into a master. But"—his voice firmed, his shoulders straightened—"it's something I'd like to try."

It wasn't an unreasonable request. There was no way Luca would get enough work through Tolliver's agency to fill his days entirely. He could spare a few hours to show this man how to hold a sword.

"Done," Luca said. "Now, I've got a question. Why do you need a best man worth six hundred gold?"

"My betrothed. Sofia. She has . . . an inconveniently talented paramour."

"Ah," said Luca. "And you wish to ensure the match between yourself and this Sofia is untainted by any suggestion that the gods might not approve."

Jay gave a sudden, unsteady burst of laughter. "You know, I'm starting to wonder if they simply *don't*. They seem to be doing everything they can to make it impossible. Including shoving you into my path."

Luca smiled, and felt un unexpected squirm of delight when Jay's mouth twitched towards the beginning of an answering smile.

"Think of it this way," Luca said. "They then shoved you right back at me. And—look at that! You're still getting what you need."

"I don't *need* sword lessons." The note of tentative shame buried in Jay's voice told Luca a lot.

"And something that you want, on top of it, for the same price. See? Good fortune."

"Don't push it," said Jay, but now he was almost smiling outright.

Luca was lightheaded with relief. He wasn't sure which god to thank for the fact that this encounter had managed to swing around from Jay looking ready to bludgeon him with the wrong end of a sword, to this, where Jay was agreeing that it was almost *lucky* that Luca had conned him the night before. But Luca wasn't about to question his good fortune either. He rubbed grateful fingers on both the hilt of his sword and the waistband of his trousers, sending out a silent twinned prayer. "When do you want to start?" he asked.

"Tomorrow? Early mornings suit me."

Luca made a face. "How about evenings? After dinner?"

"I'm the one paying *you*," said Jay.

Luca grinned. "Not for this, you're not. Technically."

Oh, Luca knew his role in this: the hired sword, bought into the service of this son of a grand House. His role was to be accommodating. To uncomplainingly do what he was told.

Luca had never been very good at doing what he was told.

"I'm paying you, and I say mornings," said Jay. "Just after sunrise. It's the only time I can spare."

"All right," said Luca. "Just don't expect sparkling conversation."

Luca returned his sword to the rack. He picked up his shirt and narrowly stopped himself from using it as a rag to wipe the sweat from his face and neck; he did have to wear the thing, after all, and didn't have many spares. He contented himself by wiping one palm on his trousers. A spark of mischief, a desire to push further, let him walk right up to Jay with his shirt still bundled in his hands. He watched to see if Jay's eyes dropped again to his chest.

They did.

Luca said, "Let's make this formal. A pleasure doing business with you, sir. My name is Luca Piere."

"My name is Mattinesh Jay."

They shook hands. Jay's hand was broad, smooth, and uncalloused as it engulfed Luca's. It was a hand that matched the coat, matched the bottle of wine, and didn't match at all the terrible urgency in Jay's manner, or the way his voice had sounded as he talked about his family. Every House went through rough patches, but Luca had never seen anyone with such a disconnect between the way they appeared and the things they said. Jay had no obvious reason to lie. He was a man with almost no money, who'd turned up to a sword agency and was prepared to gamble on a newcomer who might or might not be worth more than what he was asking, simply for—

Ah.

"She's rich, this betrothed of yours," Luca realised. "You need the bond price. That's why you're prepared to throw far more than you can afford at a best man."

Jay's lips parted in that distracting manner again. A faint tint entered his cheeks; Luca suspected it would have been a flood of annoyed scarlet in someone of Luca's own complexion.

"Yes," he said, stiff.

"Well, there's no need to worry," Luca said. "I'll stand beside you at your wedding, Mattinesh Jay. And I'll win."

CHAPTER
3

The world was kinder to Matti's senses as he walked home. The sunlight seemed less piercing, and more a promise from the gods that perhaps everything was turning in his favour after all. The last of Maha's Revenge had lifted from his skull somewhere between the look of guilt on Piere's face and the moment when they shook hands.

Matti had made plenty of bargains in his life, and he was pleased with the one he'd just completed. Whatever his criminal tendencies, Piere obviously knew what he was doing with a sword, and that was all Matti needed.

Matti certainly didn't *need* lessons in duelling. And now he had them, because the merchant in him hated letting something go for nothing when it could be leveraged instead. Silence in exchange for sword lessons.

Duelling was something between athletics and art form; for most sons of successful Houses it was considered a frippery. An amusing hobby at best. Matti was expected to have better things to do with his time than mess about with blades. But he'd always loved watching the formal duels at namings and other ceremonies, as well as the show matches that sometimes adorned other celebrations. It had nothing whatsoever to do with his work, and therein lay the appeal. Already the anticipation of it was like a silken undershirt, something not meant to be glimpsed by others, reminding him of his own satisfaction with every step.

It had been a long time since Matti associated secrets with anything *good*. All the other secrets in his life were the large ones, the ones that pulled tight headaches into existence and wove an ugly twill from his thoughts when he was lying in bed at night, unable to sleep. The secrets that had become as natural as breathing.

Matti looked at his palm, opening and closing his fingers. The sword had felt strange there: heavy and ungainly. No doubt he'd looked a complete fool with it dangling from his arm.

Piere had looked the opposite of ungainly. He had a trim torso, each muscle well-defined and visible under the pale skin, as would be expected from someone who made their living in such a physical manner. And the way Piere *moved*. A fierce economy, each motion sharp and graceful, as though the air knew to dance out of his way or be sliced apart. Matti would never learn to move like that in fifty years of tutelage, let alone a handful of months, but the desire to try was like a shout within him.

Matti was a few doors down from his own house when he recognised a man walking in the opposite direction, down the street towards Matti himself. In a few more moments they would be face-to-face.

Matti entertained a short-lived fantasy of ducking up the front steps of a neighbour's house, pretending he was paying a call, and avoiding the encounter entirely. But it had to happen sooner or later, and he'd had enough of feeling wrong-footed for one morning. He could manage this.

"Adrean," he called. "Good morning."

Adrean Vane's eyes slid onto Matti with a speed that suggested he'd been keeping them deliberately averted. "Good morning, Mr. Jay," he said, and Matti groaned inwardly as he pulled to a halt, stepping aside to leave space on the footpath for others to pass them by.

"Adrean, really," said Matti. "Stop it. I'm not going to be Mr.-Jayed by you of all people."

Adrean was as tall as Matti, though more leanly built, and his hair was straight and longer than was fashionable, with a tendency to fall across his eyes like a raven's wing. He sighed as though the informality were a struggle, as though the years that they'd known each other did nothing to make up for the difference in their status.

Perhaps it couldn't. They'd never been anything like friends, but Matti had always felt a kernel of admiration for Adrean Vane. The only son of Jay House's senior business agent, Adrean didn't care a button for trade, and had no intention of following his father into the Guild of Spinners and Weavers. He was a musician; he was an amateur duellist. He was doing exactly what he wished to do with his life.

Gloomy sigh completed, he said, "Congratulations on the engagement, Matti."

"Thank you." Matti tried to make something appropriate arrange itself on his tongue. *I'm sorry I'm marrying the girl you love? It's not personal?*

Adrean did not look inclined to interject anything that might make things less difficult. Not that Matti could blame him. From Adrean's perspective he *was* the superior Mr. Jay, swooping in and offering Sofia the prosperous House name that Adrean never could.

"I hope we'll see you there" were the words that came out of Matti's mouth, and he nearly felt his tongue spasm with the desire to suck them back in again. Now it sounded like he was rubbing it in Adrean's face.

"I can assure you that you will," Adrean said. "Good day." He gave the kind of lingering bow that was as bad as the Mr.-Jaying, stepped around Matti, and continued on his way.

"Fantastic," Matti muttered to himself. "Well done."

Between them, Adrean and Matti's own stupidity had managed to kick a fair dent in the good mood he'd been carrying home. He felt itchy and annoyed as he let himself in the front door of the Jay townhouse, hung his coat by the door, and climbed the stairs two at a time. The door to his father's study was ajar, and Matti stepped inside to find his father behind the desk. Tomas Jay was spinning his glasses with one hand, while the other combed absently through a nest of tawny curls. The patches of grey at his temples were more pronounced than they'd been a year ago.

Standing close by, and speaking in a low tone, was Corus Vane. Both men looked up as Matti entered.

"Sorry, I didn't mean to interrupt."

Corus straightened. Jay House's senior agent had his son's long face, made even longer by the fact that his own hair was neatly trimmed. "So, some good news at last," Corus said warmly.

"Yes," said Matti.

"Congratulations, Matti. Huna smile." Corus turned back to Matti's father. "I'll let Matti know if I can pin down anything more definite, Tomas. But we should assume the worst, and start strategising accordingly. This is a real concern."

"And we were so very short on those," said Tomas. He waved Corus out of the study.

"What—" Matti began, but was interrupted by a minor commotion behind him. It sounded like someone, or something, managing to collide with both sides of the doorframe at once.

"Oh, Huna's dripping—"

"*Mayanesh,*" said Tomas, equal parts indulgent and reproving.

A large walking pile of fabric pushed past Matti and into the study, where it nudged a fold of heavy wool aside to reveal the face of Matti's sister. Maya's hair was braided back, and the fabric's rub had given her a fuzzy black halo of loose strands around her face.

"Good, you're back. Someone needs to talk sternly to the supervisors at the workshop in East Quarter," Maya said to Matti. "The new colour formula's taken well, but I don't think this bolt has had more than flirting acquaintance with a burling iron."

"We laid off some of the quality control staff two months ago," said Matti. "But that shouldn't— Gods, I hope nobody's taken it into their head to helpfully start cutting corners. I can look into—"

"There's something more pressing," said Tomas.

Maya shot a look at Matti, then a sharper one back at their father. "Dad, what is it? What was Corus here about?"

"He knows not to bother you with House business," said Matti. "Is it something to do with the Guild?"

"He *was* bringing it to you, Matti, but you were out and I was handy." Tomas took longer than usual to affix his glasses to his face, and during those few seconds the last of Matti's good spirits evaporated.

"Dad," Matti said.

"It's only rumour so far," said Tomas.

"*What?*" said Maya.

"Harte House is branching out into wool."

"Wh-what?" This time Maya sounded a lot shakier.

Matti, moving with legs that felt as though he'd run the distance between the Rose Quarter and the docks without pausing for breath, went to lean on the corner of his father's desk. He splayed a hand on the leather-inlaid surface for balance, and his fingers found the deep scratch in the leather that he himself had put there when he was young, an overexcited child playing at man of business with an empty fountain pen.

He said, "What kind of wool? What's the rumour?"

"A series of rumours." Tomas began to count on his fingers. "They've approached one of the most innovative loom builders I know, with an order for something different to their usual. To handle a new kind of material. They're looking into warehouse space here in Glassport—that one's certain. Enris Harte mentioned it in passing at a Guild meeting last week, and then tried to cover for it. I didn't know what to make of it at the time, but it makes sense now."

"Warehouse space?" said Matti sharply. The Hartes were silkmakers, spanning the whole breadth of the process from raw worm-thread to finished bolt. Their farms and workshops were all well inland, and there was no demand for Thesperan silk offshore; the country of Ashfah, Thesper's closest neighbour across the sea, produced more than enough. There was nothing for the Hartes in Glassport except a market for their end products.

"And," said Tomas, in the tone of someone coming to the pointy end of a thing, "they're inquiring about hiring ships to make the crossing to and from Fataf."

"So we know the kind of wool," Matti said. There was a sensation in his throat like swallowing too-cold water. "Black libelza."

"Harte is already a luxury name," said Maya, echoing Matti's thoughts. "They've got the connections. If they keep to libelza and other kinds of superfine, if they concentrate their efforts at that end of the market . . ."

"They can more than give us a run for our money," said Tomas grimly. "They don't know the business like we do, but I imagine the learning curve would be quick for someone with Jacquelle Harte's reputation. The expertise in processing isn't there, but you can buy that, if you're rich enough."

Unspoken was the fact that Jay House had been forced to lay off enough skilled workers in the past few years to staff a moderately sized workshop. They'd be easy enough to find, to hire, for anyone looking to break into the market.

"If we could only—" said Matti, but stopped. It was useless to talk that way. If only Matti had anticipated more, worked harder, forced himself to find more opportunities where the goddess had laid them hidden in his path. If they could *only* afford to outfit another ship—to buy raw libelza wool from the auction houses across the sea in Draka—to pay the high duty on it when it arrived in Glassport.

If *only* the last ship, which had been their last chance, had made it.

"You will," said Tomas. "You *will* be able to, Matti. I know you'll turn this around. This engagement—"

"I know," Matti said. He glanced at Maya, who had unburdened herself of the rolls of fabric and was twisting her hands in her skirts. She looked back at him and managed an encouraging smile.

Matti willed his mouth to smile back, and willed the anxious, self-blaming lump of ice in his throat to go away—everything was going to be *fine,* he'd *fixed* it. Matti would turn this around. All he had to do was get married.

A voice came drifting up from downstairs. "Hello? Maya, where are you?"

"We're all up here, Mama," called Maya over her shoulder. "Dad's study."

After her footsteps sounded on the stairs, there was another rustle of fabric, and then Matti's mother was sweeping into and across the room. In most respects, she was a shorter version of Maya, though still taller than the average. Nessanesh's braid was smooth rather than a game attempt to wrestle waves into submission, and the lines of her face were deeper. The women's fashion for long sleeveless tunics belted over the basic combination of shirt-and-skirt or shirt-and-trousers was beginning to show some bleedover from shorter, more masculine styles of jackets. Nessanesh wore a brocaded jacket in green and red with stiff flared sleeves, over a black skirt edged in rows of gold floral embroidery.

"You look nice, Nessa love," said Tomas.

Nessanesh lifted a hand above her shoulder and flicked its fingers wide, a family gesture of resignation. "Nice, the man says! I suppose I am a mouse, every other day I exist under this roof. I suppose I do not know how to dress myself."

Tomas turned a look of entreaty on his two eldest children. "Twenty-five years of marriage and you see how I'm treated?"

"Twenty-five years of marriage to a Jay and he's surprised I can put a visiting outfit together," said Nessa loftily. Tomas pushed his chair out so that his wife could lower herself to sit on one of his knees. "I have been out to spread the news of our son's engagement. I have dropped it everywhere. Like a biscuit into coffee. Matti, Gerta Lourde has a tongue loose with news about changes to the fee structure at her aunt's bank. We will talk about it at dinner. How did you fare at Tolliver's?"

"Fine," said Matti. He slid Lourde House's banking fees into his list of things to worry about that evening. "I now have a best man."

"Who did you get?" asked Maya. "Was Aren Rowell available? He was best man for Ellen Jessamy, you remember, when everyone *knew* that Nicoletta Picia was going to challenge for Jacinda, and he did a great job. Ellen and Jacinda hired him again as swordguard for the ceremony when they named Ellen's nephew as their heir."

Matti ran his tongue around his mouth. "I hired someone new to town," he said. "He hasn't worked in Glassport before."

His mother looked at him. Her tone was still gentle but her black eyes did all the piercing that was required. "Six hundred gold, Matti," she said. As if Matti could somehow have forgotten.

"Don't worry, love," said Tomas. He wrapped an arm around his wife's waist. "It'd take a spectacular cheat to pull one over on our Matti."

Matti managed, somehow, to keep his face from doing anything revealing. "I know better than to buy without a sample, Mama," he said. "Hardy Tolliver vouched for his skill, and he gave me a demonstration. He's. He's very good." Matti felt his face heat.

"What's his name?" Maya asked. "Where did he work before this? If he's had any interesting victorics, especially at a wedding, there'll be gossip. I'm sure I can write to someone and find out."

"Luca Piere," said Matti. "And I don't know. I didn't ask." After all, it didn't necessarily mean anything that Piere had mentioned Guildmaster Havelot by name. And Matti wasn't inclined to trust Piere's accent any more than the rest of him; the man was an admitted con artist, no matter what else he was.

"By the way," Matti added, aiming for casual, "Wynn Amberden has bought me lessons from a dancing master, as an engagement present. It's for the Half Moon Ball. A secret."

"What a nice idea that is," his mother said. "A surprise for Sofia."

"I'll go in the mornings, instead of swimming," Matti said. He'd come up with the story on the walk home from Tolliver's; it wasn't perfect, but it was the best he could do. Perhaps nobody would have noticed, but on the occasional morning his mother was up early enough to walk part of the way to the baths with him, peeling off at her favourite bakery to smell the first trays of raskils fresh from the oven. Now he had a solid excuse to be heading in a different direction.

"I should be off to the council offices." Tomas levered first Nessa and then himself up out of the chair. "The health committee is meeting with the Guild of Physicians leadership to discuss changes to their accreditation and complaints process. And then I have an afternoon of being shouted at by Lysbette Martens and her allies to look forward to." Tomas's time as the city's Spinners and Weavers Guildmaster was split between Guild business and serving on the city's ruling council, as well as representing the Glassport branch at the annual Guildband meeting of representatives from across the Nine Free States of Thesper.

"They're still pushing for the canal project?" Maya asked.

Tomas nodded grimly. "Lysbette gave another very pretty speech, using Henry Penseil's mouth to do it, and I think they're wearing down some of those who voted with me last time the proposal was raised. This time they're selling it as an employment initiative. *Think of all the jobs!*"

"You can't blame Penseil, Dad," said Matti. "A city-funded canal all the way to the border with Barlow would be an amazing thing for his Guild. Of course he's onside."

"I can blame Henry, and I will," said Tomas. "Lysbette's self-interest is the root of this proposal. I refuse to applaud just because she's managed to point out the ways in which it will line pockets other than those of her own House, at the expense of city funds.

It's our turn to host the Negenhal next year. We can't afford to strain our budget any further. And if we must create jobs for engineers, what about fixing the plumbing in the Ash Quarter? What about fixing the *roads*?"

"They are a disgrace, the roads in that neighbourhood," Nessa agreed. "Twice this year already I have had the carriage axle repaired, as though we can afford such expense! Now I walk from the south side of Ash Bridge all the way to Kupa's stall, and one day when I break my ankle on the same holes there will be no more japetas on our dinner table." The tiny pancakes of mashed vegetables spiked with garlic and smoky burr-spice were a Yaghali dish, and only one street vendor in the city made them in what Nessa proclaimed was the proper manner.

Maya made a showy sound of pain and clutched her chest, smiling. "You can't fool us, Mama. An abyss would have to form between our house and the Ashmarket before you stopped going for Kupa's japetas."

"Even then, I think she would learn to fly," said Tomas fondly.

"At least japetas are cheap," said Maya.

The silence was short and well-worn, full of glances held for exactly long enough for the four of them to realise that it didn't matter what was said in this room. They were so used to keeping some things unsaid that the sound of them could still feel fresh and strange.

"Yes. And you do not fight for my ankles, lovely though they are," said Nessa. "You heard Kupa's brother, when we had them to dinner. Roads not safe. Water pipes not replaced since they were first laid. Children sick from sewage leaks."

"Exactly." Tomas's face was set in a way that Matti had known, and loved—and even felt a little afraid of—ever since he was a boy. "Glassport itself could easily swallow all the money that such a canal project would take, given the rate the population's growing. And that's without considering the distance between the hospitals and—"

"Yes! Enough!" Nessa slapped his arm. "We are too easy an audience for your speeches. Go and deliver them where the people do *not* agree with you."

Tomas kissed her temple and took another step towards the study door. "Speaking of Barlow, Matti—any luck with Alain Collins yet?"

"He still won't commit," said Matti. "I'll write to him again today."

Tomas nodded. "The payroll list from the weavers will be coming in at noon, and I know I said I'd try to make sense of that twenty-page report purporting to explain why everyone is suddenly charging twice as much for sea-scarlet dye as they were last year, but what with one thing and another—"

"Of course. Go. I'll take care of everything," said Matti.

"Yes, yes," said Tomas. He rested a hand for a moment on Matti's shoulder as he left the room. "You always do."

<hr>

Luca got lost twice before he found the boardinghouse.

The first time, it happened because he'd stopped concentrating on his feet and started composing letters to his mother and Perse in his head. It was a difficult exercise. Luca had trouble keeping a peaceful tone when communicating with his older brother in person, and didn't have much more luck in writing, no matter how hypothetical.

I'm fine. I'm getting by. Men far less clever than I manage to make their living by the sword; there's no reason to think I won't be able to do it.

Too defensive? Perhaps.

So I conned one of the best-looking men I've ever met out of two hundred gold, and now I'm a member of his wedding party, because the goddess has a great fucking sense of humour.

He was never going to write any of this down. Never going to

actually send it. So what did it matter? If he were being honest—
ha!—then the letter would be a lot uglier.

*Yes I know I fucked everything up and yes if I were a better sort of
person I'd be on the first coach home and I'd face the consequences,
but even on the other end of a prison sentence I'd still be faced with
the rest of my life and I can't, I won't, I can't—*

That was when Luca realised that he'd emerged into a small
square containing an unfamiliar food market, and he no longer
had any idea in which direction the harbour lay. Smells gloriously
assaulted his nose: roasting nuts, an elusive herby fragrance, hot
bread, briny seafood mingled with vinegar. Luca paused in front
of a stall selling one of the few foods he'd never seen before: small
balls of dough lifted sizzling from oil and rolled in dark sugar.
They were a shade of green that bordered on lurid.

"What gives them that colour?" Luca asked the woman behind
the stall. Her headband and trousers were both made from fabric
in a striking and deeply unfashionable patchwork pattern, moving
lightly enough to be cotton rather than wool.

"Lascari leaves." Sensing a willingness to buy, she was already
scooping several of them into a waxed paper bag.

Luca pulled out his purse and asked directions while he was
at it. The woman's answer brought out the musical hint of a far-
south Elizen accent. Luca managed to escape the conversation
before he found himself mimicking her cadences to her face, but
he muttered southerly notes to himself for a few minutes while he
was busy burning his fingers on the hot sweets and getting lost for
the second time.

That time, it simply happened because his sense of direction in
unfamiliar places was mediocre on a good day, and on a bad day
was appalling enough that he had once been accused of putting
it on in order to be obnoxious. But if his brain was hopeless at
grasping the layout of new places, his muscles at least knew what
to do. He learned a place by walking it. And he was too restless,

too curious, too bursting with novelty and the remains of guilt and fear and relief, to stay in the Tollivers' attic room all day.

The lascari balls were delicious. Luca licked the last of the sugar off oily fingertips as he walked across a crowded bridge, keeping close to the wrought iron railing, around which was tied a series of ribbons in varying states from fresh to rotting. It was an exam-time tradition common to students destined for the more academic Guilds. Perhaps there was a law school nearby.

The bridge widened into a main street lined with buildings as varied in appearance as the ribbon-offerings. These days the Negenhal was a lawmakers' meeting of the governing councils from all nine of the Free States, held every other year and with each capital taking its turn to host, but the first ever Negenhal had been little more than a series of peace talks that took hold of a war-ridden Thesper and shook it like a wrinkled blanket until it grumbled its way into the current arrangement of city-states. Before then, the city of Glassport had been a kind of passive battleground of cultural influence, sitting as it did close to the midpoint between the cities of Barlow and Harbeke.

Now it had been the capital of its own state, controlling its own territories, for nearly two hundred years. And yet to Luca's eyes and ears and nose Glassport still gave the impression of *two* cities existing . . . not side by side, but piled defiantly on top of each other, like two theatregoers refusing to relinquish their warring claims on the best seat. A distinctly Barlowian flourish to the roofline here; a street sign in Old Harbekan there, the stone engraving worn almost to indecipherability with age.

No matter its enmeshed twin origins, Glassport was the major port on the west coast, and like any centre of trade it was a loudly messy cultural quilt. The market stallholder was not the last Elizen voice Luca heard, and before long he felt confident that his ear had collected nearly all the Thesperan city-states. He even heard the soft, inky Ashfahani tongue being spoken as he passed

the open doors of an enormous blocklike building and caught a
strong whiff suggestive of a horse market.

Northern looks like Jay's were rarer, but here and there Luca
caught a glimpse—gathered fabric with lace underskirts on
display, embroidered felt caps on both men and women, dark
skin—or heard a strong accent that could have signalled either
Manisi or a citizen from the northern kingdom of Narama. Far
enough north, it was nearly impossible to place someone as hail-
ing from one side of the border or the other.

Luca ran a hand through his own hair. He'd wondered if he
should dye it, but red wasn't an uncommon colour here; there
didn't seem to *be* any uncommon colours. And he *liked* his hair.
Other people liked his hair. Mattinesh Jay's eyes had lingered
on it.

Luca did draw a few glances on the street, but most of them
were directed at his waist. The weight of the sword, his awareness
of its sheath and its balance as he walked, was both familiar and
unfamiliar. Luca had spent enough hours of his life wearing his
weapons for the weight of them to be a friendly comfort, but he'd
never had cause to wear them on the street. They'd never been the
mark of his trade before. It sent an uneasy thrill up his spine, and
made his feet feel as though they might strike up sparks against
the stones of the street.

Eventually he made his way to the boardinghouse that he'd
found on his first afternoon in this city. There were rooms enough
at every price point, but Luca had fallen inconveniently in love
with the first place he'd walked into, and had not managed to convince himself that he was willing to settle for any of the cheaper or
less wonderfully situated rooms he'd viewed afterwards. He didn't
mind waiting a week in the Tollivers' attic. He didn't mind that
the rent would take most of the money he'd both conned—and,
now, promised to earn legitimately—from Mattinesh Jay.

The boardinghouse looked like most of the other houses on

the street, tucked shoulder to shoulder with its immediate neighbours, narrowing to a pointed orange roof. The blue doorframe was carved and painted with the symbols of the Hearthkeeper god, Osta. But it was the room within that Luca cared about, because that room had a view down to the water. It was only one of the many sly fingers of salt water, the canals, that branched inland through the city of Glassport from the main harbour itself. But it was, if you stretched the term, *sea*water. Luca's home city of Cienne sprawled next to a lake studded with small islands, but the horizon was an uneven line of mountains no matter which way you looked. Glassport had the horizon of the ocean: straight and vast as a line drawn by the gods.

The trappings were important when you were reinventing yourself. Luca Piere lived by the sea. Luca Piere carried a sword. Luca Piere didn't *have* to have a family to write home to, if he didn't want one.

"Can I— Oh, it's you again," said Miss Vaunt, when she answered the door. Her eyes swept Luca from toe to head and her posture shifted. A hint of a pert smile made itself known in her cheek; her face, a lighter brown than Mattinesh Jay's, was a dense paint-splash of freckles beneath a kinked cloud of hair. "Here to tell us you won't be taking the room after all, then?"

Luca canted his own posture in response, letting his grin flirt with her cheek until it rendered up that smile. "Never fear, my sweet one," he said. "No torture yet invented by the devious minds of men could induce me to go back on my word, once given."

"That's nice," said the girl. Luca wished he could remember her first name. "Because none of those tortures you mentioned will induce Mama to give you back that deposit you laid down to secure the room."

Luca laughed. "I was merely going to ask if, by any chance, the current occupant is planning to leave any earlier than I was told?"

"Sorry," she said. "We'll have to do without the pleasure of your company at breakfast for a little while longer."

"Ah, well. Pata rewards the patient. Thank you for your time, Miss Vaunt."

Now her brows arched, knowing. "It's Dinah," she said, and threw him another smile before she closed the door in his face.

Not ready to return to the Tollivers' yet, Luca made his way from the boardinghouse to the harbour proper, following the smell of salt as it deepened and broadened into something rich with fish, with damp, with the sharp smell of wood stain, with tar and smoke and a hundred other layers beneath that. The smell of everything that could be packed into a ship's hold and carried from one place to another, there to be sold or transformed into something new.

The thrill in his feet and spine had settled into a thin whisper that threatened to become words unless Luca trod it into silence. He'd hoped to crush this whisper beneath the coach's wheels when he left Cienne. No matter. He had distance, now, and time. He would exhaust it eventually.

He strolled in a slow, winding path along the docks, looking for nothing in particular, but noticing as much as he could. He passed ship after ship and craned his neck to see if there were sailors working in the rigging, or to watch furled sails sway gently against the clouds. He noted which figureheads needed a fresh coat of paint, or had lost some detail of their design through either skirmish or decay. Many of these figureheads were clutching the reef-knotted rope and had the seaweed crown of Itsa, patron goddess of the Guild of Sailors and Shipbuilders. Other deities appeared as well; these ships were likely owned outright by, or else exclusively contracted to, grand Houses dedicated to some trade or another.

The names of the ships appeared on scrolls held by these figureheads, or were painted close to the waterline in careful script. LADY JENNY. BRIGHT MORNING. FEARLESS.

A street away from the waterfront, Luca stopped and entered a glassblower's shop, which was set incongruously between a drinking house and the office of a shipping company. His eye had been hooked by one of the pieces in the window, a beautifully made figurine of a caterpillar, each body segment a bulb of clear glass shot through with spirals, specks, or shards. It was the kind of thing Luca would usually have bought without a second thought, and gifted to his mother.

He was halfway to taking the caterpillar off the shelf before he remembered that he didn't have that kind of money any longer, and also that his mother—

Well. He didn't have the money.

Luca's fingers tingled as he used one to follow a tendril of green in the glass. He could always *steal* it. That was part of who he was now, wasn't it?

The shopkeeper, an elderly man with the most lovingly trimmed and outrageously waxed white moustache that Luca had ever seen, was engaged in discussion with another customer over a display box on the counter. He'd glanced at Luca on Luca's entry into the shop, but his attention was split at best. Luca's coat, shabby as it was, had deep inner pockets. It would take no time at all.

Luca bit down on his own cheek hard enough that he wanted to gasp as a chill skated down his spine and the memory of glass shattering, musically high and cold, rang its phantom notes in his ears. Gods, gods, how stupid could he *be*? Standing in a shop owned by one of Kusi's children, thinking about *stealing* from them, as though he hadn't already done more than enough back home to earn the ire of the Artificer goddess.

He murmured an apology of a prayer under his breath, promising another handful of coins to Kusi's Guildhall, even though the donation he'd made in a guilty panic upon arriving in Glassport had been another of the reasons he'd found himself broke enough to start running small cons.

The other customer left, and the shopkeeper made eye contact with Luca as he was putting away the box.

"Lovely work," said Luca politely, gesturing around the shop with a jerk of his head. The Elizen accent was still on his tongue, and danced out before he could suppress it. "Yours? Your family's?"

"Yes to both," said the man. "Were you looking for something in particular?"

"Just whiling away the time," said Luca. "I've a meeting soon. Hoping for a job."

The blue eyes above the moustache strayed to Luca's sword. "Serving as escort on a voyage, are you?"

"Why, yes," said Luca, pleased to have his story thus embroidered. "Yes, I am."

Five minutes later, he knew all about Rubin Nyfaert's family and had gained a sprinkling of new words and terms that might come in handy if he ever wanted to pretend at being someone who knew anything about glassworking. He'd been told a story about how Glassport was first founded—though Nyfaert referred to the city as Glashaven, a sign of stubbornly Harbekan roots— that Luca was almost certain was a pretty myth, but it was a good story nonetheless.

For his part, Nyfaert had learned that Luca was an orphan by the name of Kal and that he'd been raised by a retired sword master, and that he was keen to leave the city on a seafaring job because of delicate circumstances that might or might not involve seducing a prominent member of the Guild of Lawyers while the man's own husband slept in the next room.

It wasn't hard. It was just a matter of the right smile, the right *talk*. And if Luca could do anything, he could talk.

The Tollivers thought he was a talented young duellist trying his luck in a new city. Everyone in the drinking house, when Luca tried the pocket watch con on Jay, had thought he was a harried clerk sent on an errand. Even though it was what had gotten him into trouble in the first place, even though it had sent him fleeing here with a new name on his lips, Luca couldn't help himself. Something in him thirsted after the shining, open ease in someone's face when they were looking at Luca and believing his story. Something in him quietened, within the skins of these other invented people. These people whose skins Luca wore as easily as his sword belt might have had their own small worries, but they didn't have a disaster sprawled in their wake. Or an unwanted future hanging over their heads.

Being *himself* was a failed experiment. Luca had learned that lesson already.

CHAPTER
4

It took Luca three tries to open the street-level door of Tolliver's agency the next morning. He blamed in equal measure the lingering dawn chill of the air, the fact that if there were any justice in the world he would have been firmly asleep and intending to remain so for several hours, and the fact that Mattinesh Jay's near-black eyes were watching him do it.

Jay had been leaning against the door when Luca jogged up. Now he was a distractingly solid presence, and Luca's fingers were clumsy under his gaze.

"Good of Tolliver to lend us the room."

"Mm." It was, to be frank, a grunt. Luca's eyelids felt gummy and rose-thorned.

Tolliver hadn't questioned the fact that Luca had agreed to throw in sword lessons on top of the usual best-man contract for Jay. Even so, Luca had the feeling that if any money were kept on the premises, or if the swords in the practice room were anything more than merely serviceable, Luca might not be trusted to open the office a full two hours before Tolliver himself was usually there.

Or maybe he would, given who he'd be teaching. The shift in Tolliver's manner when he was interacting with Jay had been . . . interesting. Another puzzle piece that didn't fit.

Upstairs, they shucked off their coats without speaking, and Luca was relieved to see that Jay was wearing worn-looking trousers a good few years out of style. The current fashion was for a snug fit, which Luca appreciated on someone with Jay's physique as a general rule, but looser was better for this purpose, given that the seams were unlikely to be endangered by a bit of physical activity.

Jay was bouncing on his toes, one hand lifting to scrub through his hair, where he promptly caught his fingers in a knot and had to tug them awkwardly free. Luca, whose own hair had defeated more than one comb in single combat, could sympathise.

"So, Piere. Here we are."

"Indeed, Mr. Jay." Luca gave an incline of his body. Despite his general early-morning bleariness he felt a tickle of defiant excitement on the back of his bowed neck. He'd never been an employee before. He could imagine Perse's voice in his head, the cold surprise mingled with condemnation. *Our family hasn't risen this high for you to run around playing at being in service.*

In service, Luca thought, rising from the bow. And not playing at it, either: he was here and he had a job to perform.

"Can you—not call me that?"

"Not call you Mr. Jay?"

"Yes."

"Have you misled me as to your name?" Luca asked.

"It's not that. I want this to be something I'm doing as myself, not as a representative of my family. I don't . . ."

Jay looked uncomfortable. Luca thought about how careful, how quietly hungry, and how ashamed of that hunger the man had been about the sheer prospect of indulging in sword lessons when he didn't need them. Luca would have wagered that the swallowed segment of that sentence was: *I don't do many things as myself.*

"You prefer Mattinesh?"

Mattinesh Jay's nose didn't wrinkle, precisely, but he screwed his mouth sideways in a way that drew his nose along with it and revealed a dimple in his cheek. "Matti's fine. Just Matti."

"Well, this won't do."

"It won't?"

"We can hardly have me calling you Matti, like one of your dear friends, and have you calling me *Piere*. That's not how these things go."

"No?" Matti feinted towards that sideways expression again. "I called my schoolmasters by their family names."

"And I expect they were all grey-haired, dry-voiced old men, and not handsome young things like myself." Luca wasn't sure what he was angling for. No, that was a lie. He did. He won himself a pause, a quick flick of Matti's eyes down his body.

"Some of them were women."

"There's nothing for it. I suppose you'll have to call me Luca."

A silver trout of an expression darted across Matti's face, the barbed tail of it catching Luca's breath. He waited with unwarranted eagerness to hear his name emerge from Matti's mouth, but instead Matti just watched Luca expectantly.

It occurred to Luca for the first time to wonder if he should have come up with a *plan* for these lessons. He'd first picked up a sword fifteen years ago, and had almost no memory of how his very earliest instruction had gone.

It couldn't be that complicated. Luca knew how to do this. Matti did not. It was just going to be a matter of telling him what he was doing wrong.

Master Carriere insisted that Luca, even after those fifteen years, began every lesson with the basic forms. That seemed a reasonable place to start.

Or so Luca thought, until Matti went to pick up a sword, hesitated, and then said, "Shall I just pick any of them?"

"What? No, of course not, don't be stupid," Luca said, and recalibrated.

He found Matti a pair of leather gloves first. Luca had only seen one or two hand injuries sustained by beginners during training, but those had been more than enough. He steered Matti firmly away from the longer, more old-fashioned swords that might be used in a high formal duel, and towards the shorter ones with flexible blades and simplified cage-guards. He showed Matti— quickly pulling his own sword, to remind himself of the ratio— how to measure the length of a plain practice blade against his height and select the right one.

Then he showed Matti how to hold it. Then he showed him again. Then again. Every time he thought Matti's grip looked right, he compared it to his own unthinking grip and found something different in the way their fingers were positioned.

"Does it have to be this exact?" Matti asked, after the third time he'd extended his arm at Luca's direction and Luca had snapped, "No, now your wrist looks all wrong and it's *drooping,* come here."

Luca was not going to say he didn't actually know which of the differences were the vital ones and which were a forgivable variation. He said, "Yes," with all the confidence he could project through the way his temples had started to throb, and thankfully Matti nodded and subsided.

By that time it had been half a damn hour and they hadn't even gotten to how to stand yet, and Luca was convinced Matti was going to lose patience. The man looked as calmly interested as ever, but surely it was a facade that could snap at any second. Luca felt both jittery and tired.

"Here," Luca said, trying to rescue his mood, "let me show you a trick," and he demonstrated how to find the weighted centre of a blade by laying it across the second finger of both hands, set far apart, and sliding them slowly towards each other.

Matti copied him. "What is this useful for?"

"It's not," said Luca. He flicked the sword up and caught it by the grip.

After that he tried to show Matti how to stand. If anything, that was even worse. He racked his brain for all the tricks he knew; the piece of string drawing the shoulder blades together was one. Imagining a light shining up from the forearm to the ceiling was another.

Each of them seemed to work for a moment, in isolation, but when Matti tried to combine them, it all fell apart.

Luca, through his teeth, told Matti what he was doing wrong. And kept telling him.

Matti accepted every correction like a windless lake accepting pebbles dropped into it, one after another. After a while he began to wince and shake his head, as though annoyed at himself, whenever Luca opened his mouth.

Luca felt even worse.

"All right. I think I'm holding my weight lower," Matti said. "Is this right?"

"It's . . . not bad," Luca said, dubious. Something about the man's stance looked desperately wrong, in fact, but Luca couldn't put his finger on what it was. "Try stepping forward."

Matti took a deep breath, shifted his right foot with all the lightness of an iron dragged across cloth, and nearly fell over.

"I *told* you not to stiffen up. How can you— Oh, for— This is hopeless. You're *hopeless*," Luca snapped. He put his back against the nearest wall and slid down it to sit with his knees tucked up. He set his practice sword on the ground with a loud clash. "*Fuck*," he said, with feeling.

A difficult silence thrummed in the room. Luca did not want to look up and find out if Matti looked furious, or hurt, or dejected, or disgusted. Luca was just going to stare at the window and think about the nap he was going to have soon. Morning light was washing the room with pale streaks, and the city, which had never been entirely quiet, was growing louder.

"That was hardly called for," said Matti after a while.

Luca rubbed his forehead against his knees, scrubbing a hand through his hair, which had tangled at the nape with sweat. Matti had a point, but his mildness was not soothing Luca's annoyance. It was having the opposite effect.

"You had to insist on fucking mornings," he said.

"Hungover?"

"Hah." Luca tilted his head back again, and punished himself by thumping it against the wall. "That'd be a good reason. No. Surely you've come across the concept of people who just don't enjoy being awake this early? Is every member of your bloody household up and greeting the dawn with cheer and goodwill?"

"More or less," Matti said. "It helps that two of those members are five years old. Once they're up, everyone's up."

"Please at least tell me someone is unable to put together sentences until coffee has been served," said Luca, "or I shall be forced to assume you come from a family of unnatural freaks."

Matti didn't quite laugh, but laughter appeared on either side of his eyes, and his teeth flashed in his smile. He was unfairly handsome when he smiled. And he didn't just have one dimple; he had a matching set. "That would be my sister," he said. "Maya. No matter how tight money is, there's always enough for Maya to have her morning pot. Mama calls it the murder-prevention tax."

"She's not one of the five-year-olds, I trust."

"Maya? No, she's only two years younger than I am." Matti slid a look at Luca that was knowing enough to stop the next question on Luca's tongue. "And yes, before you ask: same mother, all of us. The twins were . . . a surprise."

In the rhythm of the conversation, this was a place for Luca to offer something in kind, as apology for snapping. Some information about his own family. He could tell the truth, there'd be no harm in it. *I'm the youngest. It's just me and my brother.* Or he could invent a vast family of siblings of all ages for Luca Piere, sword for hire. He could embroider each one lavishly with imaginary traits, and sprinkle them with freckles.

Luca looked at Matti, something uncertain and wild swirling in his stomach, and experienced the vastly strange sensation of not wanting to lie. Nor did he want to peel back the paper of himself and reveal something true. Both contrary impulses seemed to stem from the swirling, like twin trunks grown up from the same seed.

No matter. Stories were fun, being entertaining was fun, but people never really *wanted* to hear about you, especially if the alternative was talking about themselves.

"If I'm to be best man for this wedding of yours," he said, "I should know about any rituals I'm expected to take part in. Whose auspices will it be under?"

"Maha, on Sofia's side. Huna, on mine."

"Huna."

"Patron of weavers and spinners."

"I . . . yes," Luca said. "I've heard of her."

Matti had sworn by Huna the first time they met, and it had passed through Luca's ears unquestioned. He was a poor man who acted like a rich one, and who wore a coat—a woollen coat—worth forty gold at least.

Somewhere in the depth of information retained from Luca's poorly attended lessons, the name *Jay* finally caught on the appropriate hook.

"Jay. Your family makes wool?"

"Sheep make wool," said Matti, deadpan. "But yes. My family takes it from there."

"And what do you do, Mattinesh, for Jay House?"

Matti smiled. This time, no dimples swam to the surface. It was a collection of muscle movements unadorned by any kind of joy.

"Not enough," he said.

"I meant—"

"I know what you meant," said Matti. "I do a bit of everything. My father is the Guildmaster here," he added, with painstaking pride. "He can't be expected to oversee our House's doings as minutely as he used to." Matti's voice firmed even further. "I'm glad that he trusts me with it."

There it was: the puzzle piece. Guildmasters were politicians; if one was also Head of a House, their elected term was a busy few years for the rest of their family. Doing a bit of everything, in that context, meant that the man in front of Luca—who dressed himself and held himself as though embarrassed by his own size, and who had yet to raise his voice beyond a mild conversational volume—was likely to be single-handedly managing the business affairs of one of the most prominent Houses in Thesper's wool trade. He wasn't a minor member of Jay House. He was the Head in everything but name. He was the *heir*.

And he was watching Luca with the kind of look that was far more appropriate to the sword ring than anything else he'd worn so far. It was the look of someone waiting to be attacked, readying himself to absorb the blow. Luca, fascinated, watched this look until it faded.

"Thank you," Matti said finally.

"For what?"

"For not pointing out that I mustn't be very good at it," Matti said, soft, and Luca remembered in an instant that Matti's family business was failing; *not enough,* Matti had said. It was failing to the point that the scion of the House was marrying a rich daughter of another, and they could barely scrape together enough for a best man. Auspices of Maha. That was vintners and brewers, but it could mean any of a number of different Houses, and . . . now they were swimming even further into the vast and unplumbed waters of Luca's ignorance in matters of business.

Luca didn't consider himself ignorant in matters of *people*—far from it, in fact—but he was becoming intrigued by the mass of contradictions in an attractive wrapping that was Mattinesh Jay. He wanted to send testing attacks towards every corner of Matti's defence, and use them to find out the truth of him.

He could have done it subtly. But often you learned just as much from the blow that was unexpectedly direct.

"Are you a bad businessman, Matti?"

"I. No." The way Matti said it reminded Luca of a luckstone tossed in a pocket for decades: worn and small, gleaming and hard.

"No?"

"In the teeth of the evidence." Matti ran his hand through his hair. This time no knots impeded the gesture. Luca's own fingers still prickled at the sight. "I know what I'm doing. But Huna throws her coins, and sometimes they land in the dust."

Meaning, Luca interpreted, that something very unlucky had happened. Some investment gone sour, some speculation that had faltered and taken Jay House's fortunes with it. It wasn't as though people had stopped wearing wool, or using it to cover their floors and their beds.

Luca said, "I'd have thought if it was as bad as all that, your father wouldn't stand for the Guildmaster position in the first place. Splitting his attention, for the pittance of a city councillor's salary . . ."

"He believes in doing the most good that he can, for the Guild and the city. For everyone. He's the best man for the job, and so he does it."

"And all the while your House is in a lot more trouble than is generally known." Luca knew he shouldn't ask the next question. He did anyway. "Aren't you afraid I'll tell someone all of this?"

"Who? And why? You'd have to explain how you know," Matti said calmly. "Besides, I have witnesses to you telling me an easily provable lie, in order to extort money from me. I don't think you want to be arrested."

"But if I was arrested, you wouldn't have me as your best man."

"But I'd be awarded my money back, so I could afford to buy myself a reputable one."

"Ah, but they wouldn't throw in sword lessons."

Matti's smile, the proper one, appeared and disappeared as though a curtain had been tugged back by a curious hand and then dropped again. Carefully he found the midpoint of the sword in his hands, and held it across two fingers.

"And so the situation is like this," Matti said. "Nicely balanced. No, right now I'm not afraid you will upset it by ruining my family's name. What would you gain by it?"

"Nothing," said Luca. "You're right."

And he wasn't lying, he told himself. There was no reason for any of this to matter. The duellist Luca Piere had no House to work himself to the bone for, or to be married off to preserve. Or to disappoint with his personal failings. Luca Piere provided a service. His only interest was in doing his job well and being paid. Beyond that, he wasn't supposed to know, or care, about the shifting fortunes of the people he served.

Luca was going to give this man sword lessons, stand by his side at the wedding that would resurrect Jay House's fortunes, and maybe have the chance to give a display of his skill, if the expected challenge took place.

It was all very simple.

Yet Luca had the sensation that the ground beneath his feet—which any duellist needed to be solid and smooth, and lacking in treacherous irregularities—had begun to show a small but noticeable tilt.

———— ∘»☗◈☗«∘ ————

"Matti!" called Maya. "Is that you, rummaging around? We're in the sitting room."

Matti scooped semi-dried tomatoes into a bread roll and hurriedly licked his wrist as oil trickled down it. He made an apologetic face at Joselyne, the only full-time member of the townhouse's domestic staff, and took his lunch into the room that Maya's voice had emerged from.

Lunch was a generous descriptor. It was midafternoon. Matti had spent the morning going over accounts with Corus Vane, after reading and then rereading the twenty-page report on some kind of tidal event that was affecting the supply and therefore the cost of sea-scarlet shells. He'd given himself a headache and counted every pen in his desk in a vain attempt to banish it. He'd exhausted a messenger girl while negotiating, via rapid exchange of notes, a date to meet with senior members from three Guilds that wouldn't fall on a holiday or an inauspicious date in anyone's god's calendar. It was part of doing business, but there were some particularly busy times of year when it felt like trying to lay stepping-stones in a swamp.

He'd gone to a meeting at a coffeehouse with one of the buyers for a drapier in Sanoy, where his cup of coffee and his raskil fell like stones into his anxious stomach, and signed off on a refund for a portion of their last shipment, which had arrived with damp-rot affecting some bolts of superfine. And then to the workshop on the fringe of the East Quarter in order to sit down with five people who wanted to tell him, in indignant detail, why the issues with the burling finish were anyone's fault but theirs. He probably should have delegated that last one to a supervisor, but their experienced seniors were almost as busy as Matti himself.

Just thinking about the pile of papers still waiting on his desk made Matti feel lightheaded. It was one of those days when he had to keep pinching the webbing of his fingers, punishing, to keep his focus. If he closed his eyes for more than a moment he found himself dreaming about a fall—not a fall *into* anything, not with any intent, just the *act* of falling. Back and back into a soft darkness that demanded nothing and expected nothing, and was what Matti imagined a solid nine hours of sleep probably felt like.

The lightheadedness, at least, might improve if he ate something. Matti was chewing a huge mouthful when he entered the sitting room and discovered that Maya's *we* had not been family-exclusive.

Matti choked on his food, struggled to swallow, and coughed several times into his cuff before he managed to speak. "Sofia! I'm sorry."

"He hasn't eaten all day, I expect," said Maya.

Sofia Cooper flapped her hand towards a chair. "Don't mind me. Sit and finish your food."

"Sofia is here to discuss plans for the events leading up to the wedding," said Maya, as Matti gratefully sat and shoved another quarter of the roll into his mouth.

"And the wedding itself," said Sofia. "If you don't mind talking a different kind of shop, Matti."

Matti shook his head, and Sofia gave him a smile. This was the first time they'd spoken since the engagement had been finalised, and Matti might have expected it to be awkward, if he'd known she was coming today. If he'd had a chance to anticipate and fret. He glanced at Maya, wondering if she'd known, and if she'd kept it from him for that very reason.

The two of them, Sofia and Matti, had been friendly in childhood in the passing way of people whose parents were friends; Sofia's mother had known Tomas since *they* were children. They'd drifted apart as they grew up, and hadn't spoken more than polite greetings to each other in years. It was deeply strange, Matti was now discovering, to look at someone you'd always thought of as a kind of distant fixture in your life, and realise that soon you would be married to them.

There was no denying that Sofia was pretty. She had a soft figure and had inherited the colouring of her Otescan mother, including thick hair the colour of acorns in the shade, today coiled at the crown of her head. All her facial features from her turned-up nose to her bright brown eyes proclaimed a kind of delicacy that was thoroughly undercut by her eyebrows. These were thick, straight slashes across the olive skin of her face, strong and expressive, and just about the only hint to her personality that existed on the surface.

"I was just telling Sofia how much I love her outfit. If she keeps draping jewel-tone scarves like that, half the city will be doing it by the end of next month," said Maya. It was a blatant attempt to engage Matti in paying a compliment to his betrothed, and Matti would have played gamely along if he did not have a mouthful of bread and tomatoes.

Sofia, Huna save her, turned her gaze and the warmth of her smile immediately onto Maya. "You like it? It was an accident. Or a tantrum, rather. I was trying to figure out how to copy a knot that I'd seen in a portrait of Mama's grandmother, and I gave up when I'd tangled myself in the thing. Then I liked the way it looked, so I went out anyway."

Maya shifted closer to Sofia on the couch and reached out to tweak a loop of the scarf. "Keep accentuating the asymmetry. It's more striking that way."

Sofia dressed very well; Matti could see that even without Maya's unerring eye for style. He could have priced to within a few silver the skirt that fell from waist to ankle, navy blue twill shot through with white, and belted over her white shirt was a burnt-orange tunic that looked like the kind of underworked silk more usually made into gowns. Matti also knew that the bright teal scarf looped over Sofia's neck and shoulder was not in line with current fashions, but unlike his sister he wouldn't have been able to state with such confidence that it had a chance of setting a trend instead of merely being remarked upon—with varying levels of snideness—as a charmingly individual expression of taste.

The snideness would dry up entirely when Sofia had changed her young House's name for another. The Coopers needed this alliance; perhaps not as much as the Jays needed the bond price, but they needed it nonetheless. Money and success counted for a lot, but *establishment* counted for just as much, and a marriage was still one of the strongest bonds. The Jays were a very old name in their trade. The wedding would swing a brush and extend the patina of their unassailable respectability over Cooper House.

Sofia and Maya planned Sofia's ongoing conquest of Glassport fashion, while Matti ate the rest of his roll at a pace less likely to cause indigestion. By the time he was shaking away crumbs, they'd moved on to talking about how perfect the Coopers' country

house was going to be for the Half Moon Ball, and Matti plunged
into the discussion as well. The ball was a tradition common to
most Guilds and their patron deities, held two weeks before the
wedding, and it would be a larger event than the wedding ceremony itself.

"Matti has hired a best man," Maya said, when talk turned to
the wedding parties.

"That was fast," Sofia said.

"Well," Matti said. "I—yes."

As with Adrean, he was unsure how to dance around the subject. Obviously, if Sofia was going to be pragmatic about it, that
was far preferable to the alternative. Matti didn't *want* her to be
sitting here sniffing back tears.

And yet.

"You're being very cheerful about all of this," Matti said. "You
don't have to pretend. Everyone knows that, you know . . ."

"Everyone knows what?" Sofia said.

Maya made a face at her brother from behind Sofia's shoulder,
but Matti tossed caution to the offcut pile. They were going to be
married. They had to be able to talk about difficult things.

"Everyone knows that you and Adrean are—that he's—"

"Everyone," said Sofia, "can be mistaken. And they often are."

"You don't have to protect my feelings, if that's what this is."

"Protect?" Sofia's brows wavered. "Matti, I'm not lying to you."

"But he's so . . ." Matti made a gesture to illustrate the figure
that was Adrean Vane, with his big sad eyes, his talent with a sword,
and his ability to compose songs and poetry. Matti was not going to pretend that he posed any kind of serious competition to
Adrean when it came to sheer romance. If he ever tried to compose a poem, he expected the inked words would peel themselves
up off the paper and flee in protest. "And, well. I'm sorry, Sofia, but
everyone's heard the song."

"Oh, Maha's bleeding liver," exploded Sofia. "If I could snap my fingers and wipe 'Wildflowers Under Glass' from the world, I would. Thanks to the one and only decent tune Adrean has ever managed to produce, half of Glassport start whistling when they see me in the street, and the other half give me sympathetic looks." Her voice took on a dry edge. "Of course, it's such a *nice* song. And of course *his* word on the matter is more to be trusted than *mine*."

"No!" Matti looked at Maya, half an entreaty that she would make everything all right, and half hot embarrassment that she was here to watch as he tangled this conversation beyond repair.

Maya was leaning back in her seat, as though making respectful room for the strength of Sofia's annoyance. She touched Sofia's arm. "All right, ignore the fact that Matti's being an idiot. We'd never take his word over yours when it comes to your own feelings, would we, Matti?"

"No," said Matti. "But at the same time, I'm fairly sure we have to take Adrean's word for *his*."

"I—oh, I know. I do know that." Some of the fiery air seemed to go out of Sofia. "I wish that *arse* of a man would get it through his overgroomed head that I'm not nursing a secret passion for him!"

"You mean you've already rejected him outright?" That stopped Matti short. He could believe in a misunderstanding, perhaps, an unrequited love mistaken for something else. Indistinct flag colours viewed over a vast gulf of ocean. The ocean, in this case, being the fact that Sofia was a daughter of Cooper House, and Adrean carried no House's name at all, nor any particular inclination to turn his hands to enriching one.

"Indeed," said Sofia grimly. "Believe me, there's nothing romantic about someone who hears the word *no* and translates it through three books of love poems and his own daydreams so that it means *please keep chasing me*."

Matti didn't know what to say to that.

"Has Adrean told you he plans to challenge at the wedding?" Sofia asked.

"Not explicitly," Matti admitted. "But he hinted. Strongly."

"Thus the rapid hiring of a best man." Sofia sighed. Her eyebrows appeared to reach a decision and rose with a practical air. "A good one?"

"The best I could afford," said Matti, more or less honestly.

This didn't change the necessity of Luca's hiring, though it did put a different spin on things. To challenge at a wedding against the bride's wishes wasn't unheard of, but it was unbelievably rude. And rare enough that Matti had never heard of it resulting in a successful duel. The best man in any wedding party was considered the mortal arm of the deities overseeing the match; if he lost, it was a sign that the marriage was ill-fated and would end poorly, if not tragically. A successful challenger had no particular claim to the bride if she denied them, but they were a line scratched through the best-laid plans of mortals.

A sword-challenged wedding would be talked about for months.

A sword-lost wedding would *not go ahead.*

Of course, there was a general agreement that if you got yourself halfway across the bridge, the gods would be more inclined to help you across the other half. Hiring the most skilled duellist you could afford was good business sense. The gods respected that above all else.

"Then there's nothing else to be done there." Sofia appeared to dispel the entire question of Adrean Vane with her breath. "We can focus on more enjoyable things, like what we're going to wear. Have you chosen a colour, Matti? We should make the decision together, but I'll be honest: I'm hoping for gold, for my party."

An array of swatches popped obligingly into Matti's mind. He banished the vibrant sea-scarlet that had occupied his morning. It would look fine with his colouring, but unspeakably gaudy, and the rest of his wedding party would have to be dressed in the same shade.

He had a sudden flash of Luca, who would be standing beside him in readiness to answer any challenge, condoned by the bride or not. Luca wore his shabby clothes with what Matti thought was an unconscious self-consciousness; he was trying hard not to mind them, but he minded anyway. He would look incredibly striking in good fabric, tailored well.

"Green," Matti said, dressing his mental image. "Not too bright. A dark forest green?"

Sofia beamed approval. "Green and gold would be lovely. I've ages yet to source the fabric for the gowns, but it'll be Harte or Duvay, obviously." She smiled at Maya. "Though I won't even tell you how many fingers I'd chop off to be married in gallia silk. Have you ever seen a swatch?"

"Huna, *yes.*" Maya's eyes flashed with glee and they were off again.

Sofia's fingers were probably safe. Gallia worms were notoriously hard to keep alive, and there was a monopoly on their farming in their native Ashfah. No producer had ever agreed to sell either worms or raw thread to anyone outside that country, and both the export and import tariffs on the finished fabric itself were outrageously high.

Oh, Huna's eyes, Matti thought suddenly. *Did I honestly just make a wedding decision based on Luca Piere's hair?*

"Matti?"

He blinked. "Sorry. Was I supposed to be—" *listening,* he managed to snatch back from his distracted tongue, but it was fairly obvious where the sentence had been going.

Sofia burst into laughter, low and gurgling like a canal in a lock, and after a moment Maya followed suit.

"No," Sofia said. "Not really. But I've got something else that I want to discuss, Matti, if you don't mind?"

Matti thought of his paperwork again, but said, "Of course."

"Maya, could you give us a few minutes?"

Maya stood, then leaned down and touched Sofia's shoulder;

the gesture was uncharacteristically hesitant. "I'm glad it's you," she said. "Is that an odd thing to say?"

"You can't tell me you've always wanted a sister, Mayanesh," Sofia said, "because I know for a fact you already have one."

Maya had darker skin than Matti, so it was near impossible to see when she was blushing, but she had a tell: her expression blanked, her full mouth momentarily a straight line. Then it dissolved into a tentative smile.

"I don't hate my brother so much that I'd wish someone unpleasant on him" was all she said, and left the room.

It was as though some of the ease between Matti and Sofia left with her. Maya could be like that. Rose oil, their father called her. Smoothing the way and making everything seem pleasant. Maya's rose-oiling had held back angry debtors, persuaded long-term clients not to withdraw their business, and steered dinner conversations that were veering towards dangerous reefs back into calmer water. With her out of the room, Matti felt the strangeness of the situation slipping back. He looked at Sofia and thought the word *wife,* experimentally. It was like trying to hold a chunk of wet soap.

"I wanted to clear the air," Sofia said. Her hand smoothed a crease in her tunic. "I was wondering if there's a reason you were so ready to believe that this engagement is souring the barrel of some secret, desperate romance of mine."

It took Matti a long moment to realise what she was asking.

"No!" he said. "No. I'm not in love with anyone. I didn't have any—hopes, of anyone."

"Really?"

"Huna's teeth, Sofia," Matti said, "where would I find the *time?*"

That watery laugh spouted out of her again, and Matti exhaled. He'd had lovers before, but never anything long term, and nothing for—gods, he didn't know how many years. It just hadn't seemed important enough. Not in light of everything else.

But he couldn't blame Sofia for having the thought. He was

already ashamed of how readily he'd accepted one popular song and Adrean's own long-winded pronouncements as a true portrait of tragic love across class boundaries. Sofia's contentment with this engagement was a shift in the ground. Contrary to his previous assumptions, Matti's betrothed was *not* in love with someone else.

"Good," said Sofia. "I wanted to know where we stood. And"— with a quick smile as she patted her scarf again—"I *do* want to set fashions, and to know more about what goes into them. If I have to marry, then I'm very pleased for it to be into Huna's service."

"I'm glad." And he was. They would be fine. There was no need at all for this sour taste in Matti's mouth, or the irrational skitter of his pulse. He remembered, like a phantom kiss on his fingers, the sensation of the sword he'd demonstrated with for Luca. *Balanced.* It was just a matter of keeping it that way.

"So there we are. My parents have bought your name for me, and your prestige for Cooper House."

There was a knock on the sitting room door and Joselyne, apologetic, came in brandishing a handful of letters. "Afternoon post, Matti," she said. "I'd have left them on your desk, but there are two Sally-eyes in the pile and another red besides."

Matti accepted the papers, turning them in his hand to confirm that two of them bore a red wax seal with a spot of white wax in the centre, mimicking the flower that bestowed the nickname, proclaiming not only that the sender considered them urgent but that they were requesting a reply within a day.

"I should deal with these."

"I won't lie and say I was just leaving," said Sofia, "but I've kept you long enough."

"Thanks," Matti said. "For . . ."

Everything. Saying yes. Making it easier for Matti than it could have been. *Being* easier than she could have been; Matti had seen enough precarious business marriages that he knew he should be grateful for something like this, where the liking was simple and, if they were luckier than they deserved, perhaps the love could be built.

Sofia lifted her chin, elegant above the bright splash of her scarf, but reminding Matti of the sturdy prow of a ship. She could have parted crowds and waves. "We do what we have to do, right?" She smiled at him. "We'll make the best of it."

CHAPTER

5

Blackmail or no blackmail, employee or not, Luca sincerely wished he had insisted on holding these lessons in the evenings. The pin in the alarm clock he'd borrowed from the Tollivers was set to an hour of the morning that Luca had previously only seen from the other side, after the occasional giddy night of dancing and flirting and drinking until the sun's first rays split the sky.

At least it *was* light. Luca shuddered to think how awful this would have been in the cold months with their longer nights.

"You get used to it," Matti said, while he was removing his coat.

"I'd rather not, if it's all the same to you."

Luca bounced on his toes and circled his wrists and shoulders to begin limbering up, while Matti went through the process of choosing a sword and then came to stand in front of him. Luca didn't know if he was envious of or annoyed by the way Matti held himself: calm and still, as though he were waiting with unconscious ease for the attention in the room to centre upon him, knowing he wouldn't have to lift a finger. And he *didn't*. They could have been in a packed Guildhall, or the busiest market in Glassport, and Luca wouldn't have wanted to look at anything else.

"All right. Show me a ready stance," Luca said.

Matti lifted his sword. It took him a few seconds of shifting his feet and consciously adjusting, but the position he ended up in was a lot better than anything he'd managed the previous day.

"That's . . . actually, that's not a complete disaster."

"I practiced. Before bed."

"I assumed you don't own any swords."

"I used my hairbrush."

The image sprang helpfully into Luca's head: solemn Matti, wearing nightclothes and brandishing a hairbrush in front of his dresser, like an indignant girl trying to defend herself from unwanted advances.

"Your *hairbrush*," he said, struggling not to laugh.

"Yes, all right, but I *don't* have anything else. The handle's about the right width," Matti said weakly, relaxing out of the stance.

"No, hold it," Luca commanded, and took a closer look at Matti's grip this time. "That'll do. Let's try the basic forms. The first one is moving from ready stance to a guard in the winter quadrant. Don't worry—I'll fix everything as we go."

A lot easier to say, it turned out, than to do. Luca's optimism crashed to the ground like a dropped glass after ten minutes of trying to explain the concept of holding a soft guard position to allow for a middling parry.

"So if I come at your winter quadrant like *this*," he said, demonstrating a slow low strike directed upwards, "and you parry too shallowly, I'll have time to adjust and get inside your guard. Parry too widely, and you'll have too far to move the next time."

"You're . . . circling." Matti was looking at Luca's feet, instead of minding his guard.

"What?"

"In the duels I've seen, everything has happened in a straight line. More or less."

"I'm teaching you informal style," Luca said. "Because—well, I don't know. That's what's used in wedding duels."

"There's more than one style?"

Luca had the strong urge to go and bash his head against the wall. "Thesperan duelling has three. The duels at most kinds of ceremonies are formal style, along a linear plane, because they're for an audience. High formal has even showier movements, and it uses longer swords. If you're trying to do what you've seen someone do at a ceremony, for fuck's sake, *don't*." He demonstrated the form again. "It's supposed to be small. Like this. You see?"

"I see."

The skin of Luca's throat warmed at the intent way Matti's gaze travelled over his body. He knew what it was to be looked at, and he did know the difference between looks and *looks*. He felt his tongue flick out and wet his lips.

"Though," Matti went on, "*seeing* doesn't seem to be helping me *do* anything properly."

"No, it isn't," said Luca, too distracted by Matti's hot eyes to be polite. "Aren't you getting frustrated?"

Surely he must be, by now. Surely not even Matti's still-waters act could be kept up indefinitely. But Matti just shrugged. The anger that Luca had seen on the day Matti hired him had clearly been tidied away into the same deep inner pocket that Matti used to hide . . . whatever it was he felt and thought when his eyes stayed too long on Luca's thighs or Luca's wrists.

"I'm supposed to be bad at it. I'm a beginner. And clearly I have no natural gift for it, if you think I should be picking things up more quickly."

"Do you want to stop?"

Matti's brow furrowed. "I didn't say that."

Luca furrowed right back at him. "As you pointed out when you asked for these lessons, Mr. Jay—"

"Matti," said Matti immediately.

"—As you pointed out, Matti, the point isn't to turn you into a duellist. You're supposed to be *enjoying* yourself, unless you're harbouring a passion for suffering that you have so far failed to tell me about."

"Yes," Matti agreed.

"Yes to the suffering thing? If that's the case, I can start whacking you from time to time with the flat of the blade. All part of the service."

That won him the feinting flicker of a smile. "Yes to the enjoyment."

Luca looked at him dubiously. "Are you sure?"

"Yes."

Luca bit down on the urge to apologise. He wasn't sure what he would have been apologising for. "All right."

Matti sighed. "I could be focusing more carefully. My mind's on other things. I'm sorry."

That at least was something Luca might be able to fix. Master Carriere had a simple technique for those days when Luca brought anything more than himself into the practice room and let his preoccupations and temper intrude on the lesson.

"Tell me about those things," he said.

"What?"

"Talk. Get it out, whatever it is, and pretend that it's all piling up on the floor and can't climb back into your head. Then kick it aside and we'll try again."

It was no more rational than the piece of string between the shoulders, but there was something about these ridiculous images that stuck in the mind and made them effective.

"It's a business problem." Matti gave one of his brief, humourless smiles. "They're all business problems. But this one woke me up at midnight and wouldn't let me sleep again. Do you know anything about locality laws when it comes to product supply? Legislation that says, for example, that only wool farmed and processed in Barlow territories can be sold in Barlow city."

"It doesn't matter what I know." Luca pointed at the floor. "There."

"For months now, the Guild of Spinners and Weavers in Barlow has been dancing around the idea of loosening their locality laws and letting the Houses in Glassport into the market. Their winters are colder than ours, and a lot of their land that used to support sheep was bought up in the canola boom. Their suppliers can't keep up with demand from the tailoring houses in the cold months. But they're afraid once they let us into the market we'll crowd them out, and it's pointless to limit legislation by dates because winter fashions start appearing in the shops at the start

of autumn, and we're producing and selling even earlier, and—"
Matti took an audible breath. He was staring at the floor, at least,
as though he could see the whole mess of it piling up there. "Collins, the Guildmaster, is dragging his heels. Partly because he
doesn't like something my father's doing on the Glassport city
council."

Luca nodded, encouraging, when Matti glanced up at him as
if to check that he was still in the room. "Your father the Guildmaster."

"It's a long story." Matti rubbed at the back of his own neck. It
looked like an unconscious motion, one that leached a small fraction of the tension from his shoulders. "Lysbette Martens is the
Mason Guildmaster, and her House has a share in a red marble
quarry up near the border with Barlow territory. She's pushing
for the council to approve the construction of a new canal in that
direction. It would save Martens House weeks of transport time.
Dad's blocking the vote on its approval."

The pieces were sliding into place, even for someone with a
mental map of Thesper as hazy as Luca's. "And I suppose half the
Houses with headquarters in Barlow love that idea," Luca said.
"Including this Collins."

Matti nodded. "A direct channel to a major port, and one that
they'd barely have to pay a bronze for, given how much of it would
be within Glassport's borders? Yes. But Dad's not going to change
his vote. I think Collins does *know* that, but he's irritated, so he's
holding out on this deal. He wants a sweetener. Some kind of
guarantee that the demand in the Barlow wool market year-round
will support Jay House increasing the supply, and—we haven't got
anything to offer."

Master Carriere had always stayed silent and uncaring when he
made Luca do this. The audience wasn't supposed to participate.
The point wasn't to find a solution.

"You need a third party in this deal," Luca said, unable to help
himself. "Demand doesn't just appear from nowhere."

"I know that," Matti said, impatient. "But there's only so much you can do with summer fashions in a city where—"

"Forget fashion." Luca hesitated. Once again he had that twin urge: to be truthful and to avoid the truth. He found a truth that wasn't the example he'd been thinking of, but which would do in its place. "I ran a con, in another city," he said. "I bought cheap feathers and lavender in bulk, got a friend to make useless dangling ornaments from them, and then sent around copies of a fake decree from the Hearthkeeper Guildband that said it was a new part of celebrating the month of Osta's Dance. Every inn and hotel and boardinghouse in the city bought them at a ludicrous price from my friend's stall, and hung them from their doorframes."

He didn't mention that he'd donated all his profits as a gift to the Hearthkeeper Guildhall. He hadn't wanted to offend Osta, and hadn't needed the money. He'd just been—bored, and trying to prove something to himself.

He said, "The point is, you can legislate demand. Legitimately. Use this Guildmaster's voice on Barlow's city council. You just have to find a group that—"

"Lawyers," said Matti suddenly.

Luca, his rhythm thrown off, stared at Matti's newly lit eyes for a moment before the meaning fell into place. "Courtroom gowns?"

"Yes. They've got to wear them anyway, they buy new hoods and trim year-round because the colour depends on Katu's religious calendar, and if there's a mandate on wool percentage in the fabric—and *that* wool coming from Barlow territories, to protect the local industry—I think it's worth trying. The Lawyer Guildmaster in Barlow is—Joan Murtagh, I think? She certainly won't mind being owed a favour by a trade Guild."

"There," Luca said. Satisfaction hummed through him. "Better?"

"I . . . thank you." Matti smiled at him: a real one, this time. "You know, perhaps you're wasted on this sort of thing," he added, gesturing with his sword.

Luca's hungry enjoyment of Matti's smile stuttered to a halt. The words struck as if on a bruise, far too close to the imaginary version of Perse that Luca kept hearing when he made the mistake of slowing down, of letting his thoughts settle. Matti had managed to land a blow within his guard because Luca had forgotten that he wasn't supposed to be himself. Because Matti made him forget to lie.

He said, waspish, "By all means. Let me toss my sword out the window *right now*—"

"I didn't—"

"—and get a job staring at numbers in an office somewhere, shall I? And you can bloody well be your own best man. Best of luck with that."

There was a long pause. A knotted rope had tightened in Luca's throat, and he had to breathe deeply to loosen it. Matti touched his own mouth with a thumb, not moving his careful gaze from Luca's.

"I meant it as a compliment," Matti said. "I'm sorry. If it's any consolation, you'll most likely get to whack me with the flat of your blade sooner or later, given how bad I am at this."

Damn it. Luca was terrible at staying angry at the best of times, and the knot in his throat was dissolving under the unexpected warmth of Matti's teasing. He felt his mouth twitch. "I'm counting on it."

"Now. Winter guard," Matti said firmly, and lifted his sword. "I'll try it again."

———— ·⟫⊛·⊕·⊛⟪· ————

It wasn't as though the hairbrush solution was ideal.

But even if Matti could afford to buy a cheap, dulled sword to practice with, his chances of getting it into the house without someone noticing and asking questions was approximately nil. So he practiced with the brush, every night before bed. Despite his exhaustion it never felt like work. It wasn't staring at numbers, or forcing his mind to the ends of various options, or writing letter after letter to debtors, to buyers, to the tailors and fashion houses who were placing orders that would not be able to be filled this season. *Next year,* Matti wrote, over and over again. They were having temporary issues with the supply. No call for concern. Next year, Jay House would be back on its feet.

Matti couldn't spit all of that onto the floor and forget it. Instead, he didn't allow himself into bed until he felt like he'd managed to recreate at least a flimsy echo of what Luca had shown him that day.

Now, after fifteen lessons and fifteen nights, he had a tentative hope that he might be starting to improve.

Luca never stopped complaining about the early hour, but every day he seemed more awake when he unlocked the door. And he was obviously trying to keep a handle on his temper; not that he was always successful. The dwindling of Luca's patience could be measured in the restlessness of his feet, and the amount he fiddled with his hair and clothes when he was watching Matti.

And Luca did watch. A lot. Nobody in Matti's life had ever paid him this much single-minded attention, for any reason. It was often uncomfortable, and sometimes downright unnerving. Not least because if Matti had managed to work out the unconscious cues of Luca's body, he wondered what Luca had managed to read in his.

Because Matti had never paid anyone else this much attention either. When he closed his eyes in bed, prepared either for swift sleep or for awful, grimy hours of insomnia—rarely did he manage a middle ground—he saw the tendons of Luca's wrist shifting as he demonstrated a parry. Luca's hair catching merry hold of the sun as it rose, or the colour of a tarnished coin when the day was overcast.

Today, Luca was trying to teach Matti another of the basic forms: a simple exchange of blows that would apparently press the memory of the action into Matti's muscles like a seal into wax.

Matti already knew that this would take a lot more repetition than he had time for, but he was happy to see how far he could get.

If he could just understand how to do it in the first place.

Matti winced as the sword's handle jerked against his gloved fingers, jarring them, and his blade scraped Luca's with a pathetic *ching* as it wobbled off in the wrong direction. Luca's sword touched the side of his neck and lifted again, insultingly fast, then lowered.

"What is so fucking difficult about elbow *out*, blade *across*?" Luca demanded.

Matti rubbed sweat from his forehead with his cuff. "Show me again."

"I've shown you ten times, you just aren't doing it right."

"Then show me another way!" Matti said, needled. "If I'm not learning, whose fault is that? Haven't you ever taught anyone anything before?"

Luca opened his mouth. Closed it. It sounded like it cost him something to say, "No."

Matti thought about everything he'd ever taught Maya, from making spice biscuits to reading an auction-house report. He thought about how much he treasured the light of Merri's smile, the crack of Marko's laughter, when he could spare the time to teach them anything at all.

How did you get through life without passing anything on, but only absorbing for yourself?

Only stealing, Matti thought, remembering the pocket watch.

He said, "Well, you need to try harder."

Luca's voice rose. "You think I'm not trying?"

Matti liked to think that he was a levelheaded man. But if there was one thing he lacked patience for, it was people who tried to wriggle out from beneath their responsibilities, and suddenly he found Luca's dramatics more tiresome than entertaining. "I didn't say that."

Something ugly flashed in Luca's expression. "I'm good at this," he said, low. "I'm very good at it. And two weeks ago you could barely tell one end of a sword from the other. So what the fuck do you know?"

The unfairness of that crystallised. Matti's voice hardened. "I know that when a lesson is going this badly, you can blame me or blame the hour of day all you want, but at some point you have to admit that some of the problem is *you*."

A bark of laughter escaped Luca. He snatched the sword from Matti's hands and returned it to the rack. "All right. This has officially stopped being fun. I'll think of something else for you to work on tomorrow, but we're done for today."

An unfamiliar tide of anger rose in Matti. He didn't manage to swallow as much of it as he wanted, before he opened his mouth. Somewhat to his shock, what came out was: "No. I've bought your time, and that means I decide when we're done."

Luca pivoted with a predatory grace that seemed to make a mockery of Matti's own efforts. It made Matti angrier.

"Really, Mr. Jay," Luca said, an acid bite to his tone.

"I'm not paying you to have fun. I'm paying you to be here."

"Even if we both agree that we're not getting anywhere?"

"Yes," said Matti. "Even if I tell you to stand there and do *nothing*."

"That would be wasteful." The acid was sliding into sarcasm now. "Like I'm *wasted* as a duellist? You don't strike me as someone who's fond of waste, Mr. Jay. If it's your precious time, are you sure you don't want to demand something else?"

"Stop calling me that."

"I am but your humble servant, *Mr. Jay*," Luca said, silky and obnoxious.

"Luca."

"You told your family you're taking dance lessons in the mornings, is that right? We could turn that lie on its head. Turn it into truth."

Matti's breath caught as Luca slid into his space. One of

Luca's hands landed on Matti's shoulder and the other took hold of Matti's fingers. Matti felt both points of contact like splashes of warm water, and couldn't help the sway of his body towards Luca's.

He felt the reaction, the sudden tightening of Luca's hand, as Luca noticed.

"You've bought me?" Luca said. His eyes were close and insolent. "You own me? Will you tell me to show you a dance?"

Matti said, "No," even as his own free hand burned with the need to put it at Luca's waist. It would be easy. Luca's chest was rising unsteadily and his gaze kept falling to Matti's mouth.

"You could tell me to do all sorts of things," said Luca. The mocking anger was by now a mere shell around his words, turning them into something that hovered between question and promise.

Into Matti's mind, vivid and explicit, crashed a host of impossible possibilities. Luca's talented hands beneath Matti's clothing. Luca going to his knees. Luca in his arms, Luca's skin against his; Luca writhing and restless and demanding. Matti barely repressed a full-body shudder. He could feel Luca's breath on the underside of his own jaw. Luca's thumb shifted minutely against the side of Matti's finger, and Matti wanted to beg him to continue. He bit down on his tongue.

"But no," Luca said. "You'd rather I did nothing."

Matti didn't trust himself. He held Luca's gaze through a tiny gap of air that seemed dry and dangerous: high-summer grass awaiting a burn. Finally he managed to say, "Yes."

It was partly a lie. He would *rather* give in to the joke that wasn't a joke, pull Luca fully against him and kiss the cleverness from that mouth until nothing came from it but gasps.

Partly, it was the truth. Matti didn't know swords, but he knew how to hold a bluff until it wasn't a bluff any longer. He was not going to budge, and he wanted to see if the shifting currents of Luca would part around him.

Luca pulled both of his hands away. He took two steps back

and then dropped to the floor like a child awaiting a story, cross-legged, casual. He stretched one leg out. He folded it in again. He drummed his fingers on the floor. His gaze was level and annoyed. "If you're done being ridiculous—"

"We're not done," said Matti.

He didn't say, *You're the one who sat down. I didn't tell you to do that.*

"All you're doing is—frustrating us both. For nothing."

"Yes."

"Why?"

Because you don't want to.

"You took my money. Today, this is what I want."

Luca scratched the back of his neck. Plucked at a dusty fold of his trousers. Rolled his shoulders, clasped his hands.

Matti's arousal was settling, but it refused to vanish altogether. He watched the taut twitch of Luca's body and felt nearly as taut himself. This was ridiculous. But this was Matti's time and he was going to do nothing, *nothing,* he was *allowed.* The pleasure of that was almost as sharp and shameful as the pleasure of enforcing idleness in someone as restless as Luca.

And it wasn't a complete waste. Matti knew it; Luca knew it. Something was being brought into balance.

When Luca settled, it was like the hand of a wound-down clock finally coming to rest. He gave a shuddering breath, dropped his shoulders a few inches, and—stopped. His head didn't bow, but his chin lowered a little as the muscles of his throat relaxed.

Matti had to breathe through a sudden, absurd impulse to reach out and touch Luca's hair. He didn't even know what the motion would indicate. Gratitude? Praise? Apology?

Or was it just that he'd wanted to do it since the instant he first laid eyes on the man, and this was the first moment it had seemed anything other than unsafe?

Luca's hands rested on his knees. He had delicate fingers, dry knuckles.

I did that, Matti thought, and it was like an ember rising from his feet through his stomach and chest. *That is mine.* His pulse picked up and there was a hot taste in his mouth: *fear,* Matti thought then, the realisation coming right on the bright heels of the possessiveness. *I'm afraid.*

When Matti was no more than the twins' age, he and his mother had travelled north so that Matti could meet his grandmother, Nessanesh's mother. Lailanesh had been unwell, though Matti had not realised this at the time, and she had died not long after.

They had travelled by sea for part of the journey. Matti remembered someone lifting him, hands firm at his waist, so that Matti could sit at the very front of the ship where the bowsprit jutted out over the parting waves. Matti had felt the wind tossing spray into his eyes, and his small terrified heart had deafened him and shaken him and delighted him all at once. A *clean* fear, an exciting one. Very different to the grubby, bone-weary fears that had dragged at Matti since the day he learned to read his father's worries in the furrow of Tomas's brow; the same day those worries first whispered into Matti's ear and began to steal his sleep.

Now only Luca's gaze was twitching, side to side. And then it too settled, until Luca was gazing steadily into an unknown distance at the level of Matti's knees.

Most of Matti shivered and shrank from the way he felt, watching Luca Piere go still. But part of him blinked open eyes that had been shut, it seemed, for a very long time, and that part insisted: *No, cling to it.*

It hurts, but it might wipe you clean.

Matti walked to where his coat was slung across a table, and checked the time on his watch where it was in the pocket. It was an excuse. It was something to do while he conquered his heart rate and made sure his face was composed. His ears were pricked for the slightest sound from Luca, but none came.

He slid the watch back into the coat pocket, turned, and went to offer Luca a hand up. He'd braced himself, but he still wasn't prepared for the echo that slammed into him, shook his bones, when Luca looked unblinking and unsmiling up at him from the floor. They were in an empty practice room, not a crowded drinking house, and Matti hadn't been tricked into stepping on anything. But he felt some of that same disorientation, that same sense of being hurtled into the unknown.

Luca put his hand in Matti's and pulled himself to his feet. He cleared his throat.

"Show me the third form," Luca said. "You've done that before, and it takes you through the same position that you were struggling with. I didn't realise. Do it slowly and I'll show you where to pause."

Matti didn't trust himself to smile without laughing.

He said, "All right," and the moment moved on.

CHAPTER
6

The velvet tunic was new enough that the collar itched Luca's neck.

"Aleit," said his employer of the moment, "we're almost ready to go in. Stop messing around, love, you'll smudge your dress."

Aleit Martens was full of the nervy excitement of being thirteen and the centre of attention, and her eyes were wide as Ilse, Luca's fellow swordguard, walked her solemnly across the Guildhall's foyer and back again as though she were a much smaller child, Aleit's satin shoes balanced on Ilse's boots. At her mother's words, Aleit released Ilse's hands. Luca caught Ilse's attempt to suppress a wince as the girl leapt energetically off Ilse's feet and landed on the carpeted floor.

A small procession arranged itself in front of the large double doors leading into the Guildhall proper. In front came the Martens parents and their other two children: a young boy, sulkily well-scrubbed, and an older girl a few years past her own naming who looked superior and calm whenever she remembered not to look envious. Behind them was Aleit herself, brown hair hanging straight from two pins sparkling with glass flowers. She was muttering to herself under her breath, rehearsing her responses.

Bringing up the rear came Luca and Ilse, the ceremonial swordguard, both wearing the damn high-collared duellist's tunics over equally new trousers. Luca wasn't sure the maroon velvet was doing him any favours, given that he was probably pink with the midsummer heat. At least he was wearing clothes that weren't ancient, and he'd be allowed to keep them afterwards.

The bright trill of a glockenspiel sounded, and the doors swung open to reveal a hall full of well-dressed people, all turning their heads with a smile.

Ilse caught Luca's eye and mouthed, *"Houses,"* with a hint of an eye-roll.

Luca twitched his mouth in reply, and they stepped forward in Aleit's wake.

Ilse was tall, with dark gold hair braided in sections, and couldn't have been more than nineteen. This was her first proper job as a duellist on Tolliver's books. And as far as she knew, she and Luca were in a similar situation: comfortably Houseless, able to look on this kind of high ritual as something belonging to a sphere of existence that was only relevant inasmuch as it provided employment and entertainment. Most people, Ilse had pointed out, managed to swear themselves into the service of a Guild with much less fuss than this. The gods only expected this kind of performance from those with the money to pay for it.

Luca wondered if he should throw in some gawking for the sake of it. It wouldn't be hard. The Mason Guildhall had an intricate patterned floor in varying shades of marble, and the room was dominated by a huge glass-faced clock, hung between two soaring windows, showing off every whir of its shining cog entrails and the huge teardrop of quartz that acted as pendulum. Beneath the clock the Deputy Guildmaster stood on a wide, slightly raised stage.

Luca managed to catch the younger Martens brother's eye as he took his place on one side of the stage, and he gave the boy a solemn wink. Luca had been nine at Persemaine's naming ceremony, enduring his mother's arm around his shoulder—as she tried, without much success, to stop him from fidgeting constantly—and gazing at Perse's hair, which was newly cropped short to go with the new name. For a while Luca had assumed that everyone was given a fresh name at their naming, even those who weren't also settling into a new set of pronouns. And though he couldn't blame Perse for shedding *Persemella,* he was worried that he wouldn't be able to come up with anything better than his own.

He didn't remember being nervous at his own naming; he hadn't taken it very seriously. He'd enjoyed the gifts, the attention, the sense of performance.

"Aleit Martens, blood daughter of Martens House," said the Deputy Guildmaster. His voice flowed out across the hush of the hall. "Do you come here on your own feet, and offer your service with your own willing hands?"

"Y-yes," said Aleit. "Yes, I do."

Not a natural performer, this girl. Her excitement had given way to a voice that stumbled on the responses as she accepted the protection and rights of her House and swore herself into the service of Arri. The Head of Martens House stepped forward. Luca, remembering Matti's business problems, had been keeping an ear out for the name Lysbette. But this was a man, old enough to be Aleit's grandfather or great-uncle. He winked fondly at the girl as he handed her a lit candle—beautifully carved back and twisted to show the layers of coloured wax, like a split precious stone—welcoming her into the protection and service of their patron.

Luca kept a hand on his sword hilt, trying to channel his energy into an unobtrusive tapping of one fingertip against the leather-wrapped metal so that it didn't manifest as an unprofessional shifting of his feet. He was older than nine, now. He *could* stand still if he really had to.

That thought triggered a memory, and the memory sent an entirely different kind of restlessness creeping through his body.

You took my money. This is what I want.

Matti hadn't pushed any further since that day, nearly two weeks ago now. Luca kept catching Matti's eyes on him, more intimate than the act of instruction would require. But Matti hadn't *said* anything, and so despite being tempted to do some pushing himself, Luca had let it rest. He wondered if Matti had scared himself with that exhilarating thing that had tried to come into being between them, like two stones struck and sparking.

You took my money.

The extent of the arousal that spiralled through Luca whenever he thought about it was, frankly, baffling. It wasn't just that he found Matti attractive. It was that the arousal was shaping itself around a thread of shame, despite Luca's best rational efforts to tell himself there was nothing shameful in service jobs. *Duelling is barely two steps up from acting,* Perse had said once, knowing full well that Luca had spent a difficult few months in childhood, before he understood the implications, trying to talk their mother into letting him join a theatre company.

Luca couldn't help the kernel of hot humiliation, the feeling less-than, that Perse's words had managed to plant in his chest. He ignored it, but he couldn't budge it.

And yet. Some kind of yearning had come free in him, unlocked by his anger and the moment when he'd realised he was trying to step up to the challenge in Matti's voice. It felt like a game, and a heady one. Luca wanted to play, wanted *more,* and it was taking all his willpower not to snatch it.

He had to remember the sword, balanced on Matti's fingers. Upsetting the balance they'd hammered out for themselves would be risky. Someone might end up bleeding.

At least the unmentioned spark added a certain spice to the sword lessons, which were progressing like a recalcitrant horse being guided down a wide path. Every two steps forward also involved a step to the side, as well as the occasional detour back to the point where Matti seemed to have not only forgotten all the techniques and habits that Luca had shown him, but to have somehow invented terrible new ones since the previous morning.

The basic forms were improving through sheer dint of repetition. But Luca felt like a limp rag at the end of each lesson, having wrung himself out trying to think of new ways to explain things that seemed obvious and clear. He was not at his best, in that room, throwing himself against someone else's limitations and seemingly taking all the damage himself. He wanted to show hardworking, overscheduled, inhumanly responsible Matti that he was allowed to have fun, that he could *unbend,* he could *laugh.*

And he might have managed it easily if they were in any other situation but this. If they'd met at that drinking house with no agenda, if Luca could have bought a handsome man a drink, as he'd done on many other nights in his life, and sat next to him and sparkled and charmed and coaxed those dimples out, then leaned over and pressed his fingertips into them; whispered *let's leave now* against Matti's mouth.

It was just a wistful fantasy. Matti would still have been celebrating his engagement. And the disastrous foot they'd started off on was Luca's own fault.

And that was the problem, Luca thought now, sweeping the crowd in the Mason Guildhall with unseeing eyes. Never before had Luca been in the position of suspecting that he liked someone else a lot more than they liked him. Nothing to do with *desire*—that was there, there was no missing it. But he didn't think Matti had much of an opinion of him as a *person,* and that rankled. People liked Luca. It was one of the things he'd always relied upon.

Luca forced himself out of that depressing rumination. The ceremony was wrapping up. Aleit had blown out her candle and was smiling broadly now that her spoken part was over. The silence that settled was expectant.

Luca cleared his throat and stepped down to stand on the cleared piece of floor in front of the stage.

"I challenge the worthiness of Aleit Martens to take her place as a full member of the Masons Guild, under the patronage of Arri. Will anyone defend her claim?"

"I will," said Ilse, and she drew her sword as she stepped forward in turn.

There was a sprinkling of polite applause. Luca snuck another sideways look at the Martens boy, who seemed to have perked up. Finally, his expression said, they were getting to the good bit.

Unlike serving as best man, there was no expectation that standing swordguard at a naming ceremony would involve any risk of serious combat. Perhaps it had, long ago, when the gods guarded their followers more jealously and the Guilds were closer to clans. When a duellist was the purposeful arm of the gods and the law, settling real disputes, standing up for real challenges where the fate of more than a marriage might hang in the balance.

These days most of the job was symbolic, although with a duel in formal style there was at least a guaranteed chance to show off.

Luca settled his shoulders, focused his attention, and attacked.

He went in for a daring overarm strike, slowing it down at the last instant when he wasn't sure if Ilse had caught his signalling of the attack early enough to parry successfully. That won him an exasperated look down Ilse's nose, and Luca grinned back at her. The next time, he didn't slow down at all. After weeks of matching Matti's beginner's level, this was like a good clean stretch of a muscle. Luca hadn't realised how easily he would become rusty, even doing his own exercises every day.

They weren't expected to draw it out. After a few minutes Luca raised his eyebrows at Ilse and got an infinitesimal nod in return, and he made sure to over-rotate his body on the next stroke, leaving a clear opening. She stepped in and took advantage with enough speed that Luca heard an appreciative murmur, and then Luca was standing very still with Ilse's blade beside his neck.

"Withdraw your challenge," said Ilse.

"Withdrawn," said Luca cheerfully.

"Arri smile!" called the Deputy Guildmaster, and his words were echoed back by the audience.

Luca withdrew with a bow. Ilse kissed her hand to Aleit, who was looking just as excited as her brother, and who nearly forgot to clasp her hand over her heart in acknowledgement. Now the

applause was full and wholehearted. Everyone was probably looking forward to the food. Some kind of delicious smell had already
begun to infiltrate the Guildhall, and Luca could see dishes being
set up on long tables along the back wall.

Their role fulfilled, the swordguard exchanged a look and
made their way by unspoken accord along the edge of the crowd
to where the food was. Ilse was rapidly waylaid by a girl no taller
than her waist, who had a stubborn and starry-eyed look as she
gazed at Ilse's sword. Female duellists were becoming more common but were still a minority. Ilse had treated Luca to a litany of
complaints about the fact that they were still called *best men* if they
stood up at a wedding, and still expected to defend against claims
on the bride. If there even was a bride. Weddings of matched
gender had been legal across Thesper for almost thirty years. Luca
had always assumed that in the absence of any expected sword-
challenge, the couple simply flipped a coin to decide who took a
best man to the altar.

"Are you really a sword fighter? For *work?*" Luca heard, before
he unashamedly left Ilse to her tiny admirer and followed his nose.

He filled a plate with spiced fish and steamed bread, and then
was held at bay from a bowl of what looked like whipped goat cheese
with lacha syrup by an ancient man with a voice that creaked like
warping floorboards. This man was very keen to tell Luca, with
much waving of a serving spoon in illustration, that when he was
a lad he'd attended a naming ceremony where the two members
of the swordguard were *notorious rivals,* and the duel ended in the
defender skewering the challenger between the ribs. The sentiment
that Luca and Ilse's more modern swordplay had been disappoint-
ingly tame in comparison was unspoken but strongly implied.

Luca watched flecks of cheese fly onto the floor as the man
demonstrated the fatal blow in question. "Fascinating," he said
brightly.

"Oh, it was for a House under the Guild of Smiths, and everyone agreed that Buri wouldn't mind a bit of blood at a naming."

"Luca Piere, at your service," said Luca, extending the hand not currently burdened by a plate. The old man looked at it, brow creasing. Luca sighed. "Do think of me if any member of your family has need of a sword." He gave up on the cheese, snatched a few pieces of dried fruit, and escaped to a corner of the hall where small knots of people could provide him with shelter. He leaned against the wall, nudging the pommel of his sword into a more comfortable angle with one elbow.

"- –compete with Jay House for quality, but a reputation hinges on courtesy and fair dealing as well."

Luca looked over. A bearded man with black hair and good posture was listening to a shorter one, who had a broken nose and a marked cowlick that made him look boyish. They were smartly dressed and looked no different to the rest of the naming-day crowd, except that their heads were bent together and their bodies angled in a way that suggested a private conversation. Not too unusual. They could have been gossiping; that was what one did at these events. But the shorter man's eyes darted in sharp arcs, as though he were wary of eavesdroppers.

Luca was careful to lower his own eyes to his plate before he could be caught watching. *Dried apple,* he made his expression say; *how interesting.* And dried cubes of a pale yellow fruit Luca didn't recognise. He turned one of the cubes with his fingertip and kept his ears pricked.

"Hm. The Jays have no connections here, but you can't be too careful," the taller man said after a moment. "There are Guild offices down the corridor. We can speak more freely there."

The two men, plates still in hand, slipped through a curtained doorway in the very corner of the hall and were gone.

This felt like a test. Luca looked down at the pattern beneath his feet, a wonder in green and white and yellow marble. He followed the spiral of it with his eyes, in polite acknowledgement of Arri, and then looked back up at the curtain. The gods didn't give their gifts outright. They dropped opportunities into your path and it was up to you to seize them.

But was this an opportunity to behave himself, or an opportunity for action?

You want to believe the latter, a voice in him whispered. *You want something to give to Matti Jay. You want him to owe you something, or at least for you to owe him less.*

Another voice, softer and more thrilling, added: *You want to lay a gift at his feet. You want to see if he will smile at you.*

"Fuck it," Luca decided under his breath.

Keeping his own plate of food for disguise, he ducked through the curtain. He crept along the corridor beyond, which was lined with portraits and boards with gilded lists of names, proclaiming various Guildmasters and prizes. He heard the two voices again, now coming from the other side of a half-open door.

"—business with Donna and Jenny."

"It *was* a success," said the voice of the taller man. "It's just going to take longer than our hostess wanted."

"Sim says she's losing faith." His companion had a nasal voice, as though suffering a summer cold. "She doesn't trust us to finish them off."

"She doesn't trust anyone," said the other. "That's how she is. But she'll get her fee eventually, as long as your lot keep the moths out and your mouths shut."

"I still don't see why we can't speed things along further. Just a few words in the right cars about empty coffers—"

"No," sharply. "The Jay family keeps secrets like watertight barrels. They could count the possible sources of a leak on one hand. It's too much of a risk."

"Like this wedding? All that nice, new Cooper gold poured into those selfsame coffers?"

A pause. "I told you that was a risk. At worst it's a . . . setback."

Luca looked down and found his knee jigging. A piece of dried apple was close to jolting its way off the plate; he put it in his mouth. He glanced up and down the corridor, but nobody else seemed inclined to leave the party.

"It could be enough to put them back on their feet," argued Nasal.

"They were on their feet before."

A shiver went down Luca's spine at the gentle malice laid over those words like gleaming soap scum on a basin of water.

"True enough," said the other. "True enough. Now. You have terms for me."

"Six silver for heavy uniform serge, dropping to five after three years held exclusive. Blankets at materials cost if they'll take it undyed and if they hold the uniform contract exclusive for ten."

Nasal whistled. "It'll draw blood, going lower than that. But we can take the hit, if it shuts them out. You're sure that's the final word? They won't come back with a counteroffer?"

"Here. In writing."

"I'll pass it on."

Luca considered creeping closer to the door and sneaking a peek through it. But there was a sound of movement, as though the two men were gathering themselves to leave, and even though the conversation didn't sound like it was over, Luca was not up for his usual level of risk-taking. Not here, where he was *lying low.* He moved at once, thankful for the practiced silence of his feet, and slipped back into the Guildhall.

The crowd and the hot food had increased the hall's temperature, and Luca's velvet tunic now bordered on stifling. He tasted some of the unfamiliar fruit—it was wonderful, a burst of sweetness—and located Ilse's blond head easily where she stood in a cluster of children. Children made good camouflage. Luca headed over to them with his free hand prominent on his sword hilt like a lure laid for fish.

What did he have, really? A conversation heard without context, opaque as steel. Hints. And no reason to give Matti this dubious and poorly wrapped gift of information, beyond the fact that Luca's mouth ached whenever Matti's nose crinkled and his lips feinted in the direction of smiling.

It was something to keep in his pocket, Luca decided. That would do for now.

CHAPTER
7

"Stop!" Luca's voice cracked. For a moment Matti wondered if he'd actually made the man *cry*, through sheer incompetence, and what it meant that he didn't feel particularly bad about it. Was embarrassment at one's own ineptitude something that you could become immune to? But then Luca scrubbed a hand over his mouth and winced. "I'm parched. I need a drink. Hold that thought. Or don't, actually—get whatever thought was driving *that*"—with a wave up and down Matti's body—"and grind it into tiny pieces. Then scatter those pieces to the wind."

"Poetic," said Matti.

"Sleep deprivation makes me eloquent," said Luca, with half-hearted waspishness. He went over to the table in search of water.

Matti found himself grinding the dulled tip of his sword down against the top of his boot, and had to pull the blade away hastily before he managed to bore through the supple leather. He had the tense, grumpy alertness that came when one poured a bucket of coffee onto the smouldering embers of fatigue, and he was already anticipating the crash that would come midmorning.

What did Luca know about sleep deprivation? He'd probably been out drinking and gaming, or else had actually been in bed at a reasonable hour and was just whining to hear the sound of his own voice. Matti had spent six hours in bed and had only slept for four of them, his mind holding his exhausted body above the waves of sleep like a gaudy float above a fishhook. No wonder his hands and feet were being particularly stupid this morning. No wonder Luca was discovering new heights of obnoxious impatience.

Luca was still *trying,* Matti forced himself to remember; Matti could see the effort making murals of his compelling face. He would let his tongue dance in abusive circles, which Matti was learning not to take very seriously, but he would still slow down. He would explain the four quadrants of guard and how each attack or parry was based in one of them. He would show Matti as many times as it took.

And because Luca was bothering to put in the effort, because Matti had stopped believing that Luca didn't consider him *worth* the effort, Matti was prepared to do his part. He wasn't afraid to step in firmly when Luca skipped a step or seven, or when Matti didn't understand. Matti was prepared to ask for the concept to be simplified again, and again.

Matti's parents had encouraged him to ask questions from the time he understood language. They'd let him sit in on meetings and conversations and would dissect them afterwards for him, one step at a time. In the afternoons, he would feel grown-up and serious walking the floors of the carding houses, running small fingers through samples at auctions, and letting the sharp warm smell of the dye vats fill his head up with aches. He'd loved to follow the shining end of a pen down a column of numbers while his father took the numbers apart, patient, and shared a smile with Matti that said he was forgiven for pretending to understand, because he would, truly, in time. And so Matti did.

There was no shame in questioning. There was no shame in learning slowly, no matter what Luca thought.

And Matti needed these mornings. They were his haven, a space made safe by the fact that its boundaries were so clearly defined. Here in this room, in the morning light, as the day's heat took hold. Here where Matti was learning the scuffs and scratches of the floor like those of his father's desk.

Here where the end point was visible, where a line could be drawn on the calendar on the date when Matti would be married and these lessons would end.

Which was a *good thing*. Matti was engaged to a girl whose money he would use to drag his House back into prosperity. He had a best man who would prove the gods' blessing on Matti's marriage and then disappear into whatever lively stream of sword-play and criminal activity he'd dwelled in before he decided to tug Matti into its shallows.

A best man who Matti wanted with a slow, awful burn of hunger, which he was ignoring as he ignored hunger when he worked through lunch, or when he needed to make Merri smile by sliding oil-dipped bread off his own dinner plate and onto hers. It wasn't the hunger of the truly desperate; it couldn't hold a candle to the hunger of the beggars who sat on the bridges by day and curled themselves into doorways by night. It was bearable. It would pass.

It will pass, Matti told himself now, as Luca took a swig from the leather bottle of water. Luca's exposed throat moved as he swallowed, and Luca's impossible hair was dark with sweat where it met his skin.

Matti moved his sword to his left hand and wiped his palm, using the friction on his thigh to centre himself so that he didn't do anything stupid like . . . ask. Suggest. Oh, why not face it: *command* his money's worth, for the pleasure of watching Luca go still.

"Let's try something else," Luca said, when he'd wiped his mouth clear of water and offered the bottle to Matti, who shook his head. "Take guard."

Luca probably had unconscious tells that an experienced sword fighter would be able to spot, but Matti knew that he only noticed a signal when Luca was giving it deliberately. He managed to parry a clean lunge and was proud of the speed with which he got in the return blow, even though Luca brushed it aside with the wrist equivalent of an eye roll. The next attack, Matti had less success with.

"Oh for fuck's—that was just a high cross-strike in autumn! I showed you the block for that last week! You *had* that."

"Do it again, I'll get it this time," said Matti, but the second time was even worse, and he knew by now that this kind of thing was like damp-rot. It started with him not being able to manage a new move, and then crept its way backwards through his meagre repertoire, infecting everything, making him second-guess even the simplest positions.

At least Luca knew better by now than to suggest they stop.

"Here," snarled Luca, backing up. "For the tenth fucking time. Front foot pointed across for stability, back leg bent for ability to disengage, you're aiming to catch and constrain their blade at the third-point of your own, and you *hold*."

Matti took a deep breath, let it out, and did what Luca had done. Or so he thought.

"Pata's blistered hands, you towering dolt, that was even *worse*. What do I have to do? Translate this into another language? Draw a picture in the dust on the window? No, I'm honestly asking, what do you *want* from me, when—"

"I want you to be *quiet*!"

It came out of Matti like beer from a tap, shocking him. He hardly ever raised his voice like that.

Luca was looking at him, eyes wide. As Matti opened his mouth—either to apologise for snapping or to compound the insult, he wasn't sure—Luca raised a single finger: wait. He lifted that hand and made an elaborate mime of sewing his own lips closed, knotting the thread off at one end and flicking the invisible needle away.

"Yes, all right," said Matti. "Thank you. Now, *think* about it. What am I doing wrong? How do I fix it?"

Luca gestured indignantly to his closed mouth.

A crackle of something, an inconvenient thrum of power, found its way under Matti's skin at the sight. It was absurd. Just because Luca was standing there with his lips held together, making an arrogant show out of his obedience. Matti wanted to push his tongue against Luca's mouth, force it open, feel those invisible stitches give way. He would almost expect to taste blood. The thought of it made muscles clench at the back of his neck.

"You've made your point," Matti said.

Luca shrugged.

Matti said, "Show me again."

Luca settled into the position. It was strange not to hear him break immediately into a fluid stream of description as to how the feet should be placed, the weight distributed, the precise angles of elbow and shoulder. Matti watched him uncertainly. Luca gave a get-on-with-it flick of his sword tip.

Matti copied him, trying to hold everything in his mind at once. He concentrated hard on his grip, but knew by the time he'd corrected it that the angle of his pelvis was wrong.

Luca tapped his foot, and looked down at his boot until Matti looked down too. Luca moved that foot a few inches outwards and then bent his knee more deeply. Matti did the same. When Matti looked back up, Luca had a smile on his face; Matti felt himself mirror it without thinking, the muscles of his face just as attuned to Luca's body as the rest of him.

Piece by piece of anatomy, Luca adjusted, and Matti copied. They held every small change for long enough that Matti's body settled into it before the next change came. In between, Matti drew his eyes constantly back to Luca's. After a few minutes he felt that he could have turned away and, if given a box of pencils, sketched every fleck of colour in Luca's irises from memory. They were an odd kind of hazel. The central ring of amber-brown turned to a cool dark grey at the edges, with barely a hint of green in between.

Finally, Luca drew in a deep breath. Matti followed suit before he could ask if he was supposed to. He echoed the held breath. He echoed the long, nearly vocalised exhalation that Luca gave.

Somehow Matti had forgotten that Luca was the only one making a game of silence; the quiet had layered itself inside his throat as well. Even more than usual, the world was here in this room, in Luca's insistent gaze, in the moments between Matti's heartbeats.

Luca made a *stay* motion with his hand and dropped the stance himself. Matti held it. Luca walked around him in a slow circle. Matti's legs and shoulders had a heat in them, a fierce ache, but it wasn't unbearable. He held.

At the end of his circle, Luca reached out with his free hand. The touch of his fingers beneath Matti's jaw was almost a static shock. Luca lifted Matti's chin by a bare fraction of an inch, and his own face broke into a stunning smile. He nodded.

Matti let everything loosen and drop, shaking the aches gratefully from his arms and legs. His hands were sweating within his gloves.

"Now what?" Matti's voice scraped as if he'd been shouting instead of staying silent.

Luca pursed his lips and made a let-me-think kind of waggle with his head. Then he rolled his shoulders and took up a different position, one that Matti hadn't seen before. It looked like another high parry, this one with a twist of the torso and oddly grounded feet.

Matti dutifully fell into his best approximation of that position, waiting for Luca to again take him through the details one by one, limb by limb. But this time, Luca straightened out of it, sheathed his sword, and stepped close, as though he were going to circle Matti again.

Matti would have sworn that nothing could make his nerves as musical, nothing could set him on so perilous an edge of sensory awareness, as the mirror-dance they'd been doing.

He would have been wrong.

Luca's touch started at his elbow and trailed up his forearm, stirring the black hairs there, until Matti felt as though his skin itself were shivering atop the tense block of his muscles. At the wrist, at the edge of the glove, Luca nudged Matti's arm into a slightly different alignment. Matti swallowed hard and kept his gaze on the contrast of Luca's pale fingers against his own skin. He had a feeling that meeting Luca's eyes now would be a match set to powder.

Matti held. Luca touched him again, this time with both hands, one in the small of Matti's back and one flat and low on his stomach. Matti had to close his eyes. He surrendered to the gentle pressure that adjusted the tilt of his torso. When the hand on his back stroked—slow, gloriously slow—up his spine, he knew what was coming.

Luca pinched his fingers together, right between Matti's shoulder blades. *Imagine a piece of string.*

Matti pulled his shoulders back and down. The touch smoothed out, a caressing stroke of Luca's palm like a reward, and then moved on to prod Matti's hip.

How long had it been since someone had touched him with real purpose? An empty eternity, sang Matti's body. His breath felt very loud.

At the end of his circuit, Luca touched Matti's jaw again, exactly where he'd touched it at the end of the mirror-pose exercise. Like a blow falling onto an existing hurt, the contact was worse— better?—than all the preceding ones. It shot sparks down Matti's neck, down and farther down, and he felt the air helplessly leave his lungs.

Luca stepped away, and Matti finally looked at his face. Luca had a curve to his mouth that bordered on wicked, and it banished the last of Matti's flimsy doubt that Luca didn't know exactly what he was doing. That he wasn't getting just as much torturous enjoyment from it as Matti.

Matti realised that he was moving. He'd transferred the sword to his left hand and was removing his glove and reaching out with his right. For some reason it was vitally important that he satisfy his curiosity, that he explore that wicked smile, and just looking at it didn't seem enough. He had to touch it.

Luca's lips were soft and dry, and under Matti's touch they

slipped open a crack. Matti's fingers were touching Luca's teeth, barely. Matti had to concentrate to inhale fully, as though an action that had been easy and unthinking for every moment of his life until this one had suddenly become a matter that required as much effort as a new parry. He had no idea what he was doing, but he knew he did not want to be doing it alone.

"Talk to me," Matti said.

Luca took a shuddering breath. His tongue flicked out nervously and found Matti's fingertips, and both of them froze.

After a moment Luca reached up and took loose hold of Matti's wrist, and—did not push it away. Did not move it at all.

Matti was a man in a trance. Two of his fingers slid over Luca's lower lip, into the wide mouth, up to the knuckle. All he could think was that he would search out the words in Luca's mouth, hook them out into the air. But Luca took Matti's fingers between his teeth instead, scraping gently, no more than a light reminder that he was allowing this intrusion. His tongue made small circles that Matti felt with the heady, ticklish warmth of caramel spilled from the spoon. Luca's strange greenless eyes held his, and the light circle of Luca's fingers could have been an iron manacle, for all the possibility that Matti would have been able to pull free.

"Talk to me," Matti said again, barely hearing himself.

Luca's teeth sank deeper into the flesh of Matti's fingers. They were not sharp enough to break skin, or to dent Matti's nails, but it was painful. Matti gave a low sound and Luca tugged Matti's wrist away; tugged Matti's fingertips out of his mouth. Luca licked his lips, looking pupil-blown and wary. He dropped Matti's hand. He took an abrupt step back, and then halted.

They gazed at each other. Matti felt stunned. His fingers were wet. He was beyond aroused. It felt as though all the blood in his body had divided itself between his cock and the pulse in his neck, where it fluttered demandingly. His lips were parted; he wanted to drink an ocean.

Luca's chest was rising and falling rapidly and he bit down

on his own lower lip, an action that sent another spike of need through Matti, then shook his head as if to clear it.

"I think that's enough swordplay for today," Luca said. Matti took some comfort from how raw his voice sounded.

"Right." Matti inhaled and held it. He forced himself to think past the dizziness of desire. Part of him screamed to address this—*talk to me*—but he didn't have a clue where to begin, what he could possibly say to open that conversation. And Luca's body language now was that of someone seeking an escape. If Matti pushed, or if he said the wrong thing, he could drive a fist through the glass pane of everything. The lessons. The flirting. The lightness of Matti's chest as he climbed the stairs every day, anticipating the moment when Luca would smile in greeting.

Matti said only, feebly, "Same time tomorrow?" He began to turn away.

"Wait. Matti." Luca's gaze was hooded now, and warm rather than hot. He sounded uncertain. "Have a drink with me, tonight."

"A drink?" Matti felt thrown off-balance all over again. "In a drinking house?"

"Or anywhere," said Luca. "I don't—I mean, you're probably burying yourself in papers, but I thought—wouldn't you like to see if we can get along any better when we're not pointing swords at each other?"

This fell precisely nowhere in the contract that Matti had signed, nor in the bordering-on-blackmail agreement that he and Luca had made. He had no idea what fell under Luca's heading of *getting along*. He wanted to find out.

"I can't . . ." Matti hated, *hated* the taste of it on his tongue, now more than ever. "I can't afford it. My bond price isn't a line of credit, you know. It doesn't come due until I'm married."

"I was thinking," Luca said, like a man walking on a fence, "you could come over to my boardinghouse. I think I can stretch to a bottle of something mediocre."

Matti would have to tell his family another lie. He would have to leave some paperwork undone. This was probably a terrible idea.

"Yes," said Matti in a rush. "Yes, I'd like that. Sofia is coming for dinner tonight, but—after that?"

"Right." Luca touched his own mouth, right where Matti had touched it. Luca's smile was sudden. "Good."

"Tell me the address," said Matti.

———— >>∞◦◦∞<< ————

A war was taking place in Matti's head as he knocked on the door of the Cooper townhouse.

Or perhaps it wasn't anything so grand as a war. A scuffle, or a skirmish. Whatever it was, it had been going all day, since he left Tolliver's with the phantom heat of Luca's mouth on his fingertips. Anticipation of the evening to come had been battling everything else that tried to snatch Matti's attention. He'd nearly made a fool of himself in more than one meeting, thoughts whirling in skittish circles around the prospect of being in a room with Luca with, as Luca had said, no swords between them. Nothing good ever came of wanting anything this badly, but gods, Matti was on fire with the thought of it anyway.

More than the bond price wouldn't come due until the day of the wedding. Matti would have cut off his own foot before being unfaithful to a *spouse,* but between business partners an engagement was no more than a statement of intent, and he and Sofia had already established that neither of them had any romantic expectations. Nobody would care if Matti slept with a different person every night until he was actually married. They might *talk,* but it wouldn't reflect badly on Sofia.

Nobody would care if Matti—if Luca—

Matti did his best to squash those thoughts down as the door opened. Sofia had a leather bag looped over her shoulder, along with a goldenrod scarf that picked up the pinkish hue of the dusk light. To Matti's relief, she didn't ask him to come in. He wasn't sure his tattered concentration was up to making polite conversation with his betrothed's parents while fantasising about someone else entirely.

"You really are taller than you need to be, Matti." Sofia looped her arm through his. "Has anyone ever told you that? I suppose not. It would seem normal in your household. You Jays are a family of giants."

"We have our uses. Fetching objects pushed to the back of high shelves, for example."

"Good to know," Sofia said lightly.

A not-quite-comfortable silence descended. Matti wondered if Sofia was, like him, trying to furnish an imaginary picture of domestic life. Not much would change for Matti, materially speaking. The house was designed to hold multiple generations; the current Jay family rattled around in it, and if times had been prosperous they might have opened the dust-closed rooms and invited some of the closer cousins to live there.

After the wedding, he and Sofia would move into one of the larger rooms. Matti was getting better at imagining it. Sofia would be a valuable addition to his House, with her clear eye for fashion. She would fit into his family's life. They liked her. *He* liked her.

But he looked down at her firm brows and the pretty braid of her hair, and nothing stirred within him. The pressure of her hand tucked through his arm did not make him feel both hot and cold at once. He could imagine kissing her, but the thought didn't turn like a key in the lock of his jaw, leaving his lips parted and famished.

Which would have been fine—expected—even comforting, on one level—if his body had not so recently remembered what all those sensations were like.

It was not a long walk from the Coopers' to Matti's house. The Rose Quarter was trapped neatly by the bracket of the river Rozen from which it took its name, unable to creep outwards as the city grew; it remained the same handful of prestigious streets lined with townhouses standing elegantly shoulder to shoulder like a line of spectators at a horse race, all too polite to allow so much as a wisp of lace to intrude on their neighbour's space. Sofia needed an escort about as much as she needed fashion advice. Still, Matti was doing the done thing. This was a chance for eyes to fall on the two of them, and for those eyes' owners to remember that Matti Jay and Sofia Cooper were about to ally their Houses.

"I ran into Adrean yesterday," Sofia said presently.

"How . . . did that go?"

"Oh, I'm as beautiful and precious a delicate wildflower as I ever was, and he remains just as devoted to rescuing me from the dire fate of a loveless, mercenary marriage."

For a long time Matti had been operating under the assumption that Adrean knew Sofia rather better than Matti did. He had been even more wrong than he had realised. Sofia *looked* delicate on first glance, but one only had to spend a single conversation weathering the force of her eyebrows to realise that there were twenty more fitting adjectives in the *D* section of the dictionary alone.

Matti steeled himself and asked, "Did he say anything about the wedding itself? About challenging?"

Sofia smoothed fretfully at her scarf where the breeze had untucked it from its neat draping. She didn't answer. Matti returned a nod of greeting from one of the senior clerks from the city council offices as they passed her on the footpath. They turned onto Matti's street. A lamplighter had done one side of the street but hadn't finished the other, giving the view a lopsided flush.

"I feel a bit of a failure," Sofia said finally. "I honestly don't think I could be more clear, but it's like everything I say to him gets translated wrong and he hears, *I'm playing aloof, I do love you really.* And then I get angry and he says I look magnificent and, well, usually I walk away before I slap him. I hope your best man *demolishes* him," she added, fierce.

"Yes." Matti coughed. "So do I."

"Maha willing." Sofia touched her fingers to her wrist in a reflexive gesture. The gold chain that dwelled there was delicate as thread. Matti had never seen her without it, but hadn't realised it might have religious significance.

Sofia followed his gaze and launched into a practiced explanation: the piece of jewellery had been bought when she was born, and dropped into a bottle of moonwater, where it had stayed for a year. At her first birthday the bracelet had been removed from the bottle, and then both bracelet and bottle set aside until her naming ceremony, where she'd donned the one and been the first to drink from the other.

"You drank straight moonwater at your naming?" Matti shook his head at the thought. He liked jenever, but he'd never been quite masochistic enough to develop a taste for the notoriously strong potato spirit.

"I did," said Sofia with pride. "Mama gave me the world's most elaborate talking-to about how I had to keep my face composed for the ritual, but apparently I still looked like I'd just sat down in a pile of horse manure."

"I had the same talk before my naming. My mother doesn't believe in gods, but she does believe in ceremonies. She says that shared behaviour *is* power, and that even though most of the rituals are weak versions of older, stronger things, as long as they still hold society knitted together, they should be followed." Matti smiled. Nessanesh Jay lived right on the sceptical edge of the wide range of belief that ran through Glassport, but she delighted in ritual nonetheless. It only seemed paradoxical until you understood how much she enjoyed observing the currents of society, like a bargeman calculating the best way of navigating a river. In this city the depth of your faith was your own business. What mattered was how you acted.

Sofia looked up at Matti. "You never seemed like you had to be told to behave yourself, as a child."

"I was clumsy, and nervous about it. Dropping the promise-cloth during a naming under Huna isn't as bad as having your wedding sword-challenged, but it's not a good sign."

"Your mother has a point," Sofia said thoughtfully. "Some Guilds already lean more lightly on the idea of the challenge than others, you know, and one day there'll be someone who turns and laughs down the challenger in the middle of the Guildhall, and who goes ahead with the wedding anyway. Someone will be first." Sofia sidestepped a puddle and a dull clinking sound came from the bag over her shoulder. Her voice lowered. "But that won't be you, Matti, I think. And as long as I'm poised to take your House's name, it won't be me either. Neither of us can afford to be shunned as inauspicious."

"Sometimes," Matti said, "all I want is a single day where I don't have to think about what I can *afford*."

He felt himself misstep, the panic in his throat communicating itself somehow to his feet; he felt the moment when Sofia's grip on his arm steadied him and carried him onwards. It was a rose-oil kind of moment and he was grateful for it, but his shoulders had gone tense at the realisation that such a thing could slip out of him.

Sofia said, abrupt, "It's even worse than you're telling anyone, isn't it?"

Matti's silence lasted long enough to bring them to a halt in front of his own house—not because he was about to deny it, but because he was surprised that she needed to ask the question. The negotiation of his engagement was the one part of House business that he'd been happy to leave entirely up to his parents, to the point where he didn't even know how honest they'd been with Daniela and Raufe Cooper.

He knew the price that had been negotiated, though. For a moment he could hear Luca's voice. *You've paid for me? You own me?*

Matti swallowed a sour, unpleasant feeling.

"It's pretty fucking bad," he said bluntly, watching her eyebrows. They twitched, but not in an insulted way.

"Then I'm glad I could help," Sofia said, and then—oddly—burst out laughing, the kind of laughter that shook her whole body.

"You're clinking," Matti said, because he didn't know what to say about the laughter.

"Oh, Maha, look at me. I don't know what's wrong. The whole thing's just so . . ." Sofia took some gulps of breath and calmed down. She patted the bulky shoulder bag. "Gifts for your table. There's a whole speech to go with them, but I'll save it until we're inside."

The remnants of the laughter lit Sofia's eyes, and there was a vivacious shape to her mouth that Matti liked. All of a sudden it seemed important that he *should* like it; that he prove himself able to feel the way he should, about the person he should. On the uppermost step of the townhouse he turned Sofia with a hand at her shoulder, feeling nearly as inept as if she were a sword, and searched her eyes hungrily for those glints.

Sofia tilted her face up to meet his gaze fully. She looked startled but not displeased, and Matti leaned down and kissed her before he could talk himself out of it.

This close, Sofia smelled thinly of cloves and mirth-flower. Her mouth was gentle and welcoming, and after a moment she put a hand at the side of Matti's face and kissed him back.

It was fine. It was perfectly fine.

When the kiss broke Matti took a breath, angry with himself in an indefinable way, and straightened up again.

"I wasn't expecting that," said Sofia.

"I'm sorry," said Matti at once.

"No, don't be." Her eyebrows wavered, thoughtful, and then she smiled. "We should get used to the idea."

Somehow her brisk tone was far better than if she'd tepidly attempted to assure him it had been *nice*. Matti's annoyance collapsed into gratitude.

"Even so," he said. "Maybe I should have waited until after dinner."

Sofia laughed and shook her bag to elicit more clinking. "I'll take it as a compliment that you didn't need Maha's courage to find me worth kissing."

Matti rubbed the first two fingers of his right hand against the side of his leg as he opened the front door with the other. After dinner wouldn't have worked, regardless.

He had plans for after dinner.

CHAPTER
8

Dinah Vaunt was making admiring eyes at Matti's back as Luca came to collect him from the front hall of the boardinghouse. She shot Luca a look that promised him extra daisy-cakes for breakfast if he spilled all the details about his handsome visitor the next morning. Dinah was eternally hungry for gossip, even by Glassport standards, and clearly didn't care about the extent to which Luca's stories were true so long as he built them around a skeleton of plausibility, so that she could then pass them on to her own friends.

He couldn't blame her for looking. Luca had grown accustomed to seeing Matti in practice clothes, loose trousers and old tucked-in shirts, and now that they were in the latter half of summer there were fewer opportunities to see him in that mouthwatering wool coat.

Here and now in the Vaunts' house stood Mattinesh Jay, scion of Jay House, with the expensive and self-collected appearance that had drawn Luca's eye on the evening they met. The toes of his boots were polished. His waistcoat was a simple but glowing amber-brown, like spirits poured into a glass and whispering the song of their oak barrel home. The almost-curls of Matti's hair were brushed smoother than they'd ever been inside the practice room. He looked as though he'd taken care with his appearance. There was a wine bottle in his hand.

No wonder Dinah was lingering in the door, flashing her eyes and drinking him in. Luca's own eyes ached as though he'd walked from a dark lane into a sunlit square. He wanted to look, and look. And after he'd looked his fill he wanted to set all the speed and talent of his hands to seeing how *dis*ordered he could make Matti's neat appearance.

"I'm upstairs," Luca said.

"A pleasure to meet you, Miss Vaunt," said Matti. He followed Luca to the staircase and up.

Luca concentrated on the smoothness of the banister beneath his hand, and the familiar place where the Vaunts' spoiled cat liked to sit in a puddle of sunlight and dig her claws into the runner that protected the stairs, leaving a patch of the woollen rug fluffy and indistinct. Neither he nor Matti spoke until the dimness of the long corridor had given way to the lamplit interior of Luca's room. There were three other bedrooms for boarders on this floor alone, and although there were no objections made to visitors, disturbing the boardinghouse's other paying occupants was rude.

The room looked smaller than usual, in the yellow light. Cosier. More intimate. A shiver of anticipation brushed fingers across the nape of Luca's neck.

"So," he said, as the door closed behind Matti, "family business let you escape for the evening?" And then could have cheerfully stabbed himself in the leg, because the last thing he wanted to do was make Matti feel guilty for taking a break, when he was doing it at Luca's request.

"Yes."

"What was the excuse? Did you tell them you're so bad at dancing that I'm demanding remedial lessons? Late at night? Because they *might* suspect some kind of ulterior motives on your dancing instructor's behalf, in that case."

"Is that what they are," Matti murmured, "your motives?"

"Ulterior?" Luca clutched a hand to his chest. He needed to do something with it so that he didn't just reach out and drag Matti's mouth against his with a handful of Matti's shirt. "How dare you, Mr. Jay."

"Actually, I told them the truth. I said I'd offered to get to know my best man better, over a drink." Matti looked rueful.

"My mother's quite hopeful at the idea that I might be making a friend. It's not something I've ever been very good at."

Luca gave that the dubious expression it deserved. Matti was so *likeable*. You could cut him in half like fresh bread and he'd be warm all the way through. Albeit with seams and flecks that were of great interest to Luca, half of whose mind was still dwelling in the incredulous and satisfied flash that had devoured Matti's eyes as Luca's tongue slid over his fingers.

He waved Matti into the single chair in the room, which at least had a cushioned seat.

"I did say I'd provide the drinks," Luca said. "Mediocre or otherwise. So I'm forced to assume you've either taken to robbing wine traders or repurposed a wine bottle in order to bring water, which I'm sure our heads will thank us for later considering the likely quality of what I managed to pick up."

"Actually," Matti said, and held out the bottle.

Luca sent fervent thanks to Huna and Pata both that he didn't drop the bottle taking it from Matti's hands as soon as he caught sight of the label.

"Fuck me sideways, is this a joke? They're not due to release another Diamond Blend for three years yet."

"You're good with wine."

"My brother's enthusiasm is hard to escape. He could talk his way blindfolded through the cellars of a Vintner Guildmaster. Not that he could ever afford anything like this," Luca added, smoothing the lie over the preceding truth like butter. "He'd probably stab me in the kidneys without remorse and step over my corpse on his way to find a set of clean glasses if he knew I was about to drink something this good."

"This is from the last release. It was a gift. Benefits of the engagement."

Luca set the bottle down carefully. He shot a look at Matti over his shoulder. "A gift like this, you're probably meant to share it with the person who gave it to you."

"I did offer!" Matti said. "Sofia laughed and said she'd tasted the blend to death before it was bottled, and then my parents insisted I take one of the bottles with me when they heard I was going out tonight."

"No kidney stabbings at all," Luca marvelled.

Matti darted his eyes around the small, cramped room, but there was no judgement in them. "My mother pointed out that the heir to Jay House would hardly expect a serviceman to buy him his drinks."

"Keeping up the illusion."

"Exactly."

Luca winced at the bitterness in Matti's tone. He'd borrowed a corkscrew from the kitchen, along with a couple of sturdy glasses, and he poured for them both. The wine was so purple-dark that you couldn't even compare it to blood.

His fingers touched Matti's as he handed the glass over. He couldn't resist a stroke over Matti's fingers, long enough to be un-mistakably deliberate, and then looked right down into Matti's eyes.

Matti paused with the wineglass poised a few inches from his mouth. He took a drink that possibly involved a more lingering press of lips and tongue to the edge of the glass than necessary. He kept his gaze fixed on Luca's the whole time, and then finally looked down at his wine and swirled the glass.

"Needs some time to breathe," said Matti.

"That makes two of us," said Luca, without thinking.

Matti's mouth—wine-wet, oh, gods—twitched into one of his incredulous half smiles. Luca wondered what would happen if he leaned down right now. Climbed into Matti's lap, set a knee be-tween the man's thighs, and began the process of disordering.

He'd spent half the day cursing the impulse that had made him step back in the training room instead of sucking at Matti's fin-gers one by one. Those stubborn ink-stained fingers, now holding a glass with the unthinking refined ease that was totally missing when they wrapped themselves around a sword.

Yet now that Matti was here, in his room, Luca felt like a child carefully setting aside the spun-sugar flower from atop a cake, keeping his eyes on it while eating the rest, savouring the anticipation. And the wait felt safer. Luca didn't want to press too far, too fast, against Matti's reserve. He would step carefully.

Luca was going to take his time with this.

He removed his boots, settled himself cross-legged on the end of the bed, and took a gulp of wine. Matti was right: it would benefit from some time in the air. It was an aggressive, fruity thing that needed to soften, and that was about as far as Luca's wine vocabulary went. Perse would have been spouting comments about cherries and tannins and chocolate, and making a guess at the percentage of grape varietals that went into the famously secret blend that was the Diamond.

"Is he a duellist as well, your brother?" Matti asked.

Luca managed to keep himself from startling at the fact that Matti appeared to have read his mind. In fact, Matti had probably done exactly what Luca had done, and backtracked to the last safe topic of conversation.

"No. No, he's . . . dutiful."

Luca did some wine-swirling of his own. At the same time, he did some rapid editing and embellishing of his personal narrative. He recognised the danger of how he was feeling: affectionate and keen to impress. He couldn't afford to be too truthful.

"My father was a duellist, but my mother wants us to move up in the world. There's a branch of her cousins who are a generation away from getting the votes for House status, everyone thinks, and she wanted me to go and do clerking work for them. Do my duty by the family." Careful, careful. He was the one sounding bitter now.

"You said *was*," said Matti, looking interested. "Did your father die in a duel?"

"Nobody dies in duels these days." It was true, unless someone was unlucky or very unskilled, or had the misfortune to be the target of a personal grudge. Murder by the sword was still murder, and prosecuted as such. "He got sick, he died. Very boring," he added, light.

"I'm sorry."

"I was five. I don't remember much about him." A scrap of truth.

"And you decided you'd rather be a con artist," said Matti.

The protest was half-formed in Luca's mouth, but he let it die there. Matti looked composed. He was pressing a finger down on Luca's nerves, reminding him. Here, Luca had the advantage of home ground, but none of the authority of the teacher, and Matti was clearly aware of that.

Luca took another drink and was relieved to see that Matti did the same. The wine was incredible.

"A con artist *and* a duellist," said Luca, flippant. "All right, yes. I—I made some mistakes. Annoyed some people I shouldn't have annoyed."

Annoyed was a weak mask of a word compared to what he'd actually done, which was bring down the ire of an entire Guild and their goddess, not to mention flaunt the city's own law. But he was hardly going to admit to that.

"You, annoying?" said Matti.

Luca grinned. "Either way, I wanted to leave Cienne, so I came here."

"I wish I could do that. Just decide I'd like to see somewhere new, for a while, and go. I haven't travelled since I was a child."

"It wasn't exactly a leisure trip so much as . . . fleeing," said Luca frankly. "Even apart from the annoyed people, clerking didn't suit me. I don't like numbers."

A long sigh from Matti, who stretched his legs out in front of him and gazed at his boots. "Neither do I. Not the numbers I spend most of my day staring at, anyway. I'm sure I would like them well enough if they moved into the black column."

"Hah," said Luca. "No, I'm equal opportunity. I hate all of

them. I never liked adding and subtracting, let alone anything more complicated. I was never interested in learning to . . . be a clerk. Which is selfish, according to my family. Lazy." A shrug. "Can't argue."

"I don't think anyone gets as good as you are with a sword by being lazy."

"That doesn't count. I *enjoy* that."

Matti bent his knees again and rested his elbows on them, watching Luca like he was trying to learn a new attack. "I enjoy it too," he said. "But I'm not under any illusions that I've got any kind of gift for it. You do."

"You're not *that*—" Luca began, heroically, but couldn't keep it up. He held his glass away from his body and laughed. "Gods, Matti, you're *so bad*. I'm sorry."

"I know," Matti told the bottom of his own glass, somewhere between smug and tragic, and then they were both laughing.

Luca recovered his breath first. "I don't know why you're still going at it. I tried to learn piano, years ago, and I gave it up after two months. I could tell I was never going to be any good."

Matti pointed a finger at him. "*You've* no patience."

That irked, the bee sting of truth delivered with no sweetener. "I don't like wasting my time."

"It's not wasted if you're enjoying it."

Luca let the silence after that hang, so that Matti could hear what he'd said. Let it sink in. That statement was a few steps down the road from the Matti Jay who'd had to wrestle his own guilt to the ground in order to ask Luca for lessons that he didn't need.

"I don't enjoy being bad at things," Luca said finally. "Does anyone?"

"Mm." Now Matti was the one leaving the silence, as if *he'd* scored a point, though Luca couldn't work out what it might be. After a while Matti went on, "I don't know. It makes it so satisfying when I do get something right, when I can feel myself doing it the way you do it. And it's fun. Compared to everything else I do in my day. It's . . ."

"Different?"

"An escape." Matti gazed at Luca, eyes fathomless and black, the lamplight making him look so brutally lovely that Luca felt a flutter like insect wings in his chest. Then Matti looked down at his wine as if betrayed by it.

Luca's throat crowded with possibilities, with thirst, and with an unexpected willingness to maintain the rhythm of their conversation. He still wanted to bury his fingers in Matti's hair, to turn his careful steps into a dance with a clear destination. But growing alongside that was the urge to crack himself open and whisper something true into the air between them. He wanted to draw all of Matti's secrets out and turn them in his hands; he wanted to show Matti his own.

Strangely, the question that emerged from this muddle was: "What happened? *Why* is your House in such trouble?"

Matti stood up instead of answering immediately, and held out his hand for Luca's glass. Once he'd refilled them both and reseated himself, he said, glum, "What didn't happen? There was the drought, ten years ago—that hit the farmers worse than us, of course, but two of our major suppliers ended up selling their land and giving their flocks up for meat, and everyone else's prices soared to the clouds at auction. We had a run of bad sales. Kept losing contracts that were up for renewal. One thing after another, we kept slipping and slipping, and then one day we were too deep in the rut to get out."

"But you managed to hide this, somehow." That was the part Luca was stuck on. "Doesn't that turn into dishonesty, at some point?"

"We kept our name." Matti closed his eyes and drank. "Down in the dust with Huna still kicking us for whatever offence we'd caused, but we kept our name. Jay House still meant something.

Fair dealing. Good quality. After a while the name was most of what we had, so . . ."

"So you propped it up."

"It's not lying," Matti said, soft. "And now we're out of it. Or we will be. A marriage is the best solution. My father was meant to marry Sofia's mother, you know. Back when that kind of money might have stopped all of this from happening in the first place."

"Why didn't he?"

"He went north," said Matti. "He visited his mother's family in Cantala, and he ducked up to Manisi as well, to look into opportunities for Jay House to open an office there. And when he came back, he was married to my mother. He doesn't regret it, but he might feel guilty about it. I don't know. He never talks about might-have-beens. He says what's done is done." Another drink. Matti's controlled voice was growing new notes of expression. "For a while I wondered if that was why he ended up taking the risk that he did, on the black libelza."

Luca pressed his lips together, took a breath, and reminded himself who he was pretending to be. "What's that?"

"Wool," said Matti. "Good wool. Libelza sheep aren't bred or sold outside of Draka. They produce wool with a finer crimp than any of the Thesperan breeds, and it's called black but actually it has almost no natural stain and it holds dye like—" He gave a silent laugh into the back of his hand. "You don't care. You don't need to care. It's wool. And one of our agents bought five of the best fleece lots seen in years, at auction in Hazan, and the ship carrying them here from Fataf was lost with all hands somewhere in the Straits."

The easiest trade route to Glassport from Draka, which was directly to the north of Ashfah, went through the southern Ashfahani port of Fataf. Luca's usual struggle with mental geography almost made him overshoot the sudden cliff-drop of that story.

"Gods," he breathed. "But surely the insurance—"

"It hadn't gone through," Matti said. "Clerical error. Papers lost in the wrong pile, or delivered to the wrong office. Something like that."

Luca chewed on his lip. You'd have to have a skin of stone, or else no faith at all, to think that such a flood of misfortune didn't represent *some* sort of judgement on the part of the goddess. Still, he couldn't blame the Jays for trying to hide it. He'd probably have done the same.

Matti went on, "It might not have mattered. After the cost of the fleece we could only have afforded to insure for half value anyway. We have some other ventures underway now—I've written to Murtagh and Collins, with the robes suggestion—and we're about to bid on an army contract here too. But to keep afloat in the meantime we've sold everything outside of the city that isn't the ground beneath our factories, and there's a huge loan coming due with Lourde House that we can't extend any longer. So when we lost the ship . . . that was it, really." This smile didn't look like any of Matti's real smiles. "That was when my parents first went to talk to the Coopers."

Luca pulled himself out of the fit of smothering guilt that was trying to overcome him at this reminder of how seriously Matti took his responsibilities. Nobody would ever accuse *Matti* of not doing his duty by his family. He was about to duty himself right into a dull marriage. Luca wanted to grab him by the shoulders and shake.

"Did they even bother to ask you about it?"

"Don't be stupid," Matti said. "I told them to do it."

"You *told* them?"

"I knew it was coming. It was the only option. And not a day too soon either. There's word Harte House is expanding to wool, and Huna knows we can't compete with them on the luxury end of the market while fighting off the Keseys at the other end."

Luca, very carefully, set his empty glass down on the floor by the bed. A tension like a plucked clothesline flooded his arms, or tried to; the wine was getting in the way. The net effect made him momentarily queasy. He'd controlled his face by the time he was looking at Matti again. "Harte House. The silk traders."

"They're buying up warehouse space and booking ships from Fataf." Matti sighed. "It was only a matter of time before someone else with enough capital looked at getting libelza to Glassport."

Luca changed his mind about his glass. He held out a hand for Matti's as well, and went over to the desk to refill them. The purple stream of wine shook unevenly as it left the bottle. *Well then,* Luca told himself savagely. *There's no point in being honest now. Ulterior motives wouldn't even begin to cover it.*

"Sounds like someone should tell the Hartes they aren't guarding their secrets as well as they should," Luca said.

"Now I've managed to get us talking business. I'm sorry. It's like a pigeon that won't get its claws out of my shoulder. And spends half its time shitting down my back," Matti added, in the ponderously wry tones of the tipsy. "Are you holding my drink hostage, Mr. Piere?"

"Yes," said Luca at once. "Your drink for the chair."

Matti's eyes darted to the floor, and lingered there for long enough that Luca had a heart-stopping memory of sitting cross-legged on the floor of the practice room. Then Matti moved himself, pivoting easily on one foot, to take the place where Luca had sat on the end of the bed.

As usual, Luca hadn't thought far enough ahead of his tongue to decide what he was going to do, but it seemed obvious. He lifted the chair by the looped frame with his free hand, and moved it to its usual position beneath the desk.

Then he sat himself right back on the bed, at the midpoint between the headboard and Matti.

Matti looked at him, suddenly still, like someone mastering their balance. Luca looked back.

"I've complied with my end of the bargain," Matti said.

Luca hastily handed over the glass. While he was pouring, Matti had unbuttoned his cuffs and shoved them untidily up his arms. Luca saw Matti's arms every day, but not like this, emerging from the otherwise immaculate shell of such a good shirt. He gazed at them, trying desperately to convince himself that he still wanted nothing more than what he'd wanted when he first asked Matti over to share a drink.

It was no good. Somehow, Luca had managed to step himself right past the opening for simple physical pleasure and all the way here, into this space of quieter and stranger and more devastating intimacy.

Matti had trusted Luca. He had bared part of himself that had nothing to do with the shape of his arms, and Luca felt helpless to resist doing the same. It was like throwing a sword aside and laughing out an invitation to strike; in its own way it was as heady and delicious as every other stupid, impulsive, pleasure-seeking thing Luca had done in his life. He had just enough wits left to scramble for a truth that wasn't going to spell disaster.

And he had one, right in his pocket.

"I have something to tell you," Luca said.

"This sounds serious."

"It might be. It probably is."

And Luca told him what he'd seen and heard at Aleit Martens's naming. Matti listened without interrupting. His brow furrowed and his whole body went tense when Luca mentioned the terms of the contract, though Luca couldn't have remembered the exact numbers in question even if his boots had been held over a fire.

"You're sure?" was all Matti said when Luca had finished. "You really heard all of that?"

"Why would I lie?" Luca managed to swill down the irony with another mouthful of wine.

"Serge and blankets."

"Yes."

The furrow between Matti's brows was deepening. No wonder. Luca had just proved the existence of a gaping hole in Jay House's much-needed secrecy.

"Almost nobody knows those terms," Matti said. "We decided them, Dad and me. It's our holdout line, in the negotiations with the city quartermaster. Those negotiations aren't even due to *start* for another week. The tall man, can you tell me anything else about him?"

Luca closed his eyes, trying to call it up. "I don't think he respected the other one, the one he was reporting to. Something about the way he spoke to him. But he was doing a good job of playing polite. Hm. Black hair, pushed away from his face. High forehead. Fair skin. And a beard."

"A beard?"

"Is that strange?" After only a moment of thinking about it, Luca realised that it was. Facial hair was still an oddity in Glassport. The fashion for it had been rising for nearly two years in Cienne. It was irritating for Luca, who refused to tolerate the uneven bramble of a beard that improved his appearance not one jot, and of course it was downright inconvenient for his brother; Persemaine had about as much chance of growing a pair of wings. "More salt-and-pepper than the hair on his head. Neat." Luca demonstrated the rounded *V* shape of it with his fingers.

Matti was silent, looking at his wine as though a portrait of the man had appeared there. "Tell me again what they said. From the beginning. You must have misunderstood something."

"I know I'm just a *failed clerk*," Luca said, landing on the words with drunken sarcasm, "but I'm not an idiot."

"It can't . . ." Matti looked bewildered.

"You know who he is."

Matti drank off the rest of his glass in two long gulps, and then winced. "Corus Vane. He'd know the terms if anyone does. And he looks like that."

"Wait." Luca struggled with a slippery fish of memory. The wine was getting its muffling breath into his bloodstream. He felt light and unserious. "Vane? Isn't that the person I'm supposed to, you know." He made a few sword-swishing motions.

"His father," said Matti. "*Corus Vane*. It makes no sense. He's one of the most senior agents working for our House. His fortunes live and die with ours—why would he be working to undermine our success?"

"If he's doing it, does the why matter all that much?"

"The why always matters."

Luca sighed. "I know. I do know that."

"He could be compromised," Matti said. "Blackmailed. And you said they mentioned their hostess?"

"Not by name." Luca could almost see the dart of Matti's thoughts, like lantern kites slicing the night sky at a midwinter fair. "But we were in the Mason Guildhall, and I did think—"

"Lysbette Martens."

Luca shrugged. "Is there any other reason your House's agent would be at a Mason Guild naming?"

"I don't know. But Lysbette wouldn't care about the details of our army contracts. She doesn't like Dad, but why would she— and if Corus— Oh, fuck everything, I've drunk too much to think about this properly. Why did the wine have to be so good?"

Luca snickered at the plaintive note in Matti's voice. "Blame your betrothed, Mattinesh."

"Corus has known my father for a long time. Practically since Maya was born. I thought he'd have come to us, if he was in trouble."

"Gambling debts, maybe," Luca contributed. "Or he could have just been bribed. Not much help you can be there. If it's money. Sorry," he added, stumbling into the belated realisation that this had not been a particularly sensitive thing to say.

"No, you're right." Matti was about to run a hand through his own hair, Luca could tell. Yes! There it went. "Martens House has money to spare. Fucking Huna's fucking tits. Sorry."

"Fuck off, Matti," said Luca, delighted. "Don't *apologise*. This is amazing. Swear away." He drained the rest of his own glass, set it down one last time on the floor, and followed the gentle yearning of his body to be horizontal. He didn't realise the full implications of this until his feet hit the headboard—he bent his knees to compensate—and his cheek landed on a warm, helpfully pillow-height surface that was, he realised after some investigative nuzzling, Matti's leg.

The leg in question tensed for a brief moment. Luca didn't think he was imagining the catch of Matti's breath above him. Luca wriggled over until he was looking directly upwards, and clasped his hands tight over his own stomach. They weren't done talking business, after all. Part of him still mourned the loss of opportunity, but he could hardly throw this gift of information in Matti's lap and expect the mood to remain flirtatious. He'd known that. He'd done it anyway.

The fact that Luca had also thrown *himself* in Matti's lap, and would very much have liked to explore the possibilities of this position, was not to be helped. He'd made his choice, and he couldn't even find it in himself to regret it.

Matti blinked down at him.

"I hope you don't mind," said Luca, in his most dignified company voice.

Sure enough, Matti's natural courtesy rose to the fore: "No, by all means," and Luca settled his shoulders with a sigh.

"Then please do continue with your obscenities."

A pause. "Fuck you," said Matti, slow and polite, and Luca laughed. "The problem is, what do I do now? If, if you're right—"

"*If?*"

"It wouldn't be smart to just confront him." Matti spoke even more slowly now, like he was dragging his thoughts through a muddy field. "If I know and he doesn't know that I know . . ."

In the pause, Luca yawned. The yawn rose and infected Matti, who lifted a hand to cover his mouth.

"And if I'm going to tell the rest of my family, your word's not enough to go on— Oh, I believe you," Matti said, with a smile down at Luca. "But I need harder evidence. Proof. Exactly who he's working with, and how Martens House is involved, if at all. A sense of what he might do next."

"I'm not tailing him for you," said Luca. "You haven't paid me enough to be a private investigator on top of everything else, and as wide and glorious as my skill set is, I'm not exactly—"

"I wasn't going to ask you to—"

"I *could* break into his house. Look for evidence."

A pause. Luca beamed up at Matti, pleased with his own wine-fuelled brilliance.

"You could what?"

"I have many talents." A small voice in Luca was trying to say something about the fact that he was *lying low,* that was the *point.*

But Matti was looking thoughtful, and one of his hands came to rest with its fingertips just touching Luca's scalp, which prickled with a sudden eruption of yearning heat. The small voice was going to be outvoted.

"And what'll that cost me?" Matti said.

That landed like a slap. It shouldn't have hurt, Luca told himself; he had only himself to blame. This was the nature of their relationship, even if that fact felt as slippery as memory, lying here in the aftermath of unfamiliar honesty with Matti's thigh so warm beneath him. Luca bit the inside of his cheek. "Did I ask for anything for telling you this?" he said. It came out harsh.

"Did you want something?"

What stung was the knowledge that he *had* wanted something in exchange, even if that something was . . . intangible, soft, and undefined. Something like the fact that Matti had made no move to push Luca away, even as he asked the price.

"No," Luca lied. "No, there's nothing I want."

"You're just doing me a favour."

"I . . ." Luca was suddenly tired beyond belief. He felt dizzy and endangered. He should sit up, move away. He let his eyes fall closed. "Matti, I found out through the luck of the gods, and I thought you should know, so I told you. And now I do want to know the *why*, so I'll help you discover it. There. That's what I want."

A long silence. Luca kept his breathing steady, his muscles softening into the bed. The feeling of danger passed.

The touch by the side of his closed eyelid was so soft that it felt like a stray piece of hair. Just as Luca was trying to persuade his sluggish arms to lift and brush it away, the touch firmed, becoming the recognisable contact of fingertips. A sigh came from Matti. "All right. Thank you. So this is why you asked me over for a drink. To tell me this. I thought . . ." Matti's hand smoothed down the side of Luca's face, then up again, curling slowly though some of his hair.

Luca heard himself make a truly embarrassing sound of comfortable bliss. The dark behind his eyelids was cosy and his head was heavy. The slow movement of Matti's fingers was hypnotic. He didn't ever want it to end.

"You thought," Luca mumbled. "Hm? Were you saying something?"

A soft laugh. Luca considered opening his eyes to see the face that went with it, but he was so very comfortable, and his eyelids were heavier than the rest of his head combined. "Nothing in particular."

If the fingers had stopped, Luca would have complained, but they didn't. He let out a long, slow breath. He felt rocked by waves.

After some time he heard Matti say, quiet and distant as though through a wall, "What are you doing in my life, Luca Piere?"

Making it more interesting, Luca said, or meant to. But he didn't manage to say it aloud. Halfway between the thought and the action he was falling asleep.

CHAPTER
9

It turned out that every house that Luca had broken into before now had stood on its own piece of land, with at least a slip of space on either side, whereby one could get at convenient windows or at least find access to a back door. That was the sensible way to build houses, Luca had declared.

That was a waste of good inner-city real estate, in Matti's opinion.

Here in Glassport even the grandest houses lived happily pressed up against one another, and Corus and Adrean Vane did not live in a grand street. Their small dwelling with its dull brick facade was cramped among a long row of similarly dull ones, without even the hope of a back garden. It backed directly onto a row of shops the next street over, and anyone trying to access the second level would have to dance on the roof of one of those shops.

"Which I am not opposed to *in theory*," Luca had said thoughtfully, "but it's hard to think how the thing might be accomplished with any sort of stealth."

All in all, Luca had seemed relieved when Matti mentioned that his father held a spare key to the Vane house. It was a normal thing for a friend to do for a friend: a small and domestic gesture of trust. The irony wasn't lost on Matti.

Matti was breathing hard by the time he met Luca at the arranged spot. He'd been waylaid by his mother on the way out of the house, picking up a conversation they'd been having about a new chemical additive for fabric crabbing, which a friend of hers at the university in Manisi had written to her about. Matti had then almost forgotten the all-important key, and had to make an excuse to duck back up to Tomas's study to fetch it from the safe.

His mind was scattered. He hadn't slept well, anticipating the usual business meeting with their most senior agents, including Corus Vane. The meeting had taken place that morning. Matti kept pulling his memory of it worriedly through his mind like a rough strand through sensitive fingers, wondering if he'd somehow given away what he knew. He'd had a lot of practice keeping his emotions and his thoughts to himself, but he'd never had to be on guard against this kind of resentment before. It was almost *hatred,* a word with hot spikes to it. Matti was unused to spikes.

Soon enough he'd know if it was justified.

"We *must* stop meeting at these odd hours," said Luca upon Matti's arrival, with an absurd glance up through his pale lashes. "I'm going to start suspecting your motives are the ulterior ones."

"Noon isn't odd," Matti said, though it was, a bit. One hardly thought of crimes as being committed in the middle of the day. The sky was cloud-strewn and glutinously bright. A voice calling instructions in a tired, cranky tone drifted through an open window above their heads. A man carrying a toddler trudged down the street away from them and passed another man, struggling with a covered handcart, who paused every so often to wipe his fingers on his trousers and glare at the cart's handle.

Matti was overdressed for the neighbourhood. Luca, slouched against the wall in an uncharacteristically casual posture, wearing a plain shirt and no waistcoat, was not.

"Would you have preferred daybreak?" Matti asked.

"I was awake at daybreak on your account *anyway.* Sword lessons and counterespionage in a single day, all on your behalf. I am a professional, you know. I could have been seeking out actual paid employment."

"I think you're glad of the entertainment."

Luca flashed a smile at him, sharp-edged. "And you? What was the excuse you used this time?"

"I invented a meeting."

"Scandalous behaviour, Mr. Jay." Luca straightened and looked pleased, as he did at any suggestion that Matti might be unbending. Luca thought Matti's sense of duty rendered him hopelessly stuffy and dull; there was no getting around that. It was a terrible idea for Matti to be doing things just because they called up a smouldering glee in Luca's grey-brown eyes.

Matti felt he was on a downhill slope of some kind. He was fighting the incline the whole way, but the ground was smooth and treacherous beneath his feet, like frost on long grass. He'd crossed a boundary marker when he let himself stay in the boardinghouse room for a precious stretch of time after Luca had fallen asleep, reluctant to move his leg and lower Luca's head to the bed. At first Matti had been breathing his way through a mood that kept switching back and forth between relief and disappointment. He'd anticipated . . . well, *something*. The ice on the slope was the way Luca glanced at Matti's fingers; the way Matti went tense when Luca was close, awash with wanting.

But after a short while of sitting there with Luca's soft wild hair under his hands, Luca's restlessness dissolved into sleep, Matti had just looked. He'd let his eyes travel over Luca's closed lids and the constellation of pale freckles that he knew half by heart. He'd felt like a child having crept down to the pantry after a festival feast, stuffing small handfuls of leftover sweets into his mouth.

He'd felt that there was nothing disappointing at all about the chance to sit there, on a narrow bed in a rented room, with Luca Pierc asleep in his lap, for the long bittersweet hour before he surrendered to the reality of his life and crept out of the boardinghouse.

That was the angle of the slope. Matti didn't know what to do with it. It was dangerous, that much was certain.

"I didn't have to come at all. I could have just given you the key this morning," he said, turning to lead the way towards the Vane house.

"Not a chance," said Luca. "Everything about this approach works better if it's Mr. Mattinesh Jay wielding the key."

"What about the neighbours? What do we say if someone asks what we're doing?"

"Nobody is going to *ask,* because you have a *key.* And even if they do, I can think of five good stories off the top of my head!"

"Pick one," said Matti.

"Stick with the truth. Your father is this man's employer, and you own a key to his house. People can make whatever assumptions they wish. Or, if you absolutely must have something lined up . . . your father wants to surprise Mr. Vane on the next feast of Huna with a new piece of furniture, or a set of woven wall hangings, as thanks for his many years of loyal service. You're sneaking in to measure the place up and make a decision about what would match best."

Many years of loyal service. Yes. The resentment pricked at Matti's heart again.

"And you are . . ." he prompted.

"A serviceman." Luca curled his shoulders in, looking as he did when he was showing Matti a mocking version of Matti's habitual posture, which was—apparently—just one of the endless sources of pain that Matti provided as a student of the blade.

The street was deserted, though faint sounds of habitation floated in the air, when they knocked on the front door of the Vane house. There was no answer. They weren't expecting one; Corus had left for an overnight trip to the town of Loford to threaten some sense into the head of an enterprising toll-taker who'd illegally hiked up the levies on commercial goods passing through the canal lock. Corus was good at putting out those kinds of fires.

As for Adrean, Matti knew that he spent as little time here as possible. He split his time between a duelling club in an equally grubby corner of the city, and the back room of a coffeehouse, where he could commune with like-minded artists and compose odes to the beauty of other people's betrotheds.

The door went unanswered. Matti let them into the house. He wouldn't have wanted to spend much time in there, either, given the choice. It was clean but there was a dingy smell to it, as though some sort of damp had set in and never been fully banished, and the lack of windows made the interior dim.

"If I were taking bribes, I'd hope to live somewhere nicer than this," said Luca.

"Not everyone cares about that," said Matti, though he'd been thinking the same thing. "If you don't do business out of your house then there's no reason to show it off, especially if you care more about—I don't know. Transient things. Food. Experiences."

"Sword lessons," said Luca, throwing him a smile.

"I'm sure he's paying for Adrean's," said Matti. "All right. Where do we start?"

"The only items I've liberated from houses have been valuables, not secrets. He's your employee. You decide."

They explored. The stairs creaked loudly as they climbed, sending tension shooting up Matti's spine. The townhouse was two storeys and narrow, and the third bedroom that served as a study was barely larger than the laundry room at Matti's house. The wallpaper in the study was a greyish blue that once might have been stripes, faded and stained, and a tidy desk was shoved up under the window, the external side of which was crusted in enough dirt and cobwebs to create an uneven pattern of light on the desk's surface.

"And the gods smile," said Luca softly. He was crouched in a corner of the study, running his hands over a squat document chest with a padlock attached to the front. "There weren't any other keys on that ring, were there? No. Too easy." He didn't look discouraged. He pulled a small roll of fabric from his pocket.

Matti had the absurd urge to laugh. "So," he said, "this skill set you mentioned."

"Turn your back, oh respectable son of a respectable House," Luca intoned.

Matti would rather have crouched down and watched Luca work, half out of sheer curiosity and half out of the desire to watch

Luca's clever hands do something new. But he turned his attention to the desk instead. He hesitated, feeling as grubby as the window. He was about to go through another person's private papers.

"I can hear that moral crisis you're having from all the way over here," said Luca.

"It's just that—"

"He's your *enemy*, Matti. You're not doing anything he wouldn't do to you."

Matti could call up any number of occasions when Corus Vane had stood next to Matti's desk, or Tomas's desk, and stirred the papers there with a casual finger, casting his sharp gaze over their contents as though he had every right to do so. Because he *did* have the right. He was trusted.

That was enough for Matti's conviction to solidify within him, as resentment stole between the bricks of his doubts. The few loose sheets on top of the desk were full of nothing in particular, each one a quilt of scribbled abbreviations and times and lists of names and places, all in Corus's narrow hand. Matti read them carefully but could find nothing unusual or striking among those references he recognised. They were the usual sorts of notes busy people wrote for themselves as reminders, or as thoughts arose in the midst of other work.

The drawers held pens and ink cartridges, stubs of sealing wax, string and scissors and buttons and loose wine corks. A wooden ruler with the name VANE etched shakily into it. Folded newspapers. A pile of yellowing letters, the edges of the paper curling up, which Matti realised with a guilty stab were signed *Isabeau*. Isabeau Vane. Adrean's mother, Corus's wife, and dead for many years now. Matti hurriedly returned the letters to their drawer and neatened the ribbon that held them together.

Once he'd poked into every corner of every drawer he slid the last one home. "Nothing much here. Would he even keep physical evidence that would be incriminating?"

"Locks are usually there to safeguard something," said Luca.

Matti turned in the chair to look at him. Luca was sitting on the floor with one leg stretched out and the other bent up, the foot of it tapping rapidly, one arm hooked around his knee as he leaned close to the chest and jiggled two pieces of metal in the padlock.

"Progress?" Matti asked.

Luca glanced over at him. "Patience, *sir*."

Matti's face heated. The query had come out in his clipped business voice, the one he used with Jay House's employees. Corus's paperwork had put him in that mood.

He ran a hand through his hair, but he had no excuse to turn back to the desk. He watched as Luca bent his head to the task again. One lockpick was returned to the roll and a new one selected.

Matti went over and knelt down himself, holding the padlock firm and steady against the upended chest. He could feel the delicate work of the metal picks, tiny scrapes and vibrations like a line of violins over the ragged drumbeat of Luca's foot and the occasional soft huff of Luca's breath as he frowned at the lock.

Matti felt the moment the tumblers gave way. He lifted his hand.

Luca said, "Hah," sounding smug as he twisted the padlock and pulled it clear so that he could right the document chest and flip the lid up.

Matti had been lowering his expectations during his fruitless search of the desk, telling himself not to hope for anything. This was a gamble. Life didn't always serve up what you wanted, let alone what you needed. The goddess might look at you, down in the dust, and not hesitate to compound your woe.

The bundle of papers in the chest was less a bundle and more an uneven pile, from Luca turning the chest and righting it again. Luca unceremoniously split it in half, handed one resultant sheaf to Matti, and settled his own on his knees, where he began to leaf through it with the air of a schoolmaster hoping to be surprised by the quality of an essay.

Part of Matti still couldn't believe he was doing this, but Luca's impulsive efficiency was like being bundled along by a strong wind. And Matti honestly couldn't think of any other options. If they didn't find anything pointing at betrayal, Matti would at least be able to tell himself that he hadn't ignored the possibility, and he'd shoulder the guilt of having doubted one of his House's senior agents.

He skimmed his eyes over Corus's personal documents one by one. Some related to the lease on this house, or the accounts Corus held with one of the banking Houses. A piece of paper with an embossed border turned out to be the wedding certificate of Corus Vane and Isabeau Perrault, signed in dark purple ink.

When Matti found what he was looking for, it took him a while to recognise it as such. It was five pieces of paper clipped together, looking almost like a journal: a column for the date, and then a brief entry of words. The ink of each entry was the subtly different shade that came with different ages, sometimes switching from blue to black, and the dates themselves were often months apart.

Each entry was short, and although some were cryptic enough that Matti couldn't immediately tell what they referred to, those that he did understand were damning. They ranged from *Allowed overcharging for Haxbridge mordant* to *Delay in labour hire to move goods from transport.*

The chemist in Haxbridge who supplied the Jays with mordants had been increasing his prices gradually over the past few years, but that wasn't unusual. And there were always a few bales of raw wool, or a few bolts of completed fabric, lost to damp-rot whenever a large amount had to be moved from place to place. Nothing on here would have showed up on its own. None of it *had.* All were small oversights, small tweaks, small mistakes that wouldn't be recognised as mistakes, affecting every aspect of the Jays' business from carding to spinning, crabbing to dyeing, weaving to sales. Together they were a field of tiny holes poked in the base of a barrel, letting water leak slowly out.

The last entry read: *Passed on details of planned neg. with CQ over new contract.* It was dated a few weeks prior.

City quartermaster, Matti thought. He felt numb.

"Your face has gone strange," said Luca, breaking across the cold ocean of Matti's thoughts. "I take it you've found something?"

Matti passed the pages over. "It's as though he's keeping an account. Something that will be totted up."

Totted up and paid for, one way or another. This wasn't the kind of simple or even complex embezzlement that every House was familiar with and knew to be on their guard against. None of these actions would have gained Corus anything on their own, nor allowed him to skim anything off the House's profits. They *diminished* those profits, every single one. Given how much Corus's own earnings and status stood to fall as Jay House teetered on the brink of ruin, they were the actions of a man suspended on a tightrope and sawing at the rope with a knife. Dangerous and incomprehensible.

Unless he knew he had a net to tumble into.

"Huna's swollen *tits,*" said Luca, turning a page. Even lacking Matti's familiarity with Jay House's dealings, Luca didn't seem to have any difficulty in following the implications. The story the ledger told was hardly complicated. Any child past the first few years of school could have drawn a diagram with the words *increased materials cost* in one circle, and the words *decreased market share* in another, with an arrow leading from the two to another drawn around the words *oh fuck.* Or the child-appropriate equivalent.

"Yes, indeed," said Matti. "What about your pile? Is there anything that would link Corus to Lysbette Martens?"

"No, but—does the name Kesey mean anything to you?"

"Yes." Matti's heart gave a sharp kick. "They're one of our major local competitors. Kesey House. They'd benefit—they *did* benefit from some of these, almost certainly, and they're in the running for that Glassport army contract." They were one of only two other Houses who'd be interested in undercutting the Jays on that front, in fact. It shouldn't have been a surprise. The nauseating fury that Matti felt at the back of his teeth was unexpected.

"Simeon Kesey?"

"He's their Head of House. What is it?"

"Simeon. Sim," said Luca, thoughtful. "*That* was the name. I'd forgotten. It does make a lot more sense for a local wool House to be behind this than Martens."

He handed Matti back the clipped pages and picked up an envelope, unsealed, from which he slid out a single sheet of folded paper. It wasn't Corus's handwriting; this was the painstaking lettering of someone who didn't have to write many documents as part of their daily routine. Matti glanced down at the signature. The name was vaguely familiar, but Rivers was a common surname in Glassport, and Rob a shortening of many different first names.

Rob Rivers, by his own scribed admittance, was a worker on a Kesey House carding floor. Matti's family employed plenty of carders; it was a job that called for strong hands and patience, and no imagination. The document was a concise statement. It said that as supervisory carder in his shift, Rivers had been provided with sacks of what were clearly a combination of hard waste fibres and pulled wool. He and his team had been instructed to card these fibres along with the high-grade fleeces they were working on, and to send these on to the spinners with no alteration to the grading label.

Rivers concluded his statement with an awkwardly phrased but damning admission that this practice had been introduced *after* the advent of mandatory labelling of finished fabrics, and that the majority of fabric being produced by Kesey House carried a classification label that overstated the percentage of long, high-crimp fibre by at least twenty percent.

"What's pulled wool?" asked Luca.

"It's from animals slaughtered for meat," said Matti. "Pulled, as opposed to shorn. You would use it for—rugs, maybe. Not for fabrics." He stared at the paper, trying to process. His mind was churning with the attempt to take this in on top of the preceding shock. "Is Corus working for the Keseys or against them?"

"It's collateral, I'd say," said Luca coolly. "The kind of man with the brains and guts to turn spy for a rival, in such a senior position, would be smart enough to make sure he held something over the head of his true employer. Just in case they backed out of their end of the deal."

"This kind of mandatory labelling is recent," Matti said. "It came out of the Guildband two years ago. All the Guildmasters in delegation voted on it, so the same standards apply across the whole continent." Regulation, for the most part, was left up to the individual Guilds to enforce at the level of the Guildband, the same standards being applied across Thesper. "Some of the other fabric industries have started taking it up as well. But it was my father's idea first," Matti added, with a stab of pathetic, bittersweet pride.

"Is there some kind of objective test?" Luca asked. "How do you prove this kind of fraud?"

"With difficulty," Matti admitted. "Once a fabric's been crabbed, getting a sense of the average fibre length that went into it is so inexact as to be useless, if the percentages are tweaked on that level. Ah, it's to do with—interlocking," he said, at Luca's questioning look. He laced his own fingers together, then flattened the fingers to the back of each opposite hand. "Crabbing means wetting the fabric, at heat, and keeping a constant tension as you pull it over rollers. The fibres lock down and the pattern won't get distorted when you process the fabric further."

"Fascinating as that is," Luca said, "if you can't *detect* something like that, the whole labelling system turns into an honour code, doesn't it?"

Matti shrugged, uncomfortable. "Investigation would be based on reports from buyers, when the fabric doesn't hold up to wear over time. But the penalties laid down in the bylaws are very strict.

And I don't . . ." He struggled. "There's no honour in producing poor product. It tarnishes your entire House." Most people in trade would rather face a penalty from a city council than go against Guild law. A city-state didn't hold anything against you, once you'd paid for your crimes. But to have your reputation blackened within your Guild could break the spine of a House, or destroy an independent merchant's dreams of aspiring to House status.

Luca was looking at him in a way that Matti couldn't interpret. "Then the question is, if they're willing to stoop to espionage and sabotage, do you think the Keseys would draw the line at committing fraud on top of that? Especially if it would be difficult to catch them doing it."

"I don't know," said Matti. "But it'd be easy enough to find out if this man Rivers is still—"

"What are you doing?"

"Was there anything else in your pile that I should see?"

"This was the important one," said Luca. "And again, what are you doing?"

Matti was tidying the papers back into a single pile, which he placed neatly in what seemed the most likely place in the chest. He'd been absorbed in the enormity of what they'd discovered, but now he wanted to be elsewhere so that he could process it.

"Corus can't know we've seen these. Besides, it's not as though we can take any of this out of here."

"Why not?"

"Because it's *stolen,*" said Matti. "Because any magistrate will ask how we got it, and we got it by trespassing and then picking a lock!"

"Not even to show your parents, then?"

"They'll believe me."

Luca glanced up at him in a way that wrung something in Matti's chest. Luca was surprised. Luca, quite transparently, would not have been able to rely on the fact that he would be trusted, not even by his own family.

Matti had to remind himself, with an effort that felt like lifting his sword at the end of an exhausting hour, that *he* didn't trust Luca. He'd gone into this venture with that fact held high in his mind. Holding it there now felt . . . well, like the same effort. Something heavy held aloft for no true reason. A set of words with no emotion beneath it.

"We—*I*—need to think about this before doing anything," Matti said.

"Never been my specialty." Luca's expression gained a sparkle. "You said it yourself, Matti. If you're aware he's a spy and he doesn't know, there are all sorts of ways you can play—"

"Stop."

"I'm serious, what—" Luca's eyes flew wide as Matti's hand covered his mouth.

Matti had his other hand uplifted, straining his ears. "I thought . . ."

In the quiet, noise came again. This time it wasn't the rattle of a key in the front door that Matti had heard the first time, but the distant creak of that door opening, along with the abrupt sound of a conversation in progress. The words were not discernible. The speaking voice, however, was.

"That's Adrean," said Matti.

Luca took hold of Matti's wrist and tugged Matti's hand away from his face. Matti's heart seemed to have taken up residence in his throat, threatening to choke him with a surge of panic.

"Move," Luca said softly. He closed the chest and reached for the padlock, fastening it again. "We can't stay in here. Move, Matti."

Matti stood, rubbing his hands on his thighs, trying to focus. Luca was right. The tiny study wouldn't have been a good hiding place for a child, and it held absolutely no possibilities for two grown men.

Luca set the chest back in position where they'd found it, cast a glance at the desk as though to reassure himself that Matti hadn't left its contents strewn over the floorboards, and then led the

tiptoeing way out of the study and back into the dark upstairs hall.
One of Luca's hands was clamped hard around Matti's forearm.

Adrean's voice mingled with that of another young man. The
two of them were moving around.

"In here," Luca said, barely more than a breath now, "I saw—
yes," as he pulled Matti into the larger of the two bedrooms. There
were sheets of paper scattered thickly on both the bed and the
corner desk, and a battered-looking guitar leaned against the wall,
along with a collection of weapons that had clearly seen better
days.

"This one's Adrean's room," Matti whispered. "We should try—"

"No. We'll have to risk it. The one in the other bedroom's
not big enough." Luca had led them right up to the wardrobe of
scratched dark wood. He made a gesture, the meaning of which
was plain.

"You must be joking." Matti wasn't sure what he was protesting. The ridiculousness of the entire thing, probably.

"Do you have a better idea?"

"You're enjoying this," Matti accused, but he *didn't* have a better idea, and the footsteps on the stairs were getting louder and
closer. He sent out a prayer that the hinges wouldn't creak, tugged
the door of the wardrobe open, and stepped up and into a sparse
flock of hanging clothes.

It wasn't a large space. Matti crammed himself back and sideways to make room, but the speed with which Luca stepped in after him caused an unfortunate rebound effect, like apples bumping
in a barrel of water. The beginning of a hissed curse fell from Luca's
mouth as Luca began to overbalance back out of the wardrobe,
grabbing at coats. Matti's pulse pounded in his temples. He did
the only thing he could think of and snaked an arm around Luca's
chest, pulling Luca awkwardly back against himself.

"Door," Matti said, a strained breath against the top of Luca's ear.

Luca shifted around to hook a toe beneath the wardrobe door
and yanked it towards them with enough force that it snicked

closed. A sudden and stifling darkness enveloped them. The wardrobe smelled of fabric, not all of it clean, and there was a mothball edge to the air.

Silence. Matti strained his ears for the sound of footsteps or voices. His breathing and Luca's both seemed abominably loud, quick and out of sync. His hand was pressed over Luca's heart and he could feel it faintly shoving at his palm through bone and flesh and skin and shirt.

Matti nearly bit his tongue when something touched the back of his hand, but it was just Luca's own hand, flattening Matti's even more firmly against his chest. Matti sucked in a long breath, which was perhaps a mistake. His nose and lungs filled with the smell of Luca's hair.

The footsteps were definitely in the upstairs hall now. Their conversation was still hard to make out.

The pressure of Luca's hand lightened. Now Luca's fingers were moving on the back of Matti's hand, making slow circles and patterns; for a moment Matti wondered if Luca was making letters, trying to communicate, but the patterns were aimless.

Or *not* aimless. Matti realised that this was Luca's outlet—that Luca's restlessness was beginning to bubble up, trapped as he was in this small space. Luca was already shifting his weight from foot to foot, small movements that did nothing for Matti's composure or the tingling fire that was beginning to crawl through his body.

Before he could stop himself, Matti moved his free hand to the side of Luca's waist, his smallest two fingers curling around and encountering the jut of Luca's hipbone.

He'd wanted Luca to be still; instead a shudder went through Luca's whole body and he pressed back farther against Matti. There was no way, no way at all, that he would have missed how Matti was hardening in his trousers. Or how he hardened further, helpless, at the feel of Luca's arse sliding up against him.

This is not the time, Matti wanted to yell at his own anatomy. But Luca was all slim muscle and there was no air between their bodies, barely enough room to slide a letter opener, and Luca's escape-artist hair was in Matti's face, tickling his nose and mouth. If Matti bent his head, he could nose at the place where Luca's collar rose. He could stir the hair at the nape, imagining what Luca might be feeling: the sensation of hot breath on skin. This was it, the crest of the icy slope, and Matti was moving too fast to stop now.

That tingle of fire had become an unbearable crackle. Luca's breath was coming rapidly. If Matti moved the hand on Luca's hip only a little, he would be able to discover if Luca was just as hard as he was. Luca would be trapped between Matti's body and palm. He could try to move, but Matti would have him pinned; Matti could make him shudder again, and again . . .

Matti's own cock twitched. Luca stilled, and then melted even farther against Matti in silent encouragement.

Matti was going to lose his mind here in this wardrobe smelling of sweat and mothballs. He had never been so aroused in his life. He was—

"—slap in the face, on top of everything else."

"But you're going to go anyway?"

"I won't turn down the chance to see her. To talk to her."

Luca's fingernails dug painfully into Matti's hand in unnecessary warning. The voices of Adrean and his companion were suddenly loud and comprehensible. They were in the room.

"Do you need a hand?" The man who was not Adrean sounded bored.

"No, it's here somewhere."

Papers were rustling; someone was moving from place to place. Desk to bed, Matti presumed, looking for whatever it was. He had no idea whatsoever what he would do if Adrean opened the wardrobe. He tried to imagine it and his mind was a pale sheet of terror.

"Besides," Adrean added, "I'll get to meet this best man that nobody seems to have heard of."

Luca's head moved in a kind of twitch, knocking against Matti's chin. Matti winced.

"I still don't know why he didn't go for the best the city has to offer," said Adrean's friend.

"I told you, it's an insult," Adrean said. "And a calculated one. He could afford the best, and he's gone for something less. He's saying I'm not worth it. Well, that's his folly. He's not even seen me fight. He knows nothing about duelling. I'll destroy this newcomer, whoever he is."

Luca was now shaking with what Matti suspected was laughter. Matti pressed his fingers warningly into Luca's hip. It wasn't that funny.

Though Matti was relieved, despite everything, to know that Adrean didn't suspect how badly off Jay House was. That Corus had kept that secret, even from his own son.

"*Where* is this shitting— Oh, here we go." Yet more rustling.

"Take your time," said Adrean's friend, with a hint of sarcasm. "I don't know him, but from what people say about him, Mattinesh doesn't seem like that kind of person."

"The Jays are good at seeming," Adrean said, scathing, and for a panicked moment Matti wondered if he'd been wrong about what Adrean knew. But Adrean went on, "They're the same kind of snobs as the rest of them. Think their shit smells of heartsease and honey. Tomas offered me a job, a few years back, did I tell you? *Ah*. Found it. It's only a draft, but I think it's the best I've done this year. Better than Hattie's incoherent mess of a song; I can't believe she found someone willing to put music behind that drivel."

A noncommittal hum from the other man. "What kind of job?"

"What? Oh, something for a handful of bronze in the logistics office," said Adrean. "Everything my father's done for that family, and that was the best they could do. The man looked as though he thought he was doing me a favour. Patronising prick. And Matti's no better. He's always disliked me—boring, self-righteous prig that he is. He's jealous."

Luca's silent laughter had subsided. Now his fingers slid against the gaps between Matti's own, back and forth.

"Hardly surprising," offered the other, "given everything."

"It's not just Sofia. He can't stand to think that some of us have talents and interests outside his precious House, or that Sofia might prefer someone with a *personality* to someone who thinks that his name should get him everything he wants."

Matti felt as though he'd been punched. Anger at the unfairness of it, mingled with a tiny ember of guilt—he *had* been jealous, on one level, Adrean was right about that—wanted to burst out of him. As for the job, Adrean had never expressed any interest in trade; he still appeared to have none. *Anyone* with no experience would start at the lowest rank of clerkship. Matti wanted to throw the wardrobe door open and defend his father, defend himself.

He wondered if this was how Luca felt all the time: this unbearable need to move.

The reassuring caress had stopped. Luca's fingernails dug in again. This time Matti clung to the warning, forcing himself to focus on the sting of pain. Some of the rage seeped out of him as the subject changed back to the poem that Adrean had written, and the possibility that the other man might help him compose a tune to go with it. Matti was afraid they'd settle in for a long discussion, but it seemed the visit to the house had just been to recover the paper, and they were heading out again.

Matti's muscles had begun to cramp. He forced himself to stay still while the two men left the room, and while their footsteps faded back down the stairs. Eventually the front door closed with a slam.

Luca removed his hand from Matti's and pushed the wardrobe door open. Matti's eyes creased at the sudden light. Luca stepped down with a single soft foot, then another, head cocked. Matti listened hard until he'd convinced himself that there was nobody moving or talking anywhere downstairs.

Then he followed Luca out of the wardrobe, and they stood an arm's span apart on the floor of Adrean's bedroom. The lack of Luca's warmth on Matti's front was as momentarily unpleasant as the light had been.

"What an insufferable little glob of worm spit," said Luca. His voice was clipped and dismissive, as Matti had never heard it before. "What a self-satisfied arse." Now Matti could hear that the haughty control was a milk-skin over some other emotion. Luca doubled over, hands on his knees, and gave a long spout of laughter that sounded like it was being wrung from him. For a moment Matti remembered Sofia, shaking and laughing and apologetic on the street outside Matti's house. "That was a close one," Luca added.

"You *did* enjoy it," Matti accused, but weakly. He could still feel the delirious buzz of anger and desire and alertness in his own veins.

"Oh, certainly. By all means. I live for the thrill of danger. I *relish* the prospect of being discovered committing acts of criminal daring on someone else's property." Some more of that laughter that seemed to come from Luca's gut and shred his pipes on the way out.

"I'm sure it was very inconvenient for you to have to manage me as well." Matti didn't know what to think. This was Luca's chosen career, or at least a large piece in the strange patchwork of things that comprised that career. Luca had moved swiftly and decisively, and hidden them in the only possible place, and they had remained secret. It hardly seemed like something that would warrant this reaction.

Luca straightened. His mouth was loose with laughter as he stared at Matti, that direct and stripping stare that found all of Matti's faults. Now it was doing nothing but making Matti remember, with perfect clarity, how Luca's hair had smelled and how his nails and fingers had felt on Matti's hand.

Luca swallowed. Matti watched his throat move.

"Manage you," Luca said. "As if I'd dare. Come on. This part is known as *making our escape.*"

Matti's pulse and erection had both settled themselves by the time the escape was properly made. They let themselves out via the front door, locked it, and strolled—with a casual pace that took all of Matti's concentration to maintain—two streets away.

Luca ducked into a small courtyard between townhouses. The same kind of yard could be found all over the city, small spaces for neighbourhood children to play skipping games and skin their knees and generally burn off some energy after school. This courtyard was shielded from the street by a wall topped with wrought iron detailing. It was empty, ramshackle, with the small piece of earth gone to knee-high whistleweed and dry dead grass. What had been an area of paving stones was now a battlefield of broken rock where a tree's roots had erupted in knots, forcing their way through.

Matti was settled. In fact, Matti was feeling quite calm about the whole business as he sat down on the yard's tiny bench, greyish wood flecked with the old white of pigeon and gull droppings. Now he would think. He would plan. He would decide on the next step.

"Matti," Luca said. He sounded uneasy. He didn't need to. Matti was calm.

Matti was—looking down at the tree roots, the turbulence of the pattern, the way the flat stones had given way to the simple brutality of nature, cracked right open and lifted their dusty insides to the sky, and—

And then it was Matti giving way, as though some insistent buried force had been straining against the rock of *him* for hours, maybe years. His vision blurred. He could hear the air sucking in fast through his nostrils. He leaned his elbows on his knees and willed himself to find normality, but he was brittle and breakable and this, here, stupid and small, was his breaking point. What a fucking joke.

"Matti?" Luca sounded outright alarmed now.

"It's not just because of me." It came out somewhere between a gasp and laughter. It sounded worse, even more uneven and strange, than Luca's laughter in Adrean's room. "It's not—my fault. Oh, Huna. Oh, fuck."

The pause seemed to stretch on for minutes, while Matti shook with a relief so tangible it was like walking into crashing surf. First it refreshed you, and then your feet were swept away and your mouth filled with salt.

Finally Luca said, incredulous, "You mean, your family—your House? You thought it was all because of *you*? But you told me— you said you knew what you were doing. You said it was an accumulation of bad luck."

Matti didn't know what to say. He couldn't have said it even if he did know. His arms were shaking from the shoulders down, and his chest felt overfull, like a pair of bellows being prised wider and wider and never allowed to close and blow. Stars danced behind his eyes. His heart was going to explode. He was going to die here on this bench covered in bird shit while Luca Piere watched over his last breaths.

"Responsible fucking Matti Jay," said Luca, with an odd tension in his voice. "You don't do things by half measures, do you?"

And then there was a warmth against Matti's forehead, and two more on his shoulders. Luca had stepped close and he was tugging Matti against his own body.

The first instinct in Matti was to wrench himself away—to try harder, try *better*. To centre himself, regain control, and be the person he was supposed to be. He could cope. That was what he did.

"All right. Um," Luca said. "I think . . . deep breaths? Probably? Breathe, Matti. Nobody's looking, you can take your time."

The hands on Matti's shoulders tightened, guiding him, settling Matti's forehead against Luca's lower ribs. A button of Luca's shirt was a small, hard focus point against Matti's skull. There were fingers brushing through his hair, thumbs at his temples, soothing.

This was worlds away from the agonising closeness they'd shared inside the Vane house. This was a touch that offered no increase in tension but instead seemed designed only to calm, to warm, and to be a small haven where Matti could press his nose into fabric and inhale thinly past just enough pressure, feeling the dreadful bellows of his lungs begin to slowly relent.

He knew, intellectually he *did* know, that he couldn't be single-handedly responsible for his House's failures. That certainty was held firm by a part of him rooted in the fact that he was loved unreservedly, that he was respected.

Matti was coming to realise that this part had been at war, for a very long time, with the part of him that had nothing to do with intellect and everything to do with his parents' decade-long worry, and with knowing that he would do anything and everything to rescue them from it. That everything he could do, everything he *had* done, was not enough. Love was a sword with two edges.

Take your time.

Matti wasn't sure how long he sat there, breathing, with his face against Luca's stomach and Luca's fingers stroking his scalp. When he felt fully himself again, his head was aching gently. He could smell Luca's body through his shirt. Matti lifted his head and pulled away, half expecting to see damp patches where his eyes had been, but the shirt was dry.

Luca stepped away as well, giving Matti space. Matti ran a hand through his hair once, and then again. He braced himself for eye contact.

"I'm—"

"If you fucking apologise to me for that," Luca said at once, "I will break your nose with my knee."

Matti was startled into a snort of laughter. He made a decision, then, between one second and the next. Luca had done so much for him today. He was going to do something for him in return, even if the importance of it was lost on Luca. It would balance the columns of obligation, remove some of the weight.

Matti said, "Instead of coming to Tolliver's tomorrow morning, meet me somewhere else."

"I see, I see. Is this what I am to you now? Pick one lock for a man and suddenly he has a list." But Luca was smiling, tentative.

"No locks to be picked. I promise."

He was gambling on the same curiosity that had dragged Luca along today. The need to know *why,* and *what,* and *how.*

"All right," said Luca, easy. "Tell me where."

CHAPTER
10

The dawn air off the ocean was like the breath of a generous cool beast, brushing Luca's cheeks as he approached the sea's edge. It was welcome. Summer seemed to be holding the land in jealous claws as they headed into its last few weeks.

The preceding night had been warm enough that sleep had eluded Luca even with the window cracked. He'd ended up fetching water from the kitchen and dipping his fingers into it, then creating hopeful cool trails down his own face and neck. Even then he'd lain there for some time, shifting his aching shoulders against the pillow. He and Ilse had been hired for a high formal show match at the Woodworker Guildband dinner, and Ilse had clearly been practicing how to get the best advantage out of her height and reach.

It hadn't helped that every time Luca closed his eyes in bed he was back in the intimate darkness of Adrean Vane's wardrobe, balanced between Matti's hands like a sword on two fingers. That every time Luca trailed his own wet fingertips over his skin he imagined Matti doing the same thing, and felt hotter and more breathless than ever.

Now, as though Luca's imagination needed any more fodder, Matti was sitting bare-chested on a stone bench with his feet only just touching the choppy green-grey water.

The sea bath had clearly been a natural basin in the rock, once, and it had been encouraged and shaped by human hands. Now it was a roughly rectangular pool, long enough to swim respectable laps in, and ringed with a low hump of stone in which wooden posts were set at intervals. Sluggish white-capped waves swilled over the ocean-side border and into the pool, but the backwash was weak, and a net was strung between the posts. Even in the half-light of morning it would be safe to swim without fear of being swept out to sea.

The crags of rock lifted, beyond the bath, to form a rough headland dividing these rock pools from the calmer and broader curve of coast which was Glassport Harbour proper. On the other side, the wave-washed ledge stretched out for a good hundred yards before lowering to a short stretch of unattractive pebbled beach. Only a half-hour walk from the busiest part of the harbour, this was a strange, tucked-away piece of the city, barely feeling like city at all. The closest people to Matti and Luca were the fishermen, their boats already dots heading towards the horizon, and the dockworkers and sailors whose cries were faint as birdsong as they drifted from the unseen harbour.

"This wasn't the kind of swimming pool I was expecting," Luca said.

Matti had been looking down at his feet. When Luca spoke, he lifted his head, and the smile that broke over his face was like the moment when a lock surrendered to Luca's picks. Something gave way before it. Some small piece of machinery fell in Luca's chest with an audible click, some unseen hinges opened, and a soft unfamiliar happiness flowed through the crack.

Before now, Luca's experience of Matti's smiles had been that they were sidelong things, unconscious or grudging or hard-won. And now Matti was bestowing this one upon Luca, allowing it to light his features to something extraordinary, as though Luca deserved it. As though Luca need do nothing more than exist for Matti to be glad to see him.

Luca paused in his steps and smiled back. The ocean breeze stroked his cheeks again and he thought: *Oh.*

Then he thought, making the words deliberate and large in his mind: *It's not real. The person he thinks you are isn't fucking* real.

Which was the fun of it, the point of it. Luca had to remember that.

Matti stood and made his way to the edge of the pool. The bathing trunks began beneath his waist and reached to just above his knees. Luca's interested gaze had enough time to stray across Matti's broad shoulders, down the solid line of his torso, and follow the trail of black hair south from his navel. Then Matti rolled his shoulders and loosened his neck, an unselfconscious motion, and dove smoothly into the water.

"All right," said Luca resignedly, to the breeze, and to the dark moving shape of Matti beneath the surface. "That's . . . fine."

Matti resurfaced with his hair flattened to the sides of his face. He let out a gasping, satisfied exhale. "It's cold," he called, "but you get used to it quickly. Come on."

"At least it's summer," Luca said, and began to undress. He found the small pile of Matti's own clothes, along with a cloth bag containing towels, and set his own things down next to it.

Matti swam closer. "Yes, in winter it's quite bracing."

Luca paused in the act of removing his clothes. When Matti had told him where they'd be meeting, he'd gone out and bought a cheap pair of trunks. They were itching his legs beneath his trousers.

Luca said, aghast, "You swim here in *winter*?"

"I swim here every day," said Matti, as though he weren't confessing to the deepest form of bodily insanity. "Before you, anyway," he added. "There are usually a few days when it's too dangerous, but it's not that bad." He rested his arms on one of the rocky edges. Wet Matti was no better for Luca's composure than dry Matti. "It doesn't get as cold here on the coast as it does inland."

Luca imagined stripping off and diving into the freezing lakewater in the coldest mornings of Cienne's winter. All the skin tried to crawl off his body in horror. He slowly finished undressing and tested the water with his toes. It was no cooler than the sensation of trailing one's hand through a fountain.

Matti laughed. "Just dive in, Luca."

Luca shook water from his foot and took a moment to choke down the ironic role reversal of Matti being the one to advocate flinging oneself headlong into an experience. He felt as though he'd been dared, and he'd never been very wise in the face of dares.

The water was like a light slap, and Luca held his breath hard against the urge to gasp it out at the shock of coolness. He surfaced for long enough to take a breath and then submerged himself fully again, eyes shut, willing his body to acclimatise. The bottom of the pool was smooth rock with a thin layer of sand. Luca had barely nudged it with a toe before he found himself bobbing towards the surface, where he trod water awkwardly. It had been a long time since he'd swum, and he'd never learned much more than the minimum required to stay afloat. Muscles in his legs and arms, which he considered fit and strong, were already beginning to protest that they were not used to moving in this particular way.

"That end is shallower," said Matti.

"I see," Luca said. "You wanted to see *me* flail around for a change. Hilarious. Please imagine I can spare a hand to make the gesture I want to make."

Matti grinned at him and took off for the indicated shallow end with a loping stroke of his arms. Luca followed in his wake with less speed and less dignity. He felt better with his feet solidly beneath him, though his body had already embraced the water's temperature and the air now seemed the cooler of the two environments, prickling at Luca's neck as the seawater trickled down it.

He joined Matti at the edge of the pool, looking out at the horizon. The lightening sky was grey-blue, streaked with pale gold clouds like smoke rising from the jewelled fire of the sun. Luca looked sidelong at Matti, whose face was still, but it didn't strike Luca as the stillness of hidden things. He looked almost at peace.

Luca drew his fingers back and forth in a shallow puddle formed in the rocky barrier, crossing and recrossing his own ripples. The intimacy of this, the generous sharing of something private, was settling over him.

"You did this every morning?" Luca asked. "Before we started having sword lessons instead?"

"My physician told me to."

"Really?"

Matti began to run his fingers through his hair, made a face when they caught in the wet strands, and settled for pushing it slickly back instead. "I used to get nausea so bad that I couldn't eat in the mornings. Then I started having dizzy spells. The physician told me to exercise every day. He said it would improve the flow of blood to and from my head, and it would feel more solid. And this was easiest." Matti looked out to sea again. "It doesn't cost anything. I can do it without anyone else around, before the day properly starts."

Luca began to ask a question, stopped, then decided to ask it anyway. "Do you enjoy it?"

Matti looked back at him, eyebrows raised. "I like the quiet. And it did make the nausea and dizziness better. I didn't do it to enjoy it."

"No." Luca's heart wrung like a lemon being squeezed for juice. "No, you wouldn't." He thought about the way Matti's shoulders had shaken yesterday: the quiet, violent breakdown of the wall behind which Matti had been storing years and years of tamped-down guilt and worry. Luca added, forcing himself to sound playful, "And instead of following your physician's orders you've been listening to me go on and on about feet positions and reading your opponent's signals. It probably hasn't been helping, has it?"

"No! I mean, yes, it's been . . . fine. Just different. I don't focus on anything when I'm swimming, and I have to focus *all the time* when I'm with you. But that's just as good, I think. In its own way."

"Good," said Luca. "I'd hate to think I was shoving *more* things into the tangle that goes on up there." He meant to poke at Matti's forehead, but somehow the gesture gentled itself. Luca found himself with his fingertips soft at Matti's temple, his hand barely hovering above the side of Matti's face.

Matti leaned into it. After a moment his eyes fell closed: not a flutter, a definitive fall, just as he'd fallen to sit down on that bench when they'd left the Vane house. It had the same exhausted air to it. Matti's cheek was wet. Luca's throat felt tight.

"You are. You do," Matti said, very soft. "You tangle me up."

Luca pulled his hand away. Or at least he planned to. The plan had barely communicated itself to his body when Matti's own hand rose, trapping Luca's beneath it just as Luca had trapped Matti's yesterday. Matti's eyes opened. His lashes were spiked with water.

That was enough for Luca. He had been wanting for weeks, and now the desire was large enough and unbearable enough that he couldn't find it within himself to do anything but take, as he took most things that he wanted, in the end.

He stepped even closer, used his hand to angle Matti's face slightly downwards, and kissed his way through the film of salt water to the heat of Matti's mouth beneath.

If Luca had tried to count the number of people he'd kissed in his life, he would have run out of space on his hands and feet, with a fair few digits representing those whose names he couldn't remember. He certainly hadn't gone to bed with all of them. But he'd seldom held himself back from the impulse of the moment, if the slightest spark of attraction was there, and some of his fondest memories were of the nights when he'd flirted himself into a man's company and then into his lap, taken all the kisses he wanted, and then melted away, buzzing and satisfied, before midnight.

There had been, in short, a lot of kisses. Some of them disappointing, but most of them enjoyable, else Luca would have abandoned the activity; he didn't stick with things when he wasn't getting anything from them.

He wondered, now, whom Matti Jay had been kissing in the years before Luca elbowed his way into his life. For all Luca's thinking about it—and he *had* been thinking about it—he'd assumed that Matti might have been too busy, too self-sacrificing, to be particularly proficient in this area.

Matti kissed in a way that was unhesitatingly hungry and exploratory, a way that Luca had never known he wanted. Luca wondered if he was now doomed to spend the rest of his life trying to chase this kiss down and replicate it.

Luca still had one hand at Matti's jaw and another at the back of Matti's neck. They were standing waist-deep in water and Luca felt as though he was fully submerged once more: buoyant and breathless and aware of his skin's boundaries. The heat of Luca's desire and the heat of Matti's body, his arms wrapped around Luca's back, were battling the coolness of drying skin, and their attack was two-pronged and deadly. Matti didn't taste of salt anymore.

"Wait," Matti said, during a pause for breath.

Luca had waited long enough, thank you. He tried to communicate that with a murmur of complaint against Matti's jaw, which was unshaven and rough, shadowing Matti's face in a way that frankly had no right to render him more attractive than ever and yet was managing to do so.

Gently, Matti pushed Luca backwards, his hands on Luca's shoulders. He wasn't making eye contact.

"Stop," Matti said softly. "Just stop."

"We *have* stopped," said Luca, with more of an edge than he'd intended.

Matti gave something that wasn't quite a laugh. "I—it's not you."

"Remember yesterday, when I threatened to break your nose?" Luca said. "I'm not saying it's not going to be more of a challenge, now that you're standing instead of sitting, and I am possibly even more useless with my fists than you are with a sword, but if the words *it's me* are the next things to emerge from your mouth, I'm going to do my level best to punch them back in again."

Matti gave a sudden sunburst of a smile and touched Luca's mouth. He did it absently, as though his hand was acting freely from the rest of him: a touch like an exploration of new cloth's texture, like a finger between pages, marking the place in a book. Luca's whole body tried to sway into the smallness of it. He would have paid every bronze he'd ever earned, every gold in the coffers of his House, to hear Matti say *be quiet,* or *be still,* and to keep on looking at Luca like this while he waited for Luca to comply.

"I meant, I was talking to myself," said Matti. His smile slipped as Luca, figuring he had nothing to lose at this point, opened his lips enough to be an unmistakable invitation.

"I don't want you to stop." Luca's tongue slid against Matti's finger with the words. *Come on,* he begged silently. *Let yourself have this.* "If that isn't absurdly obvious."

"Luca." Matti's hand dropped to his side. "We're not—I'm not—"

Luca didn't know where that sentence was heading, but he liked his chances of throwing a log in its path. "Matti. I'll steal a lot of things, but I wouldn't *actually* steal someone's husband. But you're not married yet, are you? And it doesn't have to be serious. I don't think either of us is looking for serious. We don't even have to do anything more than . . . this."

He lifted his mouth to Matti's again, and Matti didn't resist. Luca directed the kiss this time, making sure it was the sort he was good at: teasing little bites, very light, very swift, promising something deeper but never delivering. He was rewarded with a moan, a thrum of breath in Matti's throat where Luca's hand rested.

"You want to," Luca said, letting the words catch his lips against Matti's. "I want to. It's not complicated."

"You're such a liar, Luca Piere," said Matti, with such helpless affection that the flare of Luca's nerves was over almost before it began.

Oh, yes, he felt on one level like he was drawing Matti into another deception, but nothing he was saying was untrue. It *could* be simple. The warm, lockpicked ache in Luca's chest was his own business.

"I'm not," he lied.

"Of course it's complicated. You're . . . complicating. A complicating factor."

"How flattering."

The look Matti was giving him shifted from apologetic to sarcastic. "Yes, I know. But—oh, Huna, I wish things were different, but it's not just the engagement. It's everything else. It's that I'm already lying to my family, and now there's this business with Corus and the Keseys."

"Are you telling me," said Luca, "that you would have fucked me if I'd just kept my damn mouth shut?"

Matti's eyes widened and his lips became a line. Luca lifted his hand from Matti's neck to Matti's cheek to see if he could feel the flush. Matti pulled Luca's hand away, but kept hold of it, which seemed a good sign.

"If you'd kept your mouth shut about Corus that night at your boardinghouse, we'd never have found ourselves shut in a wardrobe the next day," said Matti, dry.

"There was a bottle of Diamond Blend and you were *on my bed*, Matti. I'm pretty sure I could have improvised if necessary."

Matti squeezed his hand. "I mean it. There's too much going on. I don't—I don't do well, when I feel overwhelmed."

"Complicating *and* overwhelming," said Luca. "I love it. I shall adopt it as my motto. I will have it embroidered on my—"

This kiss was sudden, a deluge. Matti's hand at the back of Luca's head created enough force that he was nearly crushing Luca's mouth against his own. Luca felt one of his feet slip, sand on rock, and wondered if Matti would ever believe it had been accidental when the slip brought him right up against Matti's body. They were pressed together from mouth to groin. A hot splash of longing coaxed Luca to let himself slip farther down, all the way to his knees, depth of the pool be damned. He could feel Matti stirring against him.

And then he felt the firm shove as Matti released him and pushed him away, where the water caught him and kept him from overbalancing.

"Yes," Matti said, uneven. "Overwhelming."

Luca didn't know he was arranging the next attack in his throat until it vaulted out, catching itself on the sharp points of his desperation. "You could have had my trousers down and fucked me in that wardrobe, you know. I got myself off last night, thinking about it."

"*Luca.*" Matti's tone was halfway between commanding and pleading. He didn't have a parry. Luca had expected as much. "That's not fair."

Luca opened his mouth to point out that he was a cheat and a con and he'd never pretended to play fair; that what wasn't fair was Matti putting his hands on Luca, Matti kissing him like he wanted to devour Luca whole, and then *not following through*. But here Matti was, decently telling him the truth, even though neither of them wanted to hear it.

And Luca was going to have to do the decent thing, too, wasn't he?

"Gods damn you, Mattinesh," he said. "I know. I'm sorry."

"I'm sorry too," said Matti. "Really."

"So. What do we do now?" Luca waved an arm to encompass the pool, the distant flock of birds against the sky, and the two of them, standing there shirtless and aroused and wet. He hoped his gesture managed to communicate what he was thinking, which was: *What a fucking waste.*

"We could swim laps? That was my original plan for this morning."

Luca weighed the likely indignity of his poor swimming skills against the urgent need to burn off his desire. He wanted to throw himself back at Matti and start the argument up again. He'd win, that was the awful thing. He *knew* he'd win. He could talk faster than Matti could muster denial, and he could *feel* the effort with which Matti was trying not to rake his gaze up and down Luca's body.

All he'd have to do would be to get his fingers onto Matti's cock, pick one of many provocative facial expressions, and beg. Shamelessly, explicitly. Beg.

"Laps," Luca said, mouth dry with salt. "Why not?"

CHAPTER
11

Luca's boardinghouse was on the way back to Matti's from the sea bath. The route took them along the edge of the harbour front, and the sun was heavy with promise where it fell between masts and buildings, so that Luca's hair dried quickly and his skin had the lightest itch of clinging salt. It would be a hot day.

The streets were already alive with morning traffic: streams of people in and out of coffeehouses, some clutching leather folders if they were heading into those places most favoured for breakfast meetings. Shutters were being banged back from shopfronts, dust being rubbed from windows, signs and chairs and display tables being carried outside. Shopkeepers were the same everywhere; Luca could see the marks either chalked or engraved in the stone of the footpath, proclaiming where the space allocated to each shop began and ended, and he could see the glances exchanged as people edged their wares right up to the last breath of space in their domain.

Master Carriere had told Luca a story once about a famous duel that was fought by two masters, back in the previous century when hired swords were still a legal way of settling disputes in most city-states. The duel was famous for the brilliant sequence of forms that had finished it—the Galfi Feint, named for the victor—but the reason it had been fought in the first place was that the owner of a pottery shop, senior in his Guild, had spent a year in silent furious battle with an equally senior woodcarver who held the title of the adjacent shop. The subject of the dispute had been the slow encroachment of the potter's space by a single leg of the woodcarver's table.

It was a good story, the way Master Carriere told it, even if Luca did associate it with not being able to lift his arms above the shoulder and bruises on both of his knees from the merciless week it'd taken him to learn the Galfi Feint.

Matti's face was composed, eyes bright and moving, taking things in. Not for the first time Luca wondered if Matti had been born with that resting expression—so blandly, pleasantly unreadable—or whether it was something he'd had to cultivate.

Neither of them had discussed this outright, the fact that Matti was walking Luca back to his boardinghouse. The fact that they were here, together, in public, and not skulking in courtyards or playing at housebreaking. Matti had simply fallen into step with Luca as they left the pool, and Luca hadn't thought to find it odd until they were suddenly among people. Everything that they'd done together before now had been a secret of one kind or another. There was something unsettlingly blatant about this, walking as friends walked. A wary shock like new skin exposed to the light. Luca half expected to feel the drag of gazes following their progress. It felt *remarkable*. People should be remarking.

Sunlight hummed along Luca's nerves and his mind was reliving the feel of Matti's arms around him, Matti's mouth on his: half pleasant reverie and half the equivalent of scratching away a scab to watch the blood well up.

"Matti!"

Matti pulled to a halt. Guilt flashed for only a moment on his face before he turned.

The young woman who had hailed them was leaning out of a doorway, her wavy black hair and full skirt both swinging with the abruptness of her motion. She said something over her shoulder, into the shop, then stepped down onto the footpath.

"Maya," said Matti. "What are you doing here?"

Even without that confirmation, Luca would have picked Maya Jay as being a relation of Matti's. She was a fraction taller than Luca, long-limbed in a way that only just stopped short of gangly, and her impeccably tailored shirt was tucked into a bright red skirt with gold trim. Her skin was darker than Matti's, her face a longer oval, adorned with some of the same features. Luca wondered which of their parents had passed on that distracting, demanding mouth.

Maya's mouth was lit with Matti's rare smile, as though she had an endless supply of them in the bag slung over her shoulder and was happy to give them away for free. She bestowed one on Luca, along with a curious raise of her eyebrows, then looked back at her brother.

"I'm visiting Joyce Amberden. She knows Marko likes their cherries, so she put some aside for me. Are you going to introduce me to your friend, Matti?"

"Um," said Matti, looking at Luca.

Luca, remembering how Matti had frozen up at the sound of the Vane townhouse's door opening, decided that some kind of intervention was needed. He crafted a smile that was hopefully both winning and professional, fired it at Maya, and said, "I'm his best man."

At exactly the same time, Matti said, "He's the dancing master I've been seeing."

"Well," said Maya, after a moment. "This is interesting."

Matti gave Luca a look through which naked betrayal and panic were clearly trying to escape.

"I'm sorry," said Luca, "is your sister not going to be *at* your wedding?"

"I." Matti's mouth opened. Closed. "I didn't think of that," he said, sheepish enough that Luca burst out laughing.

"*Very* interesting," said Maya. She cast a pointed look at the cloth bag in Matti's hand, which held his damp towel.

Luca was going to let Matti handle this. Matti's family was clearly everything to him, and watching him interact with them was going to be illuminating. Luca felt like a critic at the theatre with a pen and paper poised, hungrily ready to take notes.

"Luca is my best man," admitted Matti. "We've been swimming."

"Ah!" said Maya. "The mysterious newcomer."

"That's me," said Luca.

"Luca, my sister Maya."

"My name is Luca Piere." Luca extended his hand. It was the traditional framing for a business deal, and he was enjoying himself too much to drop the theatrics.

Interest glittered in Maya's dark eyes. There was a pause a little too long for good manners before she extended her own hand. Her nails were painted yellow, with red tips. "My name is Mayanesh Jay." As soon as she'd released Luca's hand she turned back to Matti. "Your best man is giving you dancing lessons?"

"Sword lessons, actually," said Matti. "It's a long story."

Maya smoothed her hands over her skirt and adjusted the lay of her perfectly symmetrical collar. "Have you two had breakfast?"

"I was just heading home," said Matti. "I have to—"

"No," cut in Luca. He tried another of his smiles on Maya. The strangeness of the morning had expanded and he felt an exhilarated, almost pugnacious urge to push at where this would take them. It was as though he and Matti had been existing in a glass bauble that had now been smashed, letting the world in. "We haven't had breakfast."

"Good," Maya said. "I want to hear this long story. Erneska's is nearby, and they make good raskils."

"Lead on," said Luca.

Maya disappeared back into the shop to bid farewell to her friend, and Matti grabbed Luca's upper arm and tugged him close. A quick, interested thrill sped over Luca's skin.

"Will you let me do this by myself?"

"No chance," said Luca. "I want to talk to your sister, she seems like fun."

"Luca—"

"What are you going to do, Matti?" Luca reached up and

removed Matti's hand from his arm. "Haul me up in front of a city magistrate? I had hoped we'd moved on from the mutual blackmail stage of our relationship."

"No. I'm not going to do that. But if we're telling Maya the story, I'm not leaving that part out."

"Of course not." Luca smiled. "I still can't believe you forgot I'm going to meet your whole family eventually."

"I was . . . distracted." Matti's gaze dropped clear as windows to Luca's mouth.

Luca, leaning into the boundaries of what was fair and unfair, and reflecting that Matti had nobody to blame but himself—the man could have had at *least* two orgasms before breakfast, if he hadn't been so stubborn—let his tongue flick over his lips.

"How much are you going to tell her?" he asked, waving his fingers to indicate the entire Corus Vane debacle.

"I think—"

"Shall we?" Maya emerged from the shop again with a small basket slung over one wrist, linked her arm through her brother's, and set off. Luca walked close behind the Jays. The pair of them strode fast, with their long legs. More than that, they shared a kind of unthinking self-possession that bordered on arrogance as they dominated a fair portion of the busy footpath, collecting admiring or resentful gazes from the people who stepped aside.

As they were paused waiting for two carts to clear a road crossing, Maya turned and offered the small basket to Luca. "Cherry? They're very good."

Luca took one. "Thanks."

"Matti?"

"Not for me," said Matti.

Maya cast another glance over her shoulder at Luca that was probably meant to be as casual as her voice when she added, "I asked Joyce to send the order for the twins to the house. These were a gift."

After a moment, Matti took a cherry. Luca bit into his own,

rolling the sweet flesh of it around his mouth with more care than he'd ever taken over a bite of fruit before. Cherries were expensive, but not so expensive that Luca had ever thought twice about buying them. He tried to imagine denying himself something so commonplace, to the point where it would become a treat. He wanted to march back to the grocer and buy up their whole supply and shove it into Matti's broad hands until they overflowed.

Erneska's turned out to be a bakery close to Tolliver's agency. Their tables were full; Maya bought three pastries and led the way to the closest park. She settled them on the grass in a precarious patch of tree shade that was going to sneak off over a pond if they stayed there too long, and handed out breakfast.

Luca had eaten raskils in Cienne, but had discovered since arriving in Glassport that nobody in the harbour city considered the cheese-and-herb pastries, in the shape of a curling snail shell, to be *real* raskils unless they were made locally. The one from Erneska's was certainly the best example he'd ever tasted, with an audible buttery crunch to the browned edges and melting threads of cheese still so hot that Luca burned his tongue on the first bite. He set it down to cool.

"So, Mattinesh and Mayanesh," he said. "What are the twins called?"

Maya wiped crumbs from her mouth and shot Matti a thoughtful look. "Marko and Merri," she said. "Yes, both with the *nesh* attached."

"It's a naming convention of the mountain people outside Manisi," Matti explained. "Where my mother's mother was from. Mama kept it going when she married into Jay House."

"And where are you from, Luca Piere?" asked Maya. That Jay smile really was disarming, and it didn't help that Luca was already attuned to it. He wanted to smile back. He wanted her to *like* him, and it had happened very fast.

He swallowed down the urge to ask Matti's sister if she'd ever considered a career in confidence trickery, and took another bite of his raskil. For a few seconds, mind lulled blank by the dappled sunlight and the warm food and the lingering smashed-bauble giddiness, he couldn't remember if he'd lied about this to Matti. Or if he'd told Matti the truth. Or if it had even come up in conversation.

"Cienne," he said, once he'd lost even the excuse of a full mouth. "And what brought you here?"

"The usual," said Matti. "Seeking his fortune. Seeking other people's fortunes."

Luca sighed. "Am I going to be given a chance to defend myself in this story?"

"No." Matti licked grease from his finger, which was cheating.

Luca raised his hands in surrender, picked up his own raskil, and settled in to eat while Matti outlined events for Maya, everything from their first meeting in Audry's drinking house. No mention was made of uneasy tensions around Matti having paid for Luca's time—or just how close and excruciating that wardrobe had been—or of Matti's tongue in Luca's mouth, Matti's fingertips bruisingly good on Luca's spine, at the sea bath that very morning.

Everything else, Matti included. Luca managed to restrain himself to only the most important and entertaining of objections when Matti started telling part of it wrong, or when Matti prompted him for details regarding what he'd overheard between Corus and the Kesey House agent.

Maya sucked in her breath when Matti described exactly what they'd found in Vane's document chest, but didn't interrupt. She waited until Matti had stopped speaking.

"Corus," she said then, like a stone dropped into a well.

"I know," said Matti. They shared a look. "I'm going to start reversing what he's done, at least the parts that I can manage quietly. The mordant will be an easy fix; I know you've been saying we should take that business to the chemists in Manisi."

"Start by just threatening to do it," said Maya. "You might

worry the Haxbridge people enough that they undercut their own price." She paused. "You . . . haven't told Dad and Mama?"

"It was only yesterday. And . . . I'm afraid to." Matti said it so quietly that it was almost lost in the noise of hooves and wheels from the closest street. "I can't put that on them as well. It's my job to keep things off their desks."

Luca expected a protest from Maya, something along the lines of: They deserve to know. They *need* to know. Instead, she nodded.

"You want to tell them when you have a solution," she said.

"There's an easy solution," Luca said. "*Fire* the bastard. Drum him out of your House."

Maya ignored that. "Is there any real proof to link Lysbette Martens to what Corus and the Keseys have been doing?"

"Apart from the fact that he was meeting someone at her Guildhall?" said Luca. "No. Not directly." It annoyed him. It was a loose thread that he couldn't help wanting to tug, though he didn't know how it might be done, short of yet more snooping. And letting oneself in the front door of an empty, shabby house to which one had a key was quite a different matter to breaking into a Guildmaster's dwelling.

Oh, yes. Luca was intimately familiar with that difference. His guts twisted with memory and the next bite of raskil had a sour foretaste.

"Leaving that aside, what about the letter about the fraudulent labelling?" asked Maya.

Matti nodded firmly. "Proof first. I should try to track down this Rob Rivers, and get more of the story out of him. See if he'll swear to it in front of the Guild authorities. And then we can—"

"Or we could simply go and see the process for ourselves," said Maya.

Luca felt off-balance. The Jay siblings had a rhythm to their conversation, a way of turning their bodies to each other, that made him feel achingly jealous in about three directions at once. Maya's face was animated, her grin sparkling.

"And by *we*," she added, "I meant me and this con artist best man of yours, Matti."

"Excuse me?" said Luca, at the same time as Matti's "What?"

"Please." Maya turned the sparkle on Luca. "Are you telling me you couldn't talk your way into a little manual labour? I can give you the lightning course. A day on the carding floor should give us what we need."

A niggling part of Luca was not sure about this, but it was immediately swamped by the part of him that didn't know how to turn down a challenge. "I'm in," he said promptly.

"But—" said Matti.

Luca raised his eyebrows at him. By the way Matti's face changed and his gaze swung between Luca and Maya, Maya was doing the same thing.

"Are you sure?" Matti said.

"I know you can't spare the time," said Maya.

"And besides," said Luca, "you'd open your mouth and sound like you've been giving polite orders your whole life, and it wouldn't work at all."

There was only the smallest twitch of Matti's jaw to indicate that he was thinking about exactly the same *polite orders* that Luca was.

"All right," Matti said.

"I've just thought of something." Maya fluttered her fingers in Luca's direction. "Does this mean you *haven't* been going to dancing lessons?"

"Not even one," said Matti. His grin flashed, sheepish, and Luca felt his own mouth mirror it.

"Huna's lungs, Matti." Maya threw a hand to the level of her head and flicked the fingers wide as though to banish water from them. "Your Half Moon Ball is only a few weeks away. You do remember that, don't you? Mama and Dad think you've been spending all this time diligently learning to spin Sofia around the floor. What are you going to do? Prod her with a sword instead?"

Matti looked so comically struck, so totally *betrayed* by the fact that he had managed to overlook this one vital thing in his meticulously planned life, that Luca burst out laughing. He let the laughter tip him backwards into the grass, shading his eyes against the sun. A piece of tension that had been winding in resentful knots around his heart since Matti rejected him in the pool was finally easing.

Matti glared down at him. "That's not helpful."

"I'm imagining you doing your terrible version of the intermediate forms in the middle of a ballroom," Luca said. "While your poor, neglected betrothed weeps in a corner."

Maya's laugher, high and rich, mingled with Luca's.

"*Still* not helpful." Matti's shoulders were stiff.

"I'll help," Maya said. "You won't be as good as you should be, but I can teach you the basics. We'll just pretend you're a terrible dancer. Unteachable."

A hint of humour appeared, finally, as Matti glanced at Luca.

Luca wasn't going to disappoint him. "No pretending necessary. He's a disaster," Luca assured Maya. "You might want to find yourself a pair of those wooden shoes they used to wear in Harbeke."

"A disaster? Matti?" Maya looked at her brother with effortless admiration. The sight of it stuck in Luca's throat. "I find that hard to believe."

"It's true," Matti said. "I'm awful."

Maya scooped up some raskil crumbs and ate them. "Well. Let's at least make sure you look like you've seen the steps before."

"I have to get home." Matti climbed to his feet, brushing crumbs from his trousers, and the other two did the same. "I'm already behind on work."

"After dinner," Maya said. "I'll come up to your study. You can spare an hour, if it means not making a fool of yourself in front of all our friends and the luminaries of two Guilds."

"No arguments." Matti kissed his thumb and flicked her ear

with it, which was probably the most adorable thing Luca had ever seen.

"I don't get one of those?" he demanded.

"Family only," said Matti. "Sorry."

"Go away, Mattinesh," said Luca. "I'll see you tomorrow morning."

Matti's gaze flicked between Luca and Maya, but he nodded and left.

"I should be going as well," said Maya. "I've a friend in town from Otesca and I need to drag every detail of next season's fashions out of her, so Matti can advise the dye buyers. We'll be taking a coach tomorrow, by the way."

"We— What?"

"The Kesey carding houses are mostly out of the city. I'll send you a note." She dug in her shoulder bag and came up with a handful of loose pencils and a notebook. "Where are you staying?"

Startled into truth before he could come up with an excuse to refuse it, Luca gave her the boardinghouse's address. Maya wrote it down and walked away, sunlight finding the faintest hints of rich brown in the black hair that fell down her back.

⁓ ⋙ ⟨ ◈ ⟩ ⋘ ⁓

"I remember this one," Maya said. "*Tales from the Sun's Fountain.* Dad used to read it to us before bed."

Matti rubbed his eyes, wondered belatedly if any of the ink smudges on that hand had been fresh enough to transfer to his face, and then decided he didn't care. He was used to pushing through this feeling, but he was grateful for the excuse to lift his blurry gaze from the papers in front of him to the side of his study, where Maya was drawing a thoughtful finger across the spines of books. The shelf was an armspan wide and stretched from ceiling to floor. Maya's profile was sharp with shadows in the golden light of the lamps.

"I haven't read any of them for years," Matti said, wistful. He'd never been a particularly keen reader, but there were remembered favourites from childhood—*Sun's Fountain* among them—which he'd find running through his head sometimes, stories tangling themselves up with the columns of numbers and his dread of the next day's stress.

There were vacant spaces in all the private rooms of the Jay house where items had vanished over the past five years, transmuted into money to bridge a necessary gap. The books had remained: not valuable enough to sell, and beautiful enough to feed the eyes when the tongue was missing cherries.

"If you're wondering where a dozen of them have gone, there's a pile next to my bed that I kick over about twice a week." Maya came to the desk, glanced over the papers that Matti was working on, then got a hand beneath his elbow and encouraged him out of his chair. "You've yawned twice and told me *just another minute* three times. We're going to get started before there's a real danger of you falling asleep on your feet halfway through."

"When did *you* learn how to do this?"

"Joyce and Verity love dancing, and they could never persuade their brothers to practice with them, so they used to show me what to do."

Matti squeezed her hands and resigned himself to yet another session of physical ineptitude. "I'll try not to tread on you too often," he said. "Where do we start?"

Despite his fears, after nearly an hour of instruction, Maya pronounced him not bad at all.

"You're picking it up quickly enough," she said, once she'd coaxed him through a wissel-step and a catskill and the slower, more stately and romantic turns of a sehassa. They had no music to accompany them, but Maya beat time with her palm against her thigh or spoke the beats aloud as they moved.

Matti had surprised himself as well. Maya was a more patient teacher than Luca, and had a knack for adjusting her explanations as necessary. But Luca's lessons had done *something* for Matti. He was used to being prodded into place or concentrating on a sequence of movements. He knew how to make his body do something over and over again, striving for the eventual rendition that would feel correct.

"I suppose Luca has been teaching me to dance," he said dryly. "In a manner of speaking."

Maya released his hands and pushed her hair back from her face. She'd tied it back but, as usual, wisps of it had escaped, and the situation hadn't been helped by the number of times she'd spun beneath Matti's arm.

"I never knew you were interested in learning to duel. You never mentioned it."

"I just took the opportunity when it arose."

"You *created* the opportunity by applying pressure at the right moment," she said, approving. "Mama and Dad would be proud."

"I didn't know you liked to dance," he offered in return.

"It's not what I'd choose out of all the activities in the world," she said lightly. "But it's fun. And no matter how long you harp on about its many virtues, I'm *not* taking up swimming."

Maya's aversion to water had led their parents to call her *kitten* until the day of her naming, when she haughtily turned around and proclaimed that her proper name had been approved in front of Huna, now, and she'd be asking Huna's revenge on anyone who insisted on using any silly animal nicknames. Even now she hated getting caught in the rain, and she declared her intention of cutting her hair short at least once a season—more, in summer— so it wouldn't take so long to dry.

"What would you choose, then? Out of all the activities in the world."

"Honestly?"

"Of course."

"I wish we could keep horses. Obviously it's impossible in the city. But when I was seven or so Mama took me visiting at the

Coopers' country house—where the ball's going to be—and Daniela taught me to ride on Sofia's pony, and I loved it. I kept nagging to be taken back."

Matti tried to imagine his elegant urban sister on horseback, leaping hedges and galloping through muddy fields. It didn't seem to fit. But then, nothing about the image of Matti with a sword in his hand really fit either.

"I wish I could have made that possible," he said.

Maya's gaze slid away. It bordered on awkward, and Maya was seldom awkward. Maya always knew what to say. Matti felt even worse for having somehow transferred his awkwardness to her by saying aloud the kind of thing that the two of them usually left unsaid.

"Don't you dare dwell on it," said Maya. "I have plenty of things. I like sketching, it's not as though pencils cost much, and you know I love the work I do choosing our dyes and working with the designers on our weaves."

"Yes," said Matti, although he hadn't known that. He'd never heard her apply the word *love* to anything about Jay House's business before. He'd always known that Maya was ten times as artistic as he was, and it had been one of the many anxieties in Matti's tangle, that she should have space to stretch her talents. He always made himself consider that when he was thinking of asking her to do a factory visit or answer letters from tailoring houses. It didn't matter if Matti had no time for anything outside work. *He* had no artistic talents; nothing was going to waste.

Say what you would about Corus Vane, at least he'd managed to give his son that freedom.

"One day," Matti promised Maya, "I'll buy you a horse."

"I'm a member of this House as well. One day I'll buy myself *three* horses." Her wide, familiar smile appeared as if from behind a cloud. "I suppose I'll let you and Sofia buy the country house where I stable them, though."

This reminder of his engagement landed on Matti with a small jolt, like someone flicking the crown of his head. The nearness of the Half Moon Ball really had snuck up on him. Sofia was in the house every other day, talking with Maya, their heads bowed over various things that Matti had never been asked to involve himself in. The last decision Matti had made was in regards to the cut of his wedding suit.

He wondered, suddenly, if his sister and his betrothed were creating the same kind of space from responsibility for *him* that he'd been trying to create for his siblings. If there were things that he should have been paying attention to, which they'd carefully handled without him, while he was—

While he was playing around with swords. While he was waist-deep in water and kissing his impossible best man.

Matti covered his guilt by taking a few steps to stand in front of his desk, where he lifted himself to sit on it.

"So, do you think I'll manage not to disgrace myself?" He indicated their recent dancing lesson with a wave of his hand.

"We'll do a few more sessions. And Sofia doesn't know you're meant to have been having these lessons. She'll not hold it against you if you're not perfect."

"When I think about all the other children of rich Houses I could be marrying, I'm lucky. I'm glad that we're getting to know each other," Matti said, and realised it was true. "I would have been glad to have her as a friend years ago."

"More friends are a good thing." There was something in Maya's tone that Matti couldn't parse. "And you've managed to make one in Luca," she added. "Do you think he dyes his hair that ridiculous shade?"

"I," Matti said, and somehow found the taste of salt water in his mouth and his mind full of the image of Luca lifting himself out of the sea bath, rivulets of water running over the muscles of Luca's upper back. Luca twisting around to sit on the rock, all freckles scattered across a milky chest and a line of the same dark copper running down from his navel. "I mean, no, I—"

"Huna *wept*," Maya breathed. Of course it was too much to hope that she'd missed his lapse in composure. "Matti, are you—are you and he—"

"No!" Matti was so very, very glad that he was able to deny that both forcefully and honestly. More or less. He'd not let it get that far. He'd pushed Luca away. "No, I'm not sleeping with my best man."

"But you wouldn't mind," said Maya, analysing.

"I—no." It came out like a deflation, through the sheer relief of being able to admit even that small amount. "He's . . . attractive. But it doesn't mean anything. I can cope with it." Matti spoke more firmly. "And Sofia's the person I'm going to marry."

Maya started to speak, but a yawn took over her face and set one off in Matti as well. They looked at each other ruefully and Matti became aware of the sandy heaviness of his eyelids.

"I'd better get to bed," he said. "Early morning."

"Of course," said Maya. "*Dancing* lessons."

Matti laughed. Despite his tiredness, he felt lighter. Sharing his accumulated secrets with Maya had been like an extra shoulder being inserted under a shared load.

"Yes," he said. "Exactly."

CHAPTER
12

The overwhelming smell on the carding floor was one that Luca had never encountered before. It was a thick, warm, unsettling scent with a dusty edge. Luca had never had cause to encounter livestock except when walking past a butcher's shop, but in the last hour he'd firmly attached to this smell the mental label of *sheep*.

Luca inched his stool closer to Maya's so that they could speak without being overheard. It was probably unnecessary; the air was busy with chatter beneath the harsh hum of carding combs moving against one another, a sound that was as unfamiliar as the smell but which Luca had already resigned himself to hearing in his sleep for the next three nights.

"I could have done this on my own," he said.

He was lying, but he wanted to get a reaction out of Maya. What he got was a long, unimpressed glance. Better than nothing.

"And I'm sure you'd have been able to plausibly describe your previous experience in this industry," she returned.

"I wouldn't have bothered. I'd have come up with a tragic story about the sickness that claimed my parents, and my desperate need for work in a new place, and sworn up and down that I would take half pay until I learned what I was doing," Luca said promptly. "There might even have been tears."

Maya looked back down at her work before he could see if he'd won a smile. Her manner towards him was cooler than it had been yesterday. No amount of semiflirtatious, semicomical effort on Luca's part, as they'd travelled out of the city, had managed to bring out the same fountain of smiles and energy that she'd displayed in the park, laughing over raskils. Today she was doing a good impression of her brother's wary reserve, and Luca didn't know what to make of it.

The Kesey House workshop was in a village in Glassport territory, the name of which kept slipping out of Luca's mind. Some single-syllable dullness like Mud or Lud, with two inns and wide, potholed streets and the comfortable air of a place devoted to cottage industry. The workshop was a repurposed barn, high beamed, divided into sections with long rough tables. Lined along one wall were large sacks full of raw fleece. Floor walkers with clipboards directed the transfer of this wool to smaller sacks, set beside the stool of each carder so that they could pick up handfuls at a time and work it.

The carding combs were each the size of a book, a thatch of metal teeth set in leather pads with wooden handles. There was a dance to it, a rhythm of the top carder against the bottom one, a flick of the elbow to turn them so that the fibres were worked back and forth.

It's just like a new form, Luca told himself. *A new feint. Observe, and learn.*

After a while he felt confident enough in the motion of his hands that he struck up conversation with the person seated on his other side, giving up on Maya for the moment. Yolente was a square-jawed woman who looked his mother's age and who wore a hair wrap of green cotton with glass beads sewn along its edge. The beads winked in the sunbeams that slanted down from the high barn windows.

Yolente, Luca learned, lived the next town over, and she was an itinerant: a worker who moved from Guild to Guild, following the available jobs for which no experience was needed, swearing herself briefly into one patron's service and then moving on. It sounded like an uncomfortable way to make a living, even though Luca knew that for the people who followed that path it was often the best of a series of bad options.

Luca wanted to ask her if she ever found it confusing, living under a patron's auspices without having grown up with them. Keeping track of the relevant rituals and calendar days, and then entering the employ of a new Guild and doing it all over again. He wondered if she swore by a different god every time she stubbed her toe. But asking about it would betray too much about himself, so he contented himself with "Do you ever wish you'd stuck with a single Guild? Stayed in the employ of one House, or tried to build a business?"

Her shrug was eminently pragmatic. "Building's for those with means. Must is must. I do what I can and the gods've never come down too hard on me."

"How do you like working for the Keseys?" Luca asked. He nodded in Maya's direction. "My girl and I wouldn't mind finding somewhere to put down roots for a while."

"They don't pay as well as I'd like," Yolente said, lowering her voice. "But at my age I've got to settle to something, hey? You have to put in five years solid under most Guilds before you qualify for even their most basic retirement pension. Last year I was working a market garden owned by Amberden House—the pay was better, and I liked the open air—but my back's not what it was, and only getting worse. At least this is easy on the bones."

"As long as your bones are intact," said the young woman on Yolente's other side. She'd clearly been listening, and now nudged a fall of light brown hair over her shoulder and sent a glance towards the workshop supervisors. She introduced herself as Susanna, and added in a low tone, "Kesey House is mean as cats when it comes to worker safety. They cut corners. I carded for the Jays for a while. *They* pay physician fees if you're injured on the job, and even give out a quarter wage if you're too sick to work, as long as you're expected to improve and come back."

"You lost your job?" Luca asked.

"The workshop closed." Her shrug was as fatalistic as Yolente's had been. "It happens. Wasn't happy about it, but I'd rather be let

go plain and simple than be squeezed slowly for my juice by working longer hours for fewer coins and fewer rights." Her mouth
thinned. "You and your girl should try elsewhere, if you've the
option to. I'm staying because my parents need me here, but I've
told my sister to go to the city. Beg a weaving apprenticeship if
she can, under a different House of Huna's."

An approving nod from Yolente. "That's sense. And it's a pity
the Jays aren't doing so well. He's not bad for a House man, that
Tomas Jay."

Luca swallowed a sudden bubble of alertness and managed not
to look at Maya. She'd knotted and wrapped her own hair, and
sworn up and down that she hardly ever left the city and that
most of her own work for her House was with those people they
contracted to do the dyeing. Even so, Luca figured there was still
a possibility that a prior employee might recognise her.

"Jay?" Luca managed, with nothing more than mild enquiry.

"The Glassport Guildmaster. I voted for him," Susanna added,
with the air of a proud parent watching their child perform on the
piano. "And I'll keep right on voting for him, as long as he keeps
on giving a pube of the goddess about those of us who aren't living
with a House stitched to the back of our names."

Luca swallowed a burst of laughter, bent his head, and applied
himself to his work. He watched the practiced way Yolente transferred a hank of carded wool to the leather back of the comb, then
rolled it between the flat surfaces until it was a pale tube like a
piece of drainpipe or an oversized cigar. Each tube was flicked
into a basket at her feet, and periodically these baskets were emptied into a fresh set of sacks, which were carried out of the workshop. Yolente told Luca, noticing his gaze, that the spinners had
their own workshop nearby.

"We don't do the dyeing or the weaving, here," she said. "The
wool goes elsewhere for that."

Luca would have liked to try his orphan story out on Yolente, but he stuck with Maya's cover story instead: that the two of them were roaming itinerants making their way south. Luca embroidered a little when conveying this to Yolente. He implied that they were all but betrothed, fleeing some vague shadow of family disapproval.

"The cobbler here in Nud's got some of that northern blood," said Yolente. "He's not as dark as your girl, though, and he's not got her way of speaking."

Maya's accent yesterday had been pure Glassport. Today, begging them work, she'd spoken in an accent Luca hadn't heard before, a musical variant on Naraman with off-kilter rhythms. Now that they were ensconced among the other workers, that accent had mellowed, but it was still present.

Currently Maya was listening, with a lot more smiles and nodding than she'd displayed since Luca met her at the coach station in Glassport that morning, to the woman seated on her other side. When that woman left her seat to empty her basket, Luca turned back to Maya, angling his body intimately.

"We're friends, aren't we?" he said softly. "Smile."

Maya's smile was toothy but insincere. "Do you have friends, Luca Piere, or only marks?"

Luca pressed the side of his thumb against a sharp spike of his comb. He had friends, and he missed them. Under normal circumstances he was sure he'd have made plenty more of them here in Glassport by now, but the combination of keeping his head down and his cheerful self-embroilment in Matti's affairs had meant he'd not taken up the opportunities to socialise with people like Ilse, beyond where employment brought them into contact. Part of why he'd enjoyed Maya's company so much, the previous day, was how much he *liked* meeting new people and feeling that happy crackle of potential that had nothing to do with sex. It made her actions today sting all the more.

"Does Matti have friends?" he asked instead.

He was looking to sting in return. Sure enough, Maya's mouth thinned. "What do you mean?"

"I mean he doesn't have anything in his life but his House. Doesn't that bother you?"

"I'm not going to feed you information on my brother."

"I think you will, Mayanesh," said Luca. "Because I think you care about him."

"Just like you do?" She was quick. She'd snatched the unsaid part of Luca's sentence from the air and turned it into a challenge.

"Yes," Luca said, defiant. "I do."

Maya lifted her combs and gestured with them. Luca had let his hands pause in their discussion. He cast a glance around to see if any of the clipboard wielders had noticed, then picked up a new handful of wool and began to work it. Yolente and Susanna had moved on to exchanging local gossip, woven through with bursts of laughter.

"He takes so much pride in his work," Maya said finally, just as Luca was wondering if he'd misjudged and prodded her too far. "He's so proud that he can handle Jay House's business."

"Yes, but at . . . wait. How old is he?"

Maya gave him an odd look. "He's twenty-four."

He looks older was going to be rude no matter what. "At twenty-four, being the senior House member surely only happens when you've lost a lot of older relatives. I know your mother's from a long way north and your father is Guildmaster, but . . . what about *their* parents? Their siblings?"

"Mama's parents are dead," said Maya, like a well-aimed lunge. "She was the youngest of eight. None of the others live outside Manisi, and none of them are of our Guild in any case. And Granddad saw Jay House through some good times in his day, but now he's . . . not very well." She gave the wool in her hands a few savage blows with the combs. "He forgets things. Grandmama looks after him well enough, but it's easier for them, in the country. They don't come to town much."

"They don't know? About your House's fortunes?"

Another violent series of back-and-forth motions. "Dad doesn't want to worry them."

"Imagine that," said Luca. "I can't think where Matti gets it from."

Maya's dark eyes held his. Her mouth moved, a tremor in its firmness. "He's not alone. Matti. He's never been alone. We all do our bit."

"And what's your *bit*?" His tone was bordering on rude, but he was increasingly angry on Matti's behalf.

"Dad calls it rose-oiling," said Maya. "It was a joke, but I do it deliberately. I don't know if he knows that. Keeping things peaceful and smooth. Like the oil on wool." Maya sniffed a handful of the wool she was working with and made a face. "Only this oil's been cut with goose grease," she said, disapproving. "Cheap habit."

Luca, who'd initially had to overcome the urge to shudder at the unexpected greasiness of it—he'd thought wool was dry, clean stuff—raised his eyebrows in query. Maya explained: in one corner of the workshop, workers were dribbling oil onto the handfuls of wool torn from teased fleeces, pressing and massaging the oil through the wool before putting it in sacks for the carders. It made the carding process easier. "Just like hair oil. It's easier to straighten the fibres when they're greased."

"Rose-oiling," said Luca. "I see."

"It's a talent. And I've learned to do it better. Mama has a different style to me. She asks questions—she pretends to be ignorant. And then she just keeps asking and keeps asking until the needle of the conversation is pointing the way she wants it to point."

"My mother," Luca said, and stopped. He could *feel* it, especially in contrast to her earlier coolness: the easy smoothness of Maya's manner. He'd nearly let something true slide out. He filtered that truth in a way that felt safe. "She's not that kind of person at all. She's got no patience for fools, and if she doesn't approve of what you're doing, you'll know it."

Maya rolled some wool and flicked it expertly into her basket. "Is that why you left Cienne?"

"No," said Luca. He didn't realise until the word had escaped that it was, in an oblique but very real way, a lie. He tried the same flicking motion. The roll of wool fell forlornly onto his knee. "She's not like that with me."

"I'd do more," Maya said abruptly. "I'd *like* to. I know every step of the business."

"Then do it," said Luca.

Maya's look was wry. "You have met my brother, haven't you? You know him, at least a little. What do you think happens when someone offers to take part of his duties out of his hands?"

Luca thought about it. Winced.

"Exactly," said Maya. "Believe me, I've offered. But I can't oil my way past the fact that Matti sees his job as keeping the rest of us as happy as possible. Not to mention that asking Matti if I can help, in his mind, is a suggestion that I don't think he can do it. And he *can*." She gave a vicious swipe of the carders. "No matter what he thinks of himself. Nobody could have done more."

"Just because he can," said Luca, "doesn't mean he should."

He wondered for a moment if Maya was going to look stricken, but though her face flickered with too many expressions to count, Luca didn't see guilt among them. She did glance around, and Luca shifted his stool even closer to hers, a silent encouragement. They were keeping their voices soft, and everyone around them was still engrossed in their own chatter; Luca didn't want Maya to clam up again, not when she was providing him with so many edge pieces to the puzzle of Mattinesh Jay.

"You don't know us," she said, low and deliberate. "You're a con artist and a serviceman. You don't have a clue what it's been like."

"I know *Matti*," Luca said. "A little. Just like you said."

Maya took a long breath. She let it out as she rolled her wool and let it drop into her basket. "It's complicated. Perhaps Dad— but look, the Guildmaster position is *important*. It's bigger than just our House. Dad thinks that the divisions that have formed in the last few decades between workers and House members have made the Guild lopsided, left it open for corruption, made it harder for us to work towards the same goals. The previous Guild-master made things worse. He barely acknowledged that people like—well, like this," she said, nodding around the workshop, "should have a voice in the Guildband, let alone the governance of Glassport and its territories."

"Susanna over there voted for your father."

"He's popular," Maya said. "Well . . . not among some of the other Houses. But every member of a Guild has a vote." And no matter the power wielded by the Houses, they were always going to be outnumbered in their own Guild by those without, as Susanna had put it, a House name stitched to their own.

"He's making himself unpopular on the council as well, from what Matti's said."

The side of Maya's mouth tucked itself into something fond. "Oh, yes. He spends most of his days irritating people. I imagine the two of you would get along well."

Luca decided to let that one go. "He's blocking some kind of canal project?"

"Blocking a proposed *waste of money* just because Martens House doesn't like how long it takes them to transport red marble overland before they can load it onto barges on the Rozen. So, Mr. Piere," Maya said, a flash of unexpected steel entering her voice, "do you think Dad should have been selfish? Refused reelection? Stepped back from the council and let people like Lysbette Martens fill their pockets with city money that could go to fixing water pipes in the Ash Quarter? Focused on our personal fortunes, and let all of that slide?"

Luca was thinking that this whole damn family could have done with being a bit more selfish. He thought again about Matti, who'd quietly shouldered all his House's failures and who thought it was up to him to keep trouble off his parents' desks so that they could—be happy. Be idealists. Be a voice for people like Susanna, who were trying to do their best for *their* families in turn.

Gods, if only this was as simple as swords. There was a raw, gnawing feeling in Luca's chest that he recognised by now as the guilt of being held up to someone else's example and found desperately wanting. Even if the only person doing the comparison was him.

"Maybe he should have, yes," he said. "If your personal fortunes were failing so badly."

"Huna throws her coins—"

"And sometimes they land in the dust," finished Luca. "Matti gave me that one as well, when he was telling me about the lost ship."

"The *Isadonna?*" Maya sighed. "Nobody's ever pretended the crossing from Fataf is a smooth one, but only five ships have ever been lost in the Straits with all hands. *Five.*"

At the name, something stirred, a sluggish niggle in the back of Luca's mind. It was like trying to see an after-flash of light in the corner of his eye; when he tried to bring it into focus, it dissolved.

He said slowly, "Ships can be crippled."

"What?" Maya stared at him.

"Was Corus Vane involved in the arrangements for this—black wool?"

"Black libelza. I don't know." Maya's carders were at rest in her lap now. "It's possible. We trust him with a lot. But that's—that's a lot more than sabotaging contract bids and overpaying for mordant. That's *killing people* just to deny us a shipment."

"An important shipment," Luca said, but she had a point. The niggle threw up one more tiny, dissatisfied signal and then disappeared. "Maybe Kesey House got impatient enough to consider it worthwhile."

"If they were ruthless enough to be capable of that, I suppose fraudulent production of poor quality wool would seem like nothing at all."

Yes. They were here for a purpose beyond arguing the relative merits of letting Matti Jay throw himself onto the pyre of his House. Luca applied himself to the carding job with vigour.

"Would those be a good place to start?" He nodded at the huge sacks full of uncarded fleece.

"Start?" said Maya. "Didn't I tell you? We're nearly done."

Luca stared at her. She might have been quick, but she couldn't hold a deception; the side of her wide mouth was curling like a leaf on flames, betraying the smug expression that was trying to crack through her calm.

"All right," Luca said, when she refused to say anything further. "If I admit that you could have done this whole thing without *me,* will you tell me what the fuck it is you've discovered?"

The calm cracked; she let out a soft huff of a laugh. "I'm sure you were an important part of my disguise," said Maya. She tipped a roll of carded wool into her basket, then leaned down and, with a quick glance around that Luca could have told her was detrimental to that disguise, pulled her small sack of fleece into her lap. She dug in it quickly and pulled out two pieces of wool, which she handed to Luca.

"It's already been mixed in," Maya said. "You're right, they're probably doing it over there." She looked towards the large sacks, and the people with clipboards. "They could have had it carded separately and spun together, but there'd be a more obvious difference in the fibre lengths that way."

"Are you saying the workers aren't noticing? I certainly didn't."

"This is the first time you've touched unprocessed wool. You can't tell your elbow from your arsecheek," said Maya, and Luca felt himself smile. "These are from two different breeds. They're both shorn fleeces, not pulled, but see how this one has longer fibres? A finer crimp?"

Luca rubbed the two samples between his fingers. There was a difference, not only in the feel but in the look of them, with one of them undeniably shaggier and the other with the kind of tight, curling wiriness similar to what you saw in the hair of some of the people native to northern Draka. One of Luca's friends back home had hair like that, and so did Dinah Vaunt.

"If you say so."

"I asked Carlin if this workshop usually does blends, and she said they only started in the last year." A quick nod of Maya's head towards the woman on her other side. Luca's estimation of Maya's worth as a partner in crime leapt another few points. "It's not the job of the carders to keep track of labelling for quality control. But they know what they're working with, even if they don't know what it's being passed off as once it's made it to the fabric stage."

Luca saw the missing piece in their corroboration mission at once. "But you need to know that what's leaving this workshop is being passed off as . . . pure? Unmixed?"

"The labelling system across Thesper was standardised when the mandatory labelling laws for fabric were passed," Maya said. "Give me two minutes." She reached down to Luca's pathetically half-filled basket of carded tubes and tipped it into her own— rendering it close to overflowing—and then stood, basket tucked under one arm, and made her way over to the sacks destined for the spinning workshop. Luca kept one eye on her and tried to look industrious at the same time, wincing as he managed to graze the side of his hand with the carding teeth.

Maya emptied her basket into one of the sacks and lingered there exchanging words with a woman standing officiously near the sacks. After a short while she turned and made her way back to her stool. On the way she caught Luca's eye and nodded, once and firmly.

"Well, look," said Luca, once she was seated next to him again. "Now I've got nothing in my basket to show for all my hard work. It looks like I've done nothing at all. Are you trying to get me fired from this very important fake job which I will never show up to again, Mayanesh?"

Maya's mouth leaf-curled again, then sprang fully alight with her smile.

"There, you *do* like me." Luca threw a grin at her in return. "Admit it."

The smile faded off Maya's face. The stirrings of satisfaction and good spirits in Luca disappeared with much the same abruptness.

"Oh, shitting gods, *what?*" he demanded. "What's your problem with me?"

"Beyond the fact that you nearly ruined my brother, and all of us, with some stupid trick with a pocket watch?"

That sounded like a distraction. "Yes. Beyond that."

Maya exhaled. The tightness of her posture relaxed in a way that looked very deliberate and very much like Matti when Luca reminded him, for the fifth time during a lesson, not to hold his shoulders so rigidly.

"I don't know if you're good for him."

Luca felt his lip curl back. "Because I'm giving him a chance to have *fun,* and not—"

"No." Her voice snipped at him. "Listen to me. Matti's betrothed is a beautiful, clever woman, and he talks about her like he's glad the teacher assigned him a deskmate who isn't going to maliciously drip ink on his worksheets."

"I thought this was a business match." The word *betrothed* felt like dry grass on Luca's skin. "Finer feelings irrelevant. Are you actually annoyed because he's not pretending to be head over heels in love with her?"

"Nobody expects them to be in love going into it." Maya was looking at her wrist now, flicking and fiddling with the pearly button at her shirt cuff. "But I know he could learn to love her, if he let himself try. They'd be happier that way. Both of them."

"And how, by all the gods, is any of this *my* fault?"

Maya looked up. Luca was already conditioned to crave fierceness in those dark, thick-lashed eyes; it was entirely unfair that Matti's sister was able to wield a weapon that Matti himself was so hesitant to use, and which Luca would have welcomed.

"Because when he talks about *you,* he looks like he's found a luckstone on the street, and he doesn't know whether to keep it in his pocket or have it set in a ring."

For a long moment, Luca didn't know what he was doing with his face.

"Because I think perhaps you could still ruin us," Maya said. "That's my problem with you."

"You can't tell me this is the first time Matti's wanted something he thinks he's not supposed to have."

"Huna wept," Maya said, soft and tight. "No. I—I don't think so. But he's never let it show before."

Luca looked down at his feet, which were in motion, drumming lightly on the wooden floor. He hadn't noticed. He felt the restive sensation in them build until his skin was stuffed with the urge to run out of the door and out of this stupid village and all the way back to Glassport, where he could find Matti and stand in front of him and—what? Search his face for a luckstone expression?

Say, *I'd live in your pocket for as long as you wanted?*

Say, *Betray everything you've worked for and everyone you love. Go on. It'll be fun?*

"This is an alarming silence," said Maya. She might have been trying for dryness, but her voice still sounded like a thread pulled taut.

"You're asking something of me," Luca said. "Spell it out."

"Don't distract him more than you have already," Maya said. "I thought I knew my brother better than anyone else in the world, and now I'm seeing pieces of him that are unfamiliar, and we can't *afford* that. We can't afford the unexpected. Not now."

"I know you can't." This was torture. The gods and the Jays were in alliance to make it very clear to Luca that he couldn't have the one thing *he* wanted, and it was just making him want it *more*. "No matter what else is happening, I've been formally contracted to make sure this wedding goes ahead. A duellist's reputation is all the currency they have. I'll do my best to win."

"And that means something to you?"

"What?"

"Your reputation."

"I—"

Maya gestured around the workshop with a carder. "Duelling's not just another very important fake job?"

That buried itself in Luca's stomach like a grass-burr. His cheeks felt tight. "No. It's important." *It's all I have left.*

Maya looked at him closely for another few moments. She nodded. "All right. Do your best. Win this for us."

"I will," Luca said, and he'd never told a truth that felt so much like lying.

CHAPTER
13

Beneath the mingled blaze of gaslight and fire that lit the crowded ballroom, Luca's hair stood out like the gleam of gold thread in tapestry. It took Matti no more than a few glances over the room to pick him out. Luca was being interrogated by Merri and another small girl in an explosively lacy dress, and he looked both bemused and alarmed at the fact.

He looked incredible tonight. Matti's breath had stopped at the first sight of him, in well-fitted dark trousers and a shirt of palest dimflower blue. He wore no waistcoat, but a structured jacket of charcoal grey and a sword belt of gleaming woven leather that Matti wanted to hook his fingers through.

Matti had worried that Luca would feel ill at ease at the Half Moon Ball, knowing nobody in the room except Matti and Maya, but he seemed to think nothing of plunging into a knot of people and immediately making himself at home by throwing smiles and stories in every direction. He'd participated in the ritual called Maha's Tasting; his fingers had lingered on Matti's when Matti passed him the cup. He'd made his formal bow to Matti's parents and received the Half Moon gift given to each member of the wedding party. And then he'd flitted off to entertain some of Sofia's friends, claiming that he'd rather be admired for the sword at his waist than run the risk of being stuck in yet another conversation about looms.

Matti could have told him that the Head of Duvay House was far more likely to talk one's ear off about his precious dogs than about the silk industry, but Luca had already been halfway across the ballroom at that point, and Matti had weathered Rowain Duvay's canine enthusiasm on his own.

The air was alight and busy, crowded with the smells of food and perfume and flowers and candle wax. Gas lamps blazed in brackets conspicuously newer than the stone of the walls, but candelabras and two wrought gold chandeliers cast their own complex shadows, crammed as they were with long sturdy candles.

The Cooper country house was much, much older than Cooper House as an institution. Sofia's parents had bought the enormous building and its even more enormous grounds just after Sofia was born, and poured yet more money into rescuing it from a state of genteel disrepair. Tonight Matti had already overheard a certain amount of murmurs, most of them approving, in regards to the restoration job. This ballroom could have been primped and wallpapered into modernity; instead the dark grey stone had been washed and left bare, a striking contrast to the intricate wooden floor underfoot.

"Matti."

Matti looked back at his cousin Roland, whose amused smile was a hint that perhaps he'd been trying to capture Matti's attention for a while.

"Sorry," said Matti. "What were you saying?"

"It doesn't matter. And we shouldn't be keeping you trapped here. This is your night, after all. There are probably ten other conversations you should be having."

"No, not at all." Matti widened his smile, trying not to feel too guilty. "I'm glad to see you two again. I feel like I'm just trotting you out for rituals."

"We know you're busy," said Wynn, shrugging that off. "Roland here was just asking if you thought he would look like a pirate if he wrapped the nice green handkerchief you gave him around his head, or if it would just look like he was trying to hide his disaster of a haircut."

Roland's fair hair was cropped fashionably close. He made a noise of protest. "Don't listen to this farmer, Matti."

"We're surrounded by some of the best wine in Thesper, Roland Jay. Make yourself useful and fetch the groom-to-be another drink."

"I've barely started this one." Matti lifted his glass.

"One of the Audelet girls is getting a card game going in another room while we wait for the dancing to start," offered Roland.

"Excellent," Wynn said. "I'm in. We'll leave Matti to mingle. Don't worry, Matti—we do like the gifts, even if the colour doesn't suit *us* to perfection. We can't all be your flame-headed best man."

Thankfully Matti had remembered in time that Roland and Wynn had been present when Luca pulled his trick with the pocket watch. Tonight Luca had spun some earnest, convoluted story for them about doing errands for a family friend while he was settling in as a new duellist in town, and Matti had nodded along.

Luca's green gift had been a scarf: summer-weight, not wool. When Matti had made the presentation, Luca had fingered the silk for a long moment and then given Matti a look like he was waiting for something. For an incoherent heartbeat Matti had wanted to take it back and tie it for Luca, let his hands linger on the column of Luca's throat—wanted to kiss Luca in front of his family and everyone he knew. It was a thought as impossible as the rest of the things that Matti wanted.

"Come to think of it, Matti," Wynn added over his shoulder as they walked off, "it's a good thing the wedding party colours shook out the way they did. I don't know if I would have been able to wear *gold* boots without being laughed off my own farms."

Matti looked over at where Cecilia Cooper, the heir of Cooper House, was standing. Her boom of a laugh was easy to distinguish. Sofia's Half Moon gift to her older sister had been a short fitted tunic embroidered with grapevines in golden thread. It suited Cecilia's rangy figure, and her preference for trousers over skirts given her tendency to spend more time tromping the hillsides of the Cooper vineyards than in the city proper.

Even if Matti did have vague memories of Cecilia pushing him into a puddle as a small child, he preferred her to Tino, the middle Cooper sibling. Tino was the perfect marketing foil to Cecilia's viticultural expertise and was unfailingly pleasant, but something about his never-dimming smile rubbed Matti the wrong way, as though Tino were always trying to close a sale even if engaged in nothing more than a conversation about the weather. Matti had been avoiding making eye contact all evening.

Matti threw back a good half of the wine in his hand. Mingle. Right.

He could see one of the senior agents from Harte House's Glassport office nearby, accepting a full glass of sparkling wine from a companion, and she gave him an easy smile when their eyes met. Matti returned the smile, but he didn't have the stomach tonight to make small talk with someone representing a soon-to-be competitor while both of them pretended it wasn't about to happen. For the moment, Harte's plans to break into the wool industry had been relegated to a less urgent position on Matti's endless list of worries.

Instead he strode up to the nearest small knot of men, which obligingly cracked open to let him join the circle. Matti had just opened his mouth to deliver some polite thanks for their attendance when he realised that he was now standing directly opposite Adrean Vane, who was giving Matti a look that bordered on belligerent. Awareness of this awkward situation descended on the group like a mist. A few people inspected their drinks closely.

"Good evening," Matti said.

There was a smattering of bows and nods. Adrean was the only one who said, "Good evening," in return, and his tone matched his facial expression.

He doesn't know what his father's doing, Matti reminded himself,

but all he could think of was Adrean's sneering assessment of
Matti's personality, and Luca calling him a—

"Mr. Jay!" said Luca, elbowing his way into the circle at Matti's
side. "So sorry to intrude, sir, but your sister—the tiny one—was
very anxious for me to remind you that you promised to dance
the catskill with her, later. That's all. *Do* continue your conversation." He beamed around the circle. He was wearing the scarf in a
careless knot around his neck. His gaze landed on Adrean, where
it stayed.

A complicated series of things happened in Matti's stomach.
He wondered if it would be obvious if he trod on Luca's foot.

"Luca Piere," said Luca to the group at large. "At your service.
Well, at the groom's service, obviously."

Many of the guests would have seen Luca's formal bow as a
member of the wedding party. Even if not, the green scarf at his
throat and the sword at his waist loudly proclaimed his role. The
awkward mist thickened into something more like fog. Gazes
travelled between Luca and Adrean as though already following
the blows of the inevitable duel.

Matti urgently reconsidered throwing himself on the mercy of
the Harte agent.

Adrean's gaze was on Luca's weapon, and Luca made an exag-
gerated show of noticing this and patting the gleaming hilt.

"It's a sword," Luca said kindly. "I can see why you might not
be familiar with it. I do understand that none of Mr. Jay's friends
are any good at duelling. After all, if you were, he'd hardly have
needed to engage me, would he?"

Matti found a strangled laugh in his throat and managed to
hide it in a gulp of wine. One of the other young men in the circle, whom Matti recognised vaguely as someone from one of the
larger brewery Houses, was not so restrained. The person next to
him patted him pointedly on the back as he worked to turn the
laugh into a coughing fit.

Adrean flushed and threw his shoulders back. He gave Luca a

look of intense dislike down his long nose as he visibly struggled with the desire to explain just how expert a swordsman he was, without having to publicly admit that he was no friend of Matti's.

"It doesn't seem like it'll be the most interesting job, this wedding." Terrifyingly, Luca was still talking. "Apparently there might be a token display of mediocrity by some tiresome fellow, now what was his—"

"Excuse us, please," Matti managed, and dragged Luca away to the nearest corner with a hard grip on his arm. They collected a few curious stares as they went.

"Yes, that's it." Luca sagged dramatically against the wall. His face was still sparkling with humour above the green silk. "Now look like you're giving me a stern talking-to about being rude to your guests."

"*I am.*" Matti was trying desperately not to let his own laughter out; it was still straining against his throat, wanting to emerge and join Luca's. "That's going to be all over the party by the end of the night."

"Good. The smug fuckwit deserves it."

"I am trying to be pleasant to the Vanes," Matti reminded him. "I shouldn't act differently around them, remember?"

"Yes? And? *I* don't have any reason to be pleasant. I'm just a serviceman who's being paid to be here. *I* don't know who they are. Which is nearly true, by the way; I had to get someone to point him out to me, given that my previous experience of his charming personality was from the wrong side of a wardrobe door." Luca snuck a look around Matti's arm and his smile widened. "Now he's stalking off to the gardens. Probably to write a poem about his feelings and then set it to music."

Matti lost the battle and buried his smile in his sleeve.

"That's better," murmured Luca. His fingers touched Matti's where they were curled around the wineglass. "And that's enough time for a rebuking, I think. Why don't you find your brother and introduce me properly? I can collect the full Jay set."

They found Marko doing his best to get chocolate smears on Nessa's dress, while Merri added a reddish stain to the endeavour from some kind of fruit tart.

"Who let you two into the sweets?" Matti demanded, scooping Merri up and holding her at a determined arm's length as she tried to twist around and inflict her mess on him, with a muffled shriek full of delight and sugar giddiness and being up past her bedtime. Once she settled, he set her down gingerly, kissed his thumb, and flicked her ear. "I've brought my best man to talk to the future of Jay House, not a pair of blue-winged honey hummers."

"Merrinesh and I have already met." Luca swept an extravagant bow in Merri's direction.

Marko and Merri exchanged a look. Then Merri fixed Luca with her limpid brown eyes and broke into Yaghali too rapid for Matti to understand it.

"Oh, gods," Matti said. "Mama?"

His mother sighed. "Ten minutes ago they started. And now you have come and made a fuss over it, they will not stop until tomorrow."

"Mama will tell me if you're being rude," Matti warned the twins.

Marko rolled his eyes. "*Gnyet*," he said. Matti knew that one, at least. *Will not.* Marko was probably right too.

"Secret twin language?" asked Luca.

"My language," said Nessa.

"Oh." Luca looked from Matti to the twins. The question was plain on his face.

"I don't speak it," Matti said. "Not well. These two, however . . ."

"Ah, you had other things to learn." Nessa expertly created a fold in her skirt to hide the most egregious of the chocolate smears. She smiled at Luca, looping him into the conversation, before glancing back at Matti. "Who would you speak it to, here?"

Matti swallowed down his instinctive surge of self-blame and guilt. He also swallowed down what came next, which was a protest. *You never taught me; not like you're teaching them.* His mother had never uttered a single word of desire that Matti or Maya would be any less Glassport, any more northern. And in the Jay household, truths only had to be acknowledged when they were brought into the light.

"Your people are from Manisi, Matti told me," Luca said to Nessa. He kicked out a chair and seated himself. One foot wrapped around the chair's leg and began to beat gently, side of boot against wood.

"Not Manisi," Nessa corrected at once. "The mountains. Far outside the city."

"But still, part of Manisi territory. Right?"

"On the maps, yes. On the *papers*."

Matti opened his mouth, calculated the odds that he'd make the situation worse if he tried any rose-oiling, and closed it again. Luca was doing fine; he looked interested, making a go-on kind of motion that pulled an expression onto Nessa's face that was equal parts flattered and suspicious.

Matti pulled out the chair on the other side of Luca's and bus-ied himself with picking the nuts out of a slice of butter cake, while Nessa gave Luca the relevant geopolitical history. This mostly involved the dwindling Yaghali people clinging crankily to the mountains and ignoring everyone else while the city-state of Manisi and the kingdom of Narama had a leisurely decade-long squabble over the exact location of the border. When the armies were exhausted enough that the politicians nailed the border down to its current location so that everyone could go home, the mountains ended up formally Thesperan and the Yaghali went on pretending, to the extent of feasibility, that Manisi's formal governance didn't exist. Matti knew that things were changing, as the fingers of trade and cultural influence made their way up into the high villages. His mother's parents had grudgingly accepted the course of the future and sent their children down to be educated at the university in the city.

Luca paid charming attention to Nessa's colourful and affectionately biased version of historical events. The twins, still exchanging a fluid and incomprehensible rattle of conversation, had meanwhile settled themselves beneath the tablecloth. Matti lowered a bowl of cherries and was rewarded with Marko's widest grin. Matti began to gnaw on the cake, which was lacking in structural integrity now that he'd excavated all the nuts.

He coughed on crumbs when his mother abruptly turned her attention from Luca to himself as though responding to some inner clock strike.

"Mattinesh," she said sternly. "Hiding with your family at your own Half Moon Ball! Any moment now there will be dancing. Go and talk to people."

"I'm hardly hiding, Mama." Matti took another bite of cake. He wondered if the wedding would be a similar round of nobody letting him pause for more than a few moments, for fear that some phantom other group of guests was missing out on his company. An unpleasant curl of cold shuddered at the base of his throat, and he coughed again, pushing the cake plate away.

"You are absolutely right, Mrs. Jay." Luca leapt to his feet. Matti tried to convey refusal with his eyes, but Luca tucked a hand under Matti's elbow, and Matti stood before his brain could remind his body that it didn't have to obey the slightest pressure from Luca's hands. Not here, anyway. Not now.

"So that's the accent Maya was doing," Luca said, threading through the crowd and creating space for Matti to follow. "Hah. Outside Manisi. I think I could learn to do it, if I spoke with your mother for half an hour."

The musicians were tuning up, the crowd in the ballroom already beginning to thin at the centre like a spun bowl, making room for the dancing. Matti found he didn't mind the prospect. The mention of Maya had sent a fretful energy under his skin, remembering what she and Luca had discovered in Nud. This knowledge tucked in their pockets, where it was burning away.

Matti was at tug-of-war with himself over the fact that he hadn't told his parents. Hadn't told them any of it. He couldn't fully justify it, when he tried to arrange the facts in weft-straight lines in his head, but he also . . . hadn't told them. Anxiety dug painful fingers into his forehead at the thought. It *was* his job to deal with House matters so that they could focus on other things. Matti wanted to come up with some brilliant fix that would allow the whole situation to be presented as though wax-sealed and stamped. Problem, solution. It had been one of Tomas Jay's first lessons: if you're going to ask a question, you have to be the first one to try to answer it. No punishment for wrong answers. Just . . . try.

So Matti, in the few spare moments of his days—which still began at dawn with swords, and still ended late with lamplight and columns of numbers, and during which he was carefully placing roadblocks in the path of Corus Vane's recorded sabotages in order to halt the damage—was still playing with the idea that they'd find a way to turn this against the Keseys and the Vanes. He was trying to think like Luca. It was so tempting, to think that they could somehow *win*. Strike a blow. Trot this truth out into the light.

Matti was pulled away from his thoughts. Luca had led him over to where Sofia was holding court, glorious in a black dress, the low-cut bodice trimmed densely with gold beads and the skirt a stormcloud of chiffon. Draped over her shoulders was a scarf similar to Luca's, in a red so bright as to be almost pink. She was embracing the trend she'd begun for all she was worth.

Maya stood next to her, bending her dark head down to Sofia's brown one. A golden pin in the shape of a butterfly, like the one that adorned the label of Cooper wines, clung to Maya's pile of black hair: her own Half Moon gift. They were laughing.

The twang and scrape of the instruments was beginning to cohere into music. Sofia looked up and met Matti's eyes, and he managed a respectable bow with his hand outstretched.

Sofia collected her floating skirts, murmured something final to Maya, and stepped forward to take Matti's hand.

"Are you having a good night?" Matti asked as they made their way to the centre of the room.

"Excellent, so far."

They took up positions as the musicians settled into an anticipatory, sheet-music-rustling pause, during which a quiet fell over the ballroom. The clear space around them expanded like ripples from a dropped stone. Matti had to make an effort to loosen his grip on Sofia's hand as he felt hundreds of pairs of eyes pinned to him.

The first song whispered and then hummed through its opening bars. It was a sehassa, of course: romantic and slow, to give the celebrated couple a chance to fall into each other's arms.

"Right," murmured Sofia, with an almost military air of resolve. She showed no inclination to fall anywhere. She was clinging to Matti's hand and arm as though expecting a gale and intending to brace herself against it. "Shall we?"

The music swelled, and the dance began.

Matti discovered two things quickly. The first was that dancing was a lot easier when music was playing; it seemed to give invisible help to his limbs, rendering him much less clumsy than he'd feared.

The second was that it wouldn't have done him much good to have lessons from the most accomplished master in Thesper, because Sofia Cooper was an *appalling* dancer.

She apologised for it as soon as her mouth was close enough to his ear. Matti, who was spending half his attention making sure he didn't injure her and the other half marvelling at the fact that for once he was not the most physically inept person in a room, told her not to worry about it.

"Cee keeps saying that Cooper House had no choice but to become very rich indeed, because neither of us were ever going to be married on the strength of our dancing."

The image of Cecilia tromping across the floor as though it were a trough of first-press grapes brought a smile to Matti's face. "Is anyone?"

An answering smile that looked more genuine peeked around Sofia's pinched brow of concentration. "That's what I said."

They managed to finish out the dance in something like dignity, helped by the fact that Matti was afraid to move too much in case he took a step beyond the reach of Sofia's feet. Sofia was one of those people whose cheeks went hectically pink with exertion. The colour clashed with her scarf.

"There, you can hand me off to endanger someone else's feet now," she said.

Matti hesitated, wondering if that was a signal for him to gallantly insist on the next dance as well, and Sofia patted his arm with a rueful look. "I mean it. The wedding will be about us. Tonight is about everyone else. Let's go and do our duty."

That left Matti's mouth dry and sour, as though he'd been eating undersweetened lemon tarts. Of course tonight was about duty.

Matti danced with Maya, and then Joyce Amberden, and then found his hand determinedly claimed by Wynn, who was surprisingly just as good a dancer as his sister Joyce. A spike of mischief prompted Matti to offer a dance to Cecilia, making sure it was one of the more energetic ones, and she laughed her way through it with verve if not grace. He remembered just in time what Luca had said about Merri's claim on the catskill; it might have been a ploy to enter the conversation, but Merri's face went blissfully excited when Matti led her out onto the floor and took her through the twirls. Dancing with a five-year-old was another way to make sure nobody noticed your lack of skill, Matti decided.

He offered Marko a dance next—he'd be finding salt in his shoes for days if he did something with one twin and not the other—but Marko was yawning in Tomas's lap, and just scrunched up a tired nose at Matti's offer, so Matti took his mother out instead. Sofia whirled unevenly past them with her hands in Maya's.

After an hour of dancing there was a break for the crowd to gulp down water and yet more wine. It was getting late, and most of the children and older people among the guests had already retired to their rooms or been taken down the road in coaches to one of the inns nearby.

Matti decided with regret to steer clear of the Coopers' incredible wine for the rest of the night. It was hardly going to do his coordination any favours. He tipped some water into his palm and used it to pat down his warm face and smooth back his hair.

Roland caught Matti's eye from across the room and made a gesture with his head as he and Wynn and a few others headed over to the grand doors, which stood open to allow the crowd to spill onto the lit terrace or down into the gardens; Matti wavered, considering, but then caught sight of Luca. His best man was standing nearby, in animated conversation with a young man Matti didn't know. Luca's fingers were rubbing back and forth on the side of his own jaw. Matti wanted to engulf that hand in his own until it quieted.

And he could, couldn't he?

He waved a negative to Roland and made his way over to Luca as the music restarted and the first few couples slowly began to move across the floor.

"Mr. Jay," said the man speaking to Luca. His tone was polite enough, his bow deep enough, that he was probably not a named member of any House.

Matti nodded in return. "May I borrow my best man?"

"Of course." The man waved a hand and moved away.

"Is there another ritual you haven't warned me about?" Luca asked, bestowing his smile upon Matti. "I liked the last one. It involved gifts."

"Can you dance with that attached?" Matti gestured at Luca's sword.

"What," said Luca, wide-eyed, "you don't think I can control it?"

Matti swallowed a burst of exasperation that was far more affectionate than annoyed, and held out his hand.

Luca's expression shadowed, then sharpened, then softened. It happened quickly. Matti didn't have time to feel more than the first stirrings of uncertainty before Luca reached out and accepted his hand, and let himself be led into the dancing. It was something like a wissel-step, but simpler than the version Maya had taught Matti, with a lot of repetition and claps and turns.

"Though you're right, I've never tried to do this while wearing a sword belt before," Luca said. "How generous of you, Mr. Jay, to offer a dance to your humble best man."

"Humble, Huna's arse," said Matti.

Luca laughed at him as they fell into the steps. "Now *that*, I'm afraid, was less generous. Someone might overhear and get the wrong impression. Quick! Steer the conversation back into polite waters. We could discuss the quality of the food. Or the music."

"It is nice music."

Clap, step, clap. The laughter still adorned Luca's eyes like glittering dust. "If you say so. I can't tell one end of a chord from another. I'm just concentrating on the rhythm." Luca glanced down at their feet as they parted, moved through a couple of turns in their own small circles of space, and then joined hands again. "You're doing surprisingly well at this, by the way."

"Now who's being ungenerous?"

"You've been holding out on me," Luca intoned. "I knew it. You have a secret genius for physical coordination, and you decided to get your revenge for the nonsense with the pocket watch by asking for sword lessons and then tormenting me by pretending otherwise. What a cunning, underhanded creature you are, Mattinesh Jay." Luca's eyes were darting back and forth over Matti's face as if anxious to memorise it, and the smile that arose in response to Matti's laugh was even more breathtaking than the act of dancing. Arousal fizzed through Matti as the steps forced him to pull Luca close, almost sharing the same air, their thighs firm together.

When the dance ended, Luca was biting his lip. Matti felt hot all over.

To recapture his composure he looked anywhere but at Luca. Maya had just finished dancing with Tino Cooper, and she was giving Matti and Luca a look that Matti was too far away to read. She turned back to Tino, picking up their conversation, and then someone moved between them and Matti couldn't see her any more.

The next song was slower. Another sehassa, or something like it: stirring and lyrical and sweet. Matti felt the fall of his heart as though the bows of the musicians were being pulled clean across his nerves. He was already anticipating the glances, the expectation that he find Sofia again instead of staying here with his hand in Luca's where it wanted to be.

Where it should be, murmured something in the cool voice of the flute.

He should drop Luca's hand and find his betrothed. He should put himself in the centre of this room, to be seen, instead of lurking near its edges. He should remind himself that this was the beginning of the rest of his life, a countdown of mere days to everything his family had hoped for and a chance at sleeping peacefully through the night, next to someone he might one day be able to talk himself into wanting.

"Matti." Luca's thumbnail dug into the soft skin of Matti's wrist.

"I don't want to be here," Matti heard himself say. His voice sounded odd.

"Then we won't be here," Luca said at once. "Lead on. Did you want to go outside? Get some air?"

Matti shook his head, struggling. The gardens were lit with lamps. There were people outside.

"All right. Where?"

Matti didn't know this enormous house well, but he'd already claimed a room in it—his whole family had been allocated rooms for the night, as had every member of the wedding party and several of the other guests—and he knew his way from here to there, at least.

The glances he'd been anticipating weren't there. Nobody was looking at them. Still Matti felt a pressure on his skin like a dive into too-deep water.

Matti moved, the decision happening at the level of his muscles rather than his mind, striking out towards the closest exit. He remembered just as his arm reached its full length that he hadn't untangled his fingers from Luca's, but it didn't matter. Luca was behind him, keeping pace. Then Luca was beside him, and they had ducked out of the doorway, and Matti's own celebratory ball was already a rising roar of irrelevance behind them.

CHAPTER
14

Luca had never seen Matti like this before.

Or perhaps he had. Something like it, in that ramshackle park after they left the Vane house. An icy lake with deadly thread-thin cracks appearing and the sense of something churning beneath.

Matti kept painful hold of Luca's hand up two flights of wide stairs and along an empty corridor lined with near-identical doors. Luca's room was somewhere in this wing and on this level too. The small golden plaque on his door depicted a half-blooming rose. He remembered this, but couldn't have said when they passed it. His heart was hammering promises and threats. He couldn't spare any attention except to worry for Matti, who was vibrating like a plucked string and breathing too quickly.

Matti's plaque was a bare winter tree. Luca had barely enough time to notice that the room had been prepared, well-lit and almost overwarm with it, and that the curtains were pulled nearly all the way closed, only a sliver of dark night and their own reflections visible in the window. The door closed behind them.

And then Matti was kissing him: clumsily, wildly, crushing Luca between himself and the wall next to the door. Luca's body surrendered in a jubilant rush of heat. He took hold of Matti's clothes and kissed back, fierce and urgent, like taking gulps from a cup that would be snatched away.

Which it was, far too soon. Matti wrenched himself out of Luca's grip and stepped back. He didn't look horrified, or guilty, or even conflicted. He looked—distant, and dreadful. Full of dread.

As though kissing Luca had been a lungful of good air before he ducked his head back beneath a pool of fetid water.

Luca found himself settling into a ready stance, knees slightly bent, able to shift his weight anywhere on little notice.

Matti said, "I don't want to be in that room."

"You're not in there anymore," Luca said, careful. Almost visibly, Matti's thoughts were looping him back again and again, like circling dancers.

"I don't—"

"You're here."

"—Because all of that, down there, that's the future, and I'm so fucking sick of *pretending*. I want—" A hitching laugh. "I want it to be morning, a normal morning, I want to be in the practice room with you, doing something stupid with my feet. I . . ." Matti's breathing was erratic now, each inhalation ripping the air in half. His eyes glittered and he looked bewildered with pain.

Huna save us, Luca thought, with a despairing twist of his stomach. *Not again.*

Luca unbuckled his sword belt and set it down on the floor. When Luca got close and put his hands on Matti's shoulders, Matti flinched. Luca was expecting it—it had happened last time too—and managed not to flinch in return.

"Matti," he said, low. "Matti, it's all right." And Matti gave another of those not-really-laughs and then his arms were around Luca, warm and sturdy at Luca's waist, and Luca pressed his face for a long and incoherent moment into the side of Matti's neck. Neither of them knew what the fuck they were doing, he suspected, but Matti was the one closest to the snapping point, so Luca was the one who had to find the path for them both.

He pulled away to look Matti in the face again. Matti's body was heaving against his, but the rhythm of his breaths was steadying. His hands were on the small of Luca's back.

Don't distract him.

We can't afford it.

Everything crumbled. Luca didn't care. He was done pretending he did. He would have tried, for Matti's sake, but Matti was clinging to him and Matti deserved more than his own stupid immolation. Matti should know what it was like to have exactly what he wanted, even if it was just for one evening.

"I told you it could be simple. I'll make it easy," Luca said. Matti smelled incredible. Luca's blood was a river boiling over rocks. "Do you want me?"

"Yes." Matti's body stilled. One more deep breath in and out, and he was poised. "Yes."

"I'm here. I'm willing. I'm—" *yours,* Luca almost said, and felt himself reeling, yanking himself back from that particular precipice.

He lifted his face instead, moving a hand into Matti's hair so that he could pull Matti's mouth back down to his for a long, incandescent moment. Matti's mouth opened to the pressure, and Luca wavered on the edge of letting this kiss turn as frantic as the last, but the memory of Matti's heaving breaths stopped him. He wanted Matti to have this, but he wanted Matti to be sure.

He stepped back, disentangling himself. He made sure no part of his body was touching any part of Matti's, though he let his gaze travel over the dip of Matti's throat and the drowning darkness of Matti's eyes.

"Say yes to me again," Luca said.

"Yes."

"Say you want this to happen."

"I—*yes.*"

Luca shivered all over at the raw need in Matti's voice. "Good. Tell me exactly what you want." He managed to find an edge of humour, somehow. "Yours to command, Mr. Jay." There—the word had slipped out anyway. But in a way that felt safer.

"I . . ." Matti's voice trailed off. He swallowed.

The pause stretched out long enough that discomfort began to gnaw at the edges of Luca's desire.

"Sorry," Luca said, rueful. "I guess I misread that."

"No, *I'm* sorry—"

"We can come back to it." Luca stepped closer again, putting himself within arm's reach. "You can just . . . take." Somehow he made it sound casual, Huna only knew how. "If that's—"

Matti took.

This was more like it. Luca wrapped one arm around Matti's side and one around his neck, for balance, and experimented with how much of his weight Matti would take. This kiss was more controlled than the first, but Matti's mouth devoured Luca's with the same hunger and only slowed when it was apparent that Luca was not going anywhere. It felt more like a duel between equals than anything else he and Matti had done up to this point, as though they were trying to learn each other's movements.

Matti's fingertips dug into Luca's spine through two layers of cloth. Matti moved to kiss Luca's temple, a harsh press of lips that felt more indecent than his tongue.

"I want you. I can't decide what I want *first*." Matti sounded almost irritable. "No. I can." His eyes were burning as he reached out and unwrapped the scarf he'd given Luca earlier that evening, tugging at one end, letting it slide against Luca's skin like a caress. He tilted up Luca's chin and kissed the same place on Luca's neck, once and then again, with a faint scrape of evening jaw and teeth.

A shiver like a net being pulled tight took hold of Luca's entire front, nearly bending him double with the force of it. His body swayed, bucked, coming into firmer contact with Matti's.

"It's all right," he assured Matti. "I—*ah*. I feel adequately wanted."

Luca's jacket came off next, when Matti was done with the scarf, and landed in a pile somewhere on the floor. Luca was making a disaster of Matti's hair, Matti yanking Luca's shirt out of his trousers so that he could get his hands against Luca's back—Luca made a low noise of encouragement, because *gods,* that was amazing, the first searing touch of fingers on skin—when a thought elbowed its way into Luca's brain.

"Though if we could get down to specifics, briefly," Luca murmured, "do you want to fuck me?"

There was a single suspended moment, and then the hunger crashed back onto Matti's face like a wave. Luca's mouth curved in gratification; it *was* nice to be wanted. It was almost unnecessary for Matti to say, "Yes. *Yes.* If, ah, if that's something that you . . . want?"

Luca balanced the words in his mouth, enjoying the anticipation. He looked Matti in the eye and said, with the pure heat of honesty: "I'm fairly certain I want you to wreck me."

Matti's lips parted in something like disbelief. Luca glowed with pleasure at his own aim.

"The point of my question being," Luca went on, chasing the advantage in an unsportsmanlike manner, "do you have anything that would facilitate that?"

Perhaps he'd pushed Matti's coherence too far. He had to lift a hand and rub his fingers together before Matti caught on to his meaning, and then Matti's dark brows drew together with comical speed.

"No," Matti said. "Fuck."

Luca tucked his shirt back into his trousers. He snatched up Matti's hand and kissed it hard, once: marking his place. "I'll be right back."

The corridor was deserted when Luca stepped out into it. Luca took some breaths to clear his head and set about searching for his own rose-adorned plaque. A couple came up the stairs, loudly enough that Luca had time to arrange his face before they came into view. It was Sofia's brother, whose name Luca couldn't remember, and his blond wife. Luca gave them a careless smile, fumbling with the doorknob as though drunk, and stumbled through his own door.

By the time he emerged again, they were gone. Nobody else ventured into view in the time it took Luca to jog light-footed back to stand in front of Matti's door. As he stood there, however, laughter drifted from the far staircase, and it propelled Luca back into Matti's room like a nudge from the gods. *Don't waste your time,* it seemed to say. *He's too good for you. Leave him alone too long and he'll realise it.*

Matti was sitting on the edge of the bed. The thick bedcover had been pulled back and folded into an impeccably neat pile, a fact that struck Luca as both promising and painfully sweet. Matti stood as Luca entered. He held his hands self-consciously apart from his body, which Luca appreciated, because it brought into beautifully framed relief the fact that Matti had also used the time to remove not only his own waistcoat and shoes, but his shirt as well.

Matti had learned, eventually, under the lash of Luca's tongue, to stand to his full height. To hold his shoulders properly wide. The span of them, the broad expanse of his chest with its scattered black hair, banished Luca's breath. The small jar of grease felt slippery in Luca's hand, though it was screwed tight shut.

Luca was staring. Matti licked his lips.

"I've thought of some more things I want." Matti's voice was hoarse.

Luca said, dry-mouthed and clutching the jar as though it would disappear: "Me too."

He directed Matti back to a seated position on the edge of the bed by the firm press of fingers against Matti's chest. Luca spared only a moment to be grateful for hours spent moving Matti with his fingertips, for the shorthand of physical direction that they'd woven painfully between them. Then Matti was reaching for him, and Luca was climbing into his lap, one knee on either side of

Matti's legs. He tossed the jar so that it landed near the pillows; they'd get to it soon enough.

An exhalation jerked out of Matti in three parts, nearly soundless. Luca put his hands on Matti's cheekbones and kissed him. He was nowhere near drunk, neither of them were, but he still felt like swaying.

"Luca." Matti laid his hands on Luca's legs and squeezed, his thumbs skating close to the sensitive inner thighs.

Luca arched, encouraging. His trousers were tightening with every breath. He undid his own shirt with fingers that had been very nimble two minutes ago, but now had been somehow tipped with lead weights. Matti gave another of those helpless exhalations when Luca wrestled the garment off and to the floor and leaned in.

"Fuck," muttered Luca. "Gods, that feels good." He buried a hand in Matti's hair, felt the heat of Matti's scalp twinned to the heat of Matti's mouth as it moved over his chest, an exploration of lips and tongue and—*"Fuck"* again—a scrape of teeth over Luca's nipple.

Matti's hands had moved, tight at his waist, but Matti still hadn't mastered the art of the feint. He signalled his movements loud and clear. So Luca was ready when Matti tugged and leaned back on the bed, pulling Luca to lie on top of him and between his legs.

He *wasn't* ready for Matti to roll them sideways, and the surprise of it melted into delight. There was a moment of glorious weight, Matti stretched out hard above him. Luca twisted, to create more contact, and Matti pulled back almost at once. Now it was his turn to sit astride Luca's hips.

"That wasn't a protest," Luca said hastily. "Really, *really* not protesting. Any of it. Quite the opposite, in fact." He wriggled, getting himself comfortable on one of the pillows. He had a moment of wanting to do five things at once with his hands, and settled for framing his head with his arms, exposing the undersides of his wrists in a vulnerable way that he knew practically shouted to be taken advantage of. *Pin me down,* this posture said.

Matti's eyes locked to Luca's upturned wrists, but he didn't reach for them.

"This," Matti said. Rough, like he couldn't fit all the edges of the words in his mouth. "Yes. Fuck. This is what I wanted."

This was, apparently, to get his mouth on every piece of Luca he could expose. Luca ended up with two handfuls of the sheets, cursing as Matti worked the rest of his clothes down and off his legs. An open-mouthed kiss over Luca's navel. A gentle trail of Matti's tongue down the revealed skin of Luca's leg, to the ticklish back of his knee. Then Luca's neck, then his hip. No rhythm, no pattern, just Matti following whatever whims were seizing him.

"*Yes,*" Luca said, "gods, please," as Matti's lips passed close enough to Luca's cock that Luca caught his breath, urgent desire pooling. So far Matti hadn't laid so much as a finger on that part of Luca's anatomy.

"Please?"

"Oh, fuck you," said Luca, a bit strangled. He'd been resisting grabbing hold of Matti's hair, as Matti seemed to be enjoying directing his own explorations, but now he reached out and managed a tame tug.

Matti buried his face in Luca's side, laughing. In another partner Luca might have been batting away concern, or embarrassment, but Matti was not at all the kind of person to laugh *at* someone, least of all in bed. The joke was probably one he'd be happy to share, and Luca's mouth was already curling in response.

"I'm so pleased you're finding this amusing, Mattinesh."

Matti lifted his head. Luca felt like a piece of plain fabric taking in dye: he wanted to soak this up, thread by thread. He wanted to capture forever the loveliness of Matti's mouth, the dimples sparkling in his cheeks.

"I suppose we could call it irony," Matti said. "I'm so used to looking at the way you move. The way you respond to things. This is a lot easier than the intermediate forms."

"Matti," said Luca, breathless, "if there's a man alive who would not be responding like this, who would not be going *insane* looking at you, with you doing that, then he's either tragically committed to women or so lacking in taste that there's no helping him at all."

Matti lowered his abashed expression to drop another kiss on the inside of Luca's thigh. His hair tickled Luca's cock and Luca's leg jerked in protest.

"Be still," Matti murmured.

"I—"

"Luca. Be still."

Luca's heart was trying to punch through his ribs. He felt dizzy and alive, stretched out bare for the taking. He'd never been this hard in his life. Matti sucked, gently, at a new patch of skin.

"You can," Luca panted, "harder."

Matti glanced up. "Harder?"

"I mark easily."

"But—" Realisation. "*Fuck,*" said Matti fervently, and this time when his mouth landed over Luca's hipbone he sucked hard, drawing blood to the surface, and Luca gave up on *being still* and wrapped a hand around his own length. He squeezed once, dragging a groan from his throat, and then forced himself to let go. The grease jar was digging into his shoulder. He fumbled for it and held it out to Matti.

Matti hesitated. Luca paused in the act of bending one leg up invitingly. He choked back the first three flippant things he was going to say, and made sure his voice was casual.

"Have you done this before?"

Matti's brow creased. He sat up and looked at the jar in Luca's hand. "Not . . . this part, with men."

Luca bit his lip so hard he endangered the skin. It was stupid for him to find that so blazingly, unbearably hot. Sex was many different things. Actions were arbitrary. But Luca was selfish;

he liked things that were his, *only* his, and he was already looking forward to imprinting somewhere on his greedy, dye-hungry heart the memory of Matti's face and the sounds that Matti would make.

He realised too late that Matti was taking his silence as a judgemental one. Luca pushed up onto his elbows, almost slipping in his haste. "Matti, it's fine, I didn't mean—"

Matti stilled him, silenced him, with a firm press of his hand on Luca's stomach. One of Matti's dimples was starting to deepen again.

"Do you think I'm embarrassed?" Matti said, steady. "It's not like I have no experience at all. But yes. It's been hard to find the time."

To justify the time, Luca translated. As for sword lessons, so for . . . well, more enjoyable forms of physical exertion.

"And I haven't . . . felt like it." At that, Matti did look embarrassed. Not *getting* sex was understandable, but it was odder to admit to not wanting it at all.

"Not enough blood getting to your brain. I remember."

Matti flicked a glance at him, dark eyes transparent as smoked glass, limned in silent gratitude.

"Or maybe not enough blood getting to other places," Luca murmured. He sat up fully and unscrewed the lid of the jar himself. "Take your damn clothes off, Mattinesh, and come here."

Matti did.

In the intimate light of the room, Matti undressed was mouthwatering. His skin was like shadowed amber and he was, Luca was gratified to see, just as aroused as Luca himself. When Luca's slicked fingers closed around Matti's cock, Matti made a sound that Luca was going to remember for the rest of his life.

"All right," Luca said, soothing. Matti was bucking into his hand, kneeling over him. Luca felt like new-spun thread about to be snipped. He shifted his hips and bent his legs up—exhaled, slow—and guided Matti to his entrance.

"I do know the mechanics of this." Matti's arms were shaking, but he sounded almost amused. "You don't want—fingers, first?"

Luca had to swallow hard before he could be sure that his voice would be even. "Believe me, if that was what I wanted, I'd ask for it."

He wondered if Matti was going to argue, but Matti was back to following Luca's lead. Luca was glad of it. He was full of that sparkling-wine sensation that he loved so much, the one that came when he simply *acted*, without dragging himself down with planning. The joy was in seeing what would happen next.

The fizz of sensation carried him through the painful stretch when Matti took himself in hand and pushed, finally, guiding himself inside. Luca was endangering his own lip again. His breath was unsteady and he was—full, gods he was full—his legs bent up around Matti's hips, helping Matti the rest of the way, taking Matti deep inside himself.

Matti whispered, like an entreaty: "Luca."

"Yes, yes," Luca threw back, echo and answer. "Go. *Go.*"

Then Matti's arms were gathering him up as Matti drove into him, the discomfort rapidly melting into a pleasure that seared along all of Luca's nerves. Luca framed Matti's face in his hands, making Matti hold eye contact, wanting to see him. To watch him. He hadn't planned it, but he wanted it. And he felt something that wasn't orgasm building in his chest, like a welling of tears, as Matti closed his eyes and turned his head, opening his mouth against Luca's wrist in what might have been a kiss when it started, but ended up ragged and inelegant, a scrape of teeth.

The hot water in Luca's chest kept brimming. Luca couldn't run from it, so he did the only other thing he could: let it wash over him. He craned up to kiss Matti's neck and murmur pleas against Matti's mouth. He let himself be overwhelmed by Matti, Matti inside him and above him and anchoring him.

Matti came first, with a sudden cut-off cry that he buried in Luca's neck. Luca felt suspended in a moment, not quite fitting into his skin. He was too hot and too cold. Matti was heavy and impossible and Luca never wanted him to move, or else wanted him to keep moving forever. Luca's cock was pressed between their bodies, and Luca was reaching for it to finish himself off when Matti got there before him.

The motion of Matti's mouth on Luca's face became deliberate. They were kissing, Matti's tongue warm and demanding against Luca's, when a final squeeze of Matti's fingers dragged Luca over the edge as well.

Afterwards, when Luca had stripped a pillow of its fine case in order to give them both a perfunctory wipe, they lay side by side in the warm room, breathing. More than one of Luca's previous bedfellows had said that Luca could form a diagonal line in the narrowest or the widest bed in the world. He sprawled with a leg hooked possessively over Matti's knee, feeling tired and happy and something else, too, a niggling sense of vulnerability, as though a wind had swept through him and left a window open somewhere.

"I don't believe I feel wrecked enough," Luca said, to cover it. "You'll have to try harder next time."

Matti's breath shook out of him, not quite a laugh. "You really are an awful teacher, did you know that?"

A familiar defensiveness tried to rise in Luca and sharpen his tongue to lash back. It didn't get very far. There was too much in the way. Instead, he yawned and looked at the shadow of Matti's jaw and actually let the accusation—lighthearted as it had been—settle into him.

"Ye-es. I suppose so." He added, "Sorry."

"You've been getting better," Matti said. "At about the same rate as I've been getting better with the sword. But I do know that you're supposed to give praise every so often, as well as pointing out all my mistakes."

"Oh, *well*." Luca grinned, warming to the task. "In that case I could tell you that was still one of the better fucks of my life, and I'd dance five hundred catskills with a halitotic lech for the opportunity to repeat it, with variations, every day for the next year. And that I didn't *need* to take my shirt off to demonstrate the basic forms, that first day in the practice room when I was trying to convince you not to have me arrested, but I wasn't thinking straight because I'd never seen anyone look so glorious when they were angry as you. You are absurd, Mattinesh. In another life you'd be posing for paintings. I'm going to have dreams about your shoulders, or maybe your knees."

Too late Luca heard the note of affection in his own voice deepening, hushing, as though the long stream of his words were a plume of fragrance wrapping them intimately close. Matti hadn't interrupted. Matti was watching him with something that Luca felt he should be able to read by now, but which lived in the neutral at-rest realm of Matti's facial expressions.

"Do you want me to be quiet?" Luca asked. His lips twitched in helpless memory.

Matti smiled. "No. No, I love the way you talk. Most of the time," he added, in response to the dubious look Luca gave him.

"I talk too much."

"You talk like you're not afraid of anything. Like you could say whatever you wanted and it wouldn't matter."

Luca rubbed his thumb over the roughness of Matti's jaw and moved to press a kiss over Matti's collarbone, then another. Matti's arm slid around him, holding him close. "There are things I'm afraid of," Luca said, soft against Matti's skin.

After a moment Matti said, "Have you ever been hurt with a sword? Badly hurt, I mean?"

Caution swam in Luca's gut. "Hm? Why?"

"I was wondering about your scars." Matti rubbed a hand down Luca's back. "I suppose I thought duellists would have a lot of them, but then I realised: few ceremonial fights even go to the blood, these days. And you train with dulled blades. So." His fingers were gentling back and forth on what Luca knew was a long, thin groove that curled around Luca's side. A line of almost ghostly whiteness on Luca's already pale torso.

That one *was* from a sword, as it happened. A training session a few years back, when Luca had learned that picking up a sword while seething with anger was a recipe for disaster.

He opened his mouth to tell Matti that story, but the caution was still there, trying to call out to Luca. He was in too deep for safety. He knew that already. Nothing could prevent him from feeling nearly boneless with pleasure, helpless with longing, lying here in Matti Jay's arms.

What he could do was remember that he was a liar. That he was lying. That nothing here was as simple as it felt, and that Luca's fears had nothing to do with metal blades.

"Sorry to disappoint," he said lightly. "Childhood accident. Smashed a window, tripping on a toy, and was lucky to escape with just that cut. And one on my hand, but it healed without scarring."

"What about the ones on your feet?"

"All right," said Luca, "*when,* during the events of the last half hour—thoroughly enjoyable though they were—did you bother to look closely at my *feet*? Do you like feet? Is that it? Can I re-duce you to a panting mess by simply flashing my ankles? Because that's useful information."

Matti laughed. One of his own feet slid over Luca's, gently rub-bing. "I saw them at the sea bath."

"Oh. They're from chilblains. Two winters ago." That was true.

"I didn't think chilblains scarred."

"They don't, usually. But these ones were bad, and they got infected, and I didn't stop going to sword lessons when the physi-cian told me to stay off my feet. I hate winter."

"You complain about the summer enough. Are there any tem-peratures you *do* like?"

Luca pretended to consider this. "There's usually a few weeks in spring that are tolerable," he said. Then, sliding his hands under Matti's sides, burrowing farther into Matti's neck, "And I'm comfortable now. You're a good temperature."

"I'm not a season."

"Yes you are." Luca was sleepy, lulled by contentment. He hadn't meant that to come out. For a moment he hoped Matti would let it go, or wouldn't understand what he'd meant, but Matti could be perceptive when Luca didn't want him to be.

"You're saying you'll move on."

"Yes. I'm a season in your life, and you're a season in mine."

"Don't go anywhere tonight." Matti brushed a kiss into Luca's hair. "Please?"

"Are you joking? You were probably given the best room in this wing." Luca pressed his fingertips hard for a moment into Matti's skin: *I'm staying.*

After a pause Matti said, "It's probably not nearly as nice as Sofia's room."

Luca swallowed a sudden surge of salt at the mention of Matti's betrothed. He had the unpleasant and unfamiliar sensation of not knowing how to handle a conversation. After what had just passed between them, he hadn't thought Matti would be in the mood to talk about Sofia at all.

"Do you think she was expecting you . . . ?"

"No. My assigned room would be a lot closer to the family wing if that were the case. But . . . it's a Half Moon Ball."

Luca nodded. These celebrations were often when the eldest child of any given marriage was conceived. It was an easy matter of counting. "My older brother was probably conceived at the Half Moon point," he said. "Were you?"

"I don't think my parents had a Half Moon Ball."

"That's right, they were married in Manisi. Wait: correction." Luca lifted his head. "*Outside* Manisi."

Matti's laugh was warm. "No, they did get married in Manisi. But apparently Mama's extended family grumbled about having to make the trip down into the city for the ceremony. I don't think they gave everyone much warning."

Luca rested his cheek back on Matti's chest. Matti's fingers combed through his hair and Matti's breath was a soothing tide, lifting and lowering him. This was so easy. Family stories. Laughter. Luca felt like he could say anything in this moment and it *wouldn't* matter, nothing would matter; Matti would accept it.

But that wasn't true.

Luca's mouth, half-open on a truth, closed again. His lips burned with his name and he shifted to kiss Matti instead, wondering that Matti didn't pull away at the feel of them. But Matti's mouth was generous and sweet. Luca wanted to kiss him for hours.

They didn't have hours. Or rather, they did, but the house had the heavy quiet of nighttime; they were either too late or too far removed from the main entrance to hear the departure of the last guests. Luca's limbs clamoured for sleep even as his brain flitted from doubt to joy to doubt.

Matti slept first, his breathing softening out, his arm draped over Luca's back. Luca's body wanted to shift positions, but he was stubbornly fighting it, letting his hands and feet move instead so that he could stay under Matti's arm like—

Like it meant something.

"Fuck," Luca breathed. "I'm sorry. You deserve better. You deserve someone who can tell you the truth."

Matti took a deeper breath and shifted the angle of his jaw against the pillow on the exhale, but slept on. *Selfish, selfish,* Luca raged at himself; and answered himself, exhaustedly: *Yes, I know. Selfish. Lazy. Liar.*

"But I'm not sorry enough to let you go," he added, low enough now that he could barely hear his own words. "Not yet."

⸻

Matti woke to rain. He could hear a steady, heavy drumming on the roof, and pale light angled through the sliver of window between the curtains. A clock on the wall told him that it was the same hour he usually woke. After a year of swimming and another three months of sword lessons, Matti's mind and body knew what time they would be asked to function.

There was no set hour for breakfast. Nobody would care if Matti didn't show himself for a few hours yet.

Another steady murmur slowly resolved itself into words. Matti scrubbed at his eyes and turned, and his arm hit Luca, who was sitting upright in the bed and seemed to be drawing aimless patterns on the sheets with one finger.

"—and Jenny. But that wouldn't work. Unless. It's a lot of moving parts, but you can make parts dance if you pay them enough. Donna and Jenny—" He stopped as Matti laid a hand on his leg. The glance he directed down at Matti was not shy, exactly, but it was careful.

"What are you talking about?" asked Matti.

"Maybe nothing. Maybe something."

"You don't need to cultivate an air of mystery, you know. I'm already fascinated by you."

A smile of true delight lit Luca's face. "Really?"

Matti stretched, then pushed himself upright as well, shoving pillows until he was sitting back against them. "I have been since I first saw you." This room with its halfhearted light, the unfamiliar warmth of waking next to someone else's body, felt unreal. Anything true could be said, here and now, and it would be treated kindly. "Since I knocked you down."

"To be scrupulously fair about it, I *made* you knock me down." Luca let his fingers play on Matti's stomach. One finger scratched idly through the trail of hair, but there was no serious intent in the action. Luca was just moving because he had to move. "But when I got a good look at you from down there . . . part of me wanted to stay on my knees."

Matti closed his eyes briefly, unable to stop his imagination from running with that. He had woken partway hard and was only stiffening further at the thought. "What would that have involved?"

Luca's hand stilled. Matti looked at him. Luca was staring back, his eyes the same shade as the rain-soft light; he swallowed, and the smile began to cut across his face again.

He said, silky, "Why don't you stand up and I'll show you?"

Anticipation rubbed itself over Matti's skin, making him feel boyish. He pushed aside the covers and stood. Luca followed him across the bed, grabbing Matti's pillow on the way. He laid the pillow at Matti's feet and gave him the hand gesture that meant *hold, stay.*

"It would have involved something like this," Luca said, and threw himself backwards.

Matti's knees weakened and then locked as the instinct to help came up against the instruction to stay. And Luca wasn't hurt, Matti could see at once. Luca was sprawled playfully on the floor, seeming not to notice his nudity in a way that made Matti feel less self-conscious about his own.

"It's easier in a crowd, of course. A lot more going on. But either way, I end up down here. *How dare you, sir!* And you're apologetic, and confused, and it's a simple matter to get my watch—already broken, obviously—precisely where your foot will fall on it. It's all about reading the body's cues."

"I see."

"But then I get a better look at the mark I've chosen," Luca said. He was kneeling upright and straight on the pillow now. His hands came to rest lightly on the sides of Matti's legs. "And I'm struck instantly into repentance by your magnificence, your"—a slight smirk, a dart of Luca's eyes—"stature."

"Not to mention the fact that I appear to have forgotten my clothes when I came out this evening."

The scrape of Luca's nails down Matti's thigh might have been either encouragement or warning against further improvisation.

"Oh, sir, I should never have tried to deceive you. Will you ever be able to forgive me?" Luca's voice had a theatrical breathlessness, but the glance he directed up at Matti was that of someone daring himself to draw a finger through a candle flame. "How can I make it up to you?"

"Luca—" Matti lost his breath as Luca wrapped a hand around Matti's cock and gave it two light strokes.

"Ah," said Luca softly. "A solution presents itself." He leaned in and made a careful, agonising circle of his tongue around the sensitive head of Matti's cock.

"I think we're going to be thrown out of this drinking house," Matti managed.

Luca seemed to take Matti's ability to string clever words together as a challenge, because he abandoned all effort at teasing and simply took Matti deep into his mouth. He sucked Matti slowly, thoroughly, a steady pressure that had Matti tilting his throat to the ceiling and muttering every piece of Huna's anatomy that passed through his unravelling thoughts.

But it was Luca's own noisy satisfaction, his obvious pleasure in pleasuring Matti, that gave Matti the courage to ask for what he wanted.

"Wait," Matti said. When Luca pulled away, Matti twisted and leaned to pick up the grease from the bedside table, then handed it to Luca. "I want you to—use your fingers in me, at the same time."

"Whatever you wish," Luca said, easily. He slicked his hand and then settled his weight on his knees again. His mouth was very close to Matti's dark, straining, still-wet cock. "I suggest you hold on to something"—a grin with claws to it—"*sir.*"

Matti had just enough time to grab the frame of the bed before Luca dove into his task as though it were one of the rare sword lessons when Matti could persuade him to show off, to dance through forms and parries, and to defeat invisible enemies, while Matti watched him with a joy so hungry it bordered on peace.

This was not peaceful. Luca hummed, licked, kept his mouth

full, as his slick fingers gently rolled Matti's balls before moving to press inside him, careful and sure. Matti's knees were weak, pleasure sparking through him in bursts. He gripped the bed frame hard enough to whiten his knuckles and kept his other hand gentle at the back of Luca's head. At least, he was gentle until Luca moved his finger a certain way and a hoarse cry burst from Matti's throat, and he realised that he had tightened his grip, pulling Luca closer.

The apology was poised on Matti's numb lips, but Luca just gave an encouraging moan. Pleasure was winding tighter and tighter at the base of Matti's stomach. Slowly, he allowed himself to use his grip, pushing Luca farther down until the heat was overwhelming.

"*Luca,*" he managed, as he felt himself swaying with incipient climax. He released Luca's hair abruptly.

Luca pulled his mouth off but kept hold of Matti's cock, angling it so that when Matti came, with a wrenching groan, it was over Luca's neck and chest.

As he recovered his breath, Matti clung to the bed frame for dear life, staring down at Luca.

"I—" Matti stopped, shocked at himself. And a little amused as well.

Luca stood, curious and unconcerned. "What?"

"I. Nothing."

"Nothing?" Luca drew a finger slowly across his own collarbone and gods, oh gods, Matti was still staring. He wrenched his gaze back up to Luca's face, remembered Luca's delight when Matti had loosened control of his tongue in the past, and let himself speak.

"I was thinking I can't decide which I prefer around your neck, of the two things I've given you."

Luca's eyes widened.

Matti's face heated. An incredulous smile broke out on Luca's.

"Filthy," Luca said, admiring.

Don't think about it, Matti told himself. *Just act.*

He echoed Luca's motion, drawing two fingers through the evidence of his own release, and felt his breath stop yet again as Luca took hold of his hand and sucked the fingers clean.

"You are full of surprises, Mr. Jay."

At that, Matti made a face, then laughed, and after a moment Luca laughed too.

"Is that form of address not working for you in a bedroom setting?" Luca bit his lip, dropped his eyelids, then glanced up at Matti through his pale lashes. "Sir?"

To Matti's embarrassment, that one landed cleanly on an invisible nerve. His face did something. Before Luca could do anything to press the advantage, Matti said, feeling the slippery ease of truth in his mouth again: "I just want you to use my name. I just—like to know that you want *me*."

Luca's face smoothed out like a new-flicked sheet. It was gone so quickly that Matti could have imagined it, replaced with a slow, devastating curve of Luca's mouth.

"Mattinesh." Husky, lingering on the hiss at the end. Matti had meant *Matti,* but he felt the correction die in his throat. Nobody else said his full name like that. "*Mattinesh,*" Luca said again. "I wish I could show you how it tastes." And that was about all Matti could bear; they were kissing again the next moment, Luca shoving him back down onto the bed and bracing himself above, his legs falling between Matti's.

When they were fitted together, Luca took them both in hand, his hard cock against Matti's softening one, pushing them against each other with urgency and little finesse.

Matti winced; his sensitivity was crossing over into discomfort. "It's—"

"Too much? Fuck, sorry, I'll—" Luca loosened his grip.

Matti wanted to learn what Luca liked. In his memory of the previous night, everything had been a frantic haze by the end, Matti barely thinking consciously at all, just wanting to see Luca's face and swallow the broken sounds that Luca made against his mouth when Matti pulled the orgasm out of him.

Now he put his hand over Luca's, a careful offer, their fingers tangling on Luca's length, Matti's thumb brushing through the moisture leaking from the tip. Luca shuddered and buried his face in Matti's shoulder. The hand Luca was supporting himself on wobbled; he moved so that they were lying side by side, face-to-face.

"Here," Matti said. "Show me what to do."

And Luca did, his fingers guiding Matti's into a fast, steady rhythm of strokes. Near the end Luca's fingers stuttered, his face screwed up in something between wonder and pain, and Matti greedily drank in the sight of him as he kept his own hand moving.

"*Ah,*" Luca cried, as he spilled over both of their hands and his own stomach. His face slackened; the slits of his eyes were dark, his perfect wide mouth slightly open. Matti understood, quite suddenly, what Luca had meant when he'd talked about Matti posing for paintings. And yet he didn't want anyone else to see Luca like this.

Matti didn't know what to say. There was a bubble of something in his throat, like blown glass or hot chocolate, a tenderness that threatened to sear itself into Matti on a fundamental level.

"What with yours *and* mine, I am rather a mess," said Luca presently. He didn't sound unhappy about it. "Time to sacrifice the other pillowcase?"

"I think we can do better than that." There was a small washbasin in the corner with a single tap, and towels folded over a rail. Matti fetched one of these, dampened it, and offered it as an alternative to further degrading the bedclothes. Luca dumped it cheerfully onto the floor when he was done. Matti resisted the urge to fetch it and hang it up again.

"I should get dressed," Matti said, perched on the edge of the bed.

"You should get back in here with me," Luca said at once.

Matti opened his mouth to argue, then closed it. What changed his mind wasn't anything so sensible as the truth, which was that here in the Coopers' country house he didn't have any deadlines to meet, or meetings to attend, or problems to clear from his desk. No. What pulled Matti back into the bed was the edge of resignation in Luca's voice, as though he didn't expect to be placed above any of the other priorities of Matti's life.

Matti was full of the overwhelming urge to prove Luca wrong. To press his mouth and his hands against Luca's skin and imprint the proof there: that for Luca he had already thrown so many *should*s aside, and hadn't regretted a single one yet.

Luca's surprise was obvious in the way his eyebrows shot up as Matti slid beneath the covers.

"You were right" was all Matti said. "I've reconsidered my position."

Luca's foot slid between Matti's calves. "I like being right."

Luca's hair looked less vibrant now than it had by firelight or gaslight. Less like it could burn. And yet, somehow, warmer. Burnished and dark and everywhere at once. Matti reached out and ran his fingers through it and thought about sea-scarlet dye, and then about rising costs, and—

"Don't get any ideas," Luca murmured. "My own mother can't persuade me to get it cut."

"That's not what I was thinking."

"No? You were doing your pensive thing again." Luca touched Matti's forehead, right between his eyebrows. Matti caught his hand and kissed one of the fingertips, loving the way Luca's eyes went immediately hooded and pleased. He shoved the thoughts of business aside; they'd be there, waiting for him, as soon as Matti was back in the city. For now he was exactly where he wanted to be.

He said so, aloud, and Luca's face changed again.

"You wouldn't rather be in the practice room?" Luca said, arch. "Like you said last night? Fully clothed, no bed in sight?"

A spasm of desire filled Matti at the image that sprang into his mind. The two of them in the practice room, mostly clothed, fucking on the floor. Or against the wall, Matti's hand over Luca's mouth to stifle the cries that he would wring from Luca's throat.

"I've changed my mind." Matti settled deeper into the pillow and pulled Luca close. "I'd be quite happy to stay here, in this room, forever."

Luca's arm was slung over Matti's waist. His fingers were tapping, undemanding, on the small of Matti's back. He said lightly, "There's a lot more world to see than just this room."

This felt like they were skating close to a conversation that neither of them was ready to have.

"I'm sure I'll see more of it one day. And I've already seen more than Maya or the twins have. None of them have been on any voyages by sea, or to Manisi."

"Outside—"

"Shut up," said Matti, fond, tilting his face down to Luca's and kissing the smug smile.

It was a while before Luca said anything. He sounded thoughtful when he spoke again. "You know, I used to think all of you Jays needed to be a bit more selfish, but I've decided I was wrong about that. It took a while for me to change my mind. She's very good at that rose-oiling trick, your sister. Your House should deploy her a lot more."

"I don't understand."

"I like your family. I do. I think they love you and are proud of you, and if they knew you weren't fine, when you tell them you're fine, they'd be troubled by it."

Matti opened his mouth. His words were held back by Luca's fingers, a brief and commanding press on Matti's lips. Luca pulled himself free of Matti's arm and pushed himself upright in the bed again, as though he needed the distance.

"I also think," said Luca, with a shift of tone that Matti recognised from sword lessons as the criticism coming hard on the heels of token praise, "they're not asking the next question because it's easier not to. You're telling them the lie and they're accepting it at face value, because it's more convenient that way."

"It's not a lie."

"Of course it's a lie." Luca smoothed his fingers on that same place between Matti's brows. "Matti, you've been destroying yourself. You're not fine."

"It's not that bad," Matti said, but weakly. He thought of the physician's contemplative silence when Matti talked about his dizziness and nausea. "Fine means normal. Fine means I'm coping. And I *am,* it just feels as though . . ." He struggled, moving his hand in an effort to pluck the right words out of the air.

Luca bent one leg up, one arm wrapped around it. He rubbed his mouth on his own knee as though clearing dust from it to make way for something. Then he looked down at Matti.

"It feels like you're in a box," Luca said. "Not a cage. A box. Whenever it shrinks, it's like there's less air in there with you."

Matti wouldn't have found those words given ten hours and a magnifying glass, but Luca had glimpsed them, somehow. Luca, who had cracked the lid of the box and shown Matti how much space there was outside it.

"How. How did you know?"

Luca's mouth twisted. He glanced away. His expression was warmer when he looked back, and he lifted one shoulder in a shrug. "Don't you think your family deserves to know that the prospect of marrying Sofia has you feeling like you're closing yourself in a box? Don't you think *she* deserves to know?"

"What would it help? Then they'd be unhappy as well, and I wouldn't be any less unhappy myself."

Matti nearly stumbled over the last few words, surprised at hearing them in his own voice. Three months ago he wouldn't even have *thought* himself unhappy.

"And that," said Luca, "just about sums up the last ten years of your life, I'd wager."

"I—I really should get dressed."

Matti climbed out of the bed and dressed under Luca's unabashed gaze. Halfway into his jacket he realised he needed to shave, and did so with the soap that had been laid out on the basin, retrieving his own razor in its leather case from the bag he'd packed.

Luca stayed in the bed. He was quiet enough during the shaving process that Matti wondered if he'd fallen back asleep. But when Matti pulled his jacket on again and tugged a brush through his hair, Luca met his eyes in the mirror.

"Good enough?" Matti gestured down at himself.

"You'll do." Luca's tongue flicked out and wet his lips. It looked more nervous than appreciative. "Matti. If there was some other way to get Jay House out of this hole—"

"But there isn't," Matti said. "Even if I could snap my fingers right now and halt everything Corus has done, we're too far over the line." The familiar ache of resignation was like a swallowed stone.

"But if there was," Luca persisted. "If you didn't have to get married."

Something prompted Matti to turn around and look more closely. Luca was a knot of pale limbs, one hand encircling the opposite wrist and wringing it. He looked awkward. Vulnerable.

Matti was not sure, all of a sudden, what he was being asked. And he couldn't dredge up the courage within himself to drag this conversation even more explicitly into the realm of personal declarations. Luca was probably not offering—anything.

I don't think either of us is looking for serious, Luca had said, in the sea bath.

"If," Matti said, granting the premise despite his better judgement, "then I *would* like to see what else is out there in the world, apart from what I've been doing for the past ten years."

Luca climbed out of the bed. The sight of his casually naked body made desire throb weakly in Matti, and it settled into something soft and bittersweet as Luca walked right up to Matti and lifted his face demandingly, close enough to press his bare chest up against Matti's clothed one. Matti kissed him, wrapped him up in his arms. He had never been with anyone before who sought as many kisses as Luca, who seemed content to spend so much time on them.

"I meant it. I wouldn't mind if time stopped right now," Matti said, when he'd kissed his fill.

"Would time let me put some clothes on first?"

"No." Matti ran a hand over the lower half of Luca's spine, then down over the firm muscles. "Time would prefer you in exactly this state, Mr. Piere."

"How about in that scarf?" Luca teased. "*Just* the scarf. Nothing else. Oh, you like that idea? *Ah.* Fuck, Matti." He tilted his head back and let out a soft groan, encouraging, as Matti sucked over the pulse on Luca's neck, feeling the slightest scratch of morning stubble; nothing compared to his own. Matti burned to leave another mark on Luca's easily markable skin. He wanted to order Luca to wear the scarf for the rest of the week, and to think of Matti whenever the silk brushed over the bruise.

That felt like a step too far.

When Matti released him, Luca looked at the clothing strewn around the room and laughed. "I'll have to put my ball finery back on to begin with. I haven't got any other clothes in here. Go on, you leave. I'll make sure the coast is clear, then I'll go back to my own room and wash up properly."

"Then come down to breakfast and be charming at my betrothed's family." Matti made himself say the word deliberately. "And tomorrow we'll be back in the city."

"And in thirteen days I'll stand up at your wedding."

Yes, Matti told himself. *Remember what this is, and what this isn't.*

He almost wanted to stretch out his hand to be shaken. It felt like an amiable bargain, an agreement being made that would benefit everyone. It didn't have to be as complicated, as overwhelming, as Matti had feared. He'd always known this couldn't be anything more than a brief, precious window of pleasure.

And Matti *was* benefiting. Here was Luca Piere, gorgeous and dishevelled and fresh from Matti's bed, his lip reddened with Matti's kisses.

There was no reason for Matti to feel aching and hollow, as though hearing a mourning song being rehearsed in another room.

"And in the meantime?" he heard himself ask.

"Two good weeks in spring." Luca smiled. His rainy eyes were dark. "Figuratively speaking. Let's make the most of them, shall we?"

CHAPTER
15

"Enough. We should stop for the day."

Luca lowered his sword and wiped sweat from his forehead. Matti sounded half-winded, and he was bent over, breathing with his hands braced on his legs. He'd let Luca push him hard today, and Luca had been in the mood to push.

Honestly, Luca had half expected not to be working with swords at all, in these last couple of weeks before Matti's wedding. It was hardly the best way to take advantage of their remaining time before Matti vowed himself to Sofia and became officially off-limits.

But Matti hadn't been lying when he said he enjoyed the sword lessons. So the sword lessons continued.

And if Luca sometimes rewarded good form with a brush of his fingers against the front of Matti's trousers, or if he tested Matti's concentration during the basic forms by giving an explicit litany of how he'd fucked himself on his own oiled fingers the previous night . . . well, that was simply him exploring novel teaching methods.

"By the way," said Matti, when he straightened up. "I have something for you. A gift."

Luca thought vividly and immediately of the green scarf and the fading mark on his hip. Matti crossed to where his jacket was folded over the sword rack, and pulled something from one pocket, which he then held out to Luca. It looked like the kind of fuzzy ball meant to amuse a baby or a cat. Its true nature was only apparent when Luca turned it in his hands.

"Socks," said Luca. "Congratulations, Mattinesh, you have

achieved an originality in gift-giving previously only achieved by my brother, who I suspect only gives socks as a form of protest to people who don't appreciate his taste in wine, and—actually," as Luca's fingertips finally caught up with his mouth, "these are lovely. I've never felt anything like this."

"It's gold-foot lambswool from the Barlow territories," said Matti.

Luca inspected the socks with a greater degree of interest. The wool was so soft and slippery he wanted to rub his cheek against it, and it was dyed the blue of winter skies.

"For the cold, when it comes." One of Matti's dimples peeked through. "To prevent chilblains."

For once nothing flippant lined itself up to emerge from Luca's mouth. It was such a simple gesture and Matti had delivered it so casually. Luca remembered Maya with her precious basket of cherries, and how she'd spoken of Marko's fondness for the fruit. Luca rubbed the wool between his fingers again and wondered with an aching pang if this was what it was like to be part of Matti's family, where the language of love was these small personal details.

Was there really no way for them to hold on to a semblance of friendship, past Matti's wedding? In ten days' time, when Matti was married and Sofia's bond price paid, Matti would have money enough to pay for his own sword lessons—legitimate ones. Maybe Luca could persuade him that instead of engaging someone who actually knew how to teach, he could keep Luca on. Luca was improving. They'd both said it.

Maybe Luca would manage to be satisfied with that; maybe he would somehow manage to have Matti in his life without constantly wanting to be kissed against walls and ordered around. Maybe he would be able to touch Matti, guiding him through each motion, without longing for another kind of touch entirely. Without taking what he wanted.

And maybe the snow clouds of Barlow's winter would come and envelop Glassport in a summer's-end blizzard.

Stop planning, Luca told himself fiercely. *You'll just disappoint yourself.*

He went and took demanding hold of Matti's shirt front. "Thank you for the socks, Mr. Jay. A very thoughtful gift. It almost makes up for the fact that I can think of three better ways that I could have worked you into a sweat this morning."

Matti laughed and took Luca's face in his hands. Gods, Luca was never going to get enough of the way Matti kissed him. It was like standing in the direct beam of a lantern. Deep, hot kisses, leaving no part of Luca's mouth unexplored, until Luca was nearly gasping.

"Come over tonight," Luca said, once he'd been released.

"Not tonight," Matti said, rueful. He raised a hand above his shoulder and let the fingers fly wide. Maya had made the same gesture. Like the ear flicking, it seemed to be part of the Jay language of physical expression. "The daughter of one of our buyers is holding a dinner party. Maya and I have promised to show our faces."

"House duty calls." Luca tucked two fingers into the closest gap in Matti's shirt, just far enough to find skin. "Tomorrow night?"

Matti reached down and closed his hand over Luca's. Luca could hardly be blamed for seizing the opportunity to lift their joined hands to his mouth, letting his lips drag thoughtfully over Matti's knuckle.

"Tomorrow," Matti agreed, with a gratifying hitch in the word.

Luca went back to his boardinghouse for breakfast. He was tempted to stop by Erneska's for raskils, but he, too, was learning what it was to be aware of how much money was left in his purse, and at least the Vaunts included breakfast in the rent. His next job through Tolliver's wasn't for another few days. Luca, who had always lived on an extremely generous allowance, had discovered his least favourite part of the duellist's lifestyle: the fact that one had to rely on infrequent large payments instead of a steady income. Which meant planning. Budgeting. Doing sums.

So far Luca had chosen "just don't buy anything extravagant and hope for the best" as his approach. So far, it was working. He'd deal with any crises as they arose. He always had his less legitimate skill set to fall back on, after all.

And he was planning to give those skills a good airing today.

Luca wrote a letter as he sat at the dining table. It was quiet. The only other person eating at that time was Daz Haslai, one of the other long-term boarders: a tiny young person with wide cheekbones and the dangling Daz earrings of those Ashfahani who declined to be named either male or female. They were half a year away from finishing their physician's training, and their pile of books put Luca's single sheet of paper to shame. Crumbs of daisy-cake and the occasional drip of coffee tumbled from their lips as they read, muttered, and stabbed their finger at the pages.

Dinah Vaunt refilled Luca's cup of coffee and leaned against the table next to him, eyes unabashedly curious on his letter. Luca relaxed his hand, paused, dashed off a signature that looked nothing like his own, and then flapped a hand over the ink to dry it.

"Any exciting plans for today, Miss Vaunt?" he asked, to distract her.

"Mama's decided we'll be cleaning the windows and rugs, how absolutely thrilling. And I was meant to be meeting Stefan this evening, but apparently the theatre's director is having some sort of tantrum and all the sets have to be rebuilt and repainted before the new play opens next week, so I won't see him for days."

"The scoundrel," said Luca, sipping coffee. "Abandoning a lovely girl for such fripperies as paid employment. Allow me to comfort you in your hour of desolation."

Dinah made a threatening motion with the coffee pot. She never took Luca's flirtation seriously, and was just as likely to flirt back as to pretend offence, depending on her mood. "What about you? Going to stab anyone today?"

Across the table, Daz Haslai appeared to decide that they couldn't study under these conditions, or possibly realise they were late for a lecture; they threw back the rest of their cup and swept out of the room with their armful of books.

Luca considered a couple of amusing lies about his plans for the day, but the truth would do just as well. "I'm looking into something for my friend. The one who's visited me here a few times."

"Ooh, Mattinesh Jay." Dinah's tongue curled around Matti's name as though she liked the sound of it. She glanced in the direction of the kitchen before pulling out a chair and sitting next to Luca. She took a hard-boiled egg from the bowl and began to peel it. "Mr. Mattinesh Jay who's engaged to Miss Sofia Cooper. And you're his best man."

"That's right." Luca had learned Dinah and her friends were a rich archipelago of information about the people of the city. "What else do you know? What's the gossip about him?" he asked. "You hear everything."

Dinah shook both salt and pepper over her denuded egg and took a bite. She chewed slowly and swallowed primly. "I've got ears. *And* eyes. If your handsome House friend Mr. Jay snapped his fingers at me, I wouldn't be waiting around for an apprentice set painter, I can tell you that."

Luca's letter was dry now. He folded it carefully in three and put in inside his coat as Dinah, between bites of her egg, told him what was generally known about Matti. That he did most of the work of Jay House, which was going through a rough period at the moment—Dinah's friend Elodie's cousin's husband had been laid off as a weaver from one of their workshops—but which was still talked of as a good, solid, respected House. That this marriage was obviously a business match to help shore up Jay House's fortunes, given that everyone *knew* Sofia Cooper was tragically in love with the penniless son of Jay's agent.

"And of course everyone knows he'll challenge at the wedding." Dinah heaved an envious sigh. "Osta's open palms, what I'd give to be there. Don't you feel a *little* bit bad for your part in it?

Standing in the way of true love, all so these big Houses can keep marrying their children off for profit?"

Luca had bitten his tongue at the first mention of Adrean. "It's the job."

Dinah frowned in disapproval at Luca's lack of a romantic soul. "You said you're on business for the Jays today? Is it something for the wedding?"

"In a way," said Luca. "I'm hoping I can find a wedding gift."

"This is Glassport," said Dinah, lofty with local pride. "You'll find something. Where are you going to start?"

Luca beamed. "The library."

———— ·»·≫·◊·◊·«·«· ————

True to his word—in this instance, at least—Luca started his day at the Glassport City Library. He'd not been inside any of Cienne's libraries since he left school, but he remembered the atmosphere, a kind of busy, ponderous quiet that made him want to drop crockery on the polished floor simply for the satisfaction of the noise. The entry hall led to a pair of crossed staircases beneath a huge, arch-shaped clear window, and through a door in the centre Luca could glimpse an even larger room full of desks and lamps. In the middle of the entry hall was a circular desk.

"Excuse me," Luca said to the person seated behind it. "Do you have newspaper archives here?"

This man did not look like Luca's idea of a librarian. He was large, with hair the colour of cured leather pulled back in a rough ponytail, and he had an attractively stubborn square jaw.

"We certainly do." The librarian fumbled for a pair of glasses and put them on. "Can I help you with something?" The eyes behind the glasses swept over Luca in an appreciative way that Luca wanted to pull into his lungs like the smell of bread.

"Oh," Luca said, just the wrong side of suggestive. "I *do* hope so."

Luca quickly learned that the large librarian's name was Jem, and also that librarians and archivists fell under the auspices of

Ibur, like bookbinders and printers, although in some of the more northern cities they aligned themselves with Hazi instead. Jem himself had little patience for writers and their god.

Luca nodded his way earnestly through this explanation, admiring the thickness of Jem's thighs as the man led him into the newspaper archives and showed him the indexing system. Under normal circumstances he'd be flirting with real intent. Jem was precisely his type. But he felt only a mild, dismissible spike of interest. Trying to imagine Jem's large hands—so careful with the index cards—on his body, he ended up thinking longingly of Matti instead.

"Ships, lost at sea." Jem handed over a small stack of cards. "We haven't indexed by anything else, so you'll have to look through them to find the ones mentioning Fataf, but if it's in the *Gazette* archives you can assume it's relevant to Glassport society in some way."

"I'm sure I'll manage." Luca gifted Jem with a smile. "Thank you so much."

He'd told the librarian he was a research assistant from a university in Sanoy. At least that persona matched the shabbiness of Luca's coat. When Jem had disappeared back to the main desk, Luca laid that coat over the back of a chair—Glassport's weather was cooling, as the summer grudgingly made way for autumn, but it was warm and stuffy in this archive room—and set about finding what he needed.

Maya had been right. The *Isadonna* was the most recent of five ships to be lost with all hands, and never recovered, in the crossing between the port cities of Fataf and Glassport. All five of them had been mentioned in the *Glassport Gazette,* even if it was only a throwaway inch of space in the shipping news column. Luca jotted down their names and the dates of the reported wrecks, and didn't linger in the room. The quiet was making his ears itch.

He did linger at the entry desk on the way out, leaning on the inlaid leather surface of it to thank Jem again. No harm in leaving a good impression.

From there Luca made his way down to the dockside neighbour-hoods, where the streets narrowed and the harbour was visible in glinting slices, the air thicker with the smell of salt and fish. He asked directions to the harbourmaster's office, where he changed his cover story to that of a put-upon clerk from one of the larger insurance companies, here with a letter of instruction from his superiors.

"I might need to come back and look at the details of ships that were merely crippled, or had their cargo damaged to the point where it couldn't be sold on, but for now I'm just looking at those which have sunk without trace. Five in all. The *Good Hearth,* the *Lucretia,* the—"

"Harbour records are public access," said the harbourmaster's secretary, a bored-looking blond boy with the stained fingertips that bespoke a golden-tar habit. He barely glanced at the letter that Luca had taken such pains with at the breakfast table, and jerked his thumb in the direction of an open door. "Help yourself. Hope you've got dates, 'cause otherwise you'll be paging through the stuff until you go blind."

Luca ducked his head with the impatient gratitude of someone whose job depended on not making trouble, and scurried through the door with a mild jab of disappointment that it hadn't been more of a challenge. When he located the records room, he could see what the boy had meant. The harbourmaster's records filled a room cramped with shelves, each one holding a series of large, thick leather-bound books.

The records were, indeed, arranged by date. Nobody was watching Luca; there was nobody to see if he went straight for the ill-fated *Isadonna* and her cargo of black libelza wool, but some mixture of mischief and pride made him seek and write down the same details for the other four ships.

Date of voyage lodgement. Date of leaving Fataf. Expected date of arrival in Glassport. Date ship classified as lost. Name of House financing the voyage, if applicable. Name of House from whom the ship was hired.

After a moment's thought, Luca took down one of the newest record books, which covered the week he himself had arrived in Glassport. It took longer to find what he was looking for this time, but eventually he found a single entry noting that the *Lady Jenny* had arrived on a return voyage from Elluthe, having been hired from Lior House for the use of Jessamy House.

"Hah," Luca said to the empty room. "Maybe someone is moving a lot of parts after all."

As he was about to flick the book closed, Luca's eye snagged on the name of Mantel House. He checked the name of the shipping House, too, and smiled. This room was about as far as Luca's vague planning had taken him, but the next step had just suggested itself.

He bought a lunch of spiced fish and onions wrapped in flatbread from a street vendor, then made his way back to the boardinghouse, where he changed his worn clothes for a much nicer shirt and a navy blue jacket that he'd been given to stand swordguard at a naming ceremony. Luca's wardrobe had expanded in odd directions since he'd arrived in Glassport. He let his fingers brush over the waistcoat in forest-green satin, cool and perfectly cut and never worn, that he would don to fulfil his duties as Matti's best man.

Dinah and her mother were in the courtyard, Dinah clearly relieving her feelings in regards to Stefan by whacking the daylights out of several rugs. Luca indulged in an action that would have lost him his precious canal-view room, if he were caught, and picked the lock of another boarder's room in order to liberate Mr. Heughnessy's spare glasses from his bedside table. Heughnessy was an elderly teacher, on the verge of retirement, who loved to tell stories about his travels and about his large, ungrateful, disappointing family. Luca had spent a few evenings in the man's room, being a good audience and drinking tea. He knew exactly where the glasses were—and the bottle of hair oil as well.

Soberly clad, hair slicked down, document bag slung over his shoulder, Luca retraced his steps a few blocks, back in the direction of the harbour. He stopped in front of a large, square, redbrick building that stood just shy of a street corner. The faded lettering across the front of the building proclaimed LIOR.

Luca paused outside the front door to slip the glasses on. He took a breath and let his brother's persona settle over him. The playacting at the library and the harbour office had been more for fun and deniability than anything else. Public access was public access, and there was nothing incriminating or unusual in what Luca had discovered so far. This would be the *really* fun part.

He didn't bother to knock. He pushed the door open and strode inside.

The ground floor was a warren of desks and people and squat brick pillars in place of supporting walls. Luca imagined a wooden rod holding his head atop his spine and stalked towards the desk directly in front of the entrance.

"Hello. I'm here on behalf of Mantel House. Who can show me the way to your client records room?"

"Sorry, what do you need with our records?"

The girl behind the desk had an astonishing pile of red-blond hair that clashed badly with her yellow shirt. Mr. Heughnessy's glasses were not strong, but Luca could already feel a strain behind his eyes as he focused on her face. He tried to channel that into an expression of impatience.

"Nothing I want to explain three times. Who am I speaking to?"

"My name is Erica Lior," she said, vocally holding her House membership out like a shield.

"Very well, Miss Lior. I want to speak to your Head of House."

"He's not available right now." Erica rang a bell on her desk and an even younger woman dashed up. "Fetch Uncle Dan," Erica said. She was trying to hold eye contact with Luca, but Luca let his gaze sweep over the room and his lip twitch towards his nose as though he were finding the entire scene wanting but would never be so vulgar as to say so aloud.

The next person to stride up to the central desk, where they were beginning to gather an audience of sidelong glances, was a burly man with a brown waistcoat and the general air of a relaxed highwayman.

"Danforth Lior," he introduced himself. "What seems to be the problem?"

"My name is Persemaine Mantel. My mother-in-law is Genevieve Mantel." The two Liors exchanged a look that Luca felt was promisingly alarmed. "You may know her as the woman who is currently considering her options for when our shipping contract comes up for renewal."

"Mr. Mantel," said Lior, with a new slathering of respect over his voice. "We are quite used to doing business with Mantel House's agents in Glassport—"

"I'm quite sure you are. And I had quite assumed that *my* personal presence here now, to audit the records of your House's work on behalf of my own, would emphasise for you the seriousness with which my Head of House takes her contractual relationships."

Luca was raising his voice, even as he hammered all the personality out of it beyond the spirit of disapproval. Their surreptitious audience had become one where people were pausing halfway across the floor or looking up from their own conversations in order to watch.

"Is there some particular concern?"

"Oh, certainly, I'll just shout my business on your public floor for the world to hear, shall I?"

Lior was beginning to look grimly flustered. "Perhaps if you come this way, sir, to my office—"

Sir. Luca had this one in hand. He heaved a sigh, now enjoying himself thoroughly. "My time, *sir,* is both limited and valuable. I'm sure you understand that. Or perhaps"—with a glance up and down the man's outfit, which if Luca was honest was perfectly unobjectionable, if rather dull—"you do not."

Behind the desk, Erica Lior blanched. Her uncle weathered it better. "Our client records are stored on the next floor," he said, and gestured Luca to a corner staircase with an open arm.

Luca steered his haughty gait towards it. "And you keep duplicates offsite, I would hope." He sniffed.

Danforth Lior knew how to handle himself in front of a representative of one of Thesper's most prosperous Houses. He managed to keep his face straight as he led Luca through the building, though his temper manifested itself in the force with which he shoved the door of the record room open.

A girl wearing trousers and a lavender tunic was atop a stepladder on one side of the room. At the bang of the door hitting the wall, she jumped, and a pile of papers and folders slid from her arms and fell to the floor, where it slithered in every direction like she'd dropped a jar of papery snakes.

"Rikke," Lior barked. "Itsa's crown, girl, will you get hold of yourself?"

Rikke climbed quickly down. She was skinny and coltish with two plaits of Harbekan white-blond hair. "Sorry, I'm sorry."

"You'll give Mr. Mantel whatever assistance he requires," Lior ordered. He nodded at Luca and then strode away, transparently relieved that Luca was someone else's problem now.

Luca caught the hastily stifled poison on the girl Rikke's face as she watched Danforth Lior leave. Just as hastily, he dropped the Persemaine expression from his own. He'd replaced it with something a lot warmer by the time Rikke looked at him.

"Here, let me give you a hand," he said, and moved forward to start scooping up papers.

Rikke was nearly smiling by the time they'd set all the paper on a table. "Mantel House? I like your mirth-flower soap."

"Thank you, Rikke. It's always nice to hear that our products are appreciated." Luca jerked his head towards the door. "*He* doesn't seem the appreciative type, in general."

"No," said Rikke. "No, he isn't."

Luca smiled and levelled a sympathetic look at her over the top of his stolen glasses. It made his eyes feel better. "Some people don't realise how hard clerks work, do they?"

It was wonderful, Luca thought five minutes later, how happy people were to talk about themselves, and how much you could steer them into doing for you while the talking was taking place. In addition to mirth-flower soap, Rikke Galoys loved and had strong opinions about raskils; she swore by Agate Lane Bakery, and made a dismissive snort at the mention of Erneska's. She had worked as primary archiving clerk for nearly two years and she was not, obviously, a named member of Lior House.

"Mama was, though."

"Oh?" Luca asked, encouraging, as she passed him down a thick folder of records. She did not seem to care at all that none of what Luca had asked for so far related in any way to Mantel House. "What happened?"

"She had a screaming row or seven with Grandpa Giles. She went for an outdoor wedding, to enrage him—said she'd rather wear a name with no status than wear his for a moment longer—and Dad loved her enough to go along with it."

An outdoor wedding, so named because it involved someone leaving their House and not entering another, was remarkably rare. Most people married *in,* not *out.* Luca gave an appreciative nod. "So what are you doing back here working for them?"

Another almost-smile. "Enraging *her,*" Rikke said. "Or mending bridges. Depends who you ask."

Soon Luca was ensconced at a table with records spread in front of him, taking yet more notes as Rikke re-sorted and re-filed her mess of dropped paper. He found the records relating to the final voyage of the *Isadonna,* ship of Lior House, contracted out to Jay House. He took down the names of its crew members and some of the details of the contract, which had been signed by—yes— Corus Vane, on behalf of his employer.

The very first record of the *Lady Jenny,* which took Luca and

Rikke nearly half an hour to track down, showed it entering Glassport on a short trip from Port Gull, several months after the wreck of the *Isadonna*. The client listed for that voyage was Kesey House.

Sometimes people were just lazy enough, Luca thought. Something sweet and pleased happened in his gut, like a trickle of new-brewed cider.

The records relating to Lior's purchase of their ships were, Rikke told him, probably in a cabinet in the acquisitions office. Luca waved her offer to fetch it aside; he didn't actually need it, and it would call attention to what he was digging into. He set himself to taking down the *Lady Jenny*'s details and crew members instead. That done, he asked idly if Lior did any work for Martens House—no, was the answer, the Martenses had their long-term shipping contract with Kenninck House—and then tapped his finger on the folder for a while before asking for all the contracts with Mantel House for the past year. Other than providing cover, they'd be useless to his present purpose, but maybe he'd find something he could use to needle his brother with later. Perse hated not being the most knowledgeable person in a room.

Despite the fact that this was a lot like schoolwork, like House work, Luca's enjoyment was undiminished. Somehow it made a difference to be doing it on someone else's behalf. And nobody was standing over his shoulder, forcing him to look at rows and columns of figures and insisting that it was *easy,* that it was *essential* for Luca to understand, and if he'd just *concentrate*—

This, though. This was people. This was disguises, and slipperiness, and stories. Luca could handle those any day.

chapter 16

Six days more.

Matti regarded Luca down the length of two swords, trying to remember five things at once and knowing he was probably failing at three of them. But Luca's tongue wet his lips in a blatant attempt at distraction and Matti couldn't bring himself to care overmuch. He was going to enjoy himself here, now, while he could.

Six days more.

"You're not concentrating, Mr. Jay."

"I am," Matti protested, not quite truthfully. He would concentrate for hours on Luca's mouth, if given the option. The previous night he'd watched that mouth stretch blissfully around his cock, then let it gasp broken words against his own as Luca worked himself to completion between Matti's oiled thighs.

"Show me a Sugeen Graze," Luca commanded.

Matti forced his attention back to the present. He took a deep breath and attacked, engaging Luca's blade from the distal end and concentrating on the angle as he stepped closer, trying to keep a steady pressure as Luca resisted. He didn't fool himself that Luca wasn't making it easy for him, but there was still a pang of satisfaction as Matti finished the move, ending up with Luca's blade forced sideways in a way that would take a few seconds to recover from. Luca nodded and stepped back.

Luca thought he was silly for wanting to keep going with these lessons, but Matti still loved them for what they were, as well as the chance to tease and talk, to drink in Luca's graceful competence, to hear Luca laugh.

And there were other advantages.

"I still don't think I've quite grasped how to direct the angle from the shoulder," Matti said. "You should take your shirt off and show me again."

"*Should* I," murmured Luca. "Is that what your money buys you this morning?"

Matti held Luca's dancing gaze, feeling desire flare in his blood. "Yes, I think it does," he said. "Well?"

Luca laughed. "Land a point using that graze and I'll take it off."

Matti assumed a ready stance and Luca did the same. Matti was still mustering a verbal riposte that wasn't something too raw and too honest—*I could look at you forever, I would do this forever*—when the door into Tolliver's main office opened and a slender man stepped through it, then paused once he'd let it close quietly behind him. Luca's back was to the door. He didn't notice, didn't turn around.

The newcomer wore a grey coat, high-collared and severe, open over a dark blue waistcoat with pearl buttons that gleamed expensively in the light, and a pair of matching grey trousers whose lines had the heaviness of good wool. His slicked-back hair was the colour of old bronze and his face was familiar.

"Concentrate," said Luca in his most laughing-lecturing tone. "You're not looking at me, Mattinesh. I don't believe you're serious about winning your prize at all."

The man behind Luca rolled his eyes. "Oh, for gods'— *Lucastian Harte.*"

There was a clatter as Luca's sword fell to the ground. It was a sound so familiar that Matti looked at his own hand, momentarily confused at the continuing presence of the hilt there. Usually he was the one doing the dropping.

Matti thought about saying something. He thought about *feeling* something. He felt . . . nothing. His mind held a spreading numb blankness like a pool of ice water.

Luca had spun when the name was uttered. He was staring at the newcomer, though he kept darting little looks at Matti over his shoulder, and he looked pale, as though the ice water had come for him, too, and had started with his face. Which was to an uncanny extent the same as the face on the grey-suited man.

"Perse," said Luca. "What—what are you doing here?"

"I'd say I'm surprised," said the man thus addressed, gesturing at the sword rack with an efficient flick like a backhand slap delivered to the air, "but honestly, Luca, I'm afraid I was expecting something like this."

Luca screwed his eyes shut, then opened them. "*Perse.* I need you to leave. Just—go down to the street. I'll meet you there. I need a few minutes."

Perse looked from Luca to Matti and back. "Fine. A few," he said, frostily. "But I'll do my waiting on the other side of this door, just in case you get any foolish ideas about sneaking out the back."

Then he was gone, back through the door, and Luca looked at Matti and Luca's expression changed, *twisted,* at whatever he saw in Matti's face.

"Harte," Matti said, trying it out.

"I—"

"Lucastian Harte."

He knew the name. He'd never attached a face to it, though; he'd never had any reason to.

"Matti." Luca was standing with his palms outstretched like someone trying to soothe a horse.

For a sudden furious moment, lightning emerging from nowhere to herald the storm's arrival, all that Matti could see was a broken pocket watch with an elaborate swirling *H* on its cover.

"Pick up your sword."

"Matti—"

"I decide when we're done," Matti said, the words like shards of glass in his mouth. *"Pick it up."*

Slowly, Luca crouched and closed his fingers around the sword hilt. He kept his eyes on Matti as he did so. He kept them on Matti as he stood.

Matti felt as though something colder than metal had been set between his ribs and was being pressed, inch by inch, into his heart. Duelling had always seemed like a pleasant, archaic pastime, something in the realm of ceremony and exercise. A series of forms to be learned so that one could face an opponent, smiling, and have the satisfaction of the dance: attack and parry, feint and score.

But no—that wasn't what swords were for. That had never been what they were for. Swords were for the moments like this, when all of Matti burned with the grim desire to inflict harm. He remembered, like being struck by a reflection lunging out of a mirror, the first time he had stood in this room—furious and embarrassed about being conned into betraying his family's trust—and thrown his anger at Luca down the length of two swords.

Matti had learned a few things since then.

He picked an attack at random. The precise pattern of his feet and the calculated angle of the sword tip were things he might have been proud of, an hour ago.

Luca turned him away with a mastery that seemed like contempt.

Matti gritted his teeth and attacked again. More force, this time. More emotion. Less control. He wanted to cry and to shout, and to be anything other than this lumbering ball of need to damage. But one of the things Matti had learned was exactly how outclassed he was when Luca was fighting at his true capacity, and somehow it made him angrier when Luca just kept parrying and parrying, turning him easily aside with no attempt to strike any blows of his own, driving home Matti's worthlessness.

"What?" Matti demanded. "You'll only fight properly when it suits you?"

"I don't *want* to fight," Luca said. *Clash.* "I want to talk."

"Oh, I'm sure you do." Matti's heart ached. "Do you think I'm going to let you spin me another story?"

Luca lowered his brows and abruptly turned a parry into a movement Matti had never seen before, so sinuous and incredibly quick that Matti knew it was going to disarm him. Knowing it didn't help at all.

Now it *was* Matti's sword, clattering. Something about the showy care with which Luca then crouched and placed his own sword on the ground—the consideration shown to a length of lifeless metal—stuck in Matti's gullet and burned there.

"Stop it," Luca said, impatient. "If you'll just let me explain—"

Matti didn't want to listen. Matti wanted to fight.

He didn't realise what he was doing until it was happening. His hands felt iron-gloved as he shoved forward. If he was a mediocre duellist then he was no wrestler at all, but along with his height and weight he had the advantage of absolute surprise, and Luca tripped backwards clumsily when they collided. Matti had enough time to realise that their legs were too close together, too entangled, before he found himself toppling forward as well.

Luca gave a short cry that sounded more surprised than pained when he hit the floor, followed by a more breathless *oof* as part of Matti's weight landed on him. Matti had managed to get one arm out to catch himself as he fell, but the angle was bad, and jarring force fled up from his wrist. He put his weight on it anyway, propped awkwardly, one of his thighs still between both of Luca's.

With his free hand he hit Luca across the face.

"Ow—*fuck*," yelped Luca. He wriggled an arm in between them and tried to shove Matti off. When that didn't work, he kicked.

Matti's head was a haze of hot vengeance and something like a silent, dismayed scream. His body, however, was an idiot thing that knew exactly how it felt about having Luca writhing beneath it. It produced a quick surge of arousal, followed by an equally strong coil of disgust and hurt.

"All right," Luca panted. "Fine. I deserved that. Can I explain now? Look, I know, I *know* I didn't—"

"No," said Matti, cutting him off.

"Will you just—"

"*No.*" He wasn't going to give Luca a chance to drop more lies into his ears. He lifted the hand again; Luca flinched. Still Matti's body was responding, like a wheel set spinning and never told to stop, to the sensation of Luca stretched out beneath him. Still he wanted to drag Luca's hand above his head by the wrist, with its capable tendons, and bite Luca's mouth. Luca's coloured cheeks and parted lips, the sound of his breath, the vulnerability of his fingers . . . somehow all of this now appeared, sickeningly, like a manipulation.

And how very easily Matti had let himself be manipulated, even with his eyes wide open.

Matti shoved himself away and climbed to his feet. His wrist ached. The words that burst from him were an accusation directed as much at himself as at Luca.

"I should have known, I suppose. When I first *met* you, you were running a con! On me!" A new, awful chill grabbed Matti all over. "Of course. You knew who I was. Even then."

"I didn't!"

"I don't believe you."

"I *didn't.*" Luca was on his feet as well. He grabbed a handful of his own hair, looking desperate and furious with frustration. He was a good actor. He was almost wasted on the fabric trade.

"What was that business with the Vanes and the Keseys, anyway? Sowing discord, weakening my House? You just *happened* to overhear a conversation at a ceremony." Nausea was rising in Matti's throat. "You could have planted those papers yourself."

"Of course I fucking didn't," Luca snapped. "You know I didn't, you were *there,* Matti, *think.*"

Matti couldn't think. All his thoughts jabbed at him like needles. "Harte House is about to be in direct competition with mine, and the heir apparent shows up in Glassport and—and wheedles his way into my bed? Is that it? Listens to me talk about all my business *troubles,*" he spat, throat aching with horror. "Good information, for the bargain price of letting me fuck you a couple of times."

"Matti," Luca said, strained. "No. I came here—I—it had nothing to do with any of this. Nothing to do with your House, or mine."

"Then *why did you lie?*" Matti shouted.

Luca's lips parted. Nothing emerged from them.

The last piece of hope in Matti had shattered. Nothing was left but this shell of anger, hardening over the well of terrible hurt. "Why else would you be here, giving me lessons, pretending you need my money? You *don't* need it. Everyone knows how well Harte House is doing."

"Just like everyone knows that Jay House is only going through a rough period?" Luca flung back.

Matti's pulse drummed in his ears. That was a threat.

Luca stood straighter, shoulders back. He pressed his advantage. "I lied about my name. You've been lying to everyone for years. You're just too hypocritical to face the fact that your family is running a con greater than anything I ever pulled in my short, stupid career. *The Jays are good at seeming.*"

Matti struggled to hold himself steady, trying to absorb that. There was something in Luca's face that he recognised from their lessons. Luca had seen a weakness in Matti's guard and was going to use it to prove a point.

This is going to hurt, Matti told himself. *Brace.*

But he'd never had any hope at all of protecting himself from Luca's attacks.

"You lied *for* them and you lied *to* them, and for what? So you could have a life so fucking boring and narrow that you had to pay someone to be your friend."

"Be quiet." Matti could barely force the air out. He wished, horribly, that he hadn't caught the flash of naked regret in Luca's eyes as those words erupted like bile beneath them. "Be quiet."

Luca shifted his weight and touched his own mouth. His hand formed a fist. His eyes flashed with something uglier. "And you're right: at least you *knew* I was a con. You knew I was a liar. You're angry because you were so desperate to believe in the story you told yourself about who I was. About what this— *Fuck*." Luca half spun, as though the ground were too warm for his feet to touch it for long.

"Yes. Fine," Matti said. "I'm naive and boring and can't see my enemies when they're in front of my eyes." Luca flinched. Matti was viciously glad. "You and Corus Vane can both be very pleased with yourselves."

"Now you're being ridiculous. I'm not—"

"Not what?"

"Matti—"

"People I know call me Matti. You can call me Mr. Jay." Matti found steel in his spine, at last, and let it hold him rigid. "And I think you should leave now, *Mr. Harte*."

Luca's face moved through five different expressions. It ended on a snarl. "Fine," he spat. He left the practice sword on the floor, snatched up his own sheathed sword from the table, and didn't bother to attach it to his belt, just clutched it in his hand as he wrenched the door open and was gone through it.

"Luca—" Matti heard, and then someone running down the stairs, and then nothing.

Matti stood in the middle of the practice room, bathed in sunlight. His hands were trembling, his head still light with fury. His eyes didn't want to focus. He stood and waited for the panic to hit, waited for his breath to race away with itself and for his heart to do its best at exploding.

None of that happened. He just stood, once again ice-water

numb and shivering all over. He counted the number of swords in the wall rack: twenty-nine. He counted them from the other end: twenty-eight. Thinking was like trying to walk in a straight line after leaping off a carousel.

He had to cope with this, somehow. He had to fix it. It was his own stupid fucking mistake, and he *should have known better;* he should have known the gods hadn't meant to be kind when they shoved Luca into his path. Luca had stood here months ago and said, *I can do this for you,* and Matti's mouth had gone dry at the outrageous slippery beauty of him, and Matti had forgotten to be careful.

Matti had indulged himself. Look where it had gotten him.

A throat cleared itself. Hardy Tolliver was hovering in the doorway that Luca had left open.

"Uh. Mr. Jay. Is everything all right?" Tolliver's voice said that he knew it wasn't, but couldn't think of what else to say.

"It will be," Matti said. "Somehow."

After all, another lie could hardly make things worse at this point.

———— ⟫⟫◆◉◆⟪⟪ ————

The raskil on Luca's plate smelled of warm butter. Cheese seeped from its coils. The golden-brown pastry looked so crisp and good as to be mythical, something conjured by the gods to tempt hungry travellers.

Luca had never felt less hungry in his life.

He looked up and met his brother's eyes across the table. After Persemaine had followed Luca's stormy exit out of Tolliver's and down onto the street, he'd insisted on the two of them finding somewhere to talk over breakfast. Perse claimed not to have eaten yet, but he hadn't touched his own raskil either. Luca suspected his brother was labouring under the delusion that Luca wouldn't yell in public. Certainly *Perse* wouldn't raise his voice in public. You could probably count the number of times Perse had raised his voice in his entire *life* on your hands, and you'd still have enough fingers left to play cards with.

Perse should have known him better, after twenty-five years. Luca would yell if he felt like it. And right now he wanted to open his mouth and let his mortified fury surge out like a wave, but he kept his teeth clenched, kept it in.

If only he'd been able to exert the same kind of control over his voice in the practice room. Guilt at what he'd said had poured over him along with the sound of his own words, but what was he going to do, snatch them back? Some blows were unstoppable, once you'd begun.

"How did you find me?" Luca asked.

"There are only so many sword agencies. And you're not entirely unpredictable. And in addition to that, two days ago my mother-in-law got a deeply apologetic letter assuring her of Lior House's earnest desire to keep Mantel House's business, and begging to know what concerns arose that necessitated her sending *me* to Glassport to audit their records."

"Oh," said Luca.

"*Oh*," said Perse. "That did seem to have your fingerprints all over it. And once I got here, Mr. Tolliver was all too happy to tell me where his newest, redheaded duellist could be found most mornings."

"And so you stuck your nose in where it wasn't wanted." A certain amount of irony tried to crowd Luca's chest. "Did you really have to stand there and use my fucking name?"

"Yes, actually." Perse sat up straighter. "That's what I'm—"

"*Fuck*," Luca burst out, the disaster crashing over him anew. "Of all the people you could have— *Fuck*, Perse. Well done. You always did have a real fucking gift for ruining a good thing."

"Don't be childish." Perse frowned. "Is this about the man at the agency? Why would he care about your name?"

Luca choked out a laugh. His heel was tap-tap-tapping against the floor. "Because it means I've been spying on him, in the hopes of acquiring information about the wool industry that I can use to benefit my own House. Or take down his. Because there aren't enough people trying to do that already."

"Wool? Luca, you're not making any sense."

"I know! It *doesn't* make sense, but he's talking about it like he's heard credible rumours. Perse, we're not—I mean, Mama's not branching Harte House out into wool production, is she?"

Perse looked nonplussed. Luca felt a trickle of relief. He hadn't thought the prospect was likely, but if their mother had been considering anything of the sort, Perse would have known about it. Harte was no longer the House to which Perse owed his first allegiance, but he was uncomfortably omniscient and, more importantly, remained in close touch with their mother.

"Why would she do that?"

"I don't know. I thought perhaps it might have been one of Uncle Raibert's whistleweed schemes."

"Mama might let Raibert talk her into the occasional unwise experiment, but she has more than enough sense to draw the line at diversifying the House into a whole second line of products. And you've got some nerve to talk about schemes," Perse added.

Luca's jaw twitched. "I know."

"Sometimes I wish I'd been born the one with the same personality as Mama's favourite brother. It's the only reason I can think of why you've been so indulged."

The restlessness in Luca's legs crested. With great difficulty, he forced his hands flat on his thighs, pushing down, keeping himself from standing up and walking away. This was the usual point in any conversation with Perse where Luca got bored and angry and stormed out, making sure to get the last word, but failing to gain satisfaction from it. Perse's icy silences could strike you in the back of the neck, like a stone from a slingshot, as you were leaving the room.

"Indulged?"

"Yes, Luca. Indulged. She let you continually duck out of lessons and play at swords, and she told everyone to be patient with you, that you'd come around in time. And then when the time did come for you to finally *grow up* and start spending time on proper tasks, you just—I mean, do you even know what Mama had to *do,* to get you out of that idiotic situation you created with Andri Baudrain? Not to mention his entire Guild?"

"I—"

"Of course you don't," said Perse, withering. "You skipped off to the seaside and left your mess for other people to clean up. As per usual."

Luca's shoulder ached with potential as he imagined pulling his sword and having the point to Perse's neck, table and bakery patrons be damned. His brother would probably just curl his lip and tell Luca not to be foolish. There'd be none of that admiration that had lit Matti's eyes when Luca first demonstrated the basic forms.

Matti. Another tide of anger and despair rose in Luca's throat and then ebbed, leaving him with roughness and the taste of salt.

Luca braced himself. This was it. He hadn't run far enough or lied well enough. The consequences of his own stupid actions had taken their time in pursuit, but they'd caught up with him now, and they were about to close over him like the lid of an airless box. He said, "What did she do, then?"

"Pardon?"

Luca looked his older brother in the eye. He and Perse looked terribly, amusingly alike. Everyone had always said so. Perse's hair looked darker because he used oil to keep it smooth and flat, where Luca let it leap as it pleased. Perse dressed in sober layers and wore glasses, and Perse could add up a column of numbers as easy as blinking, and Perse was the disapproving bane of Luca's existence.

But he was, as much as Luca writhed against the idea, right about this. Luca was lazy. Luca had failed, and failed, and disappointed, and then run away because it was the easiest thing to do.

"What did Mama have to do?"

"Apart from repaying the Guild of Artificers twice over for materials and labour costs, and making a gift of new silk rugs for their Guildhall?" A pointed eyebrow rose. "Baudrain House now holds the glassware contract for the school of chemistry at the university. Mama called in a favour with Genevieve, she's got a lot of contacts there."

Luca winced. Jacquelle Harte hoarded favours like a gold-sprite from a myth. His mother would hold it over his head for years, if she'd had to waste one of them on him. And yet . . . "She made deals? That's it, no charges laid, it's all forgiven?"

"And forgotten," Perse said firmly.

Luca's cheeks burned. "Margot Baudrain saw me. She wouldn't have kept it quiet."

"No charges means no crime," said Perse. "Oh, there was some talk. Youthful spirits. An unfortunate lark, taken too far." He spread his hands in a what-did-you-expect? kind of gesture.

It was too easy. Surely. Surely it wasn't enough.

Then again, the crushing bad luck of having Perse walk in at that exact moment, with Luca's name on his lips . . . that had the scent of the gods to it, of past deeds coming due. Kusi had been waiting for Luca to build something he treasured so that she could raise an eyebrow and break it, as Luca had broken something of hers. The gods liked that kind of symmetry.

Please say we're even now, Luca thought. Prayed. *I haven't got much left to lose.*

Luca said, uneasy, "The last person who stole from Andri Baudrain was found with two broken arms."

"And I've no doubt they were a common thief. This is different," said Perse, impatient. "There's no point in pretending otherwise."

Money, and power, and a weighty name. These things had protected Luca even in his absence. Luca wondered what would have happened to Luca Piere, duellist and con artist, if he'd been the one to be glimpsed in the act of escaping from Baudrain's sprawling garden.

But nobody without a rich House's protection would be that stupid, would they? That was the *point* of the broken bones. And yet it had seemed like a game, at the time. Luca hadn't truly believed there would be any consequences to his actions until he'd locked eyes with Baudrain's daughter, as he was halfway over the garden wall, and seen the surprised recognition on her face.

"Why do you think I'm here, tracking you down?" Perse added.

"Because your adopted House doesn't need you to do anything useful?" Luca heard the nastiness slide off his tongue.

Perse pushed his glasses up his nose. "Because you can stop all this melodramatic silliness and come *home,* Luca. I was trying to *show* you that, when I used your real name instead of whatever false thing you've been living under. It's all been fixed. Nobody's going to call a magistrate on you, and you won't be hauled up in front of the Guild of Artisans either. Your housebreaking stunt can be laughed off as the childish prank it was, and you can start doing your job."

"I have a job here." Luca's lips were numb.

"Doing what? Physical labour? Giving sword lessons to anyone ignorant enough to believe you're anything but a dilettante?"

"I'm not leaving Glassport," Luca snapped.

"Luri's thumbs, Lucastian, will you just—"

"Won't even swear by Huna any more, will you?"

Perse rubbed his forehead. "Gods give me strength. Luca. Little though you may think it, I care about your well-being. I care about your future, and yes, the future of Harte House. I didn't throw aside every scrap of loyalty to our family when I got married, though the extent to which you resent me for it would seem to suggest you think I did."

"I," Luca said, and swallowed past something that was untrue. He *did* resent Perse. For doing something unexpected, when he'd always been the stable one, the dull one, the one who stayed within the lines. For vacating the manacles of his illustrious future and leaving Luca to step into them. For making Luca the heir apparent, when it was the last thing Luca was suited for. "I don't completely hate you," Luca muttered.

"I'm still your brother. I'm simply trying to help you see sense." Perse's stolid gaze bored into Luca. "Help me see *your* side, then. What have you managed to get yourself embroiled in, here, that's so important?"

Stuck with no alley to walk down but that of the truth, Luca explained. Not the part about the pocket watch con, and not the part where he and Matti had begun their relationship by ostensibly blackmailing each other. *Not* the part where he'd kissed Matti in the warm dawn and Matti had ordered him to be silent and Matti had danced with Luca at his Half Moon Ball and then made love to Luca instead of going to his betrothed's bed, and Luca had felt something inside himself shift and crumble, terrible and wonderful, and now he was barely holding himself together against the thought of how badly he'd fucked this all up.

He left out the investigations he'd been doing into the *Isadonna*'s fate; that was *personal,* that was *for Matti.* And, damn it, if Luca had been thinking clearly in the practice room, he would have tried to blurt out his half-baked findings when Matti was accusing him of—everything. Not that Matti had let him say much, by the end.

But Luca told his brother about the sword lessons, and the fact that he was engaged as Matti's best man, and most of what they'd discovered about Corus Vane's treachery and the Kesey fraud.

When Luca was done, Perse stared. His jaw looked as though it were considering dropping, which was a lot of facial expression for Perse.

Perse said, "Mattinesh Jay?"

"I didn't know he was—anyone!" Luca said. "It might sound ridiculous, but . . ."

"Oh, I believe you. I have complete faith that you've never paid a jot of attention to any of Mama's and Raibert's attempts to teach you the basic facts pertinent to the House you will someday be the Head of."

Luca pressed his hands more firmly against his legs, and his feet against the floor. Part of the action was reminding himself that his feet *could* touch the floor; that he was not a small child, legs dangling, making mutinous fork patterns in his gravy while Perse droned smugly on about the latest way in which Luca had been misbehaving at school.

"I gave him my word," Luca said. "He *needs* someone to stand up. He needs me."

The words escaped before he could remind himself that Matti had knocked him to the floor; that Matti had looked at him with hate in his eyes, and Luca had said awful things to him, and there was a good chance Matti would rather draw swords against Adrean Vane himself, and be humiliated, than speak to Luca ever again.

But that's not really true, is it? said a treacherous voice in Luca's mind. *He'll do whatever it takes for his family. He'll come back to you, because you're the best chance he's got. He* does *need you. And he'll hate you even more because of it.*

Luca felt sick. Perse gazed at him for long enough that Luca's legs gave up and began to dance silently against the floor again. Luca looked around the bakery. There was a couple nearby holding hands across the table, knuckles brushing a shared pot of chocolate. One of the women was speaking quietly, earnestly, and the other had spots of happy colour in her cheeks.

"I suppose that's honourable," said Perse finally. "But . . . a service job, really? You're a House member, Luca. You're better than that."

"Apparently," said Luca tightly, "I'm not."

"You're *smart*, I know you are. If you'd just bother to *apply* yourself—"

"I do apply myself."

Perse's eyes dropped to the pommel of Luca's sword. "Not to anything important."

"You don't know what's important to me," Luca said, dry-mouthed. "You don't— Oh, *gods*." He slid down in his chair, lifting both hands as though to scrub the sight of his brother from his eyes. As disguises went, it wasn't his best effort. He didn't think he could fake an accent or a facial expression right now if he were handed half a fortune, so covering it up was his only hope.

"Luca?"

"*Fuck*." Luca could have stabbed himself in the hand, because he sounded exactly like what he was: a man about to burst into unattractive tears.

After a long, long pause, during which Luca breathed wetly into his fingers and refused to relinquish the kind blacks and sparkling browns that were dancing on his closed eyelids, Perse coughed.

"I didn't think you cared much what other people thought of you."

"Why would you think *that*?" said Luca, bewildered. He flung his hands down into his lap and blinked defiantly at Perse. He probably looked blotchy and pinched. Just wonderful.

Perse ignored the question. "You gave him your word, you said. And you care that he might think you a fraud. He's important, Mattinesh Jay?"

"I am a fraud," Luca said, tired. "And I—yes, he's— Oh, why do I have to have this conversation with *you*, why couldn't it have been *anyone* else—" He shoved his hands up to his eyes again.

"Luca."

"Go away. Fuck off back to Cienne. If you make me talk about my feelings I'm going to sit here and choke to death on the irony, and then Mama will be forced to poach you back from the Mantels to be the House heir again."

There was a long pause. "I must say, this is a new kind of mess, even for you."

"If you're not going to leave, please at least shut up," said Luca, muffled, into his hands. "If you fucking try to lecture me about this, Perse, I swear—"

"Luca," sighed Perse.

Luca raised his head. His brother had his lips pressed together in a way that reminded Luca of Matti trying not to have an emotion. He was also peeling away one layer of the raskil's pastry coils, but in an absent way, like some people scribbled waves and stars in the margins of notes. At Luca's glance he seemed to realise he was doing it, and wiped his fingers on a napkin.

"Do you know why I married Melisette?"

Luca knew the business reasons, but he knew that there were stickier ones as well, and right now he was heartsore enough and angry enough at his brother to speak the latter aloud.

"I had rather assumed that it was because it was convenient for you to have a wife who'd already gotten herself pregnant."

Perse didn't look offended. Or at least no more offended than he usually did. "It was. But Mel didn't have to marry me. She could have had Charls on her own, and taken her time finding a partner."

Luca had to admit the truth of that. Marriage to Melisette Mantel had been a quick foothold to luxury for Persemaine Harte. Any number of people would have leapt at the chance to marry into the extravagantly prosperous Mantel House, or to form an alliance by taking Mel into their own, even if she did come with a son inconveniently fathered by someone else.

"Why, then?" he asked, when it became apparent that Perse was waiting for proof that Luca was listening.

"She married me for the same reason I married her." Perse looked down at his long fingers, folded on the table, neat. Everything about Perse was neat. "Because we were in love. We are. In love."

The word *love* sounded very strange in Perse's stuffy voice.

"You'd barely known each other a month when it was arranged," Luca pointed out.

Perse's fingers shifted. A new, passionate expression entirely failed to appear and transform his face. He was the same stern Perse as he'd ever been. As for Melisette, she was a quiet, thin woman, pale and dull as though she'd been rinsed before her colours had had a chance to properly take. Even beyond that—and Luca would be the first to admit that his tastes ran for the most part towards men, so his judgement of her looks was beside the point—Luca had never found her company interesting or her personality compelling. The idea of a whirlwind romance sat as strangely on her as it did on Perse.

"Nevertheless," said Perse.

"Well, thank you very much. What an illuminating piece of information. How kind of you to wave your apparent love match under my nose, when I've managed to get myself hopelessly attached to someone whose right to marry someone *else* I am contracted to defend."

"That's not what I—" Another put-upon sigh. "I am attempting to show you that I might *understand*— Oh, I don't know why I bother."

Silence fell. Luca's anger settled like soap bubbles. Despite Luca's dramatic claims, he was a lot more comfortable waving his emotions around than Perse was. And Perse was sitting here, once again dissecting a pastry with his clean fingernails, and talking about his feelings.

"All right," Luca muttered. "Sorry."

"So you've misled this man Jay. What are you going to do about it?"

"I don't know."

"Run away?" said Perse coolly.

Luca narrowed his eyes. "Is this a clumsy attempt to manipulate me into coming back with you after all?"

"That would be ideal, yes. But actually, it's an attempt to discover if you have anything resembling a plan."

Luca barked out a short laugh.

"Yes. Indeed." Perse pushed his glasses up his nose. "This strikes me, Lucastian, as an excellent opportunity to learn a new skill."

⊶∘≫∺⊕⊕∺≪∘⊷

Matti was almost sure that swimming would help. In the past— *the past,* as though it had been years since Luca whirled into his life instead of merely feeling like it—he'd often been midstroke, nothing in his mind but the slosh of salt and the sound of breaking waves, when a solution to a business problem would slide across the surface of his thoughts.

He wasn't optimistic. He could swim for days and not solve this. How did you *solve* the slow surrender of yourself to another person, like a dwindling stack of coins at a card table, only to look up from your empty hands to see the cold triumph of your opponent?

But it would *help.* His neck was knotted and he was queasy with worry.

There was, however, the stack of papers waiting for him on his desk, of letters to be answered and reports to be read, and the fact that he had an early meeting scheduled with three of Jay House's senior buyers. The buyers had been both chafing and chirpy since Matti's engagement was announced. They were all shrewd bargainers, but they liked having money to play with as much as anyone else, and they hated having to pass over good lots because Matti had ordered conservative practice. They smelled gold; they knew their budgets were about to be expanded, and they were going to respectfully demand to know why Matti couldn't sign off on the expansion *now.*

Matti wasn't sure he'd be at his best in this meeting, let alone able to read more than a few pages before the pain in his neck crept lovingly around to his temples. He should delay the morning's work and go swimming.

He should go home and deal with things, as he'd always dealt with things.

He should go swimming.

It took Matti a few minutes of near-paralytic indecision, during which he leaned against a lamppost and counted cobblestones, before he firmed his hand into a fist and set off for home. He'd caused this fucking mess by letting himself be distracted from his responsibilities. He could hardly justify abandoning them further so he could have a fit of self-indulgence about his feelings.

He ran into Maya, almost literally, two steps inside the front door of the house. Her smile faltered at once. "Huna's thumbs. You look awful."

"Oh," Matti said, vague as he could manage, and eyed the stairs. Maya stepped in front of them.

"What is it? What's happened?"

Matti found the words *Nothing you need to worry about* lining themselves up helpfully, but he choked on them. They were even more of a lie than usual.

Maya's mouth set into serious concern. She took hold of his arm. "*Matti.*"

"Come upstairs," Matti said. "I'll tell you."

"*Joselyne,*" Maya called, not breaking eye contact.

When Joselyne appeared she was herding the twins towards the front door, pushing string bags of lunch into their hands. Matti had arrived at the most chaotic hour in their household. He ruffled Marko's hair and flicked Merri's ear as they left, and the headache began to worsen as he did so. It wasn't just his own future he'd put at risk.

"Matti's not feeling well," Maya was saying to Joselyne. "Tell whomever comes to meet with him this morning that they'll have to come back tomorrow. If there's anything urgent they can leave a Sally-eye. Yes?"

"I'm not—" Matti protested—he'd worked twelve-hour days while miserable with fever, during the winter—but Maya squeezed his arm hard.

"Nothing that can't wait a day?" she said.

After a moment, Matti nodded, surrendering.

"Easy done," Joselyne said. "Can I bring you something, Matti? We've no chocolate, but there's tea."

Matti declined tea. Minutes later he was shut in his study, leaning against the edge of his own desk while Maya stood with folded arms and worried expression in front of him. They'd been here before, many times. Matti thought of the list in Corus Vane's lockbox, and had another moment of disorienting doubt as everything he thought he knew about the last few months wavered.

"What is it now?" Maya asked quietly.

Matti covered his face with both hands and rubbed his eyes. It was an act of cowardice, buying time, but he couldn't think of how to start.

Maya said, "Whatever it is—"

"Luca Piere's not Luca Piere," said Matti. "He's Luca Harte. *Lucastian* Harte."

There was a long silence. When Matti gathered his nerve to lower his hands, Maya was staring at him.

"Well, fuck," she said.

"Yes."

"Spying?"

Matti gripped the edge of the desk. "We have to assume so, don't we? He denied it—yes, exactly," at Maya's snort.

"What did he say he was doing, then? A nice holiday in Glassport, see the ocean, wave some swords around, pretend to be nobody?"

"He didn't say anything." Only the determination not to lie further to his sister forced out the next words. "I wasn't in the mood to let him talk."

Maya came and stood right in front of him, sliding her arms around his shoulders. Her cheek pressed against his and Matti squeezed her waist with one arm, feeling himself exhale as though it had been hours since he'd last done so.

"How did you find out?" she asked, releasing him.

Matti told her about the sudden arrival in the practice room of

Luca's brother, Perse. The one who had an enthusiastic interest in wine, Matti remembered. Unless that had been a lie as well.

Maya frowned. "Seems clumsy, to stumble into your brother's spy operation and immediately break his cover. Unless it served their purpose, somehow, but I can't think what they'd gain by you finding out *now*."

"The brother's not Harte anymore. Married into another House, a year or so back. I remember hearing about it. He might not have even known about it, if it's Harte business."

In which case it was a terribly unlucky coincidence for Luca, and Perse had certainly seemed to be seeking him out to a purpose. The whole thing was odd. Matti had the wild urge to track Luca down and fire questions at him, hooking the answers out one by one until the picture was clear. But it would be useless if the answers couldn't be trusted. The entire foundation of Luca and Matti's relationship—whatever it was—had been built on shifting, treacherous sand.

"In any case, I hope you punched the son of a whistleweed worm."

"Yes."

"I—wait, yes? You did hit him?"

Matti nodded. Maya looked fleetingly impressed.

"It's a mess," she said. "But I'm sorry. I know how much you liked him. At least you found out, and at least you didn't— Oh, Huna's dripping slit, Matti, you *didn't*."

Matti blanched, and then felt like an elderly aunt, but it couldn't have been worse than whatever she'd seen in his face to trigger the obscenity in the first place. "I didn't what?" he managed, stalling.

Maya's eyes narrowed. She spoke with deliberation. "You didn't start sleeping with your best man. Because you said you could cope with it, and I believed you."

The hot, roiling shame was back. Matti thought about the night of the ball, about Luca's head flung back and mouth open around cries of pleasure. Luca lying on Matti's chest telling stories about his scars. Luca kissing him, teasing him about the scarf Matti had bought him because of how well it would look. Matti had thought he was making bright memories to keep in a corner of his heart and bring out to admire in the years ahead. Now they were rot-tainted, like wool gone damp.

"Clearly, I couldn't cope with it!" he snapped. "I—gods, Maya, I liked him. Whatever version of himself he was playing. I liked him so much."

"I can see why," she said, grudging. "I can't *believe* him. Well, no, I can believe it of him, the good-looking, fast-talking little shit." Her frown snapped to Matti. "I can't believe *you*! I thought you *liked* Sofia, you said you were glad it was her! You didn't mind marrying her, I thought."

"I don't mind," Matti said. "I don't mind marrying where there's nothing more than friendship. Just like I don't *mind* that I've never had a chance to do what I want, I don't mind that everything's on my shoulders, that Dad's stupid need to throw himself into what's best for the Guild and the city means that *I'm* the one pulling our whole family out of this." The air was hot in his chest and he couldn't stop. "I don't *mind* that Dad married Mama for love and no money but nobody has ever thought I might want to do the same, I don't mind that the only time I've ever had something truly for myself has been—has been—"

Had been a beautiful, overly dramatic man laughing at him and teaching him badly and coming unravelled under Matti's hands, and *lying with every fucking breath*. Matti's arms were wrapped around himself, overtight and trembling, his breath starting to hurtle towards the panic that hadn't come at Tolliver's. It seemed only fitting that this was turning into a pattern, an unmendable tear in Matti's fabric left by the deliberate spikes of Lucastian fucking Harte.

Matti forced himself to breathe and to count the breaths. One, two. In and out. He'd caught it early enough that he managed to settle it.

"Matti." Maya's voice caught. "I didn't know." He'd never seen her this shocked. He'd never seen the guilt that was starting to creep across her face.

"I'm sorry," Matti said at once. "I didn't mean to—I'm sorry."

"I'm sorry as well. And we'll talk about it. Later." She reached out and touched his jaw, briefly. "Right now we need to talk to Sofia," she said, sending Matti's gut hurtling towards his ankles. "I'll go myself. The Coopers do business from home in the mornings, like us—she'll be there."

"Sofia?"

"You don't have a best man anymore, and Adrean is still determined to challenge for her. This is officially her business too."

The part of Matti that was used to keeping secrets wanted to protest that surely Sofia didn't need to know *all* of it, but he couldn't muster the energy to argue with his sister. Not when she looked that stubborn. Not when he'd already spent more anger this morning than he usually showed in a year, throwing his hurt in Luca's face and driving him to the floor. The crackling pathways of fury within Matti had turned to dull threads of hopelessness.

Maya ordered him to have some of that tea, or possibly a nap, while he waited, and she left for the Coopers' with that worried, determined look still lingering on her face.

Matti wrote off napping as impossible, but went down to the kitchen and made his own tea while Joselyne, chopping potatoes, demanded reassurance that he wasn't on his deathbed. Matti couldn't blame her, given the cancelled meetings. He escaped to the sitting room with the pot and three cups on a tray. By the time Maya returned with Sofia it was cooling and likely oversteeped, but he poured it anyway.

Maya had already explained most of the situation. For a moment Matti felt indignant at that, but then was flooded with relief that he didn't have to admit to his mistakes all over again.

Sofia didn't look angry, which seemed a minor miracle. Her brows were a dark, thoughtful line.

Still, Matti owed her an apology, and he gave it, at length.

When he was done Sofia said, in the tone of one offering a concession, "He was very charming when I talked to him at the Half Moon Ball."

Somehow it had not crossed Matti's mind that Luca might have spoken to Sofia beyond their introduction at the wedding party's gift ceremony.

"Yes," he said. "He is very charming."

"You know, Cee tried to tease me with the idea that you might be having a fling with your best man, when nobody could find the two of you for the last dance. Oh, I don't care about *that*," she said with a dismissive wave. "Not much, anyway. We're not married until we're married."

"But we still have to get through the wedding," Matti said, bringing them back to the central problem. "Tolliver might agree to refund his contract as a favour, but it's unlikely. Luca technically *hasn't* breached it, and—I'd have to explain who he is, and why I don't want him anymore."

Maya and Sofia looked at each other, and they all sat in silent agreement that the damage should be contained as much as possible.

"Maha's feet," said Sofia. She touched the delicate gold chain at her wrist. "What a mess. I'd pay the fee for another best man *myself*, but there's only the one agency in town, so we'd run into the same problem."

"Maybe we could poison Adrean," said Maya. "Then Matti wouldn't need one at all. And we can tell everyone that Luca Piere left town. Fell in a hole. Something."

"We don't know what *Luca's* going to be telling everyone," Matti said suddenly. "If he wants to ruin Jay House, he could just let half the city know how badly off we are."

"We don't know what he'll do," Sofia agreed. "Which means we can't do anything about it, so let's focus on what we *can* do."

"I can go to his boardinghouse and pull his liver out through his lying mouth," said Maya. "I've got the address."

Sofia coughed and patted Maya's hand. "And if he decides to go down the gossip route, I'll be right there handing you the pincers. I've had enough of men starting talk about my personal life. But we can attack the Kesey House situation in the meantime, don't you think?"

Matti blinked at this swerve of topic. Maya had clearly passed on—or had *been* passing on, for quite some time—more of the situation than he'd thought.

"Maya." Sofia had a brisk organisational look about her now. "You saw that mislabelling with your own eyes. That's more than a paper trail. That's true."

"Yes," said Maya.

Matti struggled with the morass of his thoughts. It made no sense for Luca to have called Matti's attention to the conspiracy between Corus and Kesey House, unless he'd decided to use Matti to take the Keseys out of the market first. That was plausible; the Jays were arguably in the weaker position. If Harte could leverage the Jays against the Keseys and then move to undercut and work against *them,* fast and mercilessly, taking advantage of Luca's knowledge, they could establish themselves in the market gap.

But why not let Corus keep on weakening the Jays, in that case? Or was that a calculated loss, to win Matti's gratitude?

"Matti," Maya was saying. "I know I said to wait, and I'll let you decide, but . . . I think you should tell Mama and Dad now."

Matti's heart slammed down. The look on his face, at the very idea of having to do this again—talk through his failings and his selfishness *again,* and to his *parents*—must have been stark and ugly, because Maya fluttered her hands immediately in a warding-off kind of motion.

"Not everything! Not while we don't know what Luca might do. But about the Keseys. And definitely about Corus."

Luca's voice whipped at Matti: *You lie for them and you lie to them.*

Enough, Matti thought. *No more.*

"All right," he said. "Yes. You're right, they should know. Dad is the right person to come down on the Keseys about the fraudulent labelling, though it's going to be hard to denounce them to the Guild without more proof than a rival House member's word. It'll look like Jay House is taking advantage of Dad's position."

"About that." Sofia raised her hand like a schoolgirl. "The problem is that you can't easily tell what went into blended wool once it's turned into fabric, is that it?"

"Yes," said Maya.

"What if you could?"

"But—" said Matti.

"I know." Sofia was smiling now. There was a look in her eyes that reminded Matti, alarmingly, of Luca. "You children of Huna are going to have to help with the details, but I think I might have an idea."

"Your mother might get the wrong idea if she finds out I've been taking you out this late at night," said Luca.

"Don't worry, Mr. Piere," said Dinah. "If she's really suspicious then *I'm* the one who'll get dragged to the Guildhall to do the handwashing ritual and pray to Osta fifteen times, for being so unprofessional as to sleep with a boarder. You'll be all right. Mama likes you. And she knows if you were paying me any attention I didn't want, I'd be giving *you* two weeks to find a new place to live. Or two hours, depending on how handsy you'd gotten," she added, with a sharp grin.

The midnight air was thin and fresh, as though it had crept in from the sea or flowed out here from the inland mountains and was making itself at home in the city while it slept. Or *didn't* sleep—the occasional hired carriage rolled by, including empty ones whose drivers gestured questioningly at Luca and Dinah, offering a ride. They'd passed a group of men almost on the doorstep of the boardinghouse, and now they still saw the occasional person on foot. People coming home from jobs, like Stefan's, that stretched on into the night. Physicians going to or returning from urgent calls. City guardsmen, making swing-footed patrols. But it was a quieting time. Even most drinking houses in this well-to-do neighbourhood would be closing up and booting out their stragglers at this hour.

Luca and Dinah stuck to the well-lit main streets, and Luca was aware of his empty belt. He'd left all his weapons at the boardinghouse. A sword would get in the way. He'd considered tucking his dagger inside his jacket before hearing Master Carriere's voice:

Wearing a weapon you can't use is asking for trouble. Luca had no training in dagger fighting without a sword in his other hand, and even that kind of duelling was considered a flourish variant on high formal, rarely requested.

It had been two days since Perse's interruption and the fight that had shattered all the happiness Luca had made for himself in Glassport. Since then he'd found himself waking early and unable to get back to sleep; he'd found himself walking in the direction of Matti's house and then turning around, cowardly. He didn't want Matti to look at him like that again. He didn't want Matti to have the chance to refuse to see him in the first place.

His best plan was to keep his mouth shut and try to make it up to Matti in actions instead of words. To that end, a hastily scribbled letter from Luca to their mother was racing its way back to Cienne under priority franking, followed—at a more reasonable pace—by Perse. Barring delays, the letter should have arrived by now, crammed full in equal weight of apologies, questions, and proposals. Every time Luca thought too hard about it, he felt shaky. But it was done. Luca would give Matti what he deserved, whether Matti forgave him or not.

"This street," he said to Dinah, and they turned onto it.

"This is exciting." She gave a skip. Her arm was firm through his.

Luca had found the Kesey townhouse during the day, then spent nearly the whole afternoon wandering the neighbourhood to hammer the route into his feet so he'd be able to find it again.

Yesterday Luca had tried to discover if there was a central record of warehouses. At the city registry he'd been told that half the warehouses in the city were rented out, just as ships were hired, for short-term use by various Houses. Temporary leases were far more common in Glassport than in Cienne, given the amount of goods entering and leaving the city via the harbour. And there was no central record of these leases; they were all direct arrangements between the Houses concerned. If Luca wanted to find out something specific, the clerk had said, he'd have to talk to the Houses directly.

Talk to the Keseys. Luca had, for a brief, wild hour, considered doing just that. It would be a tricky dance. He'd met one or two Keseys at the Half Moon Ball, and there was a high chance Simeon Kesey and any number of his senior agents had also been present, as prominent members of Matti's Guild. Pretending to be someone other than Luca Piere was out. Luca *could* try to spin a tale for the Keseys that made him out to be exactly the kind of spy Matti assumed him to be: lay out his suspicions as a form of blackmail, something to give Harte the upper hand in Glassport's market.

But secret-keeping was the best signal he could send to Matti that he had no intention of betraying him, and for once Luca was making himself think all the way through to the end of his schemes. He didn't think he could lie his way out of this without building a further teetering edifice of disaster.

No, Luca was going to do the thing that had worked when it came to Corus Vane.

He was going to break in and go snooping.

"Last chance to change your mind, Miss Vaunt," he said, slowing them down as they approached the house. He'd told her most of the truth: that the Keseys were up to no good, and that to help Matti Jay he intended to find proof in a less-than-legal way. She'd agreed to help with an alacrity that didn't surprise him. He'd recognised some of his own adventure-seeking spirit in Dinah Vaunt a long time ago. He wondered if he ought to recommend the benefits of changing your name and running away, but Dinah seemed to enjoy her life on the whole, and was a dutiful child of both Osta and her mother. Besides, it wasn't as though Luca could hold himself up as a shining example of that plan ending in any sort of success.

Dinah released his arm and shook the folds of her light, elbow-length cloak to lie neatly. She was wearing her best dress, a flattering plum velvet, and she had a dusting of gold on her eyelids, her hair in twists; she looked like a House daughter on her way home from a party.

"Don't be silly," she said. "This is much better theatre than the tedious history play Stefan's company is staging at the moment."

Luca stayed where he was. Dinah walked ahead, her shadow long and dense in the lamplight. She ran up the steps of the Kesey townhouse and lifted her hand to knock on the door. It seemed to take a long time and a lot of knocking before the door cracked open. Luca could see only a candle glimmer and the eerie underside of a man's face.

Luca held his breath during the conversation that followed, during which Dinah gestured earnestly over her shoulder and down the road in Luca's direction. Luca crouched as though tying his bootlaces, hiding himself in the shadow cast by a devotional statue that stood just off the street in another house's frontage. The story was that Dinah was nearly home and was afraid she was being followed, and she hated to disturb anyone at this hour, but could she just sit in their entry hall for a few minutes, to gather her nerves and wait for her possible pursuer to give up and pass by?

Dinah had done a version of this back at the boardinghouse that had made Luca want to applaud and cry laughing at once: high-strung, dim-witted, and blushingly trying to talk around the fact that a young woman walking home alone at midnight might have been doing something her family was unlikely to approve of.

Finally Dinah stepped forward, admitted into the Kesey townhouse, and the door closed behind her. At once Luca stood up and walked to the house, quickly and on light feet, and climbed the same steps. He had barely stopped in front of the door when it opened again. Dinah beckoned him inside.

"Asked him for a glass of water, like you said," she breathed. "He's gone for it. Quick."

As Dinah eased the door closed, Luca took in the dark entry

hall. He chose the closest doorway to the right, which after some squinting he found led into a sitting room. Only the slightest glow of moonlight and lamplight slipped through the curtains. Luca hid himself behind the door, leaning on the wall, and stood as still as possible. At once he found his fingers drumming on his black trousers, but they made no sound. He sent a prayer to Huna that his stomach wouldn't gurgle. Today was a fast day in her calendar, and Luca was feeling a desperate need to try to make amends with his patron goddess, along with all the others he'd managed to annoy. He had stuck to water and tea all day.

He remained behind the door as a stiffly polite man returned to the entry hall with water for Dinah. Dinah kept up apologetic chatter in a whisper. After a minute she claimed she felt able to continue on her way, declined the offer of a chaperone to her destination, and was gone. The front door closed a final time, and Luca heard the bolts of it slide home. The man's footsteps faded into the back of the house.

Luca's heart was racing. His palms were slick and he wanted to laugh. Dinah would find herself a carriage back to the boarding-house. Luca's part was just beginning.

He murmured a silent thanks for the fact that these enormous Glassport townhouses seemed to follow a roughly consistent lay-out, slipped back into the hall, and climbed the stairs, being slow and careful with his weight to avoid anywhere that promised to creak, or in case there was a trip-step set at a different height to the rest. By the time he reached the next floor his eyes had begun to adjust to the deeper dark. He began with the doors that were ajar rather than closed, and on his second try hit one with the look of a central office, including a large desk and some looming wooden blocks that seemed likely to hold files.

Luca eased the room's door closed. He pulled matches and a candle with a holder from inside his jacket. Illuminated, the study had a warm, chaotic, lived-in feel to it. Luca exhaled slowly and went to work.

It took him some time to work out the filing system, which was what Perse would have crushingly called *idiosyncratic*. Luca would have preferred not to be working with a naked flame, either, but it was what he had. He carefully opened and replaced books and folders full of auction purchases, payroll forms, insurance contracts, letters of legal advice, and reams of receipts for everything from dye to loom parts. He found copies of shipping contracts, but nothing that added to what he'd already discovered at Lior House's offices.

Luca yawned. His excitement had settled, and its head-clearing effect was beginning to wear dangerously thin. He pinched his own hand and forced himself to think about his discovery in Andri Baudrain's house—the shouts as the alarm was raised—the frantic chase across the garden, and Luca's lurching fright as he heard the far-off growl of dogs. The garden wall, gritty under his hands. The moment when Margot recognised him. The moment after that, dropping into the alley and barely registering the pain in his heels, when the possible consequences began to sink their fingers into his mind.

Yes. That helped.

He reached for a folder that was simply labelled CONTRACTS (MISC.). This one only held a few sheets of paper. Luca froze midway through a cursory flick and leaned closer to the candle, which had burned halfway down by now. The name LYSBETTE MARTENS sprang out at him in stark black ink beneath a fluid signature.

Luca read the short paragraph on the paper twice through. His hand twitched with the desire to fold it up and carry it away with him, but he made himself put it back. Even if it could be raised in front of a magistrate without accurate accusations of housebreaking coming into play, it was vague enough that it could be twisted any number of ways. But it was, finally, something other than circumstantial evidence. A concrete link between Martens and Kesey.

Not long after that, Luca was digging in the other pocket of his jacket for the paper where he'd written the date of the *Lady Jenny*'s arrival into Glassport. He laid it on the floor and began to flick through the much thicker folder he'd found. Building rentals. Some of them might have been temporary workshops, but by now Luca knew Glassport's harbour quarter well enough to guess at which ones were likely to be warehouses. And of those, only one of them had a date of lease commencing in the right month.

Luca had forgotten to bring a pencil. Feeling weirdly more intrusive than he had reading the Keseys' private papers, he plucked one from a glass holder on the desk and wrote down the warehouse's address. Another step closer.

The house had a slumbering deadness to it as he crept downstairs again, tiredness banished by both his buoyancy at success and the renewed risk of being out, exposed, in the halls of the house.

His fingers had just touched the bolts when someone knocked on the front door from the outside.

Luca froze. He had the giddy instinct to obey the knock's request and open the door.

The knock came again, this time a slow insistent pound that showed the knocker's intention to stand there for as long as it took. Luca's feet unstuck from the floor and he quickly returned to his hiding place in the sitting room. Mad scenarios raced through his mind. Dinah had been accosted on her way to flag down a carriage, and now she was back, truly seeking help. A wakeful neighbour had seen Luca sneak in and sent for the city guard.

"*Now* what?" came a sleepy, irritated female voice from upstairs. "Is someone trying to plague us out of our sleep?"

"I'll deal with it, Mrs. Kesey." That was the same man who'd let Dinah in. His feet scuffed against the floor as he walked to the door, slid back the bolts, and opened it.

"*What?*" he demanded. "Who are you?"

"Corus Vane. I need to speak to Simeon. It's important."

Every one of Luca's nerves pricked up, alight.

"I shouldn't have to tell you that Mr. Kesey doesn't take meetings at this time of night."

"He'll take this one, if he doesn't want his House's name dragged through the dirt in front of the rest of the Guild," said Vane.

"Corus? Have you lost your wits?" That voice, too, was raised to carry down from upstairs. Simeon Kesey had a deep voice rendered rough by sleep.

"You need to hear this, Simeon," said Vane.

Footsteps as heavy as the voice descended the stairs. The wavering candlelight that spilled into the sitting room became abruptly more complex, as another light source joined it. The front door closed.

"All right, Carstan, you go back to bed," said Kesey. "You couldn't have sent a damn message, man?"

"It couldn't wait until the morning post. And I could hardly be seen knocking at your door in daylight, earlier today," said Vane.

"Very well."

Fear throttled Luca as he wondered if Kesey would take this impromptu meeting into the room where Luca was hiding. But the light settled, as though Kesey had set his candle down on a hall table.

"It's about what you've been doing in the country workshops," Vane said. "Mixing fibres."

"Corus." There was a nasty note of warning in Kesey's voice.

"Matti met with me this evening," Vane said. "We were going over some of the recent sales to local tailoring houses. Nothing unusual. But he told me—" A sigh, as though he didn't know how to come at it. "Nessanesh has contacts at the university in Manisi. One of her sisters put her in touch with someone who does materials research there, and Nessa corresponds with them. There's a group working on all kinds of things—dyes, mordants, better ways of treating the wool at various stages."

"What does that have to do with anything?"

"A chemist has found a way to test wool fibres, from swatches, even once the fabric's been fully treated. Some kind of accidental discovery by a group looking at ways to straighten human hair, of all the frivolous things."

"This still doesn't sound urgent, Corus," said Kesey.

"Matti's got his hands on the thing. He wants it to be a surprise for Tomas, given that he was the one who shoved that legislation about mandatory labelling through the Guildband in the first place. They're planning a demonstration." A pause. "Tomorrow."

"What?"

"The feast—"

"Oh, gods," Kesey groaned. "The breakfast."

"The whole Guild will be there," said Vane. "Matti was going to keep it a secret, but apparently Nessa's been chatting, and it's already leaked out to a few people, so he wanted me to know. He's already ordered swatches. From the highest-grade fabrics."

"From—"

"Every House in wool," Vane said, inexorable. "And even the smaller independent merchants too. You see the problem now?"

Luca was fighting the dangerous urge to laugh. *Clever,* Matti. Very clever indeed. He strained to hear what happened next, but heard only footfalls as Kesey paced, and a low mutter of what could have been curses.

"Do you think it's legitimate?" Kesey asked eventually. "This technique?"

"Matti Jay is the most careful person I know. He wouldn't organise something like this unless he was sure about it."

"And you're telling me the truth?"

Luca rolled his eyes on Vane's behalf, thinking about the report from Rob Rivers in Vane's lockbox. Vane would hardly invent something that jeopardised the main source of leverage he had over the Keseys. Of course, his warning Kesey had also just done that, and Vane would need new leverage now. Luca wasn't surprised at the tight irritation when the man spoke. "*Yes.* How many times do I have to prove myself to you?"

"All right," said Kesey. Pacifying. "Our deal hasn't changed, Corus. When Jay House is ruined, you'll be plucked out of its ashes."

"And my son will bear your name."

"Yes, yes. The Jays still haven't offered, have they?"

"No," said Vane, and Luca wanted to recoil at the poisonous resentment in that single syllable.

"And they never will. It's against Tomas's precious hypocritical reformer's principles," said Kesey. "Men like you and I, at least we'll *admit* to knowing the value in a House name. And by the time we give Adrean ours, it will be worth twice the value of the name Jay."

So that was it. That kind of adoption was not unheard of, but it was rare, and the Jays seemed decent enough to be upfront about whether they would meet that kind of expectation, given that Adrean himself wasn't an employee.

Unless the expectation was unspoken. Unless it was simply assumed, seething and fermenting over the years.

That was why Vane thought it worthwhile to take down his own House: because it *wasn't* his own House, not in name. He'd sold Matti's family out for a chance to give his son what he felt he'd been cheated out of. House status.

And that was why Corus must have quietly acquired that report from Rob Rivers in the first place, Luca realised—to ensure that Simeon Kesey kept up his end of the agreement, once Jay House had been brought to its knees.

"Well," said Kesey. "You were right to bring this to me. It was Mattinesh who told you? Today, the night before the feast?"

"Yes."

Kesey paused. "Do you think . . . do they suspect my House?"

"I don't know," said Vane. "Most people wouldn't be able to tell, from the finished product, but the Jays eat and drink and breathe their business. If they had a reason to get their hands on your cloth and inspect it closely . . ."

"*Fucking* Tomas," said Kesey. "It'd be just like the self-righteous, moralistic prick, always with his eye out for someone else's faults. All right. We assume the worst. We assume Matti's grand demonstration tomorrow is either a plain prestige display, or a way to score points by exposing us."

Or a blatant lie, thought Luca. *Oh, Matti. You'd probably hate how proud I am of you.*

"Come out in front of it," said Vane. "Before the ceremony. It's the only way. You know how the Guildband feels about quality assurance. Announce you've just discovered this fraud perpetuated in your House's name, and you're shocked and dismayed. Pick someone to take the fall."

"Huna's arse," said Kesey. "No, you're right. Someone embezzling? Selling the good quality stuff on the side?"

A short, humourless laugh from Corus Vane. "You work out the story. I'm going home to bed. We've got an early ceremony to attend."

Once Vane had left and Kesey had carried his candle back up the stairs, Luca waited. He stood behind the sitting room door until the house once again had the stillness of sleep, stifling more than one yawn against his own hand during that time. Then he tiptoed to the front door, which had probably seen more post-midnight traffic tonight than in its entire prior existence, and let himself silently out.

The night was cooler than it had been, but not uncomfortably so. Luca made himself walk briskly to the nearest street corner before he leaned his shaky hands onto his knees and laughed, all the tension bubbling out of him and leaving him exhausted. It took him longer than he'd planned to make his way back to the boardinghouse, tired and faint as he was with not having eaten all day. As he approached it, his reflexes were dulled with the need to be horizontal between his sheets.

So when someone stepped up beside him and pressed a knife to his ribs, it took Luca almost two heartbeats to recognise it as such.

He halted in his steps. Cool fear drenched him. His hand fumbled at his belt and encountered . . . nothing at all.

"That's it, Mr. Harte," said the man holding the knife. The fear turned to outright ice, getting itself into the hinge of Luca's jaw and his fingertips, setting them tingling. "Keep your mouth shut, and just step over here with me."

Luca respected weapons, and respected the people on the other end of them when they handled them with this sort of confidence. He didn't even consider trying to run. He didn't recognise the man's voice, and a stranger who knew Luca's name and where he lived in Glassport could not have his basic decency gambled upon.

For a long, mind-blanking moment of hysteria, as Luca followed the knife's prod towards a dim side street, he wondered if Matti had decided to have him killed. He thought about Corus Vane saying *Matti Jay is the most careful person I know.*

Stop it, Luca told himself fiercely. *You're being stupid. You can't afford that. Open your eyes and take in your opponents, and think. You can win a point before swords touch, if you're looking closely enough.*

What he saw, with his eyes open, did not inspire hope. The dark, narrow street held three more men, all of them taller and broader than Luca. Luca opened his mouth to offer them his purse, remembered that he wasn't carrying it and also that they *knew his name,* and closed it again.

"You're a difficult one to catch up to, Lucastian Harte," said the shortest man in the alley. He stepped forward into the meagre light coming from the main street's lamps; he had a practical, rough-hewn look to him, like an unfinished carving. "But Guild-master Baudrain was quite firm on the fact that you *should* be found."

Luca's palms were sweating. They were all standing in a loose circle: men having a meeting. The knife was still tucked between two of his ribs, at the back, but friendlier now. A reminder not to move. Across Luca's mind darted a pure and specific fear of pain.

He said, proud of his voice for only shaking a little, "I thought Mr. Baudrain had come to an understanding with my Head of House."

"Due to your mother's generosity and Mr. Baudrain's respect for the name of your House," said the practical man, singsong like a child reciting vows at their naming, "he's agreed not to take charges before a magistrate, and to laugh it off. In public. But you, Mr. Harte, still need a reminder that a thief is a thief. No matter his name."

The knife had gone from Luca's ribs, but he could feel the solid threatening heat of the man behind him. Luca tried desperately to stay aware of four bodies at once, as the men flanking the speaker began to move with purpose. He found the words *I'll tell my mother* in his mouth, and managed to choke them back.

The man's lip curled as if he'd said them anyway. "Pathetic," he said. "You House brats think you can buy or bully your way out of anything. Speaking of which, aren't you going to offer me money?"

Luca thought of Matti, standing still and shocked in a drinking house while Luca held up his own broken watch.

"I haven't got any money," said Luca.

He was tensed for it, but the first blow—blunt and fast, to the side of his ribs—still came as a shock.

The ones after that were less shocking, but they hurt just as much.

CHAPTER
18

The Guildhall looked very different, that morning, to how it would look at Matti's wedding in two days' time. The quilts and tapestries covering the walls nearly floor-to-ceiling were all in different styles and colour palettes, each crafted and donated by a different House. Followed clockwise around the hall they told the story of when Huna had walked the world in disguise and been challenged by one of the old queens to weave the loveliest cloth in the world for her son's naming day. Huna had woven for a day and a night without pausing for food or drink.

"That was something out of the ordinary, wasn't it?"

Matti looked around from where he was gazing, without really taking in the details, at the tapestry donated by Jay House several generations ago. The man who had stepped up beside him was short even by the standards of people who weren't Matti's family, though a hedge of springy grey curls were doing their best to add to his height.

"Good to see you, Alfonso," said Matti. Madra House was based in the Cantala territories, where they bought and processed cotton; Alfonso Madra ran their local office and also served as the Guild secretary in Glassport. "What was out of the ordinary?"

Madra tutted. "This is what you get for standing in the corner, lad. I'm doing my duty, spreading the talk of the room to you virtuous outliers. I meant, what did you make of Sim Kesey's announcement?"

A smile surprised Matti by trying to twitch onto his mouth. It seemed like such a long time since he'd felt like smiling that he almost didn't manage to hide it. "Nobody can say that Kesey House wasn't doing the honourable thing, making a public statement as soon as they became aware of what was happening."

"Yes, indeed. Such a pity about all the bales they'll have to withdraw from sale, while they investigate just how long this buyer of theirs has been giving false instructions and pocketing the difference."

"They're maintaining the high standards of their House" was all Matti said.

Madra gave Matti a wry look of disappointment that Matti wasn't going to play along. The man had a love for gossip that could quickly turn sour-tongued and vindictive if he took a dislike to you. The Jays had always been careful to stay on his good side. "I suppose you're right. Now, look at that full plate. I'm keeping you from breaking your fast! Don't stand on ceremony with me, Matti. Eat." Madra used a tiny fork to skewer what looked like a mushroom dusted in chilli powder on his own plate, and encouragingly popped it into his mouth.

Matti smiled politely. "Another few minutes of anticipation won't make much difference, and I'll savour it all the more."

Mushroom safely swallowed, Madra gave a guffawing laugh and patted Matti's arm. "As for food, so for a wedding, hey? Not long to wait now!" Having delivered this well-meaning innuendo, he wandered away.

Matti's plate was full of all the things he usually loved, many of which his family had long been going without. Red-spiced flaking smoked fish. Chocolates with caramel centres. Tiny cheese tarts. Slices of fresh early-autumn pear sprinkled with nutmeg. Soft milk-glazed bread in an intricate knot. He'd dutifully fasted all of yesterday, but the look and smell of the food weren't rousing his appetite at all. A week ago he had been looking forward with pleasure to inviting Luca to this feast, held when they would usually be mid-lesson. Matti would have walked Luca around the walls and told him the story. Luca might have improvised his own version based solely on the wall hangings, turning the plot ridiculous when he hit some of the more abstract representations.

Except Luca, a fellow child of Huna, would have already known the story as well as Matti knew it himself.

Or Luca would have come up with an excuse to avoid the breakfast feast entirely, knowing that at least a handful of Harte House agents would be present. Matti looked around the room, trying to find their faces and drag their names out of his memory. His father would know. Matti had little reason to interact with the silk merchants at anything but these large Guild events, but Tomas would surely be friendly with some of them.

Matti gave himself a mental shake. What did he think he was he going to do, exactly? Accost a member of Luca's House and demand to know how they'd managed to stay ignorant of their House heir's presence in the city for the past few months? Luca had been, in his own theatrical way, careful. He'd avoided coming face-to-face with his own agents and the Head of Duvay, his main rival silk House, at the Half Moon Ball, though Matti hadn't recognised it as avoidance at the time. He'd certainly have kept clear of the Harte offices here in Glassport.

Besides, there had been no sign from any quarter that Luca had made himself known to anyone but Matti. No sudden surge of gossip. No whispering about Jay House's fortunes, beyond the usual. It seemed everyone in this room was still expecting Matti to stand up and be married to Sofia Cooper in two days' time, and they expected a redheaded nobody of a duellist to stand up next to him.

Matti's secrets were still secret. He didn't know what to think.

And he couldn't stay skulking in the corner with food either. There were at least three business conversations that he needed to have before the end of this feast, and one conversation that took precedence over them all.

Matti set down his plate on one of the tables but plucked the bread from it. He needed to force something down if he was going to make it through the day without fainting. He methodically pulled it to fluffy white pieces and ate them, washing them down with coffee. Then he went in search of Corus Vane, whom he found talking with Roland's mother, Tomas's younger sister.

Corus caught Matti's eye and, as Matti had expected, began to wrap up his conversation. He smiled at Matti as he did so. He'd given that same smile last night, when Matti told him the fabricated story about the new technique from Manisi. Corus's smiles had always been quick; he'd always stood in pleasant contrast to his sullen son.

Before any of this started, Matti wouldn't have thought himself naive, but now he felt wounded, ginger-peeled, a raw surface of himself laid bare to be damaged by the world. Corus Vane. Kesey House. Lucastian Harte, who'd told Matti that most people were decent, and who'd been lying about that as much as anything else.

For now, Matti smiled back at Corus. Matti knew how to do this too. He'd learned it far more thoroughly than he'd learned how to handle a sword: How to smile without meaning it. How to project calm control, when all he wanted was to throw plates to the ground and shout. The art of *seeming*.

Perhaps there weren't many decent people in the world at all.

"Matti," Corus greeted him in an undertone. "When were you thinking of doing this demonstration? Do you need help setting up?"

Matti made an apologetic face. "I'm sorry if you were looking forward to seeing it, but there's been a complication. Mama's contact at the university got greedy and made the mistake of talking to a patent lawyer. Now they've been told to keep the whole thing hushed up until they can shove the paperwork through. We're not supposed to even tell anyone it exists, before then."

Corus should have won a prize. His eyes didn't dart sideways for even a moment. The look he dragged over Matti's face was quizzical.

"Ah," Corus said finally.

Matti's next line in this was to shrug and wander away again. But anger was prickling in his palms. He made a decision more impulsive than any since he'd first told Luca, *I want you to teach me.*

"A pity, isn't it?" Matti said. "After what Simeon found out. It would have been interesting to see what happened with the swatches I have."

Corus's gaze sharpened. Matti held it.

"Matti." Corus sounded neutral. It had been driven home to Matti, during his efforts to untangle the knots and set planks over the marshes that were Corus's many small sabotages, that Corus Vane was a very smart man.

Matti would have liked to stand up on a table in the centre of the Guildhall, planting his feet between the caramels and the cakes, and yell insults at the top of his lungs. He wanted to call the man in front of him a smear of shit on the paper of the world, a fucking traitor, a thrice-cursed whistleweed worm squirming in the dirt of his own ingratitude. He wanted, more than anything, a sword in his hand and the ability to use it.

He let himself imagine that. He set it aside.

"Did you want to ask me something, Corus?" Then, when met with silence: "Or tell me something?"

They looked at each other. Matti's blood pounded a few times at the base of his throat and he watched the flickers of movement in the lines around Corus's eyes.

"I'd like to think," Corus said, very softly, a man feeling his way across wet cobblestones, "that I'm still valuable to your family."

Matti had discussed this with his mother and father, when he'd laid his findings about Corus and the Keseys bare. He'd left the vague prospect of Martens House's involvement out of it; he'd left Luca's true name out of it, for now. One crisis at a time.

At least this crisis he *was* presenting along with a solution. His mother and Sofia had refined the story about the fibre test between them, ready to be dropped into Corus's hands. Matti had watched another year's worth of worry lines carve themselves into Tomas's forehead, as the Head of Jay House sat with the betrayal committed by a man he considered a close friend. Matti felt no qualms about using Corus to carry their own deception into the enemy camp.

It was another double-edged balancing act. Corus knew exactly how badly off the Jays were, even if their fortunes were poised to change, and firing him would leave him with no reason to keep it secret. Both sides still had the ability to hurt.

"I'd like to think that too," said Matti.

Corus nodded. He didn't say anything else.

And that, Matti thought, *was your chance, Corus Vane. Whatever happens now, you've called it onto your own head.*

"Mr. Matti Jay?"

Corus stepped away as Matti turned to see who'd spoken. A tall boy stood there, perhaps fifteen, quick-eyed and poorly dressed.

"That's me." Matti let the smile rise back to his face like the bob of an apple held underwater. "What can I do for you?"

The boy held out a folded letter sealed with the green wax that proclaimed a personal missive, and Matti took it.

"Hand-to-hand delivery, already paid for," the boy said. "Now I'm done. Though he said there'd be a lot of good food around," he added meaningfully.

Matti had been wondering if the letter was from Sofia. Now a chill ran up his arm.

"Try the cheese tarts," he said, with a nod towards the tables. The boy grinned, bowed, and darted through the crowd with the air of someone prepared to inhale two platters without pausing for breath and then fill his pockets with whatever was left.

Matti went and found a chair to sit in. The moment before he sat, he realised he'd picked one set beneath a silk-ribbon tapestry, but moving to another chair on that basis would have been bordering on absurd. He sat, decisively, and broke the seal before he could talk himself out of doing so.

The lettering was slanted and uneven, as though the writer

were impatient to dash out the door and to some activity much more exciting than letter writing.

Matti,

I'm sorry I lied. I swear on Huna's hands and my mother's name that I never intended any harm to you, your family, or your House.

I'm going to make it up to you.

I'm still your best man.

—Luca

Matti's hand was halfway to closing into a helpless fist, crumpling the letter within it, when he caught himself. He smoothed it out again. The fierce shard of hope in him refused to be talked to, refused to be smothered. He missed Luca with all the hunger that he hadn't felt for the food.

He ran a fingertip beneath the word *your.*

Someone settled into the seat beside his. Maya. "I saw you with— Matti?"

Matti passed her the letter. Wretchedness sat on the back of his neck like a weight. He wanted to swim for hours and lose everything of himself in the action, and he was tired, so tired.

"Tell me what to think," he said, soft.

A long hiss of a sigh from his sister. "I can't. I'm a bit stuck there myself."

Matti looked up. Maya was looking at him as though she were seeing something completely new in his face.

"He could still ruin us," she said. "He could throw the duel."

"He could have ruined us already. He hasn't."

"He hasn't given you an explanation either."

"Are you afraid I'm going to go knocking on his door? I'm not." Saying it felt like laying steel over his bones.

Maya handed the letter back silently. Matti folded it small and tucked it into his coat.

"Then we wait," Maya said. "He's going to make it up to you? He's got two days to do it."

———— ❊ ————

"I'd avoid putting weight on that ankle for a couple of days," the physician said, straightening up.

Luca tried to find a more comfortable position on the pillows. There were no comfortable positions; he'd learned that during the mess of agonising broken sleep that had been the previous night. He tried anyway. Mrs. Vaunt had provided extra pillows in light of his injuries, instructed Luca not to bleed on them more than was absolutely necessary, and then gone off to oversee the weekly exchange of clean linens for soiled ones when the girls from the laundry shop arrived.

"A couple of days," Luca repeated.

"A couple of days?" Dinah was indignant, but also sparkling-eyed at the excitement of Luca's situation in a way that Luca was not finding altogether comforting. "He's fighting a duel! He's the best man at a wedding!"

The physician did not look impressed by this. "I'm sure his agency contract has stipulations for providing a replacement if he's incapacitated."

"I'm not incapacitated!" Luca protested. "Ow!" As he tried to sit upright, the entire left side of his rib cage flared with pain.

It was true, more or less. The physician had looked him over thoroughly and proclaimed him lucky. There was a sickly bruise across one cheekbone and wrapping up the side of his eye, and his lip had split, but they hadn't broken his nose. He had more bruises down his arms, and scrapes on his palms from catching himself against the ground, but his right hand's grip was still firm and his wrists were hale. One knee had been knocked sideways but hadn't swollen up, and the pain was already settling. Luca was most worried about the ribs—possibly cracked, possibly just strained, but it hurt like hell to move around and to lift his left arm—and the ankle. A mild sprain, when he'd landed on it and it had rolled inwards. He'd had worse. But he hadn't tried to *fight* on worse.

Luca didn't think it was luck, or incompetence. An incompetent fighter was more likely to do more damage than intended, not less; that was how people got killed accidentally, when their opponents were strong and unskilled. Andri Baudrain's men had delivered a very calculated beating indeed. If Luca had been left with any broken bones, any real damage, Luca's mother would have been forced to take action about it if she found out. Baudrain wasn't in this to create a feud.

No, Baudrain hadn't wanted to damage him. He'd wanted Luca taught a lesson, wanted him hurt and shaken and humiliated, and the fact that Luca knew it didn't mean it had been any less successful. Remembering any of it made him flinch and shiver. It had torn something casually out of him, realising how easy it was for them to hurt him and how useless he was at hurting back. His own version of fighting had never been so businesslike, so . . . *joyless*. Which was an odd thing to think. But every other physical hurt in Luca's life, even the careless slice that had opened his skin and left him with the scar that Matti had touched, had been earned for the love of it, when he was trying to improve himself.

The thought swirled through his mind: *And I'd thought I had nothing left to lose.* What kind of stupid fucking *hubris*.

"I can still fight," Luca said, holding himself stubbornly in a sitting position. "I'll show you." He swung his legs sideways over the edge of the bed—or tried to. The physician caught his good ankle and stopped him.

The physician sighed, rummaged in his bag, and pulled out another length of bandage. "If you're *not* going to be sensible about it, which I see is altogether probable—" He proceeded to show Luca a different way of bandaging the sprain, to give it as much support as possible.

"Has there been any mail?" Luca asked Dinah, once the physician had taken his leave.

"I haven't left your room since the last time you asked."

"What *are* you doing here? I'm sure you have things to do."

Dinah crossed her arms and leaned more pointedly against the wall. She was wearing a sash of woven silk ribbons in many different colours, a cheerful rainbow splash belting her black tunic over her black skirt. "You're waiting on a letter?"

"I'm waiting on part of the wedding present," Luca said, which was true. By now his mother would have responded to Luca's letter. A possible answer to at least half of Matti's problems was in some fast courier's saddlebag, drawing ever closer to Glassport, and all Luca had needed to do was bait the hook with himself.

Though this wasn't going to be one of his meaningless cons. He couldn't slither away at the first sign of consequences, or cheerfully siphon off what he wanted with one hand while making amends with the other. He was buying a future with a future. As bargains went it was practically mythic, and nobody escaped intact from myth. The gods made sure you paid in the end.

"Morning mail's due soon," said Dinah. "I'll let you know if there's anything."

"Thank you."

"*If* you show me what's in it."

"You are the worst gossip in this city, Dinah Vaunt."

Dinah's smile was equal parts smug and sunny as she let herself out.

Luca's ankle sent up pain in small warning bursts as he hobbled over to the desk, but at least it showed no signs of crumpling under his weight. He gathered pencil and blank paper and took a slow, steeling-himself breath.

He wrote a number at the top of the page, and an equation beneath the number. That part wasn't a problem. Luca knew the range of interest rates that would apply to a loan, from the safest and longest-term at a banking House to the coercive terms squeezed from the desperate by back-alley loan rats. They were just the names of numbers. Words thrown around in conversation.

The problem was that the difference between memorising an equation and being able to use it was like the difference between lifting a sword, as Matti had lifted his sword the very first morning in the practice room, and fighting your way to the end of a bout. Luca chewed on the pencil and tried to focus. He knew the principle of interest, he *understood* what compounding meant, but trying to apply it to real numbers was like listening to Matti's twin siblings natter on in their mother's tongue. It had always been that way. Perse could talk himself exasperatedly dry about how *smart* Luca was. Luca knew better.

Painfully, Luca moved the pencil. Two lines later he drew a cross through the whole thing, muttered a curse, tugged at his hair—winced, at the resulting complaint from his ribs—and started again.

He couldn't have said how long it was before someone knocked at the door of his room and then opened it without waiting for a reply. Luca flicked the pencil across the desk with a sigh. There was a number at the bottom of the paper, and his head had discovered a new kind of pain like a laundry peg being pinched between his eyes.

"Mail," Dinah sang. She held out an envelope to Luca. "Feels bulky. Come on, then. What *is* the other part of this present?"

"Something expensive," said Luca, grabbing it from her.

"Mr. Piere."

Luca grinned at the whine in her tone. "Miss *Vaunt*. You'll have the whole story, I promise you. As soon as it's all mine to tell."

Luca tore open the envelope. A tension he hadn't been aware of dissolved away as soon as his fingers touched the scrap of fabric that was folded within. He pulled it out, and the letter with it.

"What's that?" Dinah asked as he read.

"It's silk." Luca held the silvery stuff out to her, and Dinah rubbed it between finger and thumb.

"That's your present?"

Luca nodded. "It's not just silk. It's something true."

"Ooh," said Dinah. "You should write for the *theatre.*"

Luca made a rude gesture at her and continued with the letter. He skimmed it hungrily, then forced himself to go back and chew over each line, making sure he'd understood it. Jacquelle Harte hoarded her favours, and she certainly didn't give them away for free, not even to her indulged younger son. All of Luca's pain was shoved aside as he sat there, lightheaded, working through what he'd promised and what he'd won. A future for a future.

It wasn't quite enough. It wasn't everything.

He drew another piece of paper towards him on the desk. It was crumpled from having been folded in his pocket, after his time spent combing through Kesey House's files last night, and then crumpled further from the encounter with Baudrain's men. Luca smoothed the paper with his fingers, looking at the address of the warehouse. He stood up and transferred most of his weight to the bad ankle, testing its stability.

"What are you doing, you idiot? Mr. Mattinesh Jay won't be in the mood to appreciate your present if you screw up your leg, lose the duel, and stop his wedding from happening," Dinah pointed out.

"I don't think you're supposed to call your boarders idiots," said Luca, absently bouncing on that leg.

"I am," said Dinah, "when they're being idiots. Get back into bed, Luca."

Luca glanced over at her, startled. Her mouth was a curl of exasperation but there was something in her eyes that reminded him of how young she was, and how easily she'd withdraw this overture of friendship, if he let her.

"Can't do that, Dinah." Her freckled face lit momentarily with relief, and Luca added, "The wedding's in two days, as you pointed out."

Dinah gave him a knowing look that Luca, who hadn't had cause to apply the word in a personal context for sixteen years, could only describe as *sisterly.*

"Is it an errand? I'll run it. I'm going to the market for Mama later."

"It is an errand, but I need to do it myself," said Luca, thinking of his lockpicks. He touched the paper again. "Though I could use your skills at distraction one more time, if they're on offer."

Dinah laced her fingers together and grinned. "All yours. What are we stealing today? Something else true?"

"No," said Luca. "We're going to steal a lie."

CHAPTER
19

The day before he was due to be married, Matti woke up to the faint nausea that he hadn't felt in nearly a year—the nausea that the swimming had managed to banish—and also to two small lumps of bodies burrowing themselves industriously beneath his covers.

"What— Huna's arse, Merri, what are you *doing*. I nearly kicked you off the bed."

A head of mussed black hair above deep dimples appeared halfway down the bed. *"Arse,"* Merri said, savouring it.

"Arse!" echoed Marko. Both twins knew rude words when they heard them.

"Wonderful." Matti put a pillow over his face and then removed it resignedly. The household was awake. He was awake. He had things to do.

"Joselyne said we were under feet," Merri offered as explanation, and resumed burrowing.

"So you've decided to be under my feet instead," said Matti, wriggling the feet in question. Merri gave hiccups of muffled laughter as Matti's toes found the tender skin of her stomach.

"Joselyne's making lemon curd," said Marko.

Matti detected a certain stickiness to the face that his brother was currently rubbing against his shoulder and sheets, and realised that he and the twins had been tactfully assigned to keeping one another out from under feet—foot—while Joselyne put the finishing touches on the council breakfast.

By the time Matti had dressed and made his way down from the top floor of the house to the lowest, the breakfast was underway, and the smells filling the corridor were enough to banish his nausea and make his stomach rumble as though he'd never broken his fast at yesterday's feast. He and the twins ate lemon curd on thick slices of white bread with a shattering crust, and grilled cubes of lamb threaded onto rosemary sprigs, and great dollops of cherries stewed in lacha and stirred through whipped goats' cheese.

Matti watched Marko's and Merri's faces become mirrors of progressive mess, and thought: *This is what it should be like.* No more counting every bronze and feeling guilty over everything that wasn't essential. No more gradient of splendour from the perfectly kept public rooms of the Jay townhouse to the modest and half-stripped bedrooms. He set down his spoon and closed his eyes, the food souring on his tongue, torn again between anxiety and hope.

From there Matti went to the dining room to politely greet the members of Glassport's city council who had accepted Tomas's breakfast invitation. The pre-wedding breakfast was not a ritual under anyone's auspices, just a social tradition that had perpetuated itself because people liked parties and Guildmasters liked expanding the celebrations around their children's weddings. It would have looked odd for Tomas not to hold one.

That said, it was odder for the invitation to actually be accepted by anyone except the host's friends.

"Guildmaster Martens," Matti said.

He managed, he thought, to sound only mildly surprised.

Lysbette Martens had shrewd blue eyes, set deep in a bony face, and a high knot of blond braids showing streaks of silver. She wore an old-fashioned style of shirt, white cotton with narrow sleeves and folds of gorgeous lace falling from her throat, tucked into black trousers, along with a belt in pale pink leather and matching teardrop earrings of what looked like rose quartz.

She could have looked fragile, but didn't. She looked like the marble on which her House had made its fortune, and the way her face cracked and rearranged itself into a smile was disarming.

"Call me Lysbette, Matti," she said. "If you're exasperated enough while you do it, I'm sure you'll sound just like your father."

"Thank you for coming," said Matti, who had never learned to enjoy being disarmed unless it was—

Well. Unless.

"I was hoping to have a word with the groom-to-be." Lysbette glanced towards the door. "In private?"

Matti searched the room. His father was in a cluster of council members still seated and drinking coffee at one end of the table. Matti caught his mother's gaze—she was resplendent today in an orange jacket embroidered with filigree green leaves and a black scarf looped in Sofia's new fashion—and she made a subtle, resigned face at him before returning to her own conversation.

Lysbette was politely pretending not to notice his hesitation. Matti's curiosity stuck him like a burr.

"Of course," he said, and led Lysbette to the sitting room. She didn't sit. Matti didn't either.

She said, "I imagine things will be different for you, after tomorrow."

"Were you hoping to give me advice on married life, Guildmaster?"

"I know how hard you must work, Matti, considering your father's other responsibilities." The words were sympathetic. Her eyes were like cool gems. "It must be a relief, thinking of the *resources* that a bright girl like Miss Cooper can bring to Jay House. I'm sure you're the last person who has to be told that running a House with a small family is exhausting."

"We don't mind working hard," said Matti. He could feel that his guard was being tested, and he didn't know why.

Lysbette took a few steps towards the empty fireplace as if admiring the designs of the iron frame, then turned again. Her hand drifted out to rest atop the back of a chair upholstered in silk brocade.

"And next year Glassport hosts the Negenhal," she said, as though offhand. "The council will be even busier than ever, putting together the preparations for that."

"Yes." Matti waited.

"If Tomas stands for Guildmaster again—"

"*If*," said Matti. "He will. And I think you know he will." He was sick of implications and half-truths. He wanted to take a risk, to be bold—not as Luca would, but as himself. Straightforward.

He took a deep breath.

"We know what Corus is doing," he said.

Lysbette's sculpture of an expression slipped, her eyes widening, and Matti knew. She *was* involved, somehow.

It was like being squeezed between twin rollers of dismay and relief. Up until that moment Matti had half convinced himself that the Martens connection was something that Luca had spun out of nothing. A diversion to keep Matti's eyes away from what the Hartes were doing, handily invented after Matti had told him about Lysbette's possible motives to hurt Tomas and his House. After all, where was the evidence?

Nowhere, except in Lysbette's fingers clenched pale around the top of the chair. And even now she was releasing them and clasping them in front of her, well on her way to perfectly composed once more.

Matti pushed on before she could speak. That was what you had to do, with liars.

"You're paying him, too, as well as the Keseys? Sabotage can't be worth much to you, or he'd live in a better house."

Lysbette gazed at him for a while. Her chest rose and fell beneath the impeccable layers of lace. Now that she'd had a chance to recover, Matti couldn't read her as easily, but he thought there was still some surprise there, beneath the calculation.

She was probably arriving at the same conclusion that Matti had reached before he let himself speak: that even if Lysbette went straight from here to Simeon Kesey and Corus, to warn them that the Jays had found them out, it wouldn't make much difference now. After tomorrow this would all be over, one way or another.

Finally Lysbette sat down on the chair. She said, dry as paper, "Or Vane is smart enough not to flaunt wealth he shouldn't have."

"That wasn't a denial."

Half a smile appeared. "Hm. If I'd known you were fishing, it would have been. Honestly, Vane would be doing better for himself if he could keep a leash on that lazy son of his. To be relying on his father for an income, at that age . . ." She shook her head. "Not like you. *You're* a responsible boy. Tomas knows how to raise them, I'll give him that."

"This isn't about me," said Matti.

"It is about you." Lysbette's smile didn't move. "It's about Jay House. You should have adopted Adrean Vane, my dear. Then you'd never have had this problem with Corus. Anyone thwarted in their heart's desire can turn dangerous."

Matti heard the warning there, but his mind was spinning off down the path her words had opened up. House adoption? Perhaps his parents had discussed it once, long ago, but—

"Dad wouldn't," he said.

"Of course not," said Lysbette. "It would weaken his political position. Tomas Jay could never be seen admitting that House status is, *still* is, and is going to remain, the ultimate goal for anyone with ambition to wealth and influence in the Nine Free States." She fixed Matti with a wry look. "Now that you're about to be married for money, your sister had better keep a sharp eye on her own prospects. I wouldn't be surprised if Tomas encouraged her into an outdoor wedding. For the look of it."

It was like trying to follow Luca at his most sinuous, his most lazily brilliant. Matti forced himself to keep his eyes on Lysbette's, and adapted. "It's not about the *look*," he said. Even so, he thought about the shabbiness of the Vane house with a twinge of discomfort. "It's what he actually believes."

"I know," said Lysbette. She leaned her elbow on her knee, a tired gesture. "This would all be so much easier if he didn't. Arri save me from fucking idealists."

Realisation fell onto Matti. "You don't give a shit about our House," he said. "You don't care if we prosper or fail. You just want Dad off the council, so you can have your precious votes for your precious canal. You want him to quit as Guildmaster."

"And for any *normal* person," said Lysbette Martens, exasperated, "watching their House crawl to the brink of ruin would do it."

Matti thought suddenly of Corus bringing the first rumours of Harte House's expansion plans to Tomas, not to Matti. Corus would have known that Matti tried to insulate his father from business details. It made sense, if one of the people employing Corus as a spy wanted to see Tomas quit politics and scurry back to the business of his failing House.

"I won't apologise," Lysbette added. "I'm doing what I have to do to secure the future of my House."

Matti priced her outfit with two long glances, and made it obvious he was doing it. Annoyed colour appeared over Lysbette's cheekbones. Matti thought about his brother and sister, about cherries and laughter and doing without. His anger felt like moonwater lining his throat, first cold and then hot.

"Your future looks fairly secure to me," Matti said. "Will getting your hands on that marble a few weeks sooner really make such a difference?"

"You're a child of Huna. You know what it is for fortunes to rise and fall at the whim of trends. There's a demand for red marble facades in the south of Ashfah now, but who knows how long it will last? It takes long enough for ships to cross the Straits, and stone sinks faster than wool if the seas turn rough."

Matti made himself absorb that barb without flinching.

"This is how it works," said Lysbette. "When you're successful, you take your turn as Guildmaster, and you do your bit for the city. But you also get what you can for your Guild and your House. Everyone *knows* that. Everyone plays along. Except Tomas."

"So you thought you'd ruin us," said Matti, flat.

"The Keseys want to ruin you. And they also want a Guildmaster who's less concerned with working hours and industry standards. Me—yes. I want him off the council. I want a Spinners and Weavers Guildmaster with the sense to vote my way and accept my help for whatever they want in turn."

"You're being very frank," said Matti, "and I stopped fishing a while ago. You have to know I won't keep this secret."

Lysbette's sapphire gaze met his and Matti knew, before she said it, what her response would be. "Your word? My word? Would you put them in the marketplace against each other, Matti Jay? You haven't any proof against me. I think you'd have produced it already, if you did. And *I* know that your House is faltering."

That struck up a sickly echo from months ago. *Aren't you afraid I'll tell someone?*

Matti remembered the slide of his finger, careful, beneath an unfamiliar blade. Balancing. *And so the situation is like this.*

"As you said, I'm getting married," said Matti. "We won't be faltering much longer. Withdraw your support from Corus and the Keseys. Let us deal with them. Corus won't be working for us much longer."

"Do you expect me to bow out?" said Lysbette Martens. Her shoulders were perfectly straight. Luca would never have needed to pinch his fingers between them. "I can make life difficult for you in other ways. But I wouldn't have to, if you talked your father off the council. He might quit if *you* asked."

Matti was more than a little impressed that this woman had the audacity to come into his house, admit to everything she'd done, and still try to make a deal. This, he suspected, was why she'd wanted to speak to him in the first place.

Lysbette pressed her advantage into his silence. "It won't cost you anything to have this canal built. Your House might even benefit."

"That's true," Matti allowed, thinking about Collins and the Barlow wool market. "But it would cost my father something, and I'm loyal to my family."

"Is all of your family loyal to your House?" returned Lysbette. "House prosperity and family loyalty are supposed to be the same thing. It's unfair of Tomas to make you choose between them like that."

Matti squeezed his eyes shut, fighting agreement. Opened them. "Someone has to think about the bigger picture, or society collapses."

"Leave the big picture to the gods," said Lysbette. "All they want is for us to get ourselves halfway across the bridge, and they'll help us across the other half."

The idiom sounded hollow in Matti's ears for the first time. He tasted his words before he said them.

"But who builds the bridge?" he said. "And on whose backs is it built?"

Lysbette let out a long sigh. "Arri wept. You're just as bad as your father."

No, I'm not, Matti thought. *By your standards I'm better, because for a long moment there I was tempted to take your deal.*

He thought of what Maya and Luca had told him about the working conditions at the Kesey workshop. A quiet, dark trickle of poison somewhere within him, the worst of his resentment against his father, flowed out through his feet and was gone. He stood firmer without it.

"You can't build on the backs of the voiceless forever," he said. "And I wouldn't want to be part of a state that does."

Lysbette Martens nodded, as if she too had felt the finality of Matti's decision. She stood. She spread her hands with a flash of rings. "Well, young Mr. Jay. You have nothing over me. And I have nothing over you. So go and get married. Banish Corus and name a new senior agent. We'll keep playing the game, and we'll see who comes out on top."

By the middle of the afternoon, there wasn't anything left to do.

The Jays and the Coopers had visited the Spinners and Weavers Guildhall to approve its decorations—a whole new set of wall hangings had been pulled from the Guild's vast and mothballed storehouses, chosen for their depictions of romance or the predominance of green and gold in their colours—and they had spoken to Rowain Duvay. As the Deputy Guildmaster, Duvay would be performing the ceremony. He deserved to know, Sofia had pointed out dryly, that there was likely to be a response when he paused after the ritual question: *Does anyone wish to challenge against this marriage?*

The Coopers had invited Matti to lunch. The Jays had invited Sofia to dinner.

And now Matti stood looking at Sofia over the expanse of a gorgeous bedspread, a wedding gift from one of the best drapiers in the city, in the bedroom in the Jay townhouse that would be theirs to share from tomorrow night onwards. It was a clean and lovely room with small touches of personality to it that only served to make it more strange, more dissociated from anything that felt real to Matti. But this *was* what was real.

The embroidery of the bedspread was rough beneath Matti's fingers. He ran his hand over it in circles, watching the patterns blur, fighting harder than he'd fought in months to keep words inside his mouth. This was real. The happiness that Luca had brought to life within him was a lie. And the last time Matti had let himself be selfish, he'd followed the icy slope until his feet went out from under him, and he'd crashed them all into the consequences of that lie with bruising force.

"Matti," Sofia said.

He looked up. Sofia's eyebrows were worried, and for a wild moment Matti wondered if they were both on the verge of pulling back, despite everything—perhaps they could blurt it all out here, now, let their truths smash and mingle into a cleaner kind of wreckage. Ever since the conversation with Lysbette he'd felt a pressure behind his eyes as though grimy handfuls of lowest-grade wool were being crammed into his skull, just as they were stuffed into cushions. Something had to crack.

"Are you in there, Matti?" came Tomas's voice from down the hall. "You've a visitor. Your best man is here."

Matti rocked back on his feet, as though the idea of it was a blow.

"Matti." Now Sofia's eyebrows looked downright concerned. Matti had shown her the note that Luca had sent; he'd given up on the idea of keeping secrets from her and Maya, and it had been a relief. He'd lost faith in his own ability to think about the situation with the levelheaded sense he used to pride himself on.

"What am I going to do," said Matti, "tell Dad to send him away?"

Sofia said, swift, "No." She stroked a hand over her artfully draped scarf—searing amethyst, today—as if for comfort. She knew what it was to care about how things looked.

Maya was waiting for them at the base of the stairs.

"Where is he?" asked Matti.

"Still on the doorstep," said Maya. "He was polite to Dad, but he refused to step inside until you'd said he could." A quick thinning of her lips. "He was a bit dramatic about it."

"I'll bet he was." Before he could talk himself out of it, Matti opened the front door of his own house, stepped through, and closed it behind him.

Luca was standing on the second step, looking out onto the street. It was a warm, bright autumn day. In the sunlight the back of his head was like—like silk, Matti thought helplessly.

Luca turned around when the door clacked shut.

"Huna's teeth," Matti said, aghast. All his resolve not to speak first had fled at once. "I didn't think I'd hit you that hard."

Luca looked blank, then lifted a hand to the bruise that framed his left eye and coloured his cheek like poorly applied paint. Set against the vivid purpling, the grey parts of his eyes were almost blue, the brown parts almost green. *I mark easily,* he'd said.

Then, to Matti's surprise, Luca grinned. "Mattinesh," he said, "what you gave me was a slap, more or less. Don't worry. This is courtesy of someone much less good-looking than you, who mistook me for someone with a heavier purse than I actually possess. An easy mistake for a person to make, as you'll recall."

Matti found his mouth trying to smile. "I—"

"Fuck," said Luca, abrupt. "No. I knew I'd fuck this up. That's not what happened. It's what I've told everyone else happened, but . . . I'm going to tell you the truth. *All* the truth." A deep breath. "If you'll let me. Can I talk to you? Alone?"

His lower lip had been split too. Matti didn't realise he was reaching to touch it until his thumb was a whisper from Luca's mouth, and it was Luca whose breath shuddered out of him and who took hold of Matti's wrist, darting-fast, as though he were wary of the contact. Matti snatched his hand away. Luca let him go.

"Not alone," Matti said. "I don't think I can . . . I think there are other people who deserve to hear what you're going to say."

Luca didn't look happy, but he nodded.

Matti had told his parents about the Keseys, and about Corus, but not the truth about Luca. Now he told them only that his best man was visiting for a final discussion with himself and Sofia about the wedding, and about how things would proceed when Adrean Vane made his inevitable challenge.

His mother offered to have Joselyne bring in biscuits. Luca was beginning to look like a trapped cat. It made Matti feel better.

"No, thank you," Luca said to the offer.

"Then for dinner, stay," Nessa said cheerfully. "There will be one tradition or another to say that you should. Or we can invent one."

Finally the sitting room door was closed and it was just the four of them. Maya and Sofia seated themselves together on a couch, and the glances Luca darted at them would have made Matti laugh under other circumstances. They did have the air of a pair of magistrates, or a particularly ill-disposed audience at a musical performance.

Luca reached into his jacket and pulled out a sheet of paper folded into quarters, which he held out to Matti.

"What's this?"

"A very small part of what I owe you," said Luca. "Or, actually, an attempt to figure it out."

Matti's curiosity got the better of him. Unfolded, the paper was full of scribbled calculations. Many of them were crossed out or scrawled in angry lines. They began with a proposed loan, a sum of money: two hundred gold.

"I'd never charge this rate of interest" was Matti's first comment.

"Not to a friend," said Luca. "I thought I'd better err on the side of what you might charge someone you really disliked."

"Not to *anyone*," said Matti, obscurely injured. But he kept reading. He followed the calculation, the interest owing on a loan of that size over the precise time since he first met Luca, all the way to the bottom of the page. The final sum of money owing, capital plus interest, was circled.

"This is wrong," Matti said finally. "You made at least two major mistakes. Here and here."

Luca made a pained, breathless sound. "I told you I'm no good with numbers."

Maya was making demanding gestures. Matti passed her the paper to look at. "You told me a lot of things," he said to Luca. "How was I supposed to know which ones were true?"

Luca ran a hand through his hair. His eyes were wide and

entreating; the parts of his face not swallowed by the bruise were pale. He wasn't moving with his usual ease. Matti wanted badly to take Luca in his arms, to make him laugh and forget the pain. To smooth his tongue over Luca's damaged lip and hear him hiss; to kiss him until they both forgot to care if it made him bleed again.

"The truth," Matti said, only half sure he was about to hear it.

"All right. Yes." Now that the paper wasn't in Luca's hands, he clearly didn't know what to do with them, and he settled one on the hilt of his sword with relief. "I honestly didn't know who you were when I first approached you. And I was *never* trying to spy on your House. I didn't even know you saw my House as a potential competitor, until you mentioned it in passing."

"And then . . . what?" asked Matti. "Once you knew, you had to guess how I'd react when I found out."

"Yes. Thus the *not telling you.*"

"I see," put in Maya, from the couch. "That worked out so well."

"You weren't going to find out!" said Luca, firing up in return. He didn't even glance at Maya; his attention was all on Matti. "My brother's sudden appearance was not in the plan. Not that there was a plan."

"You should have told me," said Matti.

"I . . . I've tried to explain this to you, in my head, so many times. I know it sounds stupid. Of course if I could go back, I'd tell you. I'd tell you everything. But I didn't think it would matter."

"No," said Matti, hearing the cutting edge of his tone. "No, why would telling me the truth about who you are ever *matter?*"

"It didn't matter because I didn't get to *keep you!*" Luca yelled. "Because I was just the person who tried to con you, and the person giving you sword lessons, and then I was just the person you were fucking as a farewell fling to freedom, before you threw yourself away on a marriage that was going to make you miserable!"

Matti felt as though the world had paused. He couldn't look

away from the sudden wash of fear, quickly replaced by defiance, that filled Luca's face.

The silence was horrible.

There was, eventually, a very small cough from Sofia. To Matti's relief, it sounded more like someone heroically fighting down laughter than someone about to erupt with rage.

She said, "Matti, are you *sure* you don't want us to leave . . . ?"

Matti was a hairsbreadth from losing his grip and saying yes, and letting Luca keep on spinning him some outrageous story that Matti would desperately want to believe, and Matti would feel all the anger he'd spent five days nursing crumble within him as he stepped forward and got his hands in Luca's hair—

"Actually," said Luca to Sofia, "you should probably hear some of this too, Miss Cooper."

Deliriously into Matti's mind fell the idea that Luca was going to do a blow-by-blow description of exactly how Matti had fucked him—exactly how he'd sucked Matti's cock—right here and now in front of Matti's sister and betrothed. He managed to banish it as absurd, but not before he'd had to turn a sharp inhalation into a coughing fit.

Sofia's eyebrows rose like a pulled-taut archer's bow. Her voice had something of the arrow to it when she said, "Are you planning to challenge for my betrothed, Luca Harte? Do I need to hire a duellist of my own? I warn you, I can afford the best."

Luca threw a look at Matti that was raw and transparent as broken glass. It cut cleanly through something in Matti that had knotted itself irredeemably. He felt punctured, released, as though half of his heart's blood were flowing along a new route.

"There's a reason why I didn't come to see you sooner," Luca said. "I was waiting for a letter from my mother. I told you, I never thought we were competitors. But you had all these reasons, *good* reasons, to suspect that Harte House was branching out into wool. Not even Perse could tell me why Mama would be looking into hiring ships that leave from Fataf, or new Glassport warehouses, when all our raw silk is native Thesperan. So I asked her myself."

Luca pulled out a small scrap of fabric. He hesitated, then gave it to Sofia, whose brows drew together thoughtfully and then shot high.

"Gallia silk," Sofia said.

"*Gallia.*" Maya's hand was at her mouth. "But—how would your House make it? It's illegal to export the worms or the raw thread."

"The Ashfahani trade council is lifting that embargo," said Luca. "Very soon. We're buying up saplings of brindle basil and the worms along with them, we're importing them, and we're going to do everything. Pay for Ashfahani farmers to train our people. Process the raw thread. Weave it ourselves." A flash of a smile, sharp and proud.

"Huna wept," breathed Maya. "This is enormous."

"And it's secret," said Luca. "Or it has been. Mama said she hadn't planned to announce for another few weeks, but—I asked her for something I could give you."

Yet another letter emerged from Luca's jacket. This one had a broken wax seal, stamped with the same *H* that had appeared on Luca's broken pocket watch. Luca held it out to Matti. His eyes, above the letter, were tense and clear.

"Read it," Luca said.

⸻ ◈◈◈◈◈ ⸻

Matti read the letter from Luca's mother in silence. When he was done, he handed it to Maya and Sofia, whose heads bent over it together.

Matti would have worked out the gist of it from Jacquelle's reply, but Luca was suddenly glad that his own initial letter wasn't there to be gazed at too. Perhaps if he and Matti were doing this without an audience. But the total shattering of Luca's priorities and the rebuilding of them around his wretched heart were surely obvious enough, without the proof in his own hand as well.

He'd written: *I find myself owing a debt of honour. I need whatever concession, whatever advantage we can arrange, for the benefit and enrichment of Jay House. I'm asking this of you as my Head of House, Mama, and I'll owe you a favour in return. No limits.*

Knowing, of course, that there was only one thing that Jacquelle Harte now wanted of her beloved, irresponsible second-born heir.

"Luca," Matti said.

"I think it will help," said Luca.

"Yes," said Sofia. "This changes the game. This is all very promising. But Matti . . ." She paused. Next to her, Maya folded her hands in her lap as if to keep something invisible contained. Sofia said, "I want to know what *you* want to happen next. I think you owe me that much."

"What I want?" Matti sounded hesitant, as bewildered as ever at the idea that what *he* wanted might be important. It was heartbreaking.

Of the two of them, Luca was the con artist. And yet Luca knew he'd been right: Matti was just as much a liar, even if the shape of it hung differently on him. Matti was the one to whom honesty, *real* honesty, truths scraped right out of the chambers of the heart, came the least easily.

"I haven't finished with my truths yet," said Luca. He felt as though he were flinging himself off a cliff, but it would give Matti some breathing space. Show him that he didn't have to be vulnerable alone. "Though I've been going at them backwards. The gallia silk is why I wasn't spying. Don't you want to know why I was here in the first place?"

"You said . . ." Matti frowned. "I can't remember. Something about being a clerk, about what your family wanted . . ." He looked at the letter, realisation visibly falling over him.

"I can't do anything with numbers," Luca said. "It's never been a secret. My mother hired tutors. One of them locked me in a room and said I couldn't come out until I finished my worksheets; I told Mama and she fired him, and after that nobody ever forced me to do anything. I didn't see the point in working hard at something I hated, so I didn't. I went to sword lessons instead. It didn't *matter*. Perse was the one who was going to be the Head of our House."

"And then Perse married out," said Matti.

Luca nodded. His cheeks were hot. "I thought I was lazy. But I—no, I was lying about that too. I literally can't do it. And the thought of having to do it anyway, of everyone knowing I was incapable—I didn't deal with it well. Obviously."

"Don't tell me," said Matti, dry. "You did something stupid."

"I started running cons. And I robbed the Artisan Guildmaster in Cienne, Andri Baudrain. I stole the best piece in his collection, a silver inkstand with opals, and—look, I thought everyone would realise it was a joke, I was going to give the fucking inkstand *back,* but then I knocked over a sculpture of blown glass that was standing on a cabinet in his study. It was huge. Gorgeous." He breathed through a slow churn of irrational panic. It was *done.* It was dealt with. He'd wear the bruises on his face for weeks, but he could walk into Cienne without being thrown in the city jail for robbery or dragged into Kusi's Guildhall to face her justice.

He still couldn't help dwelling, for a cold brilliant moment, on the memory of time slowing down as his sleeve caught one delicate, gold-streaked flourish of glass, and the whole sculpture lurched and fell.

It had made a sound like high bells, striking the ground. Luca had laughed at the noise and at the explosion of fragments like a wave breaking over his ankles. He remembered that. He remembered laughing, and he remembered the hot fingers of recklessness and dismay that had squeezed his heart when the laughter stopped.

"It was the Guild's patron-gift," he said. There was a sharp intake of breath from Sofia. Luca tried a smile on her, and it made his lips smart. "Yes. Here's an interesting fact for you. The Artisans don't keep theirs in the Guildhall; they loan it out to the Guild-master, as a symbol of Kusi's favour embedded in their dwelling. Because I *needed* to bring an entire Guild and their goddess down on me as well. That sculpture had been the heart of the Guild in Cienne since before the first Negenhal. Before the Nine Free States. Do you know how long it takes, how expensive it is, to create and consecrate a new one?"

Not even Luca knew, really. The patron-gift of the Spinners and Weavers in Cienne was a rug of wool and silk that was hung behind glass in the foyer of the Guildhall, a miracle of geometric design in glowing shades of purple and red and blue. It was old and beautiful and revered, and if the Guildhall ever caught fire, it would be the first thing any of Huna's children would rescue.

He went on, "Anyway, Baudrain's daughter saw my face, as I was escaping, and he was going to have me arrested."

There was a silence from the Jays and Sofia that Luca couldn't kid himself was the slightest bit impressed.

Finally: "That *is* stupid. That's the stupidest thing I've ever heard!" said Matti. "What were you thinking?"

"*I wasn't*," Luca snapped. "Don't you get how I work by now? I wasn't thinking. I was *doing*. I was trying to be someone who didn't have to deal with any of my actual life, and I thought, well, that person would see Andri Baudrain as a challenge, and teach themselves to pick locks, and even if they were caught they'd laugh and be brave and get out of it, somehow." His mouth was so dry. He swallowed. "But I only got out of it because I'm the heir to a House and my mother knows how to use her connections. That's what Perse was here to tell me. And I'm *not* brave, because I ran away, figuring that would let me start over as—whatever I wanted."

"Why?" asked Sofia.

"*Why?*"

"Yes." Her brown gaze was level and calm. "What's the worst that would have happened? Yes, you'd have been arrested and tried in the city courts for robbery or trespass, and the Guild of Artificers would have claimed reparations under Kusi's auspices. Your House would have had to pay fines. Enormous ones, yes, but—was it really worth running away?"

Luca stared at her as stale panic exploded in his temples. He had no idea how to explain the sheer, mind-wiping horror he'd felt at the thought of standing trial—*twice*—while all of Cienne watched, and whispered, and knew that he was a failure and a black smudge on the bright name of the House he was supposed to inherit. It was the desperation with which he'd wanted to win Maya's approval, blown out to the scale of a city full of people he loved.

And at the time, it had landed square on top of the knowledge that he'd be just as much a disaster if Harte House's fortunes were actually placed in his hands, that he was already seeking a way to escape the path that had been laid out for him.

Of course he'd fucking run.

He was fumbling so hard to fit that into words that something even truer and more bitter slipped out around it.

"I don't know if it *would* have been fines," he said. "I don't know if my mother would have paid them. She was already losing patience, because I didn't want anything to do with House business. I thought—surely this is the line. This is where she stops indulging me."

"You thought your mother would refuse to pay? Have you serve a jail term?" Sofia asked, in a thoughtful tone that suggested she wouldn't have blamed Jacquelle one jot.

"To teach me a lesson? Yes. I was so scared she would, I didn't want to stick around and find out," Luca managed. "I told you: I'm not brave. When Baudrain's men found me two nights ago I nearly vomited, I was so scared."

"Ohh," said Maya. "And *that* explains the bruises. I was getting curious."

Matti stepped forward again, and this time Luca didn't have any self-preservation left in him at all, because he let Matti touch his mouth; he let Matti trace the edge of the bruise, and let himself drink in the concern and the tenderness in Matti's fingertips. Something was finally shining through the cracks of Matti's expression. It looked so close to forgiveness that Luca's heart soared despite himself. If he didn't think it would hurt so much, he would have thrown himself onto his knees and begged.

"Matti," he said, and realised to his horror that he was shaking.

"You're a fucking disaster," Matti said, and dragged Luca into his arms.

"*Ow,*" said Luca into Matti's neck, but he tried not to say it too loudly. Fuck his ribs, anyway. The last thing he wanted was for Matti to let go. The *first* thing he wanted was to kiss Matti, but he was going to let Matti decide when that happened again.

For now it was a sheer relief to be able to lean against someone, to have someone behave as though he were in need of comfort. He *had* been scared, when Baudrain's men found him. He'd been terrified, and it had tangled itself up with the terror he felt that Matti would never want to see him again, and now all of that was melting away.

It wasn't very long before Matti released him, but Luca felt like a new person.

Matti looked at his feet, then at Luca, and then at the girls on the couch. "Ah. What were we talking about?"

"Before Mr. Harte sidetracked us," said Maya, "Sofia was asking you what you want, Matti." She pushed back a wisp of hair. Her eyes were bright but mirthless. "Though we might have arrived at an answer nonetheless."

Matti's shoulders settled. "I want . . . something more. Something that isn't bales of wool and half-truths and lines of numbers from the moment I wake up to hours after I close my eyes in bed.

And I'm afraid it would be so easy to marry Sofia"—with a nod in her direction—"and just keep on doing what's expected of me."

"Easy?" Luca demanded. "You said you'd hate it."

"Yes," said Matti, steady and bleak. "It would be very easy to keep on doing things I hate."

The look on Sofia's face was, Luca thought, predominantly relief. She said, "I did ask you at the start of this, Matti, whether you had feelings for anyone else."

"I didn't. Not then." After a moment Matti added, "Would you have refused the engagement, if I did?"

"I don't know." Sofia sounded a little surprised at herself. "You thought I was in love with Adrean, and that didn't make a difference to you."

"No, it didn't. We needed the money too much."

"And now you don't need it? Is that"—she waved at Jacquelle's letter, which she'd set down on a side table—"enough? You'll know best of all of us."

"Enough for a reprieve," Matti said.

"There's more," Luca said. "I've got something else, something big, but—for it to have the best effect, I think the wedding should still happen tomorrow." Matti's shoulders curled and tightened at once. Luca went on quickly, "Not the marriage. But we have a perfect public forum, in front of half the Guild, and Vane and Kesey will be off guard. It'd be a shame to waste it." He added, "Will Guildmaster Martens be at the wedding?"

"Oh, Huna's tits." Matti snapped his fingers. "Luca, you don't know what happened this morning." And he told Luca about a conversation he'd had with Lysbette Martens. Maya and Sofia looked unsurprised; Matti had clearly already shared the details with them.

One last secret thrummed on Luca's tongue as the pieces fell into place, but he swallowed it. He *wanted* this to be big. This time, he wanted the glorious shattering to be a deliberate act.

"But yes," Matti finished. "Lysbette will be there tomorrow. All the council members will."

Luca nodded. "Good. I want her to see this play out. As a warning, if nothing else."

"You're saying you want them to have a wedding," Maya said to Luca, "but not get married."

"We have paid for everything," said Sofia thoughtfully. "And I do look *very* nice in my dress. How are we supposed to start this new fashion you've set your heart on, Maya, if we can't parade ourselves in front of the Guild in all our finery?"

One of those sun-bright smiles broke out on Maya's face under Sofia's teasing gaze. "I suppose that's true."

"Sofia," said Matti. "I should have asked this right away. What do *you* want?"

"I certainly don't want to marry someone who'll hate it," said Sofia promptly. "But I think what you're asking is, do I want to marry *you*. And the answer is no." She and Matti looked at each other for a few silent moments. There was a solidity to Sofia's stance that Luca admired, as though nothing could have possibly thrown her off-balance. She deserved far better than to be someone's duty, and she clearly knew it.

Matti must have seen something to that effect in her eyes, because he smiled ruefully. Sofia added, "And I have to admit, I want to see what Mr. Harte's idea of *playing this out* looks like."

"A wedding, but no marriage. Luca . . . are you going to throw the duel? Before witnesses?" A light brimming of irony touched Matti's words. "That'll be your reputation gone. You'll be kicked out of your Guild."

Luca forced himself to shrug, then swallowed a wince as his ribs twinged with pain. If Adrean Vane knew how to use a sword, and how to read someone's weaknesses, Luca might still manage to lose the duel without any pretence at all. "It's a good thing I no longer plan on a long-term career as a duellist. I'll have to fall back on silk."

"I'd rather you didn't throw it, if that's possible," said Sofia. "If Adrean challenges and *wins,* the talk will only get worse. *He'll* only get worse."

"Worse than what?" said Matti. "I thought you could handle the gossip."

Sofia didn't say anything. It was Maya who said, in a hard voice, "Some men take rejection as a negotiation. And not in a good way."

Luca felt an unexpected surge of sympathy for Sofia. He'd met men like that; he'd heard the way they talked when surrounded by what they considered friendly ears. He'd even seen the ugly side of one of them himself, after a monthlong liaison that Luca had broken off. He'd watched with startlement as the man's self-assured manner, which bordered on arrogance in a way that Luca had quite enjoyed at times, turned to vitriol and possessiveness. It was just another version of the entitlement Adrean's father had shown in deciding what he was owed for his service to the Jays, and then thinking himself justified in turning traitor when it wasn't given.

When it had happened to him, Luca had the advantage of a sword and knowing how to use it. Sofia had wit and money and a forceful personality of her own, but it clearly hadn't made a dent in the story Adrean had been telling himself—and the world—about their tragic romance.

"It's simple enough to stop a wedding at the business end," said Matti. "The Deputy Guildmaster is going to ask us if we accept each other. We just say no."

Maya narrowed her eyes at Luca. "Hold on," she said. "You said there was something else. You still haven't—"

The door to the sitting room cracked open. It was Tomas. "Dinner's on the table. And, fair warning, Nessa is instituting a no-wedding-talk rule for the duration of the meal. Are you all done in here?"

"Nearly." Luca threw Tomas a smile. "Matti, Miss Cooper, you go ahead. I want to talk to Mayanesh for another minute or two. Wedding-party secrets. Not for the bride and groom to hear."

Matti and Sofia gave him similarly suspicious looks, but they followed Tomas out of the room.

"Are you going to tell me this something else?" Maya asked, when the room was empty but for the two of them. "This mysterious big thing that you, who can't calculate a simple loan, are convinced will pull our House out of ruin?"

"Yes," said Luca. "I am. But I have some questions for you first."

Maya smoothed her skirts on either side of her and raised her eyebrows— *Yes?*

"Why haven't you offered? I'm assuming it's because you think she's had enough people's feelings imposed on her without her consent, but I'm keen to hear if it's something else."

Maya's mouth made a straight line. "What are you talking about?"

"If it helps, I don't think it'd be all that much of an imposition. Just from watching the two of you."

"You—"

"Come on, Mayanesh," said Luca. "How long have you been in love with your brother's betrothed?"

His mother's rule on conversational topics was probably the only reason Matti got through dinner without bursting. There was an awkward moment when Tomas said, "Tell us a story about your work with a sword, Mr. Piere; I'm sure you must have several," and Matti caught Luca glancing at him, just as he was looking to Luca in silent query as to whether their plan required ongoing secrecy regarding Luca's identity.

"Actually, the best story I know is one from my own sword master," said Luca. "Master Carriere used to work in Barlow, and one night in the middle of winter he was standing swordvigil for an old woman from a very rich House, who'd died suddenly of ice fever—"

And so on, into an implausibly eventful tale of mulled wine that might have been drugged, and duels fought with numb hands against mysterious masked opponents, and ghosts that turned out to be greedy distant cousins come in search of the gold that the old woman had always said she'd use to line the pockets of her deathgown.

When he was done, Luca took a drink from the glass of wine in front of him, bowed theatrically around the table, and turned to Merri, who was seated to his left.

"I saw you put that bread roll on a plate under your chair, Merrinesh."

"*Merri*," said Nessa, exasperated. "Again?"

Luca went on, "Who was that for? Do you have an invisible pet? I had one, you know, when I was younger. A cat."

Merri's face lit up. "Really? What was her name?"

"He was called Copper. What's yours? A rabbit?"

"Polina's a wolf." Merri glanced beneath the tablecloth. After a moment she said, conscientiously, "She's still growing."

The dinner conversation didn't return to Luca's past. Marko asked about his bruises, and Luca told him that he'd been accosted by some men while walking home at night, and that it looked a lot worse than it was. Luca told stories, but—as far as Matti could tell—he avoided any outright lies. Matti watched Luca laugh and drink and wave his fork, and felt something within him shift and fit together into an entirely new shape.

By the end of dinner Luca was flushed and his arm movements more expansive. He looked quite drunk, though Matti didn't think he'd had that much wine.

Nessa laughed at him. "You will fall in a canal on your way home, Mr. Luca Piere, if we send you out the door now. Sleep here. We have rooms."

Furtive excitement rose up Matti's spine. Luca was looking at him, eyes dancing.

"Yes." Matti's tongue was clumsy. "You should definitely sleep here."

"And then dunk your head in the canal tomorrow," said Sofia. "What a good thing the wedding's in the afternoon."

"Never fear. It takes a lot more than a hangover to slow me down, Miss Cooper," said Luca. "Thank you, Mrs. Jay. Very kind. I *will* sleep here."

Matti walked Sofia to her own house—she squeezed his hand, her expression a banked fire of excitement, before she slipped inside—and found his steps quickening on the way back home. He bade his parents good night, with a wash of renewed guilt at the fondness and tightness with which his mother hugged him. She wasn't one to cry, but her accent thickened as she flicked his ear and told him that she was proud, they were *so* proud, and they knew he would be happy.

"I think I will be," Matti said. Not a lie at all. No more lies. And, after tomorrow, no more secrets. "Good night, Mama."

He was not at all surprised to find Luca seated on the edge of his bed, leaning back on his hands, one foot tapping on the floor. Matti spared a moment to imagine Luca's restless energy confined to a prison cell, and was seized with the conviction that Jacquelle Harte might have been sorely tempted—and Matti couldn't blame her—but she wouldn't have done that to her whirlwind of a son if other options were available to her.

"This feels familiar." The slight slur of Luca's speech was gone. His cheeks were still pink.

"This feels ridiculous. Sneaking around in my own house, hiding lovers in my bedroom, as though I were seventeen."

Luca smiled and stood. "Now there's a story I want to hear." He came close. There was a faint limp in his step that hadn't been there before, or that he was now not bothering to mask. His clever hands slid up Matti's chest. "But later. I don't want to talk now."

Matti privately marked that one down as a lie, but an unconscious one. Nothing short of direct intervention from the gods would make Luca stop talking.

"You still have something to tell me." Matti had remembered, on his way home from the Coopers'. "You said there was some other big reason why Jay House would be fine."

Luca flicked one of the buttons of Matti's shirt back and forth with a forefinger, considering. "Will you let it be a surprise? If I swear up and down and on my mother's name that it's something good, and that I told Maya about it already?"

"Is hiding *more* things from me a good idea?" Matti demanded. "You just want to make a grand dramatic scene tomorrow, don't you?"

"Yes," Luca agreed. "I do. But you're right. I've told you enough lies." His smile slipped. "I'll tell you now, if you ask me to."

Matti wanted to know. He didn't want to go into the next day without feeling that he would have every controllable thread in his own hands.

He thought about the crossed-out lines of numbers on the loan calculation Luca had pressed into his hand.

"No, that's all right." He took a deep breath. "I trust you."

Luca's lips parted infinitesimally. He looked almost angry, for the space of a breath. Then he reached up and pressed his palms to Matti's face, hard enough to grind against Matti's cheekbones, and lifted his mouth in a quick, savage kiss. "Mattinesh. I'm sorry. I'm *so* sorry. Fuck, I didn't want to think about how much I'd hurt you."

A peacekeeping denial was obligingly ready to emerge, but Matti let it die in his mouth. It *had* hurt. It had felt like something vital had been lopped away, and the sensation of Luca in his arms now, glorious as it was, had its own fresh pain to it. Tingling and fierce like nerves being regrown.

Luca said, "I couldn't bear the thought of never touching you again."

A growl came out of Matti's throat. He kissed Luca again, burying his hands in Luca's incredible hair, tasting raw salt along the line of Luca's split lip. Luca's mouth was hungry beneath his, and Luca made little whines of desperation that settled low in Matti's stomach.

I can't lose this, Matti thought, *I can't,* and remembered that he had something to say.

"I'm sorry too."

Luca had unbuttoned Matti's shirt. His hands were sliding on Matti's chest, light rakes of his nails that left fire in their wake. "Whatever for?"

"You're leaving Glassport. You made a promise; you have to leave."

Luca's hands stopped. He groaned. "Huna's bleeding fingers, Matti, I'm about two heartbeats away from begging you to fuck me until I can't remember *any* of my names, real or fake. Can't this wait?"

That was an excellent attempt at diversion, and Matti's breath left him in a gust of immediate desire, but he wasn't going to fall for it. "Luca."

A pause. Unwillingly, Luca nodded.

"Glassport to Cienne isn't that far," Matti offered. "A few days, by coach. And I think if I refuse to take any breaks from work from now on, Maya will stab me herself."

Luca's eyes were sharp with hope. "So why are you sorry?"

"I'm sorry it had to happen at all. Your mother gave you those deals in exchange for your return to Cienne, and your word that you'd apply yourself properly to your House duties. You made that bargain. For me."

"It was probably inevitable, me going back," Luca said. "I think I always knew it. I just didn't want to think about it."

"No. Listen to me. You saw the box I was living in," Matti said, aching. "You *recognised* it. Do you think I wanted you to go back to that? For my sake?"

"It hardly compares. Yours was closing in around you for a long time. I haven't spent any time in mine—I just felt the bare outline of it, and ran."

Matti smiled despite himself. "Good instincts."

"I didn't think far enough ahead," said Luca. "Maybe I can work on it from— Look, this metaphor's getting unwieldy. Maybe I can be a different kind of Head of House to my mother, is what I meant. And different to what Perse would have been."

"You're creative," Matti pointed out. "You can talk your way around corners, and you take risks. You're a lot better at that than me."

"I am." Luca drew his fingertips down the side of Matti's neck. "Careful Matti Jay."

"You found the right angle to solve my problem with the Barlow Guildmaster in less than a minute, when I'd been tearing my hair out for a week. You have a flair for some parts of this, Luca."

"Mm," said Luca. "If only I had someone good with numbers."

A future expanded like a pool ripple in Matti's mind, so fresh and so huge that he couldn't breathe.

Luca's fingers moved to Matti's mouth. Matti kissed them and took hold of Luca's hand, adjusting his grip until it was a handshake. A bargain. A beginning.

"My name is Mattinesh Jay," he said. "Tell me what you want."

Luca's fingers stirred in his, then went still. All of him was still. It was strange enough that Matti felt like a man watching a card trick, afraid to blink.

"My name is Lucastian Harte, and I want us not to have a time limit. I don't want you to promise yourself to anyone but me."

A wave broke against Matti's lungs. "Luca."

"I want to tell you everything real about myself, because when you look at me like that I can almost believe you'll like me anyway. All of me. Even the parts that aren't—drama, and swords, and my hair, and the fact that I can make you laugh."

Their hands hung together between them. Matti clasped Luca's fingers in his own, hard, until Luca gripped back.

Matti said, "I want you to keep making me laugh. I want to keep you. Luca. I owe you my life."

"*Now* who's being dramatic?"

"Not really," said Matti. The truth felt like jenever, clean and strong in his mouth. "You broke me out of the box. The rest of my life is yours. If you want it."

"Huna's breath, how are you so fucking brave about this?" A laugh shook out of him. "Mattinesh Jay. I think you'd walk through fire."

It was an odd thought, given how Matti felt: vulnerable and raw, as though they were standing in a cold wind, stripped down to nothing but bones and undeniable things. Staring at each other over a handshake. Matti didn't feel brave. He felt like this was the only possible way to act, and these were the only possible things to say.

"I might," he said honestly. "I don't know. Are you asking?"

"I'm answering," said Luca. He lifted Matti's hand to his mouth and pressed his lips to Matti's bent fingers.

As he had done on countless days since that implausible moment in the practice room, Matti wanted to slide his fingers into Luca's mouth—and to keep them there, this time, to forget to come to his senses.

And there was nothing to stop him, was there?

Luca's eyes widened and then fell closed; his mouth twitched towards a smile before his tongue worked at Matti's two fingers, obedient to the unspoken command. They'd been to bed together at every opportunity, in the brief span of days between the ball and Persemaine's arrival, and yet Matti hadn't thought to do this. He should have insisted that they do nothing else. Matti moved his fingers gently, in and out, feeling the blunt scrape of Luca's teeth and the heady wet heat of that wide, infuriating mouth.

"Gods," said Matti, unthinking. "I want to see you do that when you're riding me."

The heat became tight suction for a moment, and Luca's eyes snapped open. He removed Matti's fingers by a tug on Matti's wrist.

"Done," Luca said. "Deal. *Yes.*"

"Take your clothes off," Matti said hoarsely.

Luca did as he was told. Matti took longer than he should have to divest himself of his own clothing, because he kept getting caught by the angle of Luca's faint-freckled shoulder emerging from his shirt, or the bruises dappling his side and legs, or the straight, bobbing arousal of Luca's cock below the thatch of dark copper curls. Luca had barely thrown his last sock aside when Matti caught his arm and drew him close. He cupped Luca's face—beneath the unbruised jaw—and kissed him, trying to make it everything he was feeling, everything he wanted to do and give and be.

Luca held on to Matti's wrists. He made small movements there with his thumbs, a glorious version of his restless tapping.

Matti kissed him deeply one more time, then kissed his cheek, then his brow bone. Light, light. Adoring.

"Now." Happiness was injecting Matti with daring. "I believe I was given some feedback, some time ago."

"Hm?" Luca had turned his head into one of Matti's hands and was mouthing the fleshy base of his thumb.

"Someone felt that I hadn't put adequate effort into wrecking them."

Luca froze. He released Matti's arms and pulled away, his eyes seeking Matti's.

"I'm not the cleverest man in Glassport, but I'm stubborn," Matti went on. "I try hard, and I don't stop."

It looked for a moment as though the impossible had happened and Luca was at a loss for words. He licked his lips. He cleared his throat.

"Oh, *please* try," Luca said finally, and yanked Matti flush against him, body to body.

The sensation, Luca's erect cock nudging up against his, was enough to threaten Matti's balance. Luca was all hot skin, his hands roaming over Matti's arse, his mouth dipping to suck open-mouthed at Matti's shoulder, and Matti almost missed the way Luca's breath caught in a grunt of pain when Matti's arm tightened around his back.

"Is it your ribs?"

"It's fine."

"I don't want to hurt you—"

"You can hurt me a *bit*," said Luca at once. His pupils were huge.

Matti coughed out a laugh. "I want you to be able to fight a duel, Luca."

"Oh. Yes. Fair point." A smile so sharp it bordered on wicked. "I believe you mentioned riding. That's mostly thighs; I think I can manage that."

Every other time they'd done this since the ball, they'd been in

Luca's small room in the boardinghouse. It felt both thrilling and comforting to Matti to lie back on his own sheets and watch Luca move naked around his bedroom, as Matti told him where in the dresser to find the bottle of oil.

"Let me," Matti commanded, when Luca knelt beside him on the bed. He held his hand out for the oil.

Luca handed it over without a murmur and sat astride Matti's hips, far enough forward that Matti's straining cock had a reprieve from the torture of contact. Luca rubbed one of Matti's nipples with his fingers, and sparks of sensation crawled across Matti's skin. He fumbled the stopper of the oil bottle, but managed to coat his fingers thoroughly.

"Lean down to start with." He could do this. He knew how much Luca liked it when Matti took charge, made his wants explicit. He put his dry hand on the small of Luca's back, guiding. "That's it. Is that all right? Not uncomfortable?"

Luca shifted until his knees were snug on either side of Matti's body. He bent all the way down, as instructed, and sucked Matti's earlobe into his mouth for a mind-curling moment. "Perfect," he breathed. "Ah—*fuck*, yes," as Matti's first finger breached him.

Matti couldn't get his finger very deep, with the angle available to him, but he wasn't interested in deep. He already knew how to make Luca shout and sob and come on his fingers alone. Now he wanted this: Luca stretched out atop him, breath coming quickly, waiting. Anticipating.

He took a handful of Luca's hair with his other hand, to remind himself not to touch Luca's sore ribs, and made small circles around Luca's rim with his oil-slick fingers.

"Matti, you fucking—*please*," Luca said, and bit Matti's lip.

Two fingertips at once, and Luca gave a gratifying moan. Still just the tips, though, pulsing in and out. Matti felt heady and powerful. Luca was hot and strong and as responsive to Matti's hands as he was to the slightest twitch of a blade.

It struck Matti anew how ridiculous sex was. But also how *good* it could be; better than he'd ever imagined. Two weeks had done nothing to rub the shine off the novelty of wanting someone this much. And now everything was layered, made more vivid, by the fact that there wasn't an endpoint. In Glassport or in Cienne, Matti would have this—have Luca—again, and again. It would keep getting *even better,* though he wasn't sure how.

Soon Luca was making needy sounds against Matti's mouth and grinding against Matti's stomach, shoving back to meet Matti's hand. Matti's wrist bumped his own cock from time to time. He was so hard he felt lightheaded with it.

"Stop," Luca gasped. "That's enough. I want you in me, right now."

Matti released him and Luca sat up. He reached behind him and took hold of Matti's cock, giving it a couple of torturous squeezes. Matti felt his abdominal muscles contract, felt the shout of his nerves. Luca knelt up, balancing himself. The crack of his mouth as he lowered himself, the audible scrape of his inhalation, was almost as good as the way he felt. Matti found he was running his palms along Luca's thighs, afraid to apply pressure and yet wanting nothing more than to shove down, to feel Luca engulf him totally.

"Just—*ah*. That's it." Small sways of Luca's hips, carrying him down. Luca's head was tipped back in simple abandon.

"Gods, you feel amazing."

"You too. *Fuck.*" Luca's stomach muscles clenched. "All right. All right." Settled, now, his weight gloriously resting on the tops of Matti's thighs, his cock leaking onto Matti's stomach. He took hold of Matti's hands and moved them insistently to his own hips. "Fuck me," Luca said: sharp and clear instruction. "Wreck me. Do it."

And Matti did his best, as he'd always done. His thumbs at the jutting bones of Luca's hips and then reaching back, taking convulsive handfuls of the hard muscle of Luca's arse. They found a rhythm, Luca rising with a powerful bulge of his thighs, Matti's firm grip grinding him down, Matti gone panting and wild with pleasure as Luca tightened and lowered and then did it again.

Matti drank in the sight of Luca's face, the slim muscle of his shoulders, the straight line of his throat. The tight pink nipples begging for the attention of Matti's mouth and yet too far away to reach.

"Oh," Luca gasped. "Forgot," and grabbed Matti's unoiled hand, pulling it up towards his face.

It took Matti a moment to focus, to remember. He was burning up. He was nothing but pulse and sweat and the pooling fire in his groin. He wanted to struggle upright and pull Luca even closer, get his hands on Luca's shoulders and yank him down; hear him cry out as Matti's length found new places inside him. But Luca was injured, and they'd begun this with other plans in mind.

Luca bit lightly at Matti's thumb before letting it slide between his teeth. The movements of his tongue were clumsy as he sucked and then groaned, kissed the pad and let Matti explore the soft insides of his slack lips. It was inelegant, uncoordinated; it was everything Luca usually wasn't. Luca's eyes were unfocused and he was working his own cock in frantic strokes. He was losing the rhythm, reduced to trembling jerks, little shifts of his body back and forth as though to corkscrew Matti even farther into himself.

"Fuck—oh, gods—" Luca came, spurting through his own fingers. Matti felt the vibrations of it everywhere at once. His thumb. His fingers tucked around Luca's jaw. And most torturous of all, the spasms of Luca clenching around Matti's cock.

It was enough. It was almost too much. Matti choked, "*Luca*," and pleasure obliterated him piecemeal: a tingling gush of heat down his legs, sparks beneath the skin of his abdomen. The sense of relearning how to inhale.

Luca swayed, his chest heaving. His fingers dug into Matti's chest, almost too hard. It took him nearly a minute to climb off, easing Matti out of him with a bite of his own lip.

"Fuck *me*." Luca sounded as drunk as he had at dinner. He performed a controlled collapse towards the space of clean sheet next to Matti, where he arranged himself on his back with a sprawl of limbs.

Matti bit back the obvious reply but couldn't think of anything clever to replace it. His mind was still clearing away the syrupy webs of his own orgasm. He dropped a kiss on Luca's shoulder instead, and moved to tug at least a top sheet up from the pile of bedclothes. It was no longer hot enough to sleep uncovered. Matti wasn't tired enough to sleep at all, yet, and knew his mind's tendency to chatter on in exhausting circles the night before anything important.

But he wouldn't mind sacrificing sleep tonight. *He* didn't have to fight any duels tomorrow. And this was only the second full night he'd ever been able to spend with Luca beside him. Every other time they'd fucked had ended in parting. Through whatever sleepless hours awaited, Matti would be able to see Luca, and hear him, and touch the storm-tossed waves of his hair as they lay bright against the pillowcase.

A slow smile spread over Luca's face when Matti matched deed to thought. Then, like a piece of wool being carded perpendicular, the smile slackened and disappeared. Luca turned his head and opened his eyes, and Matti's breath caught at his expression: shattered, and open, and young. Luca was shameless in bed in a way that Matti loved, saying anything that came into his head and never hesitating to tell Matti exactly what he wanted. It looked like whatever was brimming in his mouth now was something difficult. Something extraordinary.

There are things I'm afraid of.

"Mattinesh," Luca said, low.

"Lucastian. Luca." Matti kissed the side of that mouth as

though to sip at its secrets, its unsaid declarations. He would wait. "I want you. That's all. Just you."

———⟫⟫◦⊛◦⟪⟪———

"I hope you're proud of yourself," Luca said.

"For turning you into a morning person?"

"Bite your fucking tongue." Luca lifted his chin; Matti kissed the base of his neck, and then nipped the skin between his teeth. Perhaps Luca shouldn't have said the word *bite*. Perhaps he should say it five more times. "I will never be—that."

"You're awake now."

"Your curtains are thin."

Matti's mouth curved in a way that Luca felt rather than saw. "Do you have a pressing morning engagement, Mr. Harte?"

Matti's bedroom had two layers of curtains, and only the thinner ones had been pulled the previous night. The light in the room had the quality of a cool sun-drenched morning that was going to turn warm by noon. It would be commented on as an inauspicious sky for Matti and Sofia's wedding. Sofia's patron was an agricultural deity. Maha might have sent rain, if he'd cared to reach out and bless this particular union.

Luca sighed and twined his fingers into Matti's hair, encouraging. Matti sucked the base of Luca's neck, at first playfully, and then with enough force that Luca's flesh was drawn between his teeth. Shivers and goose bumps played cartography on Luca's skin beneath the sheets. He knew he couldn't *feel* the blood in his tiniest vessels yearning towards Matti's mouth, blushing purple and vivid in a way that would stain and stay. But imagining that he could feel it was almost the same.

"I do, actually," Luca said. "I'm giving a sword lesson."

A smile as Matti lifted his head. "I don't know if I have the time."

"Whoever said I was giving this lesson to *you*?"

The furrow of Matti's brow was a lot more enjoyable to look at when it was due to confusion and not bone-deep worry. And even better now that Luca could call it up with his words and banish it with his fingers. Matti bent his head again and bit outright at that same spot on Luca's neck. Pain throbbed beneath the smarting skin and Luca felt it go straight to his cock, both for the sensation and the possessiveness it represented.

"Hm," Matti said. "I didn't know you'd started to inflict your dreadful teaching techniques on others."

"Did you think my life revolved around your needs, Mattinesh? We poor duellists have to take our income where we can, you know. I can't be available for your every whim."

"No?" said Matti. "How much would that cost me?"

Luca bit the inside of his cheek, hard, at the jolt of need that went through him.

He managed, "A lot more than six hundred gold."

"Can I afford it?"

The second layer to that question caught up with Luca just as he was about to answer. "Yes." He leaned over and gentled Matti's mouth open, a slow tease of tongue. "Unaccustomed as you are to buying yourself nice things."

"Well, I . . ." Matti pulled away, rolled onto his back, and laughed. It was a genuinely merry sound that Luca couldn't remember having heard before. Luca wanted to put his own mouth over it, take it into his lungs.

"What?" he asked instead, trailing his fingers through the sparse hair on Matti's chest.

"Lucastian Harte," said Matti. "I gave you a scarf made of your own fucking silk."

"I worked very hard not to laugh," Luca assured him.

"You should take it as a compliment to your House. You make beautiful things."

Luca bowed his head in elaborate acknowledgement.

"And you are a beautiful thing," said Matti, softer. "You're right, I'm out of practice with luxury, but I bought you." He turned back, seeking, and took Luca's mouth with his own again. "I paid for you."

The shiver took Luca all over. He heard himself moan against Matti's lips, shameless.

Matti was braced on one elbow above Luca now, staring down at him, one thumb brushing hair back from Luca's temple. "I thought I had simple tastes. I don't care about pearls or silver. I don't need silk. I can live without cherries and bottles of Diamond Blend." Luca pressed up, incoherently wanting, and Matti obliged him with another bruising kiss. "But you," Matti breathed. "You are the most exquisite thing in this city, and I want you, and I'm going to have you."

Luca's bones were turning to water in his flesh. He felt a flush travel down his neck in the path of Matti's mouth, which laid a trail of kisses and quick nips. Matti paused to spend some time on Luca's nipples, drawing one into his mouth and rubbing the pad of his thumb in circles on the other. Luca lay there, breathing like a man about to be submerged, feeling the goodness of it crash over him in slow waves. He put a flat palm briefly to his own stiffening cock, like a command; gripping it would feel like cheating, but he needed *something*.

"Patience," Matti murmured into Luca's navel.

"Yes," said Luca, stupidly, to the ceiling. Matti's room was painted an unexceptionable pale cream. "That's me. So patient. We all know how patient I am."

Matti gave a low chuckle that vibrated. He glanced up, a measure of fierce affection delivered from between those thick lashes. The shape of him, the lovely balance of his features, struck Luca like a dart.

"Fuck, you're perfect," Luca said, hoarse. "Look at you." He got his hand into Matti's hair again, his nails on Matti's scalp. "How did nobody else get their claws into you?"

Matti scraped the black stubble of his jaw back and forth, thoughtful, on the skin of Luca's lower stomach. His hand was splayed on Luca's thigh, his thumb maddeningly close to where it might do some good.

"I wasn't looking," he said simply.

Greedy: "I made you look at me."

"I could have been halfway down the aisle, and I would have looked at you," Matti said. "I could have been halfway across the *world*." He shifted in the bed and licked a circle around the head of Luca's cock.

Luca made a sound that had nothing to do with language. His hand was still in Matti's hair. He tightened it.

Matti was in no hurry. He was curious, exploratory. He used finger and thumb to work the skin of Luca's cock, agonisingly light, while he sucked. And then Luca lost track of exactly what was happening, and stared at the ceiling some more as fingers of building pleasure worked their way up through his body. He kept hold of Matti's hair more for anchoring than for direction. His hips were trying to rise off the bed, his cock blindly seeking to be deeper in Matti's throat.

Matti pulled off. The air of the room on Luca's wet, sensitive skin was its own kind of torture. "Did you want—"

"I don't want you to *stop*, please, oh gods *please*—" He ended on what was nearly a wail, as Matti took mercy and swallowed him deep, generous strokes of tongue and then a steady pressure that sent Luca over the edge, pleasure tearing through him like scissors.

Matti took it all into his mouth, which worked around Luca as he swallowed. He pulled away and ran a finger across the crease of his own lips.

Luca lay there and tried to sort out which bits of his body he could still feel. His sprained ankle was aching. He hadn't been aware of putting weight on it, but it was possible he'd bent his legs and braced his feet against the bed at some point during that process. He couldn't bring himself to care.

"Hm," said Matti, a bit rueful. "I was going to ask if you wanted to fuck me."

"Kind of you to ask, and we'll definitely revisit the subject," said Luca. "But as you point out—" He waved a weak hand at his softening cock. "And I have to say, I'm quite enjoying this 'beautiful object' thing." He stretched, taking full advantage of the trim lines of his torso, turning his wrists up in the way that Matti loved.

It was hard to tell if Matti's eyes were darkening further, but the skin slackened around his mouth in a way that was just as good. "I can't be the first bed partner to tell you that you're beautiful."

"Obviously not." Luca grinned and batted away Matti's attempt to swat him in the chest. "Expensive, though, that's new."

This time when Matti reached out, it was with a single fingertip. He started at Luca's hairline and moved down—pausing next to Luca's eyes as though there were something noteworthy about them—skimming the centre of Luca's mouth—pressing down on the mark on his neck—and then a swift, ticklish line down Luca's side, his hip, his leg, until the reach of Matti's arm gave out somewhere near Luca's knee. Luca felt like a route being memorised; an artwork being considered one last time by its creator before it was sent for framing. It made him want to make huge, impossible, unwise promises. It took him three tries to speak.

"You've got me," said Luca. "So take me."

They ended up with Luca on his front, comfortably settled with one leg bent beneath him, head and sore ribs and arms all draped over pillows. Matti's fingers worked him open with less care than the previous night, and Matti swore gratifyingly when he lined up and pushed in, a quick blunt pressure. Luca's body tensed, then softened. Matti's hand skimmed his spine, all the way to the base of his neck and back down. He pushed in a little farther. Luca swallowed with difficulty.

"Is this—"

"For the love of everything, *move*," said Luca.

Matti did, easing entirely inside. His breath hissed. "Fuck. Luca." He drew out what felt like nearly all the way; Luca made a sound of complaint that turned to a low groan when Matti clutched his hips and slammed back in again.

Again. Again.

Luca felt safe, and admired, and yes, *taken*. It was unbelievably good. There was no urgency to his own need, nothing demanding release. Just the blissful slide of his cheek on the pillow, the firm grip Matti had on his hips, and the stretch that melted into pleasure every time Matti thrust deep inside him. Luca could have stayed there for hours, half-drunk on being fucked while Matti gasped praise and called him a lovely thing, tight, perfect, *Luca*—

Even in the moments after spilling himself into Luca, Matti was considerate. He collapsed forward but caught himself, bracing his weight on his hands, which framed Luca's neck. There was a grumble of pain in Luca's side from the shift in position, but not much.

Matti kissed the knob of Luca's spine and eased himself out and away. His hand ruffled Luca's hair. "Luca?"

"Mm."

Amused, now. "Are you going to fall back asleep? Someone is expecting a sword lesson, apparently."

"Just calculating the likelihood that I'll turn into dust," said Luca. "Scatter myself across your bed."

"You're not making any sense."

Luca managed to form a working body from the dust. He struggled upright and poked a finger into Matti's chest. "No one to blame but yourself."

Matti climbed out of bed and went to fetch something. It was his watch. He sat on the edge of the bed, tugging a fold of blanket across his legs. "Another couple of hours before my House members will be arriving."

"The long lunch. I remember. Perse stood up to call the blessing in front of all our cousins with his shirt skew-buttoned." Luca smiled. "It was the first time I'd seen him look nervous about anything. All right. I'll leave you to make yourself presentable, Mattinesh." He stood up and paused to rub Matti's unshaven jaw, lowering his voice. "But I prefer you like this. You're mine like this."

"Yes." Matti's hands closed on his waist, directing Luca to stand between his legs. "And you, like this." He learned forward abruptly and sucked another mark into Luca's skin, over the un-bruised ribs. Luca swayed on his feet. This was absurd. Nothing should feel this good.

"Clothes," said Luca reluctantly. "Sword lesson. And I need to go and tangle the sheets in the room I was supposed to sleep in, if you don't want to have to explain the fun half of the story to your parents ahead of schedule."

"I would have told them last night," Matti said.

Warmth fluttered in Luca's chest. "They might have guessed. Parents see more than you think." He suppressed a shudder remembering the time Jacquelle had sat him down, just after Luca had congratulated himself on the casual way he'd explained how he came to sleep at a friend's house the previous night. She'd given him a half-hour lecture on responsibility and safety, and being able to *talk* about things, and making sure everyone involved, himself included, was sure they wanted everything to happen.

It could have been worse. She could have told Perse to do it.

Resolve firmed Matti's expression. "Get dressed. Go and be sneaky. I'll see you at the Guildhall." A final press of his finger-tips, deliberate, in the hollow of Luca's throat. "Dress nice. I chose my wedding colours for you, you know."

"Huna's *arse* you did."

"I did!"

"I was a con artist you barely knew!"

"I know. I was horrified at myself. I told you," said Matti, steady. "Halfway across the world."

Luca put his hands on Matti's shoulders, just at the rise of

Matti's neck. He paused, face hovering a little distance from Matti's, a taut skin around the enormity of his feelings. Luca had always wanted to be liked, to know that people desired him, or simply enjoyed his company. But all of that faded next to how it felt to be accepted for who he truly was, stripped of stories. Luca Harte with all his dramatics and all his many failings.

He'd never felt so wanted. He'd never wanted to keep anything, to devote himself to anything, with the violence that he felt it now.

"It's your wedding day, Mattinesh. Are you ready?"

When Matti reached up, Luca thought for a moment he was going to fix Luca's hair; his fingers slid into the hairline and scraped with slow, careful pressure all the way over Luca's scalp and down. Luca felt like the head of a match, struck. By the time Matti pulled Luca's head down to kiss him, Luca wanted to shove Matti back onto the bed and throw all their plans out the window for the chance to have Matti inside him again, *now*.

But he liked to think he was getting better at making long-term plans.

Matti looked determined when he pulled away.

"I'm ready," Matti said. "Let's do this."

CHAPTER 21

New children of Huna's Houses were welcomed with harp strings. The songs differed between births and naming-days, between adoption and marriage, but the instrument was the same. There was a story about the affinity of materials, looms and harps both being wooden frames with something strung between.

Matti had always liked the wedding song best. There was a very simple joy in it. He tried to concentrate on the notes, to centre himself, as the procession arrived at the front of the Guildhall and arranged themselves there: Matti and Sofia, their wedding parties, and Rowain Duvay in the black-edged red ceremonial robes of the Deputy Guildmaster. Their parents and siblings formed a standing bracket around them, bowed—Matti met his mother's eyes and she twitched her nose at him, the equivalent of a wink—then stepped down from the dais. Now it was just them. The green and gold.

A hand touched Matti's shoulder.

"You're tensing, Mr. Jay," said Luca's sword master voice.

Matti forced his shoulders up and back—held them there for a count of three—then dropped them, feeling everything loosen. Luca's fingers pressed into the material of Matti's wedding coat, approving. It was easier to centre himself on that touch than on the music.

Matti glanced at Maya. She was standing between Cecilia Cooper and Sofia's friend Anne, just as Luca, Wynn, and Roland were standing behind Matti, and she gave Matti a tiny, determined nod.

Sofia's mass of curls was loose, held back only at one temple with an emerald-studded clip. The pale olive of her skin glowed against the complex wonder of the dress: cut wide across the shoulders and tight at the waist, a sweep of skirts layered upon one another in various shades of gold and white and an eye-catching flash of verdigris.

She looked even more determined than Maya. When Matti met her eyes, she grinned at him, and all at once the rest of Matti's tension settled down to a manageable simmer of excitement.

This might actually be fun, said a voice inside him that sounded a lot like Luca's.

"Children of Huna and guests to her hall," said Duvay. "Friends and witnesses. I call blessing."

The wedding ceremony was short, and the part of it that took place before the invitation for blade-challenge was shorter still. Most of the business of Sofia being released from her own Guild and House, and welcomed into Matti's, would take place after the vows had been made. Duvay called the blessing and shook out the promise-cloth, displaying it to the gathering before folding it over his forearm in anticipation. He named the parties involved. His eyes strayed to the audience and he took a deep breath before saying, "Sofia Cooper and Mattinesh Jay stand here with the intent to marry under the eyes of the gods. Does anyone wish to challenge against the marriage?"

Silence, long enough for Matti to choke on the idea that perhaps Adrean *wouldn't,* that perhaps all of this—everything from Matti's first tense conversation with Hardy Tolliver onwards—had been unnecessary.

"I do," said Adrean.

Matti had never thought he'd be so relieved to hear it.

There was a rustling of curiosity and anticipation from the crowd in the hall, but nothing that sounded like surprise. Adrean walked up the centre aisle, slow enough to be looked at. He was dressed all in black, accentuating his slender height. He held himself proudly and the hilt of his sword gleamed as he stepped forward: not the polished shine of new metal, but something well used and kept in good condition. He looked like someone about to win a duel.

"Mattinesh Jay," said Duvay. "Will you answer the challenge yourself, or will you name a best man?"

Matti opened his mouth.

"Yes," called Adrean. "Why don't you *name* the man with the sword, Matti?"

"Mr. Vane." Duvay frowned. "You've made your challenge. Very well. Now—"

"Or, better yet, why doesn't he name himself?"

Matti went cold within his clothes. He could have cursed aloud. It was easy to make plans, four people in a room, and blithely assume that everyone *not* in that room would play their parts as expected. Allowing for the other party to have wits and impulses and plans of their own was one of the most important lessons that Matti's parents had taught him, and he'd let it slip last night, seduced by the profundity of his own happiness.

"Don't worry," Luca murmured into Matti's ear. He stepped forward, placing himself a pace in front of Matti. Duvay frowned even further at this departure from the script.

Matti decided to go ahead and worry anyway.

"You sound like you have something to say to me, sir," said Luca.

"Luca Piere." Adrean rolled the name in his mouth. "The mid-range duellist from nowhere."

"The people of Cienne wouldn't like to hear you insult their city in that way," said Luca, with faint reproof. That won a few laughs from the crowd. Most likely they were starting to wonder if this whole thing had been arranged as a kind of unusual enter-tainment.

"Cienne," said Adrean. "Yes. It must have been something im-portant that brought you to Glassport."

"A change of scenery?"

"Name yourself," Adrean hissed. "Tell the man whose wedding you're *pretending* to defend what you're really doing here."

"Adrean—" Matti started.

"Why should I?" Luca cut across him. "You seem so set on doing it for me."

"There must be representatives of Harte House here in the Guildhall today." Adrean swept an arm towards the audience. "I'm sure they're surprised to see Jacquelle Harte's *son* standing up here, in a position he hasn't earned and a name that isn't his own." His voice had risen in triumph by the end. He paused, arm still outstretched, clearly awaiting the impact of his blow.

He wouldn't have been disappointed by the crowd. Voices rose. Heads bent together. People farther back in the hall stood, craning on tiptoe to try to get a better look at Luca, who was smiling faintly. Matti felt a tug on his sleeve and looked over his shoulder to where Roland looked aghast and Wynn was mouthing, *What the fuck?*

Matti waved them down, trying to promise explanations with his eyes. He wanted to focus on what was happening.

A frown flickered on Adrean's brow as he looked first at Luca and then at Matti; clearly he'd been expecting a stronger reaction from that quarter. Matti stood very still, waiting to see where this would go. Perhaps Adrean would take him as too stunned to say anything.

"A strange kind of spy you are," Adrean said. "*Lucastian Harte.* But I suppose it was an easy way for you to get access to a House like the Jays. Member of the wedding party. Invited to all the dinners. Listening to all their talk."

Matti looked at his parents. Tomas Jay was pale-faced and clearly moments from stepping forward; Matti managed to catch his eye and made with one hand a gesture from the negotiating table that he'd not had cause to use for years, as Tomas moved into Guild and city business and Matti's faith in his own abilities began to erode like a sea cliff beneath his feet.

The gesture meant *wait.* It meant *trust me.*

And because Matti had parents worth his love and his effort and, yes, worth the awful fight and draining stress that had been the last five years of his life . . . Tomas went still. Held Matti's gaze. And then, stiffly, nodded, and turned to whisper something in Nessa's ear.

Luca spread his hands in a gesture of elegant surrender. "How did you find me out?"

"The true duellists of Glassport are *my* friends," said Adrean. "Servicemen, you'd say. Beneath your notice. Once Hardy Tolliver found out who you were, the word began to trickle out. Oh, I'm sure you've enough skill to stand swordguard for children, but you're a dabbler. You're not a proper duellist. How could you be? Heir to a *House,*" he spat. "Just like the rest of them. You think you can have whatever you want. Whomever you want." He was looking at Matti now. An ugly playfulness entered his tone. "I'm afraid your best man isn't going to be worth the fortune you paid for him, Matti."

"I was afraid of that, too, for a while," said Matti. "But I'm starting to think he was a bargain." He raised his voice. "I name Lucastian Harte, my trusted friend, as my best man. Will you stand up for me, Luca?"

Luca's smile spread out across his face. "It would be my honour, Mattinesh."

And he drew his sword, the scrape of it loud and silvery in the expectant quiet of the hall.

Matti could see Luca favouring his sprained ankle, but it was no more than a faint hitch in his step as he walked up, saluted, and fell into ready stance opposite Adrean, who had drawn his sword in return. The injury might not be obvious unless you were looking for it.

Adrean looked comfortable: eyes sharp, body loose. He sprang forward, the two swords engaged—the clash loud and chaotic—a few quick motions, strike and parry—the two of them moving in a tight circle and then breaking apart again.

Matti wished he knew more about duelling than he did, or that he'd had the chance to watch Luca fight someone else before now. All he knew was how to move through the forms while his thighs screamed at him, and the names of a few moves that he could execute in slow motion. One of them might have just been demonstrated, but it wasn't like he'd have been able to tell. It had happened so fast. Adrean had clearly been hoping that surprise and speed would allow him a quick victory.

Luca, following suit, didn't allow them more than a couple of breaths before engaging again. His feet were incredibly fast, his whole body moving like a ribbon snapping in a breeze, to avoid the force of a blow and catch Adrean's blade at the midpoint with his own. Not enough leverage for it to be an easy graze. It *looked* smooth, the way he turned the trajectory of the strike, but a grunt escaped him and betrayed the effort required.

When they disengaged that time, Adrean looked wary, his knees soft in anticipation.

Luca pushed back his hair. When he smiled it wasn't his bright, wicked, usual smile. It was something unfamiliar, proud and grand. Even with the sword in his hand, that smile made him look like what he was: the son of a rich House, heir to authority.

"Are you feeling inadequate enough yet, Mr. Vane?" It was the cool, merciless voice that had found Matti's raw wounds when they'd been shouting damage at each other, and part of Matti wanted to shrink from the sound of it, even as the rest of him felt like cheering. "Finding it harder than you'd hoped to trounce this particular *dabbler*?"

Adrean's lips drew back over his teeth. He made an aborted motion with his foot, but managed to stop himself. Like any good fighter, he clearly knew that anger would make him unwise. But it was very hard, Matti knew from experience, not to be angry when every part of you was howling for the ruin of the person responsible for crushing your dreams.

"I am Lucastian Harte," Luca sang, "son of Jacquelle Harte, and heir to her House. I expect I could buy everything you own with the spare change shaken out of my second-best coat. Do you own anything? Or do you lease a damp, cheap house in a bad neighbourhood, and fill it with the mediocre scribblings of a weak creative mind?"

Matti had less than a second to admire the precision of that attack, the sheer informed ruthlessness of it, before Adrean snarled and threw himself back into the fight. This time the bout was longer, a messy and savage exchange. When they pulled apart, Luca was laughing, but the laugh caught on a gasp as his ankle rolled beneath him. It lasted only a moment. His head rose again at once, smile intact.

Adrean's eyes had narrowed. Matti swallowed a curse and took hold of his coat hem instead, rubbing it between his fingers in silent prayer.

Adrean started a series of blows that forced Luca to shift his weight quickly, constantly. The smile was faltering on Luca's face, his eyes tightening with concentration. *Watch the feet,* said that voice inside Matti that was Luca's voice. Matti looked at the distance between Adrean's feet, the wide and advantageous stance. He watched Luca lean on the sprained ankle, again and again, each time a little shakier.

And then Luca's recovery took a moment too long, too much of his weight sagging onto his good leg, and Adrean was ready. His blade flashed high, descending through the top corner of Luca's summer quadrant. Luca would have to strain cross-body to meet it, leaving himself unstable and open, unless—

Unless he lunged low, the full force of the movement landing firm on an ankle that suddenly didn't shake at all, and came up inside the reach of Adrean's arm, turning Adrean's height against him, Luca's own sword already flicking a subtle and unstoppable curve to finish, motionless and sure, with the tip just beneath Adrean's arm, ready to shove between his ribs.

Survival froze Adrean's body in place.

"Withdraw your challenge," said Luca, breathless but firm. It was a formality.

Adrean, face slackening in disbelief, lowered his sword.

Luca lowered his as well, and sheathed it without even bothering to flourish. The businesslike nature of his victory was probably as infuriating as anything else.

Luca extended a bare palm towards Adrean. "Will you shake?"

Adrean's years of training must have propelled him forward. He looked like he'd rather have grasped a snake by the tail, but he put his hand in Luca's, shook once in a jerk, and then released it.

"My Sofia," said Adrean then, turning to her. "Know that I tried. Know that I would have fought a hundred duels, to save you from being treated as a bargaining piece in this way."

"I'm not yours," said Sofia. "I've never been *yours,* Adrean. Sit down."

"Are you still afraid to speak plainly? After what I just did for you?"

"Do you want me to speak plainly?" Sofia's hands were fists in the front of her skirts. Her voice rose. "Fine. I have spent more hours of my life than I care to think coming up with ways to avoid you in the street, and trying to be polite when you shoved yourself into my path anyway. I don't want you. I didn't want you the first time you asked me, or the third, or the fifth. And if you'd done me the courtesy of taking me at my word, you could have saved yourself the humiliation of everyone here knowing it."

"Sofia." Adrean was white-faced, his voice a throb. "I never thought you were cruel."

"I'm not," said Sofia. "Cruel is when you decide that what someone wants doesn't matter, just because you want *them* and you think that means you're owed something."

Adrean looked bewildered. It still hadn't sunk in for him,

Matti could see, and maybe it never would. He was still stuck in whatever story he was telling himself.

"Sit down, Adrean," said Maya. "It's done."

Some part of Adrean knew the value of retreating with dignity, and thankfully, it prevailed. He sheathed his sword and turned his back. His footsteps rang on the floor as he walked back down the aisle. Matti didn't watch to see if he stayed in the hall.

"Done, indeed." Duvay took a deep breath. "The challenge has been met, and answered. Now——"

"Excuse me, sir," said Luca. "The question should be repeated. A formality."

"The question? Oh. Does anyone wish to challenge against the marriage?"

There was a whisper of silk on wood as Maya stepped forward, and as her skirts settled around her.

"Yes," said Matti's sister. "I do."

An extraordinary net of threads tightened around Matti's heart. He tried to exchange a look with Sofia, but Sofia was carefully smoothing the creases from where she'd taken hold of her dress.

A new, delighted murmur, like the slow startling of a large flock of birds, spread from the front of the Guildhall all the way to the back. Duvay blinked at Maya from behind his glasses. "Miss Jay?"

"Though I find myself in need of a sword," said Maya. She walked quickly to the back corner of the hall and picked up something that had been left there: a sheath, folded in a blanket. The sword she drew out looked like one of the practice blades from Tolliver's agency.

Sofia finally met Matti's eyes. With a calm deliberation that made Matti want to laugh even through his incredulity, she raised her hand above her shoulder and flicked the fingers wide. She didn't have the trick of it, but she was close. Her expression held the faintest edge of apology, but no surprise at all.

"What is *happening*," said Roland in a plaintive whisper.

Maya stood where Adrean had been standing. She looked deeply odd and yet somehow glorious, holding the sword aloft, her arm smooth and dark against the white lace that edged the short sleeves of the dress. Her stance was stiff but her grip was not, and Matti remembered belatedly: Luca shutting himself away with Maya before dinner. Luca saying, that morning, *I'm giving a sword lesson.*

Matti said, very soft, "I suppose that's one way to do it."

"Shh," Luca said, and strode out to meet Maya's challenge.

If the duel with Adrean had been like listening to the twins speak Yaghali—a few words comprehensible, here and there, but none of the overall meaning—then the one with Maya was like the first page of a familiar book. Ready stance. Take guard. Slowly, carefully, Maya engaged Luca's blade at the end and angled her own, stepping closer.

Slowly, Luca let her.

Metal spoke against metal. A Sugeen Graze. It should have ended with Luca's—no, it *should* have ended before it even began, because Luca was an expert.

Luca's sword tipped, tipped, and then Maya did something with her wrist that Matti couldn't see because Luca's body was blocking his view of it, and then—

The clatter of Luca's sword against the floor was followed by silence.

Matti heard a quick indrawing of breath from either Roland or Wynn, standing behind him.

"My goodness," said Luca. "How embarrassing."

Maya set the point of her sword to the base of Luca's neck. The alarmed way Luca's glance flicked between her wrist and her face told Matti that this part had *not* been rehearsed in advance.

"Lucastian Harte," she said. "This seems a good opportunity to warn you off."

Luca let out a delighted laugh. "Do you think you can?"

"I suppose not," said Maya. "I tried once. It clearly failed." She moved her eyes reprovingly to Matti, and then back to Luca. Her arm was starting to shake. Matti could have told her that holding anything at arm's length was the most tiring of all.

"You can't," Luca said. "I'm not sorry."

Maya nodded. "Hurt him again and I'll give you bruises worse than the one you're wearing now."

"Deal," said Luca.

Maya lowered the sword with an exhalation of relief. She held Luca's gaze. After a moment she shifted the sword to the other side and held out her hand; Luca did the same, and shook. They sheathed their swords.

Duvay looked utterly perplexed. Matti's mouth was warping itself into a helpless smile. He looked at his parents; Nessa had her hand over her eyes and was leaning against Tomas's side, shaking in what Matti very much hoped was laughter.

Luca bowed to Matti, then turned on his heel and repeated the action in the direction of Matti's parents. "My deepest apologies for failing to defend against this challenge. I realise the implications for Jay House. But I may yet be able to make amends, if the Deputy Guildmaster will indulge me for a moment . . ."

Matti bit his lip. Of course, of *course* Luca was going to make a theatrical production of it.

Luca cleared his throat. He skimmed the crowd, perhaps looking for the agents of his own House, in whose faces he was about to light an unexpected firework.

"Harte House has acquired the rights and the means to import gallia worms into Thesper," said Luca.

The firework exploded around the entire Guildhall. Luca raised both hands imploringly and managed to wave the crowd into something that was, if not silence, at least a softer morass of whispers. He went on to explain what Matti already knew from Jacquelle's letter: that the Hartes had made a contract with one of the major fashion houses in Cienne, to sell them gallia silk— exclusively—for a period of five years.

And in exchange, that same House would buy highest-grade wool fabrics from Jay House.

Exclusively. For five years.

This was the bargain Luca had won for Matti, by returning himself to Harte House. Throwing a duel, before witnesses, had just been merrily burning the bridge to ashes behind him.

"The details are in here." Luca pulled the much-read letter from his pocket and handed it to Nessa. "It bears my mother's seal. The contract is yours."

Nessa unfolded the letter. Tomas read over her shoulder. Luca had lost control of the hall's volume again, but he didn't seem to care. He stood in front of Matti's parents, fingers tapping against his thigh, waiting.

If Matti had any remaining doubts about springing this on his parents as a public surprise, they vanished at the slow creep of disbelieving joy that was lighting their faces.

"Mr. Harte," Tomas began, but Luca was already moving back to the centre of the floor, the centre of attention. Duvay threw an imploring look at Matti, as if to ask about his chances of reining in his best man before this turned into an absolute farce. Matti spread his hands. Duvay huffed.

"I have another story to tell, as part of my apology to Jay House!" Luca said. "This one is a bit longer."

The fibre fraud. The ledger of betrayal in Corus Vane's study. Matti readied himself to step forward as needed. He didn't know how Luca was going to talk around the fact of their housebreaking escapade, but he found himself fully confident that he would, somehow.

"It begins," Luca said, "with a ship called the *Isadonna*."

The breath stopped dead in Matti's lungs.

Matti was watching Corus Vane's face, waiting to see what would happen when the Keseys were unveiled and his own double nature was revealed. So Matti saw plainly the sudden freezing of the man's expression when Luca spoke the name of the ship, and the split second of incredulous dread before Corus mastered himself again.

The *Isadonna*.

A tiny seed of something almost too small and too strange to be called hope planted itself around the level of Matti's knees. Luca threw Matti a smile over his shoulder. The seed put out a shoot, and unfurled.

It's something good. Matti had been expecting—he didn't know what. He still didn't know what.

He remembered how to breathe.

"The *Isadonna*," said Luca, finding his theatrical cadence, "was a ship hired by Jay House from the shipping House of Lior, to carry a cargo of black libelza fleece bought at auction in the Drakan city of Hazan. It sailed from Fataf. It never arrived in Glassport—it was reported lost with all hands." A pause, to let everyone keep up. "But it wasn't lost. It was stolen."

The vine of hope was everywhere in Matti now. Maya didn't even look surprised. Of course: Luca had already told her.

Luca went on: "It's hard to make a boat disappear. The *Isadonna*'s captain and crew were recorded in Lior House's books under false names. They were instructed to divert to Elluthe Harbour with the cargo. It's a lot of people, to keep a secret that large, but I expect they were told that the House employing them wanted to avoid a certain type of import duty. They would have thought themselves smugglers, not thieves. And paid well enough not to breathe a word when their own ship was reported missing, and their false selves along with it. It all must have cost a large sum in bribes, to someone very senior at Lior," Luca finished, with an unpleasant smile. He raised his voice. "I admit I'm curious. How much exactly, Mr. Kesey?"

"Fuck *me*," breathed Wynn.

Matti felt like he'd taken three glasses of jenever all at once.

Heads turned. Simeon Kesey was standing. "How *dare* you—"

"How dare I?" Luca's whip of a voice recaptured the thread. "I know how *you* dared, and what, and why. Lior retrimmed and renamed their own ship, pretended to have bought it anew, and recorded a false contract with Jessamy House. The *Lady Jenny* sailed into Glassport and nobody suspected who she used to be. And then you simply unloaded the wool and stuck it in a warehouse to wait for memories to dim. For Jay House to slip into debt through the loss of that profit. Someday soon you were going to pretend that you'd made a similar purchase—expensive, luxury black libelza—and start to process it. *Stolen goods.*"

Simeon Kesey had turned a puce shade. "You fucking little—"

"It's a good scheme," said Luca. "It took me a while to find all the pieces. And it was mostly luck that I heard the names of the ships spoken together in the first place." He kissed his fingers and ran them along the hem of his green jacket. Nobody would have mistaken his meaning, here in Huna's Guildhall. Luck was the voice of the gods.

Matti's father was staring at the Head of Kesey House. "Simeon?"

"Absolute nonsense," said Kesey. "He's lying to you, Tomas. Nessa. This absurd Harte spy is making up stories. What kind of proof could he possibly have?"

"I'm so glad you asked," said Luca, bright as stars.

His hand went into his pocket again. Matti couldn't see what was in it, but again Luca went to Tomas and Nessa and held it out to them.

"The warehouse is on Tar Lane," Luca said. "It's leased in Kesey's name. I broke in, two days ago. They've not even bothered to remove the batch labels from the wool. You should be able to match them to your own auction receipts."

Tomas looked down at Luca's hand. Whatever was in it was small.

"This is. This is black libelza." Tomas stared at Luca. Then at

Kesey. A growl hid in his voice. "Was this the only way you could think to compete with us, Sim?"

"This is pure fantasy," Kesey sputtered. "Smuggling—bribes—Tomas, you know we don't have that kind of money."

"No," said Matti suddenly. Everything had fallen into place. "But Martens House does." He didn't know where Lysbette was sitting, but he didn't have to. A new ripple of murmurs and head-turning began, and at the centre of it was a blond head. Matti was part of Luca's theatre now, but part of him was still in the sitting room, facing Lysbette directly. "*This* is what you paid for. To break us. To get my father off the council so that Glassport's money can go to building that godsdamned canal."

Luca didn't give the room a chance to erupt, or Lysbette a chance to defend herself. He said, swift, "And I *expect* if we searched one or both of their offices, there'd be a contract of debt with payment promised—from the libelza profits, perhaps? Guildmaster Martens might be shy of leaving a paper trail proving interference with another Guild's business, but she's a famously untrusting businesswoman. There's no way she'd lay out that kind of expense without guaranteeing her return on investment in writing."

For a moment Matti could see Lysbette's face in the crowd, white and blank.

"I'm just guessing, of course," Luca added. Matti looked at his sparkling eyes and knew it to be a gorgeous lie. He tucked it away on the long, long list of things to ask Luca about later.

Simeon Kesey was still on his feet. Almost audibly, his nerve snapped. He spun, furious, towards where Lysbette was sitting. "You—I told you! Didn't I tell you? If you'd just accepted my *word*," he shouted, "there'd be no *proof.*"

There was a long silence. Lysbette's voice rose into it like smoke against a clear sky. "And if you'd just managed to keep your mouth shut," she said, "you *fucking imbecile,* we could have claimed it was an outlay on raw marble to build you a country house."

This was what Lysbette had been calculating, in the sitting room. When she realised that Matti didn't know about the ship and that he thought she was just another person putting wages in Corus's pocket.

Speaking of which. It was time for the last truth to come out.

"Who liaised with Lior House, Dad?" asked Matti. He had to raise his voice and repeat the question before the chatter settled; he didn't have Luca's easy command of the room. "Who was responsible for putting in the insurance paperwork that was too late?"

Tomas had been staring at Lysbette. Now he looked back at Matti and frowned.

"Corus?" said Matti. "Will you come up here for a minute?"

Luca moved aside. Now the eyes of the audience were on Corus Vane, who paused in his seat for long enough to realise that pausing was impossible. Corus stood, slowly, and came up to stand on the dais. A renewed hush fell over the hall. This was a different kind of duel, but it had been recognised as one nonetheless.

"None of the business with the ships would have worked without you," said Matti. "Your masters put a lot of trust in you, Corus."

Corus searched Matti's eyes. He was weighing his loyalties, such as they were, and Matti saw the moment when he decided to make a play for the wrong one. "Whatever sins of others you think to pin on me, Matti—"

"*Pin?* You've worked against us for years," Matti snarled, all his composure deserting him at once. "I will list your betrayals one by one, if you ask me to. Shall we start with the inflated cost of Haxbridge mordant? What about undermining our bid to the city quartermaster by slipping our terms to our primary rival? Shall we stand here and calculate *exactly* how long you've been in the pay of Kesey House?"

Corus's mouth opened. Matti stared him down.

"Oh, *please* ask if we have proof," said Luca. It was the mocking, infuriating voice that Luca had used to drive Corus's son to failure, and it worked on the father with much the same ease.

Corus stalked forward, face working in anger. Matti had no idea what he intended until Corus was standing in front of him; Matti set his jaw to receive insult and was taken aback when Corus reached for him instead, hands like claws taking clumsy hold of Matti's lapels as if to shake him.

Matti had a long, odd moment in which he wished for a sword.

And then Corus was dragged back, away from him.

"*Vane,*" snapped Roland. He'd grabbed hold of Corus's arms, forcing him back, and now speared him with a look of deep dislike. "What do you think you're doing?"

"I won't stand to have my name smeared with filth," hissed Corus. "You'll hear what I have to say, Matti."

Matti nodded to Roland and let Corus step close again, moving away from the others. Trying to have a conversation in whispers felt ridiculous, given the hundreds of eyes that were upon them, but he was prepared to let this play out.

"You'll retract all of that," said Corus, very low. "You'll do it now. Did you think I would hesitate to take you down with me? I know all your secrets. I will tell this Guild, this *city,* that your House is doing business on a ruined name. That you're failing."

"But we're not," said Matti. The sheer size of that truth was still expanding in his heart. "Not anymore. Not after today."

Corus snorted and opened his mouth, a dismissive curl already shaping it.

Matti said, "No. You will hear what *I* have to say, Corus. I can't stop you, if you're determined to expose us. And we'd cope with it." A twitch of his mouth. "We're good at coping, we Jays. But consider your own reliability as a witness, after what everyone in this room has just heard."

That struck. Corus drew himself up, breathing hard through nostrils flared with anger, but he wasn't interrupting anymore.

Matti said, "Consider that it's entirely up to me, now, how

many of your crimes Jay House might consider taking in front of a magistrate."

"Don't play coy, Matti, it's never suited you," Corus said coldly. But there was fear at war with weakness in his eyes.

Matti looked sideways. If Simeon Kesey was still here, he was making himself difficult to find. "I don't know if you still have an employer, but right now you're free. You can always run away. Move to another city. I hear that's a popular solution when you make a mistake of this size."

"I—"

"In fact, perhaps you should consider changing your name."

"You're offering to buy me off with mercy, to save your own skin." In Corus's face was the dawning awareness of exactly how cornered he was.

"Why not? Now I know you can be bought." Matti didn't smile. "Think of your future. Think of *Adrean's* future." That was a blow Matti didn't realise he'd been saving, and a good portion of his vicious anger dissipated as he delivered it, waking him up to himself. He'd won. He didn't need to be cruel.

Corus was staring at Matti like he'd never seen him before. Matti leaned close. "Be smart, Corus. Limit the damage."

It seemed an age before Corus so much as blinked. Matti was bracing himself to deal with Corus calling his bluff, bringing them all down together out of spite, when Corus cleared his throat and gave a small, stiff bow.

"I apologise, Mr. Jay, for assaulting you in such an appalling manner. I hope you can forgive me."

Matti nodded. Corus's eyes were full of the molten fury of his own surrender; pushing any further would be a mistake. Just as stiffly, Corus walked back to his place in the Guildhall, in the row behind the Jays, and—sat down. That took a kind of absolute, metallic courage. Matti couldn't help admiring it.

"If the gentlemen are *quite* finished," said Sofia.

Her timing was superb. Laughter crackled through the room.

"Apologies for the interruptions, Mr. Duvay," Matti said, returning to his place. "Please"—he waved a hand around the wedding party—"continue."

"Continue? But—wait," said Duvay, a man struggling to pull the ceremony back into order with his own two hands. "Continue with the wedding?"

"Matti, it breaks my heart to say it, but I don't believe that would be auspicious," said Sofia, with very wide eyes. "The gods were not behind your best man's blade."

"Yes. Indeed." Duvay coughed. "Mayanesh Jay, you have challenged against this marriage, met the best man named by Mattinesh Jay, and . . . won." Visibly, he was trying to remember a barely used protocol. "Were you. Uh. Were you challenging on your own behalf?"

Matti laughed and looked at his sister, waiting for her to share the joke. But Maya was looking at Sofia, and she wasn't laughing at all. She looked like someone hungry in a dream, hesitant to reach out and take the food for fear of waking.

"One moment, please!" Sofia said brightly. She stepped down from the dais, skirts in hand, and went to talk to her parents. Matti watched the resulting gesticulations for only a moment before returning his gaze to Maya, willing her to look back at him. When she did, he raised his eyebrows. Maya echoed the motion that Sofia had given him earlier: *What can you do?* Her eyes were like sunlit dew.

Matti wondered how many things he hadn't been seeing, while his gaze was fixed on his worries and on Luca.

Sofia ascended the dais again and cleared her throat in a self-conscious way. Every eye in the Guildhall was upon her.

"Yes, Miss Cooper?" said Duvay.

"If Mayanesh Jay was challenging on her own behalf," said Sofia, clear and loud, "then I offer her my hand and my family's blessing. And I offer myself into the named service of Jay House," with a quick, self-effacing smile, "if it's still prepared to have me."

More delighted uproar from the audience. Now Maya was the one to throw an imploring expression at Tomas and Nessa. Next to Matti, Luca was vibrating with what was obviously going to turn into laughter at any moment. Matti reached out and took firm hold of Luca's wrist.

"Er. Tomas?" said Duvay. "Nessanesh?"

Matti's mother dug an elbow into his father's side. When this failed to produce a change in Tomas's stunned expression, Nessa cleared her throat. "We are prepared," she said.

Luca turned to Matti. "You're standing in your sister's spot, Mattinesh."

A small amount of shuffling later, Matti—who had the giddy sense that he'd been swept up in a current, with no choice but to enjoy the ride—was standing in what was now his sister's wedding party. Luca had grandly volunteered to join Sofia's, to balance the numbers out. The entire colour scheme was a mess.

"Does anybody," said the Deputy Guildmaster, in a tone of faint desperation, "wish to challenge against *this* marriage?"

The silence in the Guildhall was an excited one, half-hopeful, as though everyone were waiting for the third act that would complete this particular drama. Luca tapped his hand on his sword hilt, a gesture that looked more meaningful than his usual restlessness.

Nobody spoke.

Duvay exhaled in visible relief. "In *that* case—" And onwards the ceremony swept.

When it was over, Sofia was Sofia Jay after all. In less than an hour she had turned from Matti's betrothed into Matti's sister. She had not dropped the promise-cloth. She had not missed a beat. Now she kept bursting into little gulps of laughter, as though she couldn't believe what had happened. Some of Maya's dark red lip-paint was still on hers, an ombre dab like a wine stain.

"I think I need to get drunk," said Wynn morosely. "Drunk enough that when Matti explains what just happened, it might make some kind of sense."

Roland laughed at him. "I think we can arrange that. Think of the wine, Wynn. Cooper House just married off their daughter."

The Coopers, along with Matti's parents, were converging on the dais, the first in what would be a long stream of people offering formal congratulations to a different couple to the one they'd arrived here expecting to see married.

"People will talk about this forever," said Luca, echoing Matti's thoughts. He sounded pleased at the prospect. "Every other wedding they attend will seem dull in comparison. Epic poems will be written about it."

"Not by Adrean, I hope," said Matti.

Luca laughed. He was gazing and gazing at Matti as though Matti were the only thing worth looking at in this hall hung with the most beautiful fabric in the world. He dug in his pocket and held something out. "Here." It was the handful of raw wool. It *was* unmistakable, when Matti closed his fingers around it. "Call it a wedding present. Or a non-wedding present."

"A warehouse full of black libelza. Is this the interest you owe me?"

Luca's eyes were nearly silver, and they blazed with happiness. "I'm buying *you* this time. You're mine, Mattinesh Jay."

The smile on Matti's face felt like it would split his lips. "Yours to command, Mr. Harte."

"Really?" Luca's hand slid around Matti's neck. People were probably staring at them. Nothing could have made Matti care. Luca said, "Kiss me."

And Matti did.

CHAPTER
22

The door to Nessa's study stood ajar. Matti rapped his knuckles on it before stepping inside.

"—*exotic mouthfuls of bliss, well worth it for culinary adventurers,*" said Nessa. "Matti! Matti, dear one, you must listen to this, nothing will make me laugh harder this week."

Matti smiled. His mother was lying on the couch tucked beneath the window, which looked out onto the uneven seam of chimneys and roof flourishes that was the Rose Quarter viewed from this height. The evening sky was the fierce blue-grey of gathering rain, with a few early stars struggling to wink through the gaps in the clouds. Nessa's head was in Tomas's lap, her plait spilling down to kiss the floor. She was half covered by the newspaper as she held it above herself for ease of reading.

"What is it?" Matti asked.

Nessa dissolved into chuckles and her tent of newspaper collapsed.

Tomas looked fondly down at his wife. "One of the food writers for the *Gazette* thinks he is the first man in the world to discover japetas."

"Adventurers! One month, perhaps two, and every eating house in the city will be making them with too much oil and charging ten silver," said Nessa. She sat up, patting down her hair. "Lucastian has left?"

Matti nodded. "And I have packing to finish. I've come to say—I thought I might not see you before we leave tomorrow, Dad, if I sleep in. I know you're meeting with the city quartermaster before the council sitting."

His parents exchanged identical looks midway between politeness and disbelief.

"I *might* sleep in," Matti said weakly. He obeyed his mother's patting of the couch cushion, and came to sit with them. Nessa swept all the papers onto the floor and took Matti's hand in one of hers.

"Perhaps it would be better to do the goodbyes now," said Tomas, "so we're not trying to shout them from opposite ends of the house in the morning. You've got everything you need? Everything on that list of yours?"

Luca had thrown the list out the window earlier that afternoon, declaring it a lesson in spontaneity. Matti had tossed him a bronze and told him that he was spontaneously paying Luca to go down to the street and fetch it back. The flood of aroused pink in Luca's cheeks had been well worth the ten minutes Luca spent complaining about it afterwards.

Rather than explain this, Matti simply nodded.

"Goodbyes, but not for long. You'll come back for Spindle Day, of course," said Nessa.

It was like a muscle tensing in Matti's mind, readying itself to make arrangements, to shift things around and calculate schedules and travel times and even start list-making about everything that would need to be organised for the foremost business day in Huna's calendar.

Matti inhaled. Exhaled. "No," he said. It felt like a new flavour on his tongue.

"No?" said Tomas.

"No. I don't know if I'll be back in Glassport then. I don't want to promise that I will."

"I'm sorry we haven't heard you say that enough," said Tomas, after a moment. "What you want, and don't want."

Matti looked down at his mother's hand, at her fingers linked through his. She'd painted her nails gold for the wedding. The paint was beginning to chip at the tips. "It's getting easier," he said. "People keep asking me now."

"Hm," said Nessa. "I will tell you a story."

Matti looked up at her, startled. Nessa glanced at Tomas, eyes sparkling as though she were about to dip a biscuit's worth of gossip into coffee.

"In Manisi I studied history, at the university. Two brothers and three sisters already there, becoming brilliant in their fields. I was to be brilliant also."

"You *are* brilliant," said Tomas.

"Hush!" Nessa rounded on him. "Is this your story?"

"Isn't it about to be?"

Nessa turned a magnificent shoulder on her husband and looked back at Matti. "A young girl buried in her books, and a man from the south swoops in and turns her world up-to-down, shoes-to-ribbons, saying he will show her something new." Her gaze softened. "And I went. I went because my heart told me that I would regret it if I did not."

Matti didn't know what to say. He said, "I'm glad you did?"

"Oh, well! So many days I have given serious thought to regretting it!" said Nessa mockingly. "I could have been Vice Chancellor by now!" But she was laughing, leaning back against Tomas, and Tomas was laughing as well. He kissed the side of her head. "No," she said. "I was right. I knew what I wanted."

"And I never found it hard to say," said Tomas, "that I wanted Nessa, more than I wanted to make a sensible match for the House's benefit. I knew my parents wouldn't mind, because it *was* what I wanted. And I truly am sorry, Matti. That we made you feel otherwise, and that we didn't notice how hard it was on you."

"Did not ask," said Nessa. She pulled her hand away and used it to lift Matti's chin. Her dark eyes swam with so much affection that for a fleeting moment Matti wanted to curl up, his own head in her skirts, as he hadn't done since he was very young. *"Ask* is what we did not do."

"I should have—no, Mama, I *should* have been more honest with you."

"We'll consider ourselves well paid," said Tomas dryly, "given what you and your sister pulled on us at the wedding."

"So," said Nessa. "You will be back whenever you are back. Go where your heart is."

Matti felt a warm knot in his throat. The Jays might be starting to learn, with tentative steps, how to haul their truths out into the open. It didn't mean he knew the best way to give his parents all the words for how he felt. For how Luca made him feel.

He kissed his mother's cheek and stood. Tomas stood as well and wrapped Matti in a firm, brief hug.

"Huna smile," said Tomas to his eldest son. "And may you weave your own fortune."

"I will," said Matti. It felt true. "We will."

⇒ ⟫⟩ ⊛ ⟨⟪ ⇐

Luca asked the coach to stop a few houses away, and walked the rest of the way to Matti's house on foot. It had rained the previous night and the street smelled of clean wet leaves, a contrast to the inside of the coach, which mostly smelled of daisy-cakes. Dinah had given Luca a whole basket of them for the journey and extracted from him in return a promise to come and visit whenever he returned to Glassport.

Matti was standing at the base of the townhouse's steps, bent over and rummaging in one of the leather travel bags on the next step up. Luca quieted his steps as he approached.

"Maya," Matti called through the half-open door of the house, "do you know if— *Oof,*" as Luca walked right into him from behind. Matti's ankle tangled with Luca's as he turned around, and Luca hissed in pained annoyance as his leg buckled and he fell.

"*Fuck,* Matti. My ankle."

"Sorry, I—" It took Matti only two seconds of gazing at Luca, who was sprawled on the ground, to narrow his eyes. Luca was so proud of him. "You little shit," said Matti, laughing.

Luca grinned and propped himself up on one elbow. He'd judged it well. His ribs had given him a pang on the way down, but the ground wasn't all that hard. It was damp and probably none too clean, but Luca was wearing the old brown coat—a kind of fond farewell, before he got home and his mother had it burned.

"Oh, no, you've turned my ankle." He fluttered his lashes. "How am I supposed to find work now? And me new to town and all."

"Ah, I see. You want me to pay." Matti's dimples flashed and he extended a hand. "Come on, get up."

Luca ignored it and pushed up to a kneeling position. "Are you sure there isn't anything I can do for you while I'm down here? For a bronze, perhaps?" Neat and deadly: "*Sir*."

"Matti?" Maya pushed the door the rest of the way open. "I couldn't hear what you were saying. Oh." She levelled a puzzled look at Luca, who sighed and took Matti's hand, pulling himself to his feet. Matti's thumb brushed the back of his hand and then dug in, hard, promising to pick the game up again later.

Matti said, "I was going to ask if Mama remembered to send a message to Daz Shana Habi, to meet them at the carding work-shop. Shana used to live in eastern Draka. They know libelza better than anyone else we employ."

"Mama did," said Maya. "And"—as Matti opened his mouth again—"I'm meeting with one of our Barlow office agents this afternoon, to make sure everything's ready for when the council lifts the locality restriction. And Sofia has meetings lined up with three fashion houses to discuss the buying patterns they're seeing as we come into winter. And I've sent Roland and Roberta to Lourde House to finalise the loan repayment." There was a glow to Maya's cheeks as she ticked these items off on her fingers, and a firmness to her chin that suited her.

She had every reason to look that way. A little more than a week ago, Jay House had acquired the bond price for Sofia's marriage, the exclusivity contract arranged by the Hartes, and their own lost black libelza, all in a single day. And that was *before* factoring in their most prominent rival in the Glassport wool market having his reputation shattered by proof of espionage and fraudulent production, and the dramatic firing of a long-term saboteur.

Huna threw her coins, and sometimes they fell in your hand, one by shining one.

Matti frowned. "I left the last of my notes on your desk, but send a message immediately if there's anything you still have questions about. I can always—"

"Matti," said Maya. "Do you think we're going to collapse in a heap without you? Is that it?"

"Of course I don't think that, but . . ." Matti shot a look at Luca. He was transparently afraid that he was doing to his sister what Perse had done to Luca: acted on his heart and thereby dumped the unwanted responsibility in his younger sibling's lap.

Maya said, "Mama and Dad are hardly decrepit. They're not going anywhere, and I'm planning to be a lot better than you were at demanding help. This isn't something I have to carry on my own. And I have *plans*." Glee entered her voice. "So many plans. We could be doing a lot more with colours, and with weaving techniques. I won't believe that every twill pattern that will ever exist has been discovered already. Black libelza will take a tighter worsted weave and create a smoother nap. Just you wait. Sofia and I are going to make Jay the *only* name in wool."

Matti kissed his thumb and flicked Maya's ear. "I believe you."

"Why wouldn't you?" said Maya, scornful. She returned the gesture and her tone softened. "You did it, Matti. You saved our House. Now go and enjoy your life for a while."

"Excuse me," said Luca. "*Who* saved your House?"

"Oh, I quite forgot." Maya looked at him. "Sofia and I deserve some of the credit. Thank you for reminding me."

"What have I done?" Sofia appeared in the doorway. She was wearing trousers and boots, which made her look a bit like her taller sister, though the blouse atop them frothed with lace at the wrists and her tunic was an intricate pattern of diamonds in shades of pink. "Hello, Luca. Are you leaving?"

"As soon as I can drag Matti away," said Luca. "I'm beginning to suspect I might have to do it at the point of a sword."

Sofia came and hugged Matti around the waist, and he smiled. "I'm glad it was you," he said.

"I'm glad it wasn't you," said Sofia. She frowned thoughtfully up at him. "Though I might need to prevail upon Luca to lend you back to me when your parents start asking me about grandchildren."

"I—you—*what*," said Matti, horror stretching his voice thin.

"It's not unheard of," Sofia pointed out.

Maya said, "We can always leave the grandchildren to Marko and Merri, when they're older."

Sofia's eyebrows lowered like thoughtful storm clouds. "I don't know. That's a lot of pressure to put on them."

Luca couldn't resist. "It's true, Matti. I think I have to agree. This is your *duty*."

There was a long, flavourful silence before Matti's face snapped into a glare. He directed it at each of them in turn. Maya was stifling laughter behind her hand.

"I hate all of you," Matti said.

Luca took his hand. "I hate you, too, Mattinesh. And now I'm stealing you."

Matti bade a final farewell to Maya, and she and Sofia disappeared back into the house. Matti stood with Luca's hand in his, rubbing the knuckles gently, not looking inclined to drop it and pick up his bags.

"You know," said Matti, "I've reconsidered."

"Oh?" Luca's heart gave no more than a little spasm. Matti was smiling faintly.

"That black libelza shipment already belonged to Jay House. *You* still owe me interest on that money you swindled out of me for your watch."

"And nobody will ever know exactly how much," said Luca. "How sad."

"Luca."

"How about I just start giving you things, and you let me know when it feels like enough."

"Things?" said Matti. "Like what?"

Luca slid his free hand around Matti's neck. Matti bent before Luca could apply more than the tiniest amount of pressure, easy as adjusting a stance, and Matti's mouth was warm and familiar. Luca tried to kiss promises into it, as Matti pulled him close. *All of this. All of me.*

"That's a start," said Matti, when he pulled away. His smile looked unthinking, effortless. It grabbed gladly at Luca's heart. "What else?"

Rain smell or no, the city and the weather had no sense of the dramatic. The sun was neither setting nor rising, and even if it had been, it wouldn't have been visible past the buildings that rose up around them.

Still, Luca looked in the direction that he guessed was their destination: Cienne, eventually, but so many roads and diversions and possibilities before they reached it.

"I thought I'd start with the world," Luca said, "and then see how you felt after that."

ACKNOWLEDGEMENTS

It will not surprise you to hear that for this book I did a great deal of fun research into the history of the wool industry, and how the stuff gets treated between the sheep's (or goat's, or alpaca's) back and our own. I apologise preemptively to the terrifyingly knowledgeable fibre-arts folks out there who have no doubt already spotted twenty errors and are ready to tell me all about them.

My research into fencing and duelling was equally enjoyable. Thank you in particular to the Met's collection of historical Italian rapiers, the six months of fencing lessons I did in my teens, and Richard Cohen's entertaining and informative history of swordplay, *By the Sword*. Thesperan duelling is a shameless mash-up of several different traditions and time periods along with a handful of details I just plain made up, which is the great thing about writing fantasy even when there aren't any dragons.

Similarly, the city of Glassport owes its history and trappings to several places, most notably Bruges and Florence with some sprinklings of Venice and Amsterdam. I stole the ocean bath from Bondi.

Despite being my fourth published book, this was the first novel I ever wrote, and it required a lot of people holding my hand from inception and through multiple rounds of edits. For support, feedback, and cheerleading at various points throughout the years, I have to thank Emily, Idrilka, Kelsey, Becca, Anna K, Amanda, Aimee, Iona, Magali, Lauren, Lottie, Everina, Jen U, Alyshondra, and Marina.

To Alex and Macey and Jenn: thank you for being there at the very beginning of this journey. Your belief in this book and your friendship got me to where I am now.

Massive thanks as usual to Diana Fox, who saw the potential in this book long before there was a place for it on shelves, and to Isabel & Brynn & Ari from Fox Literary for their invaluable feedback on earlier versions. Thanks also to Betty-Anne Crawford and David Grossman who continue to wrangle my UK and foreign rights so ably.

My wonderful publishing team at Tor Publishing Group continue to have my back in every way possible. Thanks most especially to Ruoxi Chen, Oliver Dougherty, Caro Perny, Becky Yeager, Jocelyn Bright, Ariana Carpentieri, Emily Mlynek, Megan Barnard, Yvonne Ye, Andrew Beasley, Megan Kiddoo, Heather Saunders, Jackie Huber-Rodriguez, Melanie Sanders, Kyle Avery, Lauren Riebs, and Monique Patterson. And to the Tor UK team: Bella Pagan, Sophie Robinson, Grace Barber, Rebecca Needes, Becky Lushey, Stuart Dwyer, Olivia-Savannah Roach, and Bryony Croft.

The US cover has artwork by Cynthia Sheppard and art direction by Christine Foltzer, and the UK jacket design is by Daisy Bates.

A million thanks to the booksellers, librarians, readers, and reviewers all over the world who continue to remind me that I am lucky and privileged to be part of this creative industry and its ongoing traditions, even on the stressful, dismal days when I am banging my head against the keyboard and wailing.

And as always, thanks to my friends and my family, who have always believed in me so unshakably that I can't remember a time before I believed in myself. None of the stressful wailing is your fault. I promise.

Freya Marske is the author of *A Power Unbound*, *A Restless Truth* and *A Marvellous Light*, the latter of which became an international bestseller and won the Romantic Novelists' Association's Award for Romantic Fantasy. Her work has appeared in Analog and has been shortlisted for three Aurealis Awards. She is also a Hugo-nominated podcaster, and won the Ditmar Award for Best New Talent. She lives in Australia.

*Discover Freya Marske's The Last Binding trilogy,
a historical fantasy series filled with magic, murder
and delightful queer romance . . .*

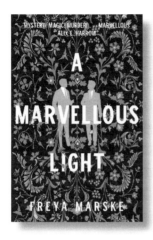 

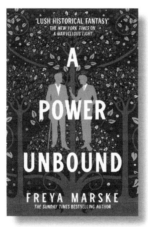

PRAISE FOR
A MARVELLOUS LIGHT

'Mystery! Magic! Murder! Long looks full of yearning!'
ALIX E. HARROW

'A dazzling debut'
SHELLEY PARKER-CHAN